The THUMB
·POINTED
Fingers

Jacki Howard
(nee Sparling)

Jackie Howard

To Andy
Happy Reading!

Lot's Wife Publishing
Staunton, Virginia
July 2008

Cover design by Gretchen Newman
Back cover photo by Jenny Howard
Interior layout by Alice Gaylor
Web design by Aimee Howard Taylor
Photo of rocking chair on front cover by Nancy Sorrells
Permission to photograph the rocking chair courtesy of the
Frontier Culture Museum of Virginia, Staunton, Va.

ISBN Number: 9781934368077
Library of Congress Control Number: 2008926758

Lot's Wife Publishing
P.O. Box 1844
Staunton, VA 24402
www.lotswifepublishing.com

Preface

One of my earliest memories is hearing tales of the "Dying Sparlings," a family story that took place in the Thumb of Michigan in the early 1900s. The events centered around my cousins, several times removed. I began to research these events in 2000 because many articles I read concerning the family did not agree with each other. After more research I found myself with documents, old newspapers, and oral histories. It was only as I compiled the information into a timeline that I began to toy with the idea of writing a book.

The book is based on facts and stories passed down through family, but I had to use my imagination to put words and thoughts into people I never knew. For those who are not familiar with the Thumb of Michigan (and I have met several people who fall into this category), take your left hand and hold it in front of you. You should see a mitten, which is the Lower Peninsula of Michigan, and your thumb is what is called the Thumb of Michigan. It is a beautiful, mostly flat area rich in agriculture and cherished by many for its lovely water retreats.

This is where my roots are and this is where the "Dying Sparlings" lived – and died.

Characters

Boddy Family
Edward
Isabelle (wife)
  Children
    Carrie
    Cora
    Lucy

Dr. MacGregor Family
Robert
Ida (wife)
  Children
    Bonnie
    Douglas

Old Pete Sparling Family
Peter
Mary (wife)
  Children
    John Wesley (J.W.)
    William
    Peter (Little Pete)

J.W. Sparling Family
J.W.
Carrie (wife)
  Children
    Mae
    Peter (Young Pete)
    Albert
    Ray
    Scyrel

Styles Family
Ed
Violet (wife)
  Children
    Aletha
    Marie

Prosecuting Attorneys
  Xenophon Boomhower
  Ernest Snow

Defense Attorneys
  George Clark
  Joseph Walsh
  Paul Woodworth

Michigan's Thumb

Map showing communities depicted in the Sparling story

HURON COUNTY Bingham Township	North	
UBLY		
Ed Hurford		
County Line Road	County Line Road	County Line Road
SANILAC COUNTY	Austin Township TYRE	Minden Township
	J.W.	
	Old Pete	Little Pete
	Big Pete	
	Ed and Violet Styles	

SPARLING FAMILY TREE

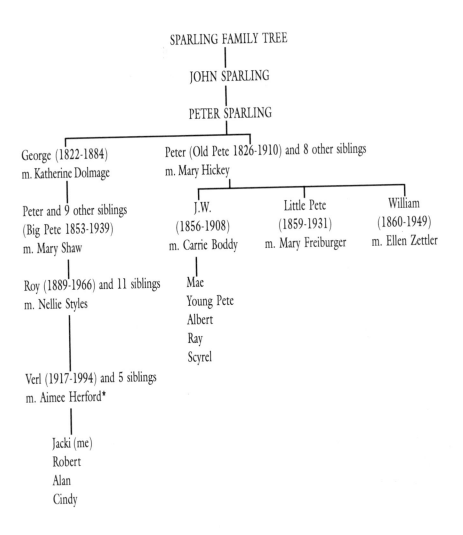

JOHN SPARLING

PETER SPARLING

George (1822-1884)
m. Katherine Dolmage

Peter (Old Pete 1826-1910) and 8 other siblings
m. Mary Hickey

Peter and 9 other siblings
(Big Pete 1853-1939)
m. Mary Shaw

J.W.
(1856-1908)
m. Carrie Boddy

Little Pete
(1859-1931)
m. Mary Freiburger

William
(1860-1949)
m. Ellen Zettler

Roy (1889-1966) and 11 siblings
m. Nellie Styles

Mae
Young Pete
Albert
Ray
Scyrel

Verl (1917-1994) and 5 siblings
m. Aimee Herford*

Jacki (me)
Robert
Alan
Cindy

* Aimee Herford is not part of the Hurford clan

There is an old saying in the Sparling family: "Big Pete – Little Pete was Old Pete's son. When they all got together they made Young Pete run." I never understood the saying, but now I believe it was coined during the time the story took place to help keep the several Peters separate. With the exception of Young Pete who never married, all the other Peters married a Mary.

Prologue

January 17, 1933

Violet wrote the number down and sank into a chair. "Yes. Yes, thank you for calling. I didn't know she remembered me. I'll call you back tomorrow for the details." So Carrie was dead. Was she finally at peace? Memories washed over Violet and drowned out all other thoughts. Events that happened over twenty years ago came back as if they had occurred only last week. "Oh Carrie," Violet said, to no one. "Did anyone really know or understand you?"

Part One
Carrie

Chapter 1

In a Sanilac County farmhouse in the heavily forested Thumb of Michigan, a daughter, Carrie, was born August 13, 1865, to Edward and Isabelle Boddy. Fourteen months later sister Cora joined them, and in 1869 a third daughter, Lucy, rounded out the family of five.

Deer, elk, bear, wolf, and wolverine also called the pristine, mostly flat landscape home. The trees were filled with hawk, owl, and wild turkey. Small towns and farms dotted the countryside.

Carrie's father stood nearly six feet tall. His plain appearance belied the fact that he had a dry sense of humor and loved to tease. And though very strong, he treated his wife and daughters tenderly. Carrie's mother had thick auburn hair, eyes that danced and twinkled, and she loved to sing as she worked.

One of Carrie's earliest memories was the move from Sanilac County to Huron County in 1870. As a five year old, she was happy and felt loved. She did not yet have the feeling of dread that would come with the many moves that followed. Isabelle had somehow managed, on meager resources, to put together a homey atmosphere in their small house. While the Boddys were never well to do, Carrie was too young in 1871 to realize that fact. Had she been aware of it, the fire in October of that year would have had a leveling effect. It raged through most of the Thumb and wrought havoc to rich and poor alike.

Without modern communication to warn of the fire's advance, they had precious little time to decide what to save and what to leave when the fire struck. Had they had the time, those decisions would have been heartbreaking. The angry fire consumed almost everything in its path. Anything spared was attributed to God's intervention, a quirk of fate, or just plain luck. Though only six years old, Carrie worked with her family in a nearly vain attempt to save what they could. This consisted mainly of throwing their belongings into the small creek that ran behind the house. As the flames became too intense, they threw themselves in the water as well.

When the fire had satisfied its hunger, the Boddy family felt fortunate to be alive. Many others were not as lucky. The acrid smell of scorched earth, burnt wood, and dead animals combined to create a lasting impression. Years later, survivors recounted the fire and its deathly stench as if it had happened only yesterday.

As the ashes cooled, the Boddys poked through the charred remains of their lives and tried to salvage what they could. Where the house had stood, they found blackened metal flatware, a copper bottom kettle, two sad irons, a lantern, and a bottle of Dr. King's remedy for coughs and colds. The barn search produced even less—nails, part of the harness, and two horseshoes. But the horse was gone; either it had run off or, more likely, burned. As the fire raged, they had led their terrified milk cow to the creek and secured her to an iron stake. Edward kept pouring water over the bawling animal and managed to save her.

From the creek they pulled Isabelle's sewing box, a trunk that held her wedding dress, and a few papers. They had saved two water pitchers, a tangled mess of sodden clothing, plates, and cups. Most surprising was the discovery of Isabelle's oak rocking chair found a few yards downstream. No one could recall hauling it to the creek. Perhaps the storm had blown it there. Carrie loved that chair. Isabelle rocked her children in it, even when they were no longer infants. It offered comfort while being cuddled and rocked in her mother's arms over a skinned knee, during an illness (measles for Carrie), or just those special times when the girls needed assurance. It had survived, but not without scars. The toe of one rocker was broken off, the cane seat was ripped, and the joints needed tightening. But to Carrie, that old chair was a sign of survival. It told her that everything would once again return to normal.

But what a little girl saw did not agree with reality. Slowly, the Boddy family replaced and rebuilt the physical. Isabelle's mental state was another matter. The fire strangely affected the loving mother who had labored hard and long to make a home. She went through the motions of daily life silently. The songs, as well as her inner spark and twinkling eyes, had disappeared in the fire's demise. Many times Carrie would see her sitting in the salvaged chair, staring blankly at a wall. If Carrie climbed into her lap, the warm hugs were replaced with nonchalant pats or by nothing at all. Carrie and her sisters found they were doing more of the household chores. Pa encouraged them by saying their mother would be well again one day, that she would come back. But rare were the times anyone saw the old Isabelle. Carrie's mother was slowly leaving her.

When school resumed, there were many days that found Carrie absent. She often stayed home to tend to her mother, her sisters, and the house. Carrie didn't mind the work, or even missing school. She held out hope that Ma would return one day. Those days became months and then years. Edward moved his family in hopes that a new residence would help erase bitter memories for his wife. Sadly, another move didn't help Isabelle and it certainly gave no comfort to Carrie who had to cope with starting anew; new schools, new friends (never to be invited home to her now cold house), new everything! As time passed, Carrie felt more alone and isolated. She often wondered if the few friends she had truly appreciated the fact that their families had remained on the same land for generations. Did they take for granted having grandparents, aunts, uncles, and cousins living nearby? She knew she had aunts and uncles, but they rarely got together. Carrie thought it would have been wonderful to be surrounded by a large, happy family.

London, Ontario. In 1876, Dr. and Mrs. Alexander MacGregor happily receive into their home a son, Robert. Mother and child are doing fine.

Chapter 2

In 1878, the Boddy family moved yet again. While they remained within Huron County, it still meant starting over. Once settled, everyday life continued as before. Pa was gone most of the day, either farming his own sixty acres or doing odd jobs in Bad Axe, the county seat, to bring in extra, needed funds.

Christmas of 1880 was surprisingly quite joyful. There was a new pipe for Edward, as well as a badger hair shaving brush. Isabelle received a pretty china vase and a new pad for her rocker seat. The girls each opened a pretty box, which held talcum powder, new mittens, brightly colored hair ribbons, and candy. At times, Isabelle seemed like her old self.

But they did not have a Christmas tree. They learned that lesson after the fire of '71. When they lit candles on that tree, Isabelle had become very agitated. Maybe next year they would try again. After all, the fire had occurred nearly ten years ago. They continued the holiday celebration sitting around the table cracking nuts and eating the meats. It had been a tradition in the Boddy family and they hoped it would assist in her recovery.

The year 1881 looked promising for the family. Isabelle continued her routine, but now with more of her old spark. There were still days that found her sitting vacant-eyed in the rocker, but such days were coming at longer intervals. Carrie watched as Isabelle began to resume her role as mother. She hoped her family would once again be the happy household it had been before the fire. The continuity Carrie craved appeared to be in sight. Now when Carrie drove the horse and wagon to town for supplies, she did not feel guilty if she stayed longer than necessary. She loved to meander through stores that sold niceties the family could not afford. Dreaming cost nothing and fifteen year old Carrie did have her dreams. She also began to notice on these trips that boys looked at her a bit longer than before. She was five feet, five inches tall, with a lovely figure that she would keep throughout her life. Her brown hair matched her brown eyes and her complexion was the envy of her sisters. And while she didn't think herself especially pretty, she welcomed the attention.

Life at home was not as exciting, but Carrie enjoyed its routine. She did chores as before and took pride in looking at the well-stocked shelves in the dirt floor cellar. There would be meat, corn, tomatoes, beans, rhubarb, and jams along with many other preserved foods. It was a good feeling to be prepared. There was also a very large root cellar between the house and barn. It was there when the family moved in.

The summer of '81 was hot and dry, and the garden needed lots of tending. That meant hauling water from the well. The heat drained everyone but they knew it would rain soon; it always did. Carrie didn't complain about carrying water. In fact, she was thankful they even had any. Some folks' wells had gone dry in the scorching heat. A few small fires broke out well south of their farm, but they had been put out and the Boddy family was not concerned. Except for Isabelle. At times she would stop whatever she was doing and carefully scan the southern sky.

Chapter 3

The first day of August brought news of more fires in Sanilac County, to the south. Now it was not just Isabelle who seemed concerned. Talk in town on Market Day had a serious tone and there was now an edge to what were previously happy outings. Carrie returned from market the last day of August prepared to inform her family of the latest news of the fires. She passed Cora and Lucy in the garden and entered the kitchen to find her mother staring out the window as the beans on the stove began to smoke. Isabelle had let the pot boil dry.

On Saturday, September third, Carrie returned with supplies from Bad Axe to witness bedlam at home. She reined in the horse and stared. Cora was running from the house clutching pillows, her father's shaving brush, and a lantern. She handed them to Lucy who turned and raced toward the root cellar. Carrie quickly left the wagon to take her packages into the house. There she saw her mother dashing from room to room, piling things at the door for Cora. Before Carrie could question the activity, she saw her mother's determined look, and her sisters' faces told her to be quiet and help. She pitched in and soon the root cellar was full of clothes, dishes, pots, and pans.

Isabelle eventually wore herself out but not before the house was emptied of everything except beds, table, and chairs. Carrie saw the glazed look in her mother's eyes as she grabbed one more thing, the rocking chair. She dragged it to the root cellar and demanded help in getting it below ground. It meant rearranging and piling things on top of each other, but the girls made room. Pa came in from the field and one look told him the long strides his wife had made toward recovery were disappearing. Her final demand was that the two rain barrels, dry as bones, be rolled to the opening of the root cellar. Once in place, she started hauling well water to them. The family silently took the bucket from her and began to fill both barrels.

Exhausted, the girls put together a supper as best they could, but Isabelle refused to eat. She just sat on the porch stoop and stared toward the south. Carrie felt helpless, frustrated, and sad as she watched her ma leaving her once again. When night fell, the heat was so intense that the fatigued family slept fitfully. On Sunday morning Carrie prepared a breakfast of fresh eggs and yesterday's bread. The wind was now coming from the southwest and while it grew stronger, it brought no relief from the heat. They were too tired that Sunday morning to undo the mess in the cellar, so they did chores and kept an eye on Isabelle.

That afternoon, a horse drawn wagon came by with a cow tethered at the rear. The wagon held a hodgepodge of articles thrown in with little planning or arranging. The driver and his wife sat on the seat while four children were stuffed here and there in the wagon among the household goods. The man asked if the well was dry and was thrilled to learn it was not. The Boddys shared water with the family and their animals. Except for the man, the family remained in the wagon.

He shared eyewitness accounts of fires burning to the west of Bad Axe. So far they had been controlled, but his farm had been devastated in the 1871 fire and he was taking no chances. He had kin to the east in Sand Beach, located on the shores of Lake Huron, and they intended to be near the water, just in case. They were anxious to move on, and after they left Edward decided to leave the root cellar as it was for now.

By noon Monday, September fifth, the heat was unbearable, and two hours later the wind had reached gale force in an ever-darkening sky. Heavy, choking smoke reached the Boddy farm and, in what may have been a final act of sanity, Isabelle threw buckets of water from the barrels into the root cellar. Before they were empty she threw two large blankets into the barrels. Her family wondered if she had sensed the approaching disaster. Maybe they had mistaken intuition for dementia. There was no time for debate as the sky began raining flaming embers. To the west they could now see a huge wall of fire bearing down on them. Without words, the girls were ushered into the cellar. Edward untied the cow and horses, hoping they could outrun the coming storm. He would never see the animals again.

Edward and Isabelle were the last to descend into the damp, soggy root cellar and each carried one of the soaked blankets. Edward shut the door over them and the family huddled together in the dark under wet, smelly blankets. The cellar felt crammed and uncomfortable, and no one spoke, though the thunderous roar of the fire that raged overhead would surely have drowned out their words. They prayed that the wooden door above would be spared. The family later learned that the fire had been sporadic. Fireballs escaped from the wall of flame and took to the air. Witnesses said those balls of fire actually bounced and changed direction. Some homes were spared by this phenomenon. This would be the only explanation as to why that cellar door had not burned and fallen in on the family.

Several hours later, when the roar had ceased, Edward carefully pushed open the door. It was near dawn on Tuesday morning. The wind had ceased and the fire had moved on, now devouring areas to the east. Slowly, the dazed family came out of the earth and looked about them. No words could express what their eyes beheld. Total destruction in every direction. There were only ashes where the house had stood, and the barn was in the last stages of its life. It would soon surrender and fall into a smoldering heap. Their farm had become a barren landscape and the family did not know where to begin. The ground was still warm, and they doubted help would be coming soon. Anything of this magnitude would surely have destroyed neighboring homes as well. They dragged things out of the cellar to dry and made meals from what had been stored there. If anything had survived in the house cellar, it would have to await rescue until all the embers had cooled. As things dried, Carrie and her sisters rearranged the root cellar. This would be home for a while.

They slept that night on the open ground. Droplets of rain woke them and heavy downpours followed. The prayed-for rain had arrived two days late. They again took refuge in the root cellar. When they emerged the next day, they searched and picked through the remains. The house cellar gave up a few canned goods and the family would not starve. Word spread and relief organizations provided tents and tools. A newly formed organization, The American Red Cross, brought in clothing and food. Once again, the Boddy family, along with hundreds more, began the slow process of rebuilding.

This time Isabelle was of no use. While the family joined together in days of tiring labor, Isabelle could be found sitting in the twice-rescued rocking chair. The twinkle in her eyes was again gone and her fiery auburn hair had turned ashen gray. As she watched her mother, Carrie pondered her own future with misgivings. Being the oldest child, she accepted, with a sense of helplessness, the burden of running the household. It was not a task she would have chosen, and Carrie knew she would have to do it alone. Lucy and Cora seemed unable to accept the fact that their mother was not what she had once been. The year that had shown so much promise had vanished.

A wagonload of lumber was given to the family and they erected a very small shed-like abode. No one complained of cramped spaces. Winter would soon be upon them and they needed the shelter. Until bitter cold arrived, the girls slept in a donated tent, surplus from the Civil War. Edward walked the six miles into Bad Axe many times to bring back contributions that had been brought to and stored in the courthouse. Families throughout the Thumb learned to improvise and the Boddys were no exception. Hand-me-down clothing that did not fit could be stitched together for curtains, towels, and blankets. In later years, people would take pride in telling how they survived the tragedy. For now, though, words used up the energy needed to rebuild. Isabelle was not the only one affected mentally. Many who had experienced both fires seemed to just give up. Physical scars would heal, but emotional wounds were another story. Edward got a loan, and life was made easier when he brought home a team of horses pulling a wagon. And behind that wagon trotted a milk cow with her new calf. Carrie could almost taste the fresh milk. Christmas would not have the luxuries of last year, but it would be celebrated. A few homemade presents would suffice. And Carrie determined she would somehow find a few "cracking nuts" to share around the makeshift table. She now knew for certain that if something needed doing, she had best plan on doing it herself.

March 1882, London Ontario. Six-year-old Robbie MacGregor runs down the lane to greet his father. Robbie takes the medical bag from his dad and together they walk up to the house.

Chapter 4

The spring of 1882 found the Boddy family in the skeleton of a new and larger house. The furnishings were rudimentary, but that would change with time. All were in the same dire straits as they struggled to resume a pattern of normality following the fire. It was almost time to plant the garden and Carrie tackled each day with renewed strength and purpose. She told herself, "If you want it done, start doing."

Carrie took pleasure in simple things; the feel of garden soil in her hands, the smell of freshly dried laundry, and the sight of the setting sun after a busy day. She loved driving into Bad Axe for supplies, and one occasion in particular would stand out in her mind. She had run into a friend, Flora, and they caught up on each other's news as they walked to their wagons.

As they approached, Carrie noticed a young man standing by her wagon. He stood about five feet ten inches tall with neatly trimmed brown hair and moustache. And his hazel eyes were fixed on Carrie as she drew closer. When she reached the wagon he offered to help load her purchases. There was no cause for concern. It was daylight and Flora was with her. Besides, he was very handsome and she had seen him in town on other Market Days. She also enjoyed the attention. He seemed to want to talk further, but there was some awkwardness. So he tipped his hat and walked away.

When he was out of earshot, Flora became giddy with excitement. "Carrie," she asked, "do you know who that is?" Though Carrie had seen him before, she knew nothing about him and said so. "Carrie, that's John Sparling. They call him J.W. and he's got his own farm near Tyre. Isn't he good-looking? And it looked like he was at your wagon on purpose!" Carrie admitted she had certainly heard the name Sparling. It was a well-known name in the Thumb but she told Flora there was no cause for any fuss. She knew the dangers of getting one's hopes up. The girls said their good-byes and while Carrie headed east toward home, her mind went back west toward town. She wondered if he really had been waiting at the wagon for her. Well, she would be back next week and perhaps she would see him again.

That week passed quickly enough. The Boddy sisters took care of the house as well as their ma, and they also helped their father in the fields. When the next Market Day rolled around, he rewarded them. "Why don't all three of you go into town for supplies? I'll sit with your ma." The girls chatted excitedly as they headed for Bad Axe. The town was flush with farmers and merchants. Carrie's sisters quickly separated from her to enjoy this outing. They traversed the entire town and relished the exciting diversion from life on the farm. Carrie, however, had errands to run, and she was coming out of a store when J.W. stepped in front of her. He tipped his hat and asked if he could walk with her.

When she accepted, he took the parcels from her and they walked slowly through the crowded town. He asked her name and admitted that he had come to town every Saturday for weeks in hopes of seeing her. Carrie could scarcely believe her ears. They reached the wagon and continued their conversation. She found out he would be twenty-six years old come fall, and owned eighty acres of land in Sanilac County. His house, as well as that of his parents down the road, had been spared from the fire due to a sudden wind change.

"My brother William lives with my folks, and my other brother Peter will soon live catty-corner across the road. We call him Little Pete."

J.W. stopped. He apologized for doing all the talking and asked how her family had made out during the fire. Carrie paused before answering. "We spent the time in a soggy root cellar—my pa, ma, and two sisters." They would have talked longer, but Cora and Lucy appeared. The girls could barely contain their curiosity as they piled themselves and their packages into the wagon. J.W. quietly asked Carrie if he would see her in town next week and she assured him she would be there.

* * * * * * *

Their whirlwind courtship commenced in June, with J.W. requesting permission to call at her home. "We could go for a ride, weather permitting," he suggested. Carrie accepted and told him she would pack a lunch.

The weather that day did cooperate and the two rode off after perfunctory introductions. J.W. drove past unfamiliar scenery. The fire had transformed large tracts of forest into fields of stumps. They observed some men digging up these remains and others building new barns and houses. It reminded Carrie of unfinished work at home, but she put those thoughts behind her and enjoyed this temporary reprieve from her day-to-day existence.

Sunday soon became their day, and both found themselves eagerly awaiting the next meeting. While J.W. had met Carrie's parents, she had never met his family. That changed when she accepted an invitation to a Fourth of July celebration at Peter Sparling's farm. Carrie was unaware that J.W.'s parents had been hinting at meeting this person who seemed to have grabbed their son's attention. "I'll pick you up early so we can have the entire day together," he said. When Carrie offered to bring a passing dish, he remarked, "not this time." Those words spoke indirectly that there would be more times and Carrie's heart skipped a beat.

Chapter 5

Carrie woke before dawn that Tuesday, excited and nervous at the same time. She did the milking and had breakfast ready for the family when they awoke. Carrie's pa didn't tease as much these days, but he did tell her, with a wink, that she was wearing out the floorboards with her pacing.

She tried to look annoyed but was secretly pleased to see her pa like he used to be before Ma. . . .Carrie pushed that concern away and checked herself in the mirror for the fifth time.

J.W. arrived at 9 a.m. and, after resting his horse, he and Carrie began their journey. He drove at a walk and, occasionally, a short trot. It was a distance of some fifteen miles and he didn't want to tire his horse. Carrie realized after an hour that she was becoming even more nervous. What if the Sparlings didn't like her? What if she did something wrong? J.W. sensed her tenseness and reached for her hand. It gave her comfort and she began to relax.

Carrie eagerly took in all the sights and was pleasantly surprised to see the roadside change from bare to tree-lined. J.W. had told her their farms had been spared the wrath of the fire but she had not expected this. Carrie vowed to never again take trees for granted.

All of a sudden other buggies and wagons filled the road. J.W. hollered a greeting to one and waved in response to another. They must be near Tyre she thought. So many people on the road and J.W. seemed to know everyone. It surprised her even more to discover they were all heading to the same destination—Minden Road. This was not to be just a small family gathering, but a large celebration. Sparlings from all over the Thumb were arriving.

As J.W. drove into his parents' yard, Carrie took notice of the house, a large, two-story white clapboard dwelling with a front door framed by two windows on each side. Tall shade trees surrounded the house on three sides. To Carrie it seemed like an oasis she had read about in school. When J.W. turned at the side yard, the largest barn Carrie had ever seen loomed into view. She thought they must have many fields to require such a huge space for storing hay and grains.

As J.W. helped Carrie from the buggy, relatives began to drift toward them. She met J.W.'s uncles. Uncle John, the veterinarian, brought his children, George, Elizabeth, and Fred. Uncle Chris introduced his family—Thomas, Maria, William, Alice, and George. Cousins abounded. William, Maria, and baby Jacob belonged to J.W.'s cousin, James.

A tall man approached purposefully. He had a full dark brown beard and short-cropped hair to match. His gray eyes hinted of mischief. His hands were huge and bore witness to hard work. In a booming voice he yelled, "J.W., is this her?" Then he laughed and Carrie felt at ease. J.W. smiled, introduced Big Pete to Carrie, and told her this cousin was known for his strength, honesty, and carpentry skills. Big Pete tried to change the subject but J.W. would not be put off. "It's all true Carrie," he affirmed. "Big Pete and his brother James are building fifteen barns and fourteen houses this summer. There's no lack of work since the fire. Right, Big Pete?" Big Pete smiled and spoke. "Now J.W., I've just met this pretty little lass and you're boring her to tears with your gab." Carrie took an immediate liking to this gentle giant. Little did she know how large a part he was to play in her life.

After Big Pete left, Carrie whispered to J.W. "I had no idea so many people would be here." He laughed, "Carrie this is only a small group. Many of my aunts, uncles, and cousins live in Canada. They don't always make it over for the American celebration, but you'll have a chance to meet them sometime."

When his brother Pete came over to meet Carrie, she commented on his nickname of Little Pete. "Well," he explained, "it helps keep us straight. You just met Big Pete and my father is called Old Pete, but never to his face." Right then, Old Pete and his Mary came over to meet J.W.'s guest. They made Carrie feel most welcome and she was very happy to be part of this day. But her head was spinning. So many people had the same name. She asked J.W. how to keep them straight. "I have already met two Georges, three Peters, two Jacobs, two Williams. Mary or Maria has been repeated two or three times." J.W. laughed, but then looked deep into her eyes. "You'll get used to it," he assured her. More words, but now less indirect, that this visit would not be the last. Carrie's heart pounded and she wondered if J.W. was hinting she might become a permanent fixture. She tried to keep hope at bay, but she also knew what she had heard. Even though she was overwhelmed with this huge Sparling gathering, she began to feel comfortable and loved every moment. She had never experienced such an outpouring of family closeness, and Carrie Boddy was thoroughly enjoying herself.

And the food! She had never seen so much at one time. Long tables had been set out and they groaned under platters of fried chicken, ham, and roast beef. There were potatoes—mashed, parsleyed, scalloped, and in salad. Fresh cucumbers, tomatoes, and scallions were set among green peppers and red radishes. Stewed tomatoes, glazed carrots, cabbage slaw, scalloped corn, green beans, and sauerkraut added to the feast. Breads, biscuits, and rolls sat next to freshly churned butter. And there were jams and jellies of strawberry, raspberry, blueberry, peach, and plum. The ladies had outdone themselves.

Desserts had to sit on a separate table. Apple, peach, and raisin pie on one end, and cakes of chocolate and lemon at the other. In between were rhubarb cobbler and Mary Sparling's sugar cookies. She made them for the children, but Carrie saw J.W. grab at least three for himself. They drank water, lemonade, and coffee. Carrie noted that the lemonade was good, but it did not have that special ingredient her mother used to add. Lemonade was simple; lemons, water, and sugar. But there was one more thing you could add to spice it up, and Carrie decided to keep that to herself. Especially now. She was not about to appear rude and possibly hurt anyone's feelings.

While the women cleaned up (would there be no end to washing dishes?), the men sat under the trees. They smoked and talked over farm plans. Carrie learned later they had also quizzed J.W. about his intentions.

Eventually, conversation came around to the Great Fire. A few Canadian cousins had not heard all the personal experiences and they were captivated by the stories.

Big Pete recalled how he and his brother James had been harrowing that day. "We got word of the fire and headed for home. Before we got there our rig tipped over and the horses were killed." He stopped and shook his head. "It was an easier way to die than by burning to death." Big Pete shuddered and rubbed his arms. Arms scarred by the fire. "We took shelter by a big pile of rocks. It was terrible. Pieces of burning wood and shingles were flying over our heads. Someday I'll show you the Bible we found. It was just lying untouched between two burned fence posts and a dead baby." Big Pete stood and walked away.

Little Pete paused before speaking. "I was one of the lucky ones. I'd been clearing land when I saw a dark wall coming toward me. I quickly soaked two blankets, put them on my oxen, and led them to a knoll. Didn't know if I was going the right direction, but as it turned out I was. I saw that firestorm pass to the south of me. Yeah, I was mighty lucky."

Others added horrific tales; bodies found with no burns. They had suffocated when the fire consumed all the oxygen in the air. There were stories of entire families killed, and descriptions of dead animals strewn everywhere.

Old Pete stood and addressed the men. "I see the women are coming from the house. It's time we changed the subject. J.W., why don't you get your accordion?"

When J.W. came from the house carrying the instrument, Carrie's jaw dropped—yet another surprise. Children left their games of tag and leapfrog to join the adults as J.W. began to play.

He sat in a chair and tapped his foot to the beat while playing familiar songs and hymns. Carrie could not take her eyes off him. He was very good and it was obvious he enjoyed playing as much as others enjoyed listening. Carrie closed her eyes and slowly nodded her head to the rhythm of the song. Goosebumps covered her arms. She didn't want the music or the day to end.

But end it did. Good-byes were shared with warm hugs that made Carrie feel accepted. Old Pete and Mary told her they were very glad she had come and to please come again.

Wagons and buggies were loaded with empty food baskets and tired children who would be sound asleep before they arrived home.

As J.W. and Carrie left the farm, J.W. turned the horse left as if to take Carrie home. But then he shouted "Haw" and the horse responded by turning left again into another farmyard. "I want to show you something," he explained as he reined in the horse. "I know it's small, but it's all mine," he proudly stated.

Carrie looked at the one-story home, again of clapboard. "I'm thinking to take off the roof," he continued, "and build another floor on top. You can see the barn is nearly done—thanks to Big Pete. Ma helped me get the orchard started." Carrie could see that J.W. was very satisfied with his homestead and she told him it was a lovely farm. It made him beam, but only for a moment. "Well, I got to get you home," he announced. "It's getting late."

Carrie paused, wondering the reason for this detour, but then began to chatter on about what a grand day it had been. She tried over and over to match names to families, but finally gave up. J.W. just sat quietly and smiled as he pulled her head to his shoulder.

When they reached Carrie's home, J.W. lingered and spoke with Carrie's pa while his horse rested. He didn't see Mrs. Boddy but knew she wasn't well and did not inquire. After he left, Cora and Lucy swarmed on Carrie. They had to know everything and Carrie happily obliged by describing it all in great detail. Long after her sisters had fallen asleep she relived the day over and over until she too finally slumbered.

Chapter 6

From then on, J.W. and Carrie were considered a couple. Her August birthday fell on a Sunday and on their outing that day, J.W. talked of the future. "I feel ready to settle down Carrie, and I believe I can support a family." It looked as though she would become Mrs. John Wesley Sparling and join a large, loving family. Her life would at long last have the constancy, consistency, and certainty she had always craved.

* * * * * * *

At the courthouse in Cass City, Tuscola County, on Thursday October 19, 1882, Carrie Boddy married John Wesley Sparling. She gave her age as eighteen, although she had only turned seventeen two months before. J.W. gave his age at twenty-five; had he forgotten his September birthday? Why did they give wrong ages and why did they wed in another county some twenty miles away? They kept that answer to themselves. Cousin Kate Sparling and friend John Davidson were their attendants and the only two people in on the secret event. An event that would not remain a secret for long.

The newlyweds first drove back to Tyre and told Mother and Father Sparling the news. Old Pete and Mary were happy to see their eldest son married and they approved of his choice. Mary prepared a light meal and then J.W. exchanged his horse for a team named Belle and Dolly. He hitched them to a wagon and the bride and groom were on their way to Carrie's folks. Isabelle had little reaction but Edward seemed to have expected it. Cora and Lucy were wild with excitement, and even a bit jealous.

Edward insisted the couple spend the night. Carrie noticed a certain sadness in his eyes and realized how much her father was going to miss her. "Belle and Dolly can use the rest," he suggested, smiling at her. Privately he felt Carrie's visits would become infrequent as time passed.

The newlyweds agreed to spend their first night as husband and wife with Carrie's family. Cora and Lucy hurriedly freshened the bed linens and tidied up their room. They would find another place to sleep.

The next morning, after a most pleasant breakfast (Cora and Lucy's doing), the young couple prepared to drive off. As Carrie climbed onto the wagon seat, Isabelle called out her name. Surprised, she looked into her mother's drawn face and detected a small spark in her eyes. "Carrie," Isabelle said softly, "we don't have a wedding present for you, but I think you should have something to remember us by." She pointed to the old rocker and told Carrie it was hers. Carrie got down from the wagon and hugged her mother tightly to her chest. She knew how much Isabelle loved that old chair. As they pulled apart from the embrace, Isabelle smiled and then, as suddenly as it had appeared, the spark vanished. J.W.'s face fell at the sight of the decrepit piece of furniture, but the look of joy on his bride's face told him to accept the gift. For whatever reason, this was special to Carrie and he didn't have to know why.

Carrie would eventually have a house full of nice furnishings, but this chair would always hold a special place in her heart. It had given comfort when Isabelle was well. It, like Carrie, had endured the frequent moves. And it had survived both fires. It needed to be used and loved. Carrie would do both. This had been a very good day for Carrie Boddy Sparling. She and J.W. left the Boddy farm and visited other family members, as was the custom, before beginning life as Mr. and Mrs. Sparling.

Chapter 7

The year 1883 was to be a busy one. Carrie adapted to her new life readily and made a comfortable home for J.W. Because his parents and brothers lived close by, this family of six shared many meals. Mary took Carrie under her wing and gave her the recipe for those sugar cookies J.W. loved. She was also there on that day in late spring to help Carrie give birth to Mae, the first child for J.W. and Carrie, and the first grandchild for Old Pete and Mary. People remarked that little Mae looked like her mother. The important thing to Carrie was that this happy family she had joined would go on forever, and even more Sparlings would be added to the clan and fill the Thumb. She had hoped this baby would bring her own mother back, but visits home proved it was not to be. Isabelle did not even offer to hold her first grandchild.

Summer brought even busier days. Tending Mae, keeping house, and working the garden kept Carrie on the go and when night fell, she slept soundly if Mae allowed. And didn't that old rocker come in handy now?

By fall, the cellar was a source of pride to the young wife and mother. Jars of jams, vegetables, fruit, and meat filled the shelves J.W. had built for her.

December brought many family gatherings, and not just at Christmas. Cousin Big Pete married Mary Shaw on December third, and settled down on a farm one mile south of J.W.'s farm. Three days later, J.W.'s brother William married Ellen Zettler. They moved into the village of Tyre, which meant they were still close by. The family was growing and Carrie could not have been happier.

* * * * * *

The next year, 1884, passed much as the one before. Mae was growing, thriving, and following her mommy everywhere.

Sunday dinners followed church services and all the Sparlings usually dined together. J.W. had acceded to Carrie's wishes to attend the large Presbyterian church in Ubly even though he preferred the small Brethren church in Tyre.

Carrie saw her own family from time to time, but was always happy to be back among her new one. Lucy was married and Cora was spoken for. Soon Carrie's pa would be the sole caretaker of Isabelle. Memories of lonely days before her marriage were put aside. She was much too occupied with what is to fret over what was and what if.

* * * * * *

Wedding bells rang again in April of 1885. Little Pete married Mary Freiburger and the couple made their home across the road from J.W. and Carrie. The immediate family that had numbered six after Carrie's marriage to J.W. had now grown to ten. William and Ellen had a son, Joseph, born shortly before the previous Christmas. That number was soon to increase to eleven because Carrie was due to give birth again in July. She and the two Marys were at Little Pete's, canning beans, when her labor began.

It was such a fast birth that her son was born there; no need to change houses when Mother Sparling and Mary were already there to help. Mother tended to Carrie, and Mary took Mae into the fields to get J.W. When it came time for a name, Carrie could not believe J.W.'s strong suggestion. Another Peter! She knew it meant the baby would be named after three very dear men, and J.W. said they could call him "Young Pete." And so they did. She had not thought days could be any busier, but was soon proven wrong. J.W. was now gone daily from sunup to sundown. He was either working on his land, or volunteering to help Big Pete raise more barns. The Great Fire had destroyed much, but it also cleared land, bringing even more settlers into the Thumb.

Carrie's day began and ended with milking. In between, she took care of her babies and worked her garden. Berry picking was an especially happy time and Carrie laughed at the new colors that appeared on Mae's clothing; colors that came from whatever berry was in season. She and the two Marys always combined their efforts when it was time to feed extra men whether threshers, wood buzzers, hay pressers, or corn shredders. The three ladies provided the food, and on really big days Ellen came from Tyre to help. If lemons were in season, Carrie was always called upon for her special lemonade. It quenched thirsts and gave her a reputation for making the finest lemonade around.

J.W. and Carrie had less time together, but wasn't that true of all farm couples? If he suggested they leave the children with his folks so they could go to town alone, she balked and said Mae and Young Pete were too little to leave yet.

Winter arrived and chores were not as intense. Crops were in and the garden was out of the dirt and into jars. Soon the cycle repeated itself. Carrie still hesitated when it came to leaving the children, and J.W. teased that she was smothering them with love. "Well," she thought, "your mother never left you." She silently vowed her children would never know that sadness.

* * * * * * *

The months became years and in October of 1887, Albert Sparling was born to J.W. and Carrie. This made six grandchildren for Old Pete and Mary. A third son, Ray, arrived on a cold March day in 1890 and brother Scyrel followed the next year. Carrie was a strong woman. Five children in eight years was not uncommon, but it often cost a woman her health, or even her life. Grandchildren now numbered ten and Carrie was proud to have contributed half of them.

London, Ontario, 1891. Fifteen-year-old Robert MacGregor is privileged to observe his father in surgery. He will definitely become a physician.

Chapter 8

Another happy gathering took place at the Sparling home in the fall of 1892. J.W. had to be persuaded, but finally agreed to an anniversary party. After all, his mother said, he and Carrie had never had a big wedding party. Carrie had never complained, but Mary knew it was important to her. J.W. relented and even got caught up in the preparations. Had it already been ten years? The house was packed. Big Pete and his Mary came with their four youngsters. Little Pete and his Mary brought their four children, and brother William and Ellen added their two young ones to the festivities. Poor Ellen. She had lost one baby in '89 and another just last August, a little boy named Peter who lived only one month. It was not unusual for babies to die, but Carrie could not begin to imagine that kind of grief and kept her children even closer to her. J.W. often watched Carrie with their children and wondered where he belonged, or if he did.

Fifteen children underfoot made for a noisy celebration, remedied when the youngsters were allowed to leave the house and play outside. Even Carrie's parents attended. Carrie could not help but notice what a handsome sixty-five year old man her father was. She also could not miss the fact that while her ma was thirteen years younger than Pa, she looked older than he did. Edward mingled well with the others, but Isabelle was content to watch the party from the old familiar rocking chair. Carrie's sisters were both married and now her pa alone watched over Isabelle. She never caused a problem, but it must have made for a very lonely existence on the farm.

As the party ended Carrie watched her father gently help Isabelle to their buggy. Carrie had thought of asking them to come live with her and J.W., but it never went beyond thinking.

That next spring found Carrie pregnant again. It was a busy time. New-bought chicks needed tending, the garden had to be readied for seed, and berry picking would soon be upon them. Carrie checked her canning supplies, and placed an order at the general store in Tyre. Ten year old Mae helped watch little Ray and Scyrel. And Young Pete and Albert handled small tasks. But most of the workload fell on Carrie. Had her mother been able to help, she would have welcomed her parents with open arms. Carrie went to her rocking chair and mulled over all the consequences of having her parents live with them. That decision would simply have to wait.

* * * * * *

December brought snow and labor pains — much more severe than during Carrie's previous births, and J.W. called the doctor from Ubly to the farm. As 1893 drew to a close, a fifth son was born and they knew right off that the infant was not well. He looked scrawny and listless, and Dr. Griffin informed J.W. that the baby's chances were dismal. J.W. would not consider a name, so Carrie secretly called him Edward, after her pa. Determined that this child would live, Carrie held him day and night in the rocker, almost willing the strength and fight for survival to pass from the chair into her son. This new life died in her arms in early January.

The grief that Carrie could not imagine earlier now came crushing down on her. Unbeknownst to her, J.W. had dug into the frozen ground by the apple orchard, and Big Pete had fashioned a small coffin. This act had even greater meaning as he had done the same for his own two year old son only eight months ago.

Eventually Carrie snapped out of her languor. She could not expect Mother Sparling to assume all her duties forever. If things were to get back to normal, she would have to regain control.

And Carrie soon realized she would be doing it alone. She and J.W. were growing apart. Intimate conversation had been a luxury before, but now it ceased to exist. The usual good night peck on the cheek had become a detached nod. If the two of them were left in a room alone, J.W. found a reason to leave. And on Sunday, Carrie went to services in Ubly while J.W. attended the Brethren church in Tyre.

But they were still a family, surrounded by family, and that would have to be enough.

* * * * * * *

Meanwhile, Sparlings continued to reproduce and fill the Thumb. There would be no more babies for Carrie to rock but she learned to accept that. Her other babies would always need her and she intended always to be there for them. And oh yes, the annual Fourth of July celebrations! Every year the number of attendees grew, but Carrie no longer had trouble keeping names straight.

The Fourth of July in 1895 was bittersweet as Big Pete announced that his family was moving to Huron County. They had bought a farm two miles north of Bad Axe, and planned to be resettled before winter. This news came as a blow to both J.W. and Carrie. Big Pete and J.W. had grown up together, fished and hunted together, and they were more like brothers than cousins. Bad Axe was not a world away, but it may as well have been. Big Pete and Mary had been very dear to Carrie and J.W., and Carrie felt they were leaving her.

But she could not dwell on that. The garden needed watering and weeding. Berries were waiting to become jam, and those darn potato bugs had to be

picked by hand. She made a mental note to ask Sam Soule at the Tyre store about something new, a powder called "Paris Green." It supposedly contained something that killed the pesky critters. Sam carried just about anything you could want or need. He was good and trustworthy, and if he didn't have what you needed, he would find a way to get it.

Carrie would soon be canning copious amounts of corn, beans, tomatoes, and cucumbers. The Sparling women—Mother Mary, Ellen, Little Pete's Mary, and Carrie combined their skills in all-day canning marathons. They still worked together when extra men were helping and needed to be fed. Time passed quickly and pleasantly for the women as they shared new recipes and an occasional tidbit about a relative or neighbor.

When they ate at Carrie's she served her famous lemonade. Mae helped in the kitchen, and Young Pete and Albert took water to the men in the fields. Ray made sure there was lots of soap and water in the washtub outside. It was easier for the men to clean up out there. Four year old Scyrel, not wanting to be excluded, shooed flies from the dining room just before the men entered. Of course the number of flies he shooed out were usually replaced with an equal number of incoming. No matter, he felt he was helping and children learned very early to help, or stay clear when hungry men were to be fed.

Early 1900 Huron County Tribune ads

London, Ontario, 1895. Nineteen-year-old Robert MacGregor resumes his medical studies at Western University. He has never doubted his choice of career to become a well-known, well-loved, and hopefully a well-heeled physician.

Chapter 9

In February of 1896, the family surprised Father and Mother Sparling with a birthday party. They would turn seventy and sixty years old respectively, and only six days apart. Their three sons and families gave them a wonderful day to remember. J.W. even brought out the accordion. The joint gift was a week's vacation. All chores would be done for them. Old Pete and Mary were free to do whatever they wanted. The festivities brought a welcome break to the winter doldrums.

Spring finally came and brought the familiar routine of so many springs before, and Carrie's children were growing too quickly for her liking. Mae, now thirteen years old, was getting prettier every day, and Young Pete would soon turn twelve. He was very strong and his voice was changing. It meant lots of embarrassment and teasing from his brothers. Carrie even heard little Scyrel mimicking the funny sounds. She told Young Pete to just wait. Their day would come and he would have the last laugh. Albert was dreamy-eyed. She often watched him as fantasies traveled through his brain. Ray resembled Carrie and he did not mind her constant naggings as much as the other boys did. It wasn't really nagging. She just always wanted to know where they were and what they were doing. Scyrel was just a year away from attending school. Her days would then be very long and lonely. Carrie always eagerly anticipated the time when her children came home from school with many stories to share over a glass of buttermilk.

Life went on, but the separation between J.W. and Carrie grew wider. She could not put her finger on the reason, but suspected it had a lot to do with the children. They never agreed on setting rules, especially for the boys. She didn't know if others could see it, but she felt it deeply. She was also having physical problems; some female troubles, and her eyes bothered her a lot. She would talk to Dr. Griffin if it got any worse.

* * * * * * *

In the early months of 1897, Carrie read of an unimaginable tragedy that occurred in the next county. A mother of five was found frozen to death only three hundred yards from her home. The woman's husband had been in the Canadian northwest for some time, and she was alone with the children, ages four to eighteen. A neighbor had driven her into town to see about an operation for her second oldest child. While there, a storm arose and it made for a very hard time getting back. When they reached the neighbor's home, the woman insisted on walking on to her own house. The horses were too exhausted for more travel and the neighbor's wife tried to reason with the distraught mother. If she would wait until morning, the horses would be rested and the storm would hopefully have abated. But logic could not sway the frantic woman who felt she had to be home for her ailing child. She set out and was never seen alive again.

The story was troubling to all, but it affected Carrie on a much deeper level and it was a story she would never forget. She did not understand why that man left his family. She rehashed the terrible event over and over in her chair.

Carrie used the rocker quite often now—if something upset her or made her sad, or if something came about that she could not understand, or control. Anything of a disturbing nature would find her there. Sometimes her family would not know the cause for her silent rocking, but they knew it would not last. She never stayed long, and when she arose all would appear to be fine. It seemed to be therapeutic and, as long as Carrie could function as housewife and mother, no one objected to her special times.

London, Ontario, June 1897. Dr. Robert MacGregor graduates as vale-dictorian of his class, and plans are made for a big move to a small town in Nebraska that needs a physician. The practice will not be lucrative, but a new doctor has to start somewhere. College has given him a hunger for the finer things in life. Shortly after settling in Nebraska, Robert meets a beautiful woman, Ida McKenzie. She is a young divorcee and Robert is immediately smitten, not only with Ida, but also with her daughter Bonnie. They become a family the following February.

Chapter 10

Market Day had long ago ceased to provide the same excitement Carrie had felt as a young girl, although she did enjoy running into a few friends. She enjoyed getting caught up on what everyone was doing, and those meetings certainly gave ample opportunity for gossip, if one was so inclined.

Now fifteen year old Mae begged to drive to town. Ubly was not as large as Bad Axe, but for a young farm girl it would suffice. Carrie really couldn't refuse, as she had been allowed such trips at the same age. The boys were helping more and more with farm chores, and soon Young Pete felt he should be rewarded with trips to town alone. It added another source of conflict between J.W. and Carrie. She felt he was too young, but J.W. said the boy worked hard and was at an age when he needed time away from home. They reached a compromise. He would be allowed to go alone to Ubly during the day. However, Bad Axe and night trips would have to wait a year or two.

Carrie could not understand why Young Pete would want to be away from home. There were three brothers here, and ten cousins within shouting distance. Surely he could find ways to amuse himself closer to home. Had she been truthful with herself, she would have admitted that it would be easier for her to keep an eye on him. The problem disappeared in the spring. Little Pete, badly injured in a hay wagon accident, was confined to bed for months. Young Pete and William's son Joe were called upon for help. The two boys assumed all of their uncle's farm work, and by nightfall were usually too tired to consider a trip anywhere but to bed.

The spring also brought a letter from Carrie's father. She tore it open, expecting bad news. But it was not her mother's death, as she feared. Edward told her that they were moving again. This time it would be quite far away. Carrie's mother had a widowed sister in the northern part of Lower Michigan and had talked Edward into bringing Isabelle there to live. He could help her with her chores and she could help with Isabelle. It meant Carrie would not have to think about adding them to her household, but it also meant she might never see them again. First Ma, and now Pa was leaving her. She took it to her chair and when she arose ten minutes later, the matter was resolved in her mind.

Sparlings surrounded her and all would be fine. Besides, she had met a new friend through church. Reverend Forester had introduced Carrie to Violet Styles. Violet was a petite woman with light brown hair. Her mouth, upturned at the corners, gave the appearance of a constant smile. Blue eyes set

East Main St., Ubly, Mich.

Postcard of Main Street, Ubly, Michigan

off a very kind-looking face. When she spoke, her voice was soft and pleasing. Violet, her husband Ed, and their four year old daughter Aletha were new to the church and only lived a few miles from Carrie and J.W. Carrie never knew why the preacher tried to bring about their friendship, but it didn't matter.

Carrie liked Violet right off and the two women soon became good friends. Before long Carrie felt she could confide in Violet things she would never share with the Sparling women. She loved them, but knew they would not want to hear anything unfavorable regarding J.W. The two ladies got together at church functions and occasionally at each other's house. They always brought mending, as idle chatter was taboo. Carrie delighted in this new friend, and the Styles were often invited to share Sunday dinner. The men exchanged views on politics and farming while the women washed dishes. Mae loved taking care of little Aletha, and the boys amused themselves on a welcome day off. A new century was just around the corner and Carrie looked forward to a new beginning.

Chapter 11

In 1900, Hawaii became a territory, cigarette production reached four billion per annum, and another Carrie (Carrie Nation) began her anti-saloon crusade. These were important events, but they meant little to Carrie Sparling. Her life, in its repetition, brought great comfort to her and she cared little for world affairs. But she did greet one bit of news with excitement. As 1900 drew to a close, Violet confided that she was going to have a baby.

Carrie was thrilled for her friend, as she knew of Violet's desire for more children. But she could not help but recall that cold day, almost six years ago, when little Edward left her. She would save those thoughts for later. She wasn't about to dampen Violet's spirits. Babies brought happy times. Ellen and William had been blessed with a fourth child just last year. How dare Carrie pity herself. Ellen had already buried three babies; rumor had it that she was now carrying a fifth child. Dear God, prayed Carrie, let this baby live. She decided to enjoy these new little ones. She could love and cuddle them, but the sleepless nights they also brought would no longer be a part of her life.

As 1900 ended, Carrie vowed she would be ready for 1901 and whatever it brought.

* * * * * * *

The new year came and everything remained the same, for a while. Farm life went by season and Carrie, having the routine down pat, never strayed from it. Never strayed, but she was shaken from it one early summer day. She received word that Violet had just given birth to a son who had lived only a few hours. Carrie told sixteen year old Mae she was going to the Styles. "Her baby has died and I need to be there. If I'm not back in an hour or so, you'll have to fix supper."

She hitched Hannah to the buggy and quickly covered a freshly baked loaf of bread, which she took to the Styles farm. She knew others were probably already there to help, but this was something she had to do.

When she drove into the yard, she found Ed Styles sitting in a chair on the porch, holding his head. Reverend Smith, the new preacher, sat with him. In the kitchen she found Violet's mother-in-law holding six year old Aletha. Violet's mother was on the way and would take the little girl home with her for a few days. Carrie asked if she could look in on Violet. Mrs. Styles nodded.

Carrie entered the bedroom. Violet turned to her and said, "We named him Earl." Carrie sat on the bed and drew tiny Violet to her. No further words were spoken, or needed. They just clung to each other and cried. When Carrie felt Violet's body sag with fatigue she knew it was time to leave.

She arrived home just as the family was sitting down to supper. As they looked up at her, she shook her head no. "I'm not hungry," she added as she went to her rocking chair. She knew Violet would eventually recover and they now had a common tragedy that drew them even closer. Carrie needed this bond, as J.W. was becoming even more distant. If he wasn't in the fields or the barn, he might go visiting his Uncle John, or even to Bad Axe to see Big Pete. He did not seem comfortable around her and always found an excuse to be away from home.

Their twentieth anniversary was next year, and Carrie knew there would be no party. J.W. had not played his accordion at the past three Fourth of July celebrations. Years before, both she and J.W. had encouraged their children to play musical instruments, and while all had begun lessons, only Ray had persevered. The others lost interest quickly, and it now appeared that J.W. had joined them. "Well," Carrie thought, "you can't stop living just because things turn sour." She would continue life on the farm as she had for nineteen years.

As promised, Young Pete, now sixteen, was allowed solo trips to Bad Axe providing his chores were done. Soon Albert began to pester for the same privileges, and J.W. gave permission. Even though she was not happy about it, she had to suppress a smile after one such outing when the boys returned from town. Albert complained that Peter was no fun any more; he was girl crazy. She did worry some when Young Pete went off alone, but if she expressed her concern to J.W., he snapped at her. "Boys will be boys, Carrie. You have to give them some privacy." She tried to stay awake until Young Pete returned home, but sleep usually won out. He never missed chores and she didn't want any more gruff words with J.W., so she let things be. Her children were growing up fast and while she accepted that, she had not come to terms with the fact that they would one day leave her.

* * * * * * *

The year 1901 became 1902, and 1903 arrived much too soon. Carrie felt time was passing her by. The days of family gatherings had dropped off a bit, but the Fourth of July was still a source of anticipation as well as a happy remembrance of past celebrations. She took comfort in that, happy that her children were still under her roof.

Burnside, Michigan, 1903. This town happily welcomes Doctor Robert A. MacGregor as he begins practice in the village. He arrives with his wife Ida, daughter Bonnie, and one-year-old son, Douglas.

Chapter 12

As 1903 progressed, Carrie's health regressed. Her female troubles bothered her more often and her eyes continued to be red and irritated. Dr. Griffin, preparing to retire, sent a Doctor Holdship to treat the Sparling family. He told Carrie to rest her eyes more at night; something easier said than done. Sewing and mending were often put off until evening when chores were done. You could get off your feet and still feel you were accomplishing something. The coal oil lamp didn't give much light and Carrie knew she was straining her eyes. Unless she gave up time during the day for this handwork, she saw no relief for the problem. The other concern might require surgery, a thought she dismissed entirely. She would never leave her children. They needed her even if they wouldn't admit it.

Peter's nightly excursions were becoming an embarrassment. More than one father had come to J.W. to tell him to "keep that boy away from my daughter." And what was happening with Old Pete? Just yesterday Carrie had seen him walking down the road in the middle of the day carrying a lantern. This morning he had surprised her when she came in from milking. She found him sitting at the table as if waiting to be fed. Carrie gave him some bread and coffee and he then agreed to be walked home, Scyrel at his side. She later talked to Mother Sparling about it. Mary said it had been going on about a month now. "Some days he's fine," she said, "and even if he does have a lost moment, he recovers quickly." Carrie put her worry aside. After all, he was seventy-seven years old and should be allowed some forgetfulness. When she mentioned it to J.W. he didn't have much to say about it. J.W. didn't have much to say about anything, at least to her.

If he did speak, it was to argue over the boys. Peter was still girl crazy, but he now stayed away from the local girls, and their fathers. Carrie thought once he found the right girl, he would settle down and all would be well. Of course, that meant his moving away and Carrie did not want that. Albert could be a good worker when he wanted, but often had to be prodded. Her concerns for her sons caused more harsh words from J.W. In one argument, he shouted, "You're no longer smothering them with love Carrie. You are suffocating the life out of them. They are young and they do an honest day's work. They deserve time away from you." That sharp rebuke brought tears to Carrie's sore eyes.

Ray overheard the conversation. He knew what his father meant by suffocating. His mother just had to know about every minute of his day and night, and while he had nothing to hide, it was unsettling. His cousins had much more freedom and he knew for a fact they did not tell Aunt Mary or Aunt Ellen everything they did. Nor did the women ask. But he felt very close to his mother and was sorry Pa had made her cry. He made a point to put his arm around her more, just a short, gentle show of affection. She had continued to encourage his music, and was as excited as he when he joined the Ubly band. If Ray was gone at night, Carrie knew he was at band practice. The older boys caused Carrie more time in her chair.

In addition to the chair, she had Violet. She and Ed now had a sister for Aletha, Marie, born in May. Carrie knew Violet would always mourn her son, but she was doing well and enjoying her little girls. She always made time for Carrie, and Carrie opened her heart and mind to this dear friend. Violet never gave advice, but she always listened. It helped Carrie to unload

Big Pete and Mary (Shaw) Sparling

her burdens and she knew Violet would never betray these confidences.

The garden of '03 kept Carrie especially busy. Overflowing baskets of green beans, vines heavy with squash, and tomato plants bent over with their fruit consumed Carrie's time with hours of canning. She also put up much of Mother Sparling's garden. Mary Sparling's health was beginning to fail and all the young Sparling wives pitched in to help. That Fourth of July celebration was one of the largest. William and Ellen now had six children. Little Pete's Mary had blessed him with eight and another was on the way. Big Pete and Mary also had eight children. This year Uncle John, Uncle Chris, and Aunt Mary were all able to return for the party. For one day at least, Carrie was transported back in time to that magical Fourth of July in 1882.

But as winter approached, her stomach hurt more, her eyes burned, J.W.'s absences grew, and Old Pete's episodes became more frequent. Nineteen hundred three was ending poorly.

* * * * * * *

The year 1904 ushered in a new President—Theodore Roosevelt, the beginning of something called the Panama Canal, Summer Olympics in St. Louis, and a new song by Hughie Cannon called, "He Done Her Wrong." Carrie still cared little for any news beyond her immediate family, the Sparling clan, and the Thumb. Politics seemed boring but she did learn that Ubly had elected a new village president; someone named Xenophon Boomhower. It was a name that got one's attention.

Carrie's sole interests involved her children, her health, and keeping the household running smoothly. Though Violet was not family, Carrie looked to her as a sister, and visits always brought great comfort.

There was some relief down the road at Old Pete's farm. William and Ellen sold their home in Tyre and moved in with Mother and Father Sparling. All those children probably added more confusion for Old Pete, but help was needed and since William did not have a farm, it was easier for him to make the move. It made sense, but also more work for Ellen. Carrie and Little Pete's Mary tried to help, but with their own large families, it wasn't always possible. So most of the care of the elderly couple was left to Ellen. If she resented it, no one ever knew. Now that the Sparlings were clustered even closer with so many grandchildren around, it was easy to find someone to follow Old Pete when he went traveling.

Ubly, Michigan, autumn of 1904. Retiring Dr. Griffin announces that his practice has been sold to a Dr. Robert MacGregor. The new physician hopes to establish a thriving practice, as he has debts to pay.

Part Two
Carrie and Doctor MacGregor

Chapter 13

In January of 1905, Dr. Holdship brought Dr. MacGregor to the Sparling farm. He had most generously handed over the care of many patients to the new physician. Everyone was surprised at the large number of new people moving to the Thumb, and Dr. Holdship felt he could not do justice to all. Both J.W. and Carrie arranged to meet the new doctor and introductions were made over coffee and apple brown betty.

Standing nearly six feet tall, Dr. MacGregor had azure blue eyes that seemed to penetrate your soul—or so Carrie thought. Clean-shaven and bespectacled, he exuded self-assurance without appearing arrogant. Carrie thought him a most charming man.

The doctor couldn't help but notice the pretty Mrs. Sparling who looked so much younger than her husband.

Dr. Holdship had already informed Dr.

Dr. Robert A. MacGregor

MacGregor of Carrie's female troubles, so that embarrassment in mixed company was avoided. Carrie gave a brief medical history of her children. "They are all healthy and strong, although Albert sometimes suffers a nervous stomach. And Young Pete has been having spells of forgetfulness." Carrie and the doctor exchanged telephone numbers.

Carrie had seen the MacGregors in church, but had not had the chance to meet them, as others crowded around to greet the new family. Now that she had met the doctor, she was anxious to meet his wife.

That opportunity occurred the following Saturday. A new preacher, Reverend Mackersie, had been appointed to the Ubly church, and a carry-in dinner was planned to welcome Dr. and Mrs. MacGregor along with the new minister. It was to be held at the schoolhouse and the Sparling family would be there. Carrie expected a fight with Young Pete who had reached an age where family outings held no appeal, but J.W. surprised her. He laid down the law and insisted the entire family would attend.

Carrie looked proudly at her children as they traveled to the welcoming party. Mae still resembled her mother, but had Grandmother Boddy's thick auburn hair, which she pulled back, tied with a ribbon. Mae was a quiet, young woman who never sought attention for herself. Always observant, she helped around the house without being asked.

Carrie ached for Young Pete. Years of acne had made him very aware of his pocked face, and he continually dabbed one cream or another on it. The acne also caused him to become shy and diffident, which contributed to a poor posture; Peter's shoulders were hunched. He wasn't unhappy, but he rarely smiled. He tried to fit in with his peers—maybe too hard.

Albert, at seventeen, was the tallest of the boys and he had his father's oval face. He appeared quiet, but in a self-confident way. Like Mae, he took notice of everything. When something needed fixing, Albert usually knew how to do it. Actually fixing it was another matter. He realized some thought him lazy, but he didn't think so. He would rather enjoy the beauty of a sunset instead of doubling his efforts to get a job done before dark. He and Peter were very close and, though younger, Albert watched out for his older brother.

Ray was the peacemaker. He hated conflict and went out of his way to please people. He loved music, and sang or whistled while he worked. His brothers often called him Carrie's pet, but he shrugged it off. He loved his family but was more at ease when playing in the band.

Scyrel's baby face belied his personality. Feisty, he never backed away from a fight if he felt he was in the right. He hated sitting still and if forced into it, in church for example, his left leg jiggled so hard the entire pew shook. When happy, his smile lit up a room. And he was usually smiling.

Carrie wondered how these children could be from the same parents and yet be so different. She was deep in thought about how quickly the years had passed when she heard a loud "Whoa!" from J.W. They had arrived at the schoolhouse.

* * * * * * *

Carrie stood in line to welcome the MacGregors and the Mackersies. The doctor still displayed a strong confident air, which was made more noticeable by his wife's lack of it. Ida MacGregor clearly did not enjoy being the center of attention. She stood nearly as tall as her husband and was quite thin. Her light brown hair had been pulled back into a chignon. She wasn't especially pretty and Carrie wondered what had attracted the doctor to her.

Carrie felt sympathy for the new families as people pressed introductions upon them. She remembered only too well how long it had taken her to put names and faces together—and those were just the Sparlings. These suppers were almost as good as family gatherings. You could catch up on so many new events. But you could also, Carrie learned, hear things you did not want to know. It was at this supper that Carrie overheard her sister-in-law Mary speak about moving to Brown City. Carrie knew Little

Pete had been hoping to acquire more land, but she assumed it would be close by. She must have heard wrong. Brown City was over thirty miles away.

She asked J.W. about the move when they got home and he verified it. Little Pete had indeed bought a 120-acre farm in Brown City and his own farm was up for sale. This could not be happening. How could anyone sell his home place? And the thought of strangers moving in appalled her. She knew they could not afford to buy the farm and doubted William would want it. Later she asked her husband, "Why wasn't I told?" And his answer stung. "It's really none of your business Carrie," he snapped. She thought her husband would have been upset to see his brother go. It was hard enough when his cousin Big Pete left, but this was a real brother. The clan would be reduced by eleven. She knew thirty miles was not impossible to travel, but she also knew the work that so many acres demanded. And Mary? She would soon have new friends. They were leaving her and nothing would be the same. She couldn't prevent it from happening, but she secretly hoped the farm would not sell and Little Pete would have to rethink his actions.

Carrie took her thoughts to her chair but she didn't stay long; a person could not dwell on troubling things with so much work to do. There were wood buzzers to feed in March and the hay pressers would be there in April. If the weather remained cool, they might butcher another hog. The canned meat would come in handy and you could never have too much lard or headcheese. She could even take some to the MacGregors.

* * * * * * *

The Fourth of July came and the party was all Carrie hoped it would be. She and J.W. had been married nearly twenty-three years. The youngsters she had met that first Fourth were now bringing special friends, spouses, and lots of babies. Carrie wondered if this would be the last time Little Pete and family attended. Their place still had not sold and he had to divide his time between farms. Some of the family remained on the old homestead to take care of crops there, and others stayed in Brown City. It was hard for them, but Carrie had no sympathy. It was Little Pete's idea; nobody had forced this move.

During the festivities, Ellen, Little Pete's Mary, and Carrie began to talk about a party in November. Mother and Father Sparling would be married fifty years on the eighth. Their main concern was the ability of the elderly couple to enjoy a large celebration. Old Pete was feeble in mind, Mary in body. The women decided to go ahead with the plans, but agreed to keep it simple.

* * * * * * *

Summer became autumn, and busy days of feeding threshers and endless hours of canning made for long, tiring days. The three Sparling wives wrapped up plans for the party one afternoon while putting up beet relish in Carrie's kitchen. Assignments were given regarding invitations, decorations, and food. Carrie suggested they invite the MacGregors but Mary and Ellen overruled her. "Let's keep it in the family," suggested Mary. Carrie didn't argue and even felt a bit sorry she had mentioned it at all.

The big day arrived. The women had strung gold and white streamers with gold bells throughout the dining room and parlor. The delicious yellow cake was devoured, and Carrie made a triple batch of her lemonade. Bless Sam Soule for finding lemons in November. Both Mother and Father Sparling seemed pleased with the party. Old Pete even remembered his brothers, John and Chris. He had no trouble remembering the old days.

J.W. surprised everyone when he pulled out his accordion. Carrie could not recall when he last played, but he hadn't lost his touch. As the party drew to a close, he played a new song that was becoming very popular, "God Be With You 'Til We Meet Again." Carrie was not the only one to wipe away a tear. The day had been a success and when everyone was gone, she rocked contentedly. Things would be all right; she just knew it. Her eyes burned, but she blamed it on the excitement of the party. Maybe she would go see Dr. MacGregor and have them checked.

Chapter 14

January of 1906 began as other years, but by the end of that month Carrie became very sick. Sick enough to take to her bed. J.W. called Dr. MacGregor and the doctor diagnosed pneumonia. "You'll need complete bed rest," he insisted. "Mae can tend the house and fix meals; the boys will have to do the milking." Carrie was too ill to resist. Ellen and Little Pete's Mary brought in food and helped Mae as best they could.

Carrie felt fortunate to have such a wonderful doctor. He charged $2.50 for each visit, but it was well worth it. He came to the farm every other day, and slowly Carrie's health returned. She looked forward to his visits, and over the next weeks she gained more trust in the man. Carrie began to confide in him as much as she did in Violet.

She especially expressed her concerns to him regarding Young Pete. The boy went out nearly every night and she worried about his health because he didn't seem as strong as he had been. The doctor tried to reassure her and he warned that stress could bring about a relapse in her own health. He reminded her, "Your son is almost twenty-one now, and anyone who burns the candle at both ends is bound to be tired." Dr. MacGregor felt uncomfortable with the situation. Peter had continued to see Dr. Holdship rather than switch to his own practice and he didn't want to interfere. He had also heard rumors about Peter in town and did not desire to get caught up in the middle. Carrie also shared other worries. "Old Pete seems to have exhausted his memory at the golden anniversary party," she told him. "Little Pete's daughter took over most of his care, but now she's needed at the home in Brown City. So Miriam, Ellen's daughter, watches over her grandfather, but that means Ellen's hands are more than full with the care of Mother Sparling, who's confined to bed." She paused for breath. "And Little Pete is about to run himself ragged working both the Tyre and Brown City farms. We hardly ever see him anymore."

Dr. MacGregor became insistent. "Mrs. Sparling, change is inevitable and you can be a greater help to others after you are well. But you'll never recover as long as you try to carry all these burdens. You are a kind lady who sees needs, and wants to fix things, but you have to realize that some things are beyond your control." Carrie promised the doctor she would do as told, but found it difficult not to worry about those she loved.

There was a bright spot in all this and his name was Ray. At dinnertime he brought Carrie's meal to her room and sat with her. He filled her in on events around town. "And the band, Ma. We're getting better every practice, and Mr. Slack just got permission to build a new bandstand." His excitement was good medicine for Carrie and she resolved to make him a special birthday cake next month when he turned sixteen. Mae and the other boys helped, but Ray always seemed to know just what she needed.

And she could always rely on Violet who came by once a week, bearing freshly baked bread. It wasn't long before Carrie went from bed to rocker, and from rocker back to her old routine. She took care not to overdo and her strength returned. Her eyes and stomach were no better, but she could get through a full day by mid-April without feeling completely drained. She even made it to Easter services and was pleased when told how wonderful she looked.

* * * * * * *

Decoration Day that year fell on a Wednesday and, though solemn, it was also a time of celebration. The family attended the parade in Ubly. Several Civil War veterans led the procession. Following them were town dignitaries; Village President Boomhower, banker Albert Sleeper, and businessman Benjamin Eilber, among others. The Ubly band came last and a lump filled Carrie's throat as Ray marched by. The parade ended at the cemetery where flowers, placed by children, decorated the graves. The assembled crowd listened to patriotic speeches and then observed a moment of silence for the departed. The band played again and everyone's spirits were lifted. You only had to visit a cemetery to appreciate the fact that you were alive.

The boys rode their horses to the event and Mae was with a group of young people who had promised her a ride home. So J.W. and Carrie went home alone in the buggy. They stopped at the Tyre cemetery on the way. Uncle John had donated the land for the small graveyard. Even though there had been no ceremony here, a few flowers had been placed on some graves. J.W. commented on the peace and quiet. "It would be a good place to rest one's bones." Carrie did not respond. She knew he was only thinking out loud. He had been most talkative in town but, once alone with her, had resumed his silence. She had grown accustomed to his reticence, but lately he had seemed even more distracted— as if his body was present, but his mind was far away.

They celebrated the Fourth of July like other years. Big Pete and his Mary arrived with their nine youngsters. The children played games as always, and the younger ones complained about being left out. Everyone ate too much but somehow found room when cakes, pies, cobblers, and homemade ice cream appeared. They tried to coax J.W. into some music on his accordion, but he begged off. "Maybe next year," he said. Carrie looked at the familiar crowd. Sparlings still filled the Thumb, reunions would continue, and her family was close, at least physically. She told herself not to complain so much. Old Pete might never get well, but Young Pete would be fine. For now at least, Little Pete and his family were around for these parties. Oh how she dreaded the end of the day.

John Wesley Sparling

Carrie (Boddy) Sparling

Albert Sparling

Peter (Young Pete) Sparling

Scyrel Sparling

Ray Sparling

Chapter 15

In the fall of 1906, Carrie experienced an abnormal amount of stomach pain and J.W. again called Dr. MacGregor. After he examined her, he spoke privately to J.W. "She won't be able to delay surgery much longer. There may be periods of relief, but episodes like this will become more frequent and more severe." J.W. said it was up to his wife to make the decision, but when MacGregor suggested surgery to Carrie, she shook her head. "You said that surgery would be done in Canada," she reminded him. "And I cannot imagine leaving my family. I'll be all right." MacGregor could not force the issue but he tried to assure her. "Your family would more than understand and, just think, you would come home free from these pains. Let me know when you're ready." She couldn't be convinced so Dr. MacGregor gave her something for the pain and left the farm.

Carrie did her best after that to hide the pain from J.W. and the children. Mae usually sensed when her mother was hurting and doubled her efforts to give Carrie needed rest. Carrie knew what Mae was doing and loved her all the more for it. But Mae was twenty-three years old. How long before she would want to have a home of her own? So far no gentleman had come calling and Mae once lamented her fears of becoming an old maid. Carrie had noticed a young man, Robert Hurford, paying extra attention to Mae in church. When she mentioned his name, Mae shook her head. "Ma, he's younger than I am. He's very nice, but I don't know if I could ever come to love him."

* * * * * * *

As 1906 drew quietly to a close, Carrie felt uneasy. There were too many unfinished issues over which she had no control. She knew J.W. was troubled by his brother's leaving. Once that move was final, she wondered if he would draw close to her again. She worried about Young Pete. It was time for him to settle down but he showed no signs of doing so. And Mae. Her daughter seemed content, but all her friends were married and some even had children. Stomach pains reminded Carrie that her own health had not improved—another concern unresolved. Carrie spent the better part of New Year's Eve in her rocking chair.

Six weeks later, matters still unsettled in Carrie's mind, all the Sparlings gathered to say good-bye to Little Pete and his family. They had moved all but one wagonload of belongings to Brown City, and it was packed for the morning trip. Everyone tried to make it a happy day, but gloom hung over the

Sparlings nevertheless. It was a poor time for William to announce his intentions, but there really wasn't a good time. He informed everyone that Old Pete's farm was to be put on the market. He and his family planned to move to Bad Axe in June.

Carrie felt numb; too numb to react. She felt the closeness of this family slipping away from her. Had she been honest with herself, she would have admitted that the closeness was mostly a memory. As William and Little Pete's families had grown, Ellen and Mary had been too busy or tired for much socializing. They still found time to get together, but the warmth of past years was missing. Carrie tried to lighten the mood and reminded everyone that the Fourth of July would be here before they knew it. "We'll have a grand reunion." She was surprised at the quiet that followed and did not see the look that passed between J.W. and his brothers.

The morning after Little Pete left, J.W. called Carrie into the dining room. He had spread some papers on the table and asked her to sit down. He explained that the papers were the deed to the farm and he needed her signature on them to transfer the deed to her name. Before she could recover from that shock, J.W. informed her that he was planning a trip to Canada. "The boys can handle the farm work and Mae is here to help you," he stated firmly. Carrie's mind raced back to the story of the mother who had died in the blizzard. Her husband had also gone to Canada.

When she asked why, he only mumbled something about always wanting to see it. When she asked how long he would be gone, he said he didn't know. It was hard enough to see Little Pete go. It was hard enough to know William would soon be gone. But it was nearly unbearable to know that J.W. was also leaving. He said it was only a temporary situation, but that didn't alter the fact that he was leaving her.

Carrie never felt more alone in her life. It was almost twenty-five years ago that she first set foot in this area. Her whole being had overflowed with joy, and she had been thrilled to finally have the close family she had always craved. How could these people throw it all away? She looked at J.W. and asked, "Who knows of these plans?" He told her she was the last to find out, which troubled her even more. But it did explain the awkward silence that followed when she had spoken of the Fourth of July celebration. J.W., having said all he planned to say, left the house and went to the barn.

Carrie went to her chair. For a long time she rocked, but this time her mind was not spinning plans. It was as blank as her stare. Then, little by little, she began to focus on all that had occurred. Shock turned into sadness. Sadness turned into anger, and anger became resolve. She rose from the chair accepting what she could not change, but with a fierce determination to change what she could. She had no answers, but she had made a decision. Carrie returned to the dining room and signed the papers with a firm bold hand.

*   *   *   *   *   *   *

The rest of February passed in a blur. Little Pete and Mary were gone. Old Pete needed constant watching. William and Ellen were kind, but they too would soon be gone and there would be no one to fill the gap. Mother Sparling was an invalid and J.W.'s mind was only on Canada. Carrie's eyes burned constantly, but she could no longer blame it on tears. They had dried up long ago. Her stomach hurt again, but she would have to live with it. Everyone around her was leaving, but she would not leave her children. They must never feel the abandonment that filled her soul.

On the last Thursday in February, as Carrie put breakfast dishes away, a buggy drove into the yard. Mae came to her and asked if she was ill. When Carrie said no, Mae looked puzzled. "Then why is Dr. MacGregor here?" Carrie had not called him, but was clearly happy to see him climb the porch steps. She and Mae met him at the door.

"I've been out to the Thomas place and since it's so close, I decided to stop and see how things are here." Mae excused herself to finish in the kitchen. Carrie offered coffee to the doctor and they drank it in the parlor. MacGregor took a sip and spoke, "Mrs. Sparling, word is out that Mr. Sparling is going to Canada. I know your boys are more than capable of handling things here but I just wanted you to know that you can call on me should the need arise." This kindness brought tears to Carrie's eyes and it was all she could do to contain her emotions. She had tried to sound at ease with her husband's leaving, but the doctor found it easy to read between the lines. This woman was very upset that her husband was going off on an adventure alone.

He changed the subject and asked about her health. She was evasive and he did not persist. As he rose to leave, she reached into her apron pocket and handed him two dollars. "I know you charge a bit more, but the notes I ordered from the bank have not arrived and I don't have any change." MacGregor looked surprised. "Mrs. Sparling, I can't accept this money. I didn't come on an official call." She pressed the money into his hands. "But your visit has had the same effect as good medicine." Seeing that she meant what she said, he took the money. Carrie saw him to the door and suddenly a severe stomach pain caused her to double over. The doctor immediately reached out to steady her and it was at that moment, Carrie in Dr. MacGregor's arms, that Mae appeared. An

63

awkward silence hung in the air until the doctor recovered his voice. "Mae, please encourage your mother to have the surgery, and soon."

The cold February morning ended. Dr. MacGregor went back to Ubly and Mae went back into the kitchen. But Carrie stood alone for a moment before joining her daughter. Strange and exciting feelings coursed through her body. How long had it been since she had been in a man's arms?

Chapter 16

Early Monday morning, March fourth, the boys hugged their father before he climbed into the wagon. Mae handed him a lunch she had packed, and kissed her father good-bye. Peter would take J.W. to catch the train at Tyre. From there he would find his way northwest to the Manitoba region of Canada. Carrie wondered if her sons wished they were going with him. If the children noticed the parting of their parents to be cool and distant, they kept those thoughts hidden. J.W. had planned to stop at his old home and say his good-byes to William, Ellen, and his parents. But just as he and Peter prepared to leave, loud voices distracted them. Old Pete was shuffling up the road toward him wearing only his union suit and carrying a lantern. William and his son Joseph were gaining ground, and Joseph carried a blanket and coat to wrap around his grandfather. Carrie thought it a tragic image for J.W. to see just before leaving. But nobody had forced this decision upon him and he would have to deal with all facets of this trip, good and bad. They guided Old Pete to the wagon and he rode in the back of it to his own farm. J.W. looked straight ahead and Carrie watched his back as it grew smaller and smaller.

Albert set to work. He and Peter had set up a milk route in addition to regular farm chores. Winter was a good time to begin and it brought in more money. As the other two boys passed Carrie, still standing on the porch, Ray gave her a little hug. Carrie hugged him back and decided to make it a special day when he turned seventeen in three weeks.

The day after J.W. left, Carrie went to Violet's. Lately she had only seen her in church and she needed this friend's shoulder. Violet knew something was wrong as soon as Carrie appeared. She put water on for tea and told twelve year old Aletha to mind her little sister in the sitting room. As the two women sat at the kitchen table, Carrie slowly began to report the recent events. Gradually, the conversation became emotional and Carrie put her head down and sobbed. "Why does everyone leave me?" she asked. The question required no answer, which was fortunate; there wasn't one. Violet had learned that Carrie never came for advice. She just needed to pour out her despair to a friend and Violet was that person. She held Carrie and listened.

* * * * * * *

March proved typical. Warm teasing of spring one day, and a cold wind-blown snow the next. Carrie had not heard anything from J.W.

but was not surprised. Dr. MacGregor usually stopped by at least once a week and, during one such call, Peter asked the doctor for something to clear his complexion. Dr. MacGregor began to explain physician ethics and when Dr. Holdship's name arose, Peter interrupted. "That won't be a problem, Doc. In fact, he just suggested to me that I switch to you; keep it all in one family." It made sense, but Dr. MacGregor had no medicine with him. He told Peter to try Vannest, the druggist in Ubly. Peter agreed, and Carrie gave the doctor a note for $2.50. He had learned not to protest when Carrie gave him money for his time, official or not. She apparently could afford it.

* * * * * * *

April passed quickly. Carrie prepared the garden, checked canning supplies, and moved jars of food from last year to make room for this year's hoped-for bounty. The milk route and farm chores kept the boys busy. No matter how things changed in Carrie personally, life on the farm remained the same. How she wished J.W. had made an effort to buy his father or brother's farms. Her boys would need their own places one day and they could have lived nearby.

Carrie continued to worry about Young Pete who had been acting unusual. He never missed church on Sunday, but went carousing Sunday night. And he might leave Wednesday prayer meeting to go to Bad Axe for questionable activity with questionable companions.

His face remained pocked regardless of any treatments he used. He began to get headaches and his memory failed now and then. Carrie knew he needed more sleep, but tried to hold her tongue. One day she watched as he walked toward the barn, and was alarmed to see him fall. His legs just seemed to give out from underneath him. Her first instinct was to run to him, but then she saw him look around and quickly get to his feet. She decided he was fine and was glad she had stayed inside. Rushing to help would un-doubtedly have caused him embarrassment.

Albert, now almost twenty years old, also liked the nightlife but, unlike his brother, had to be pushed quite often to get at daily chores. He was a good-looking young man. He stood five feet, eight inches tall, and weighed 170 pounds. His brown hair matched his eyes. He continued to suffer from a nervous stomach and, like his brother, was always putting something on his face to treat pimples. He and Peter both began to send away for patent medicines that claimed to cure a bad complexion. Ray, now seventeen, was a quiet, diligent son. He also went out at night, but Carrie didn't worry about him; the band received frequent invitations to perform. While she had no favorites, others noticed that Carrie had a special bond with Ray.

Scyrel, nearly sixteen, was almost as tall as Albert, although thinner. Very strong, he loved to exhibit that strength in roughhousing. He also made it very clear that farming was not to be in his future.

It wasn't easy being both mother and father—especially to the boys. Carrie remembered the words J.W. had drilled into her. "Boys will be boys Carrie, and they must be allowed some time to sow their wild oats."

There he was, back in her thoughts. Was he thinking of her? Would he return? And if he did come back, what would life be like? She took all these musings to her chair. She later rose, having decided to talk to Dr. MacGregor. He was a man and maybe he could help her understand her boys better.

That conversation happened quicker than she planned. Early May found Carrie in severe pain. While she had had the same symptoms before, this time they lasted three days, without relief. Mae called Dr. MacGregor, and he again urged her to have the surgery. She told him she would give it some thought. But since he was here, could he advise her on the boys? "Ray is doing all right, but the others seem to need the influence of a mature man. William is the only one nearby, and he leaves next month." Dr. MacGregor tried to reassure her. "You must be patient, Mrs. Sparling. You have good boys, and J.W. will surely be home soon. But I'll show more interest in them and their work. I could come out now and then to help with butchering or harvesting. Maybe they'll open up to me if there is anything troubling them." Carrie told the doctor she would rest, and Mae assured him that she would see to it that her mother kept that promise. He accepted a note, payable to bearer, for $2.50 before heading to the barn. Perhaps one or more of the boys would be out there.

Chapter 17

Decoration Day that year was celebrated as before with one exception. Carrie did not go to Ubly. After her children left for the festivities, she walked to the orchard and sat by little Edward's grave. Had he lived, he would have been thirteen years old.

In mid-June Carrie and her children walked the familiar tree-lined road to Old Pete's farm. They were going to say good-bye to him. Old Pete had become more than William and Ellen could handle. Mother Sparling needed more of Ellen's time and she would move with them to Bad Axe by month's end. Old Pete would go to Brown City and live with Little Pete and Mary.

When Carrie and family reached the old homestead, Little Pete was already there and had some exciting news about his oldest daughter. "Olive is to be married in December," he announced. "It'll be a big doings and Mary has started sewing the wedding dress. She sends her love and wishes she could have come with me." There were murmurs of excitement among the family, but Carrie saw that Mae looked uncomfortable and noticed her daughter went home ahead of the rest. Carrie would try to comfort her later, if allowed. Had Carrie been informed Little Pete was coming, she would have tried to organize a big meal for everyone. But as usual, she was the last to know. The visit was short, as Little Pete wanted to get his father into his new surroundings before dark. He said his good-byes and, with a very confused father in tow, took his leave. Ellen invited Carrie and the children to stay and eat with them, but Carrie lied and said she had something in the oven. When she got home there was a note from Mae saying she had gone to town and would be home later; they should not hold supper.

The day's surprise took Carrie to her chair. She thought it odd that no one had asked about J.W. Maybe he had been in touch with them, or perhaps it was just too awkward a subject to broach. And the news of a big wedding. She knew it was hard for Mae to hear about it. But it was also difficult for Carrie to think about. She and J.W. did not have a large wedding and it never mattered to her, but the word wedding reminded her that their silver wedding anniversary was four months away. She doubted there would be a celebration. She didn't even know if J.W. would be home by then. She rubbed her sore eyes and rose to get supper.

* * * * * * *

The next week left little time for rest. Berries had come on strong, more garden needed planting, the milk route was expanding, and the hay needed cutting. But Carrie and her children stopped their work to go back up the road to bid farewell to William and his family, including Mother Sparling. The new owners were scheduled to move in soon. Carrie knew she should take them a welcoming dish, but her heart wasn't in it. She had not taken anything to the folks who bought Little Pete's farm and decided not to start now. If they thought her unfriendly, so be it. She would never think of them as anything but intruders. Carrie and her children walked home; there was work to be done.

The next day Violet appeared with a loaf of fresh cinnamon bread. She knew how lonely Carrie was. They cut into the bread and made small talk. Violet did not press her beyond everyday chitchat. If Carrie needed to talk of serious matters, she knew Violet was always available. What Violet did not know was that Carrie was baring her soul more and more to Dr. MacGregor. He had been helping the boys in the hay. Sometimes he brought his son, five year old Douglas. The boy was of little help, but Dr. MacGregor thought it might cause the older boys to adopt a more adult attitude. They seemed to enjoy being looked up to, especially when the youngster tried to mimic the Sparlings as they put up hay. When Douglas was not around, they tended to dawdle, taking more breaks than necessary. Carrie made sure they had plenty of good food, and took cold spring water to them in the fields.

* * * * * * *

Ellen invited Carrie and family to spend the Fourth of July with her and William in Bad Axe. Carrie thanked her, but said they had other plans. And they did, but none included Carrie. Mae was planning to sew for her hope chest. Olive's wedding plans seemed to have given her motivation. She would be ready if marriage ever presented itself. Peter and Albert said they were going to the ball field in Bad Axe to watch a baseball game. Ray was playing with the band in Ubly, and Scyrel had gone to Sam Soule's store in Tyre. The store was closed for the holiday, but there was always merchandise to be shelved and Scyrel was thrilled for the opportunity. He had been spending his spare time at the store since his pa left and enjoyed the welcome change from farming. Besides, he knew this Fourth was bound to be strained, at best. There had been no huge family gathering this year and Carrie had been unable to hide her nostalgia for what used to be. She spent the day tending the garden, but at a very slow pace; her stomach was sore again. She made a mental note to hire a local girl, Anna Pieruski, to help her and Mae. The only Sparlings remaining on Minden Township Road were greatly relieved when July fifth dawned.

* * * * * * *

July vanished into August and before she knew it, September had arrived. Carrie had turned forty-two years of age and no one had remembered, including herself.

On a dreary Monday early in September, Violet drove into the yard. One thing or another had kept them apart for several weeks and Violet was shocked at Carrie's appearance. She looked pale and haggard. Carrie's face testified to pain, and her hug had little strength behind it. Carrie and Mae were putting up peach jam when Violet arrived—with a loaf of bread. It was a perfect time to sit and get caught up while enjoying bread and still warm jam. Carrie engaged in trivial chatter and steered away from any conversation regarding her health. Mae, sensing the need for these women to be alone, excused herself and went back to the orchard.

After Mae left the house Violet spoke freely. "Carrie, you must have that surgery. Anyone can see you're in pain and you know it won't get better on its own." Carrie smiled. "Violet, you are my best friend." She looked down at the table and began to trace imaginary shapes with her fingers. "So you have to realize that I just cannot abandon my family. I know they can manage this place without me, but I can't bear the thought of being away from them." She left her tracings and looked again at Violet. "Young Pete always seems tired and he loses his temper so quickly. Albert daydreams and always has to be pushed to keep at his chores. Scyrel looks for any chance to go to Sam's store. Ray seems to be doing fine, but I am concerned that his brothers' behaviors will eventually rub off on him. Mae is a tremendous help, but I know she would much rather be in a home of her own. Violet, I just cannot leave my children." Violet tried to be understanding and supportive, but it was hard to see her friend so overburdened. She didn't ask if J.W. had been in touch; Carrie would certainly have shared that information.

She took Carrie's hand, looked into her eyes and spoke. "Carrie, I'm very worried about you." The awkward silence was broken when Mae returned with another bushel of peaches. "Ma, we have plenty of peaches already put up, and we'll still get more from what is out there. Perhaps Mrs. Styles could use these." Violet said she could indeed use the peaches as her trees had been off this year. Mae, anticipating a few words with Violet alone, offered to carry the peaches to her wagon.

"Mrs. Styles, you're a good friend to Ma. How can we convince her to have the operation?"

"I just tried," Violet answered, "but got nowhere. Maybe Dr. MacGregor should be called."

"Humph," scoffed Mae. "He's here all the time and can't change her mind."

Violet looked puzzled. "Why is he here so often?" she asked. "Is someone else ill?" Mae shook her head. "Oh he talks to Ma for a bit and then goes out to find the boys. He's been doing this ever since—" Mae paused. "Ever since last spring when Pa left for Canada. The boys never refuse the help, but I heard Albert say the other day that Doc had taken Ma's place in having to know everything they were doing."

"Let me think on it," said Violet. "But I should go now. Your mother will be curious if we stay out here too long." Violet left and Mae went back to the kitchen. There was a lot of clean up to do after canning. "Well," remarked Carrie. "Did you two have a lot to say about me?" Mae hesitated, but only for a moment. "Ma, we're just very concerned about your health." Carrie took a clean dishtowel to the sink. "I'll be fine Mae. There is no need to fret." Mae sensed the subject was closed and got to work.

The days passed, the amount of canning decreased, and when able, Carrie worked to clean off the garden. The raspberries were near their end and anything else was a root crop, which involved no urgency. Carrie now had more time on her hands, which also meant more thoughts in her head. Today was the seventeenth and wherever J.W. was, he had turned fifty-one. He had been gone six months now. Sometimes it seemed he had been gone only a few days, but other times it felt like years. The farm was managing without him, but that didn't ease the pain of his leaving. Dr. MacGregor told her that worrying would only slow her healing. She understood that. So she rocked.

She visited the rocker nearly every day now. To think. To plan her next course of action. To remember happier days. But sometimes even the rocking chair was no help.

* * * * * * *

It was a beautiful Monday, the last day of September. The brilliant sun warmed the slight breeze that passed. It was a good day for drying clothes and it was at the side yard clothesline that Carrie heard the shouts and commotion. She walked around the corner in time to see J.W. walking into the yard, carrying a large satchel.

Chapter 18

Albert and Scyrel ran toward their father; it was their shouts Carrie had heard. Peter came racing from the north field with Ray right behind him. Mae had gone to town and missed the homecoming.

After several comments on the beard J.W. now sported, a hundred questions flowed. "How was Canada?" "Did you work up there?" "What are the people like?" "How long did it take to get home?" J.W. laughed and said he would tell them all about it later. One more question came—from Ray. "Pa, are you home to stay?" J.W. looked at Carrie and then at his sons. "Yes, I'm here to stay. But now I have questions of my own. Tell me about everything here on the farm."

Carrie said she hoped soup was sufficient for supper. "It's an easy meal for washday and I didn't know you were going to be here." J.W. nodded and then stared at her. She thought she probably looked like the tired, worn housewife she was. Had she known he was returning, she would have been wearing a nicer dress and her hair wouldn't be half out of its bun. But J.W. didn't see what she thought. He thought she looked more than tired; she looked ill. Her voice broke his contemplation. "J.W., I'm sure you have dirty clothes. Pass them over and I'll see to them." He obliged and then headed for the barn; there was so much to catch up on. Only Ray seemed to notice that his folks were very cool to each other. No hugs. No kisses. Just an acknowledgment of each other's presence. He paused and then followed his brothers and pa while Carrie took the laundry to the tub.

After half an hour, J.W. left the barn to look at the fields and saw Dr. MacGregor drive into the yard. The doctor went over to J.W. immediately and welcomed him home. "J.W., it's good to see you again. The boys did a fine job while you were gone, but I know they're happy to have you back." J.W. shook the doctor's hand. "The boys tell me you've been a great help and I want you to know I appreciate it." He looked intently into the doctor's eyes. "But I'm back now and you can have your extra time for yourself." Dr. MacGregor ignored the tone in J.W.'s voice and replied, "Of course. And maybe you can also persuade your wife to have the surgery we talked about earlier, before you left." J.W. stiffened a bit but then admitted, "I thought she looked poorly. I'll talk to her about it." Dr. MacGregor did not stop to check on Carrie as he usually did. Something told him to just leave, and he did.

Supper was a noisy affair. Mae had returned to bombard her pa with more questions. "How did the women dress?" "What kind of food did you eat?"

It appeared that a talkative evening was in store. Carrie excused herself to empty the clothesline and when she returned Mae had stacked the dishes and gone to the parlor with the rest of the family as they pried more information from J.W. Carrie decided the laundry could be folded later and the dishes could also wait. She picked up her mending basket and sat in her chair listening to the account of J.W.'s travels. It was getting dark early now and lamps were lit. By ten-o'clock, Carrie's eyes burned and she said good night. Everyone else seemed ready for a long night of catching up, but she was too tired to even pretend any interest. J.W. had said he was back to stay, but time alone would prove that. She would not get her hopes up because she could not afford to be hurt again. Nor did she have the strength to recover as she had before.

She made certain that his side of the bed was available, but didn't know if he would use it. The answer came with the crowing of the rooster. She was alone but could hear him stirring in the spare room. The same room he had slept in just before his departure last March. It appeared things were to pick up where they had left off. She made the bed and went into the kitchen to begin October.

The smell of coffee and bacon drew the family to the table. They had indeed burned the midnight oil talking, and tiredness showed on all faces. J.W. must have said something to the boys and Mae the night before because as soon as they finished eating, all found a reason to leave.

Carrie started to clear the table, but J.W. asked her to sit. "Carrie, I can see you are very ill. MacGregor said you refused the operation that could make you better. I'm home now and there is no reason not to have this surgery. You always say you don't want to leave the children but your baby is now sixteen years old. Let me call Dr. Holdship and get things started." After a long pause, Carrie spoke. "J.W., you know Doc Holdship no longer attends this family. Dr. MacGregor is our physician and he has been a very good friend to us while you were gone. He's helped the boys on many occasions, and God bless him for that. Who else came? Not Little Pete. He's in Brown City. Not William or Big Pete. They're in Bad Axe. In less than one year, we went from almost thirty Sparlings to seven. Everyone left, including you." Carrie surprised herself. She had never spoken so strongly to her husband. Apparently the words had been inside her for some time and they poured out with determination and emotion.

She rose again to clear the table, but this time J.W. did not stop her. "I will give thought to the operation, but not because you asked. The pain is constant and blood loss has weakened me greatly. If I consent to surgery, it will be my decision alone!" J.W. had no more words and he left the kitchen. So he did not witness the sobs that came when he was clear of the house. Carrie surrendered to a crying spell while she washed the dishes. Then, dishes and eyes dried, she went to her rocking chair.

* * * * * * *

Mae found her later. It took some rough estimates, but they decided she had been passed out, in a small pool of blood, on the floor by the rocker for about an hour. Mae called Dr. MacGregor and he arrived at the Sparling farm in record time. Carrie woke to find herself in bed, wrapped in stained sheets, and hearing voices outside her door. The voices took on form as J.W. and Dr. MacGregor entered the bedroom. The doctor's tone was sober. "I've called my father in London and he's making preparations for your arrival. Surgery is no longer an option. It's the only way to save your life. Don't tire yourself talking. Just listen. Ray and Scyrel have gone to Tyre to get your train ticket. Mae will assume all your chores, J.W. will watch over your boys, and I'll personally escort you to the hospital. Mae thought Mrs. Styles and Reverend Mackersie should be told and those telephone calls have been made. You have always expressed great concern over leaving your children. I'm telling you now that, without surgery, you will indeed leave them—for good!" Carrie was too weak to respond other than with a nod. The good doctor had alleviated all her concerns and she now rested in his capable hands.

The train ride to Canada was a blur. Dr. MacGregor and morphine made certain she was as comfortable as possible. A buggy met them in London and took them the short distance to St. Joseph's Hospital. Surgery took place the next morning, and Dr. MacGregor went to her room afterward. Even though groggy, she knew he was there. "Mrs. Sparling, I'm leaving in a few hours to return home, but I'll be in touch through my father. Meanwhile, you are in good hands so just concentrate on getting well." And then he was gone.

Carrie slept the rest of the afternoon and all night. She only awoke the next morning when a nurse came in to check on her. Days passed and slowly Carrie's strength returned. Soon she was sitting up and, after ten days, could get up and walk. She truly felt rested which made her realize how exhausted she had been. And the daily pain that had clung to her for years was nearly gone. Discomfort from the operation lessened every day, and Dr. Alexander MacGregor knew she was healing when she began pleading to go home. She wondered if J.W. would come over to visit and decided she really didn't care one way or the other. But oh how she missed the children.

* * * * * * *

Carrie had been away from home about two weeks. A cloudy, gray October day matched her mood. She missed her home and family. And she missed the rocking chair. She was on the verge of self-pity when a familiar voice caught her ear. The voice drew closer. No, it was two voices. Dear God, could it be? Yes! Violet and Ray entered the room loaded with goodies. They brought a new bed jacket that Mae had made, and newspapers and a magazine from Ray and the other boys. And Violet unwrapped a small loaf of bread. After hugs and tears, she peppered them with questions. They assured her that all was well at home and everyone anxiously awaited her return. Then they brought her up to date on happenings in the Thumb. The boys were busy with the milk route. Robert Hurford was coming to the farm on a regular basis and it wasn't to see the boys. The Ubly band was practicing for a Christmas program. The village had purchased a combination hand and motor fire engine. The first volunteer fire department in Ubly had been organized and Dr. MacGregor was among the first to sign up.

So much had occurred during her absence, and it made her even more anxious to be home. Dear Violet and Ray. They could never imagine what their surprise visit had done for her. A nurse offered to make tea, which they drank with Violet's bread. She hated to see them go, but knew she would soon be back among them. She leafed through the magazine; it would require concentrated reading later. Ray had brought the Bad Axe newspapers and she read every word. She noticed an article about a silver wedding celebration. Carrie didn't know the couple, but wait! What day was it? Friday, the eighteenth! Tomorrow would be her twenty-fifth wedding anniversary. She had no rocking chair to take her thoughts to, but never mind. She would not dwell on the past. It was done.

The senior Dr. MacGregor came in to see her the next day. He said how pleased he was with her progress and that he had very good news. His son Robert and family were coming for the weekend. "How would you like to go home with them Monday morning?" The pure joy on her face answered the question. Only two more days and she would be home. What a wonderful word that was—home. She thanked the doctor repeatedly and told him the people in London were very fortunate to have him for their physician.

"Mrs. Sparling, I appreciate your kind words, but I plan to retire at the end of this year. There are many good physicians here and I can still help others in another way. I'm going into the insurance business and my medical background will be a great aid." He closed his bag. "Now you must get some rest. You have a train ride to prepare for." On Sunday evening Dr. MacGregor and Ida stopped by just long enough to see if Carrie needed anything before morning. She assured them that she lacked for nothing and was more than ready for the next day.

The train ride seemed to take forever, but they soon reached the station at Tyre. Dr. MacGregor and Ida each took an arm to help Carrie, and then she saw them. J.W., Young Pete, Albert, Scyrel, Ray, and Mae. And a surprise. Robert Hurford stood beside her daughter. J.W. stepped forward and took his wife's arm from the doctor. After he helped her into the buggy, she turned back to thank the MacGregors, but they had disappeared. The buggy turned toward home, and the children followed on horseback with the exception of Mae, who rode in Robert's buggy.

Carrie didn't know if J.W. would be talkative or not, but he surprised her and broke the silence first. "You look well," he said quietly. Carrie glanced at her husband and then turned her face back to the road. "I feel wonderful and I'm sorry I put the surgery off for so long." She paused. "How is everything at home? I thought Young Pete looked tired, and what's happening with Mae and Robert?" J.W. cleared his throat. "Well, Peter does seem tired and he talks to himself sometimes. But he gets his work done, so no complaints, at least from me. As for Mae and Robert, they call him "Bert", I'm thinking they are a couple but she'll probably bend your ear over it." Carrie thought she saw the slightest hint of a smile on his face. "Daughters don't usually confide in their fathers," he said.

"Well, I'll just have to hope for a good time to talk to her," Carrie answered. "It's obvious by the look on Robert's— I mean Bert's— face that he is smitten." The conversation ended as they drove into the familiar yard which was filled with several other wagons and buggies. The look on J.W.'s face showed he was as surprised as Carrie. Violet then appeared at the front door grinning from ear to ear. Suddenly men approached the buggy. Ed Styles, Reverend Mackersie, Dr. MacGregor, Sam Soule, and neighbors John Getty and Ed Bismark greeted them. "You get into the house," said Reverend Mackersie. "We'll see to the horses."

Wonderful aromas coming from the kitchen betrayed any further secrets. Mae ushered them to the table where a bountiful feast was presented. Violet, Mrs. Mackersie, and several women from the church and neighborhood had prepared a sumptuous meal that included fried chicken, roast pork, and scalloped oysters. Potatoes, beans, cabbage slaw, corn cakes, and pickles filled the rest of the space. The table barely had room for the fresh baked rolls and Violet's bread. Raspberry pie, grape pie, fried apples, and chocolate cake rounded out the meal. Carrie's eyes teared, but they were tears of joy. What a wonderful surprise had been arranged and now she knew why the MacGregors had been so quick to leave the train station.

When all had eaten their fill, the men headed to the back yard and the women began the clean up. They would not let Carrie help, but Mae brought the rocking chair into the kitchen so her mother could be part of the happy chatter. This was a day Carrie would never forget. Her friends and family had gathered on a workday to welcome her home. One by one, the families began to leave. Ed and Violet were the last to depart. "Violet," said Carrie. "How can I ever thank you enough—" Violet interrupted her. "Carrie, we are all so glad you're well and back with us. The pleasure was on our part." She hugged her friend and added, in a whisper, "Happy Anniversary Carrie, a bit late."

Even though she had done no work that day, Carrie felt tired. The doctor had told her that her strength would be slow returning to what it had been a year ago, and she now knew exactly what he meant. But return it would! She promised not to rush things. She never wanted to be separated from her family again. Several cards and letters for her sat unopened on the front hall table, but she decided to wait until tomorrow to read them. As dusk fell, Bert headed for home, the boys did the milking, and Mae put leftovers on the table for supper. The boys and J.W. would certainly be able to eat again when chores were done. Nothing was said about Bert, but Carrie knew Mae would confide in her when she was ready. Sleep came blissfully; a precious sleep free from pain.

In the morning, Carrie woke to the smell of breakfast cooking. At first she thought she was still in the hospital. Her second thought was that she had overslept. But that couldn't be. It was barely light outside. She sat on the edge of the bed to get her bearings and then dressed and went to the kitchen. Emma Faupel, an old friend of J.W.'s parents, was busy setting out the morning meal. Poor Emma had been devastated when her husband died last April. Even though he had been an invalid for years, she had taken his death very hard.

"Emma," cried Carrie. "What are you doing here?" "Well missy," replied Emma. "The doc told J.W. that he was afraid you would overdo, even with Mae's good help. J.W. asked if I could come for a couple of weeks, just until you get your feet square under you again. You'll not be overdoing while old Emma is around. Now, how about some breakfast?" Carrie said a silent prayer of thanks. This arrangement would provide a healing time for both women.

After breakfast, Carrie went into the parlor to read her mail. There were quite a few notes wishing her well. Big Pete's Mary apologized for not being close enough to help, but Carrie knew it was more than just distance. Her oldest daughter had just married and moved away. That left eight children at home with another due in February. There was a card from Bert's parents;

she hoped to meet them soon. Sister-in-law Ellen also wrote to apologize for her absence. Little Pete's Mary sent a lovely letter about their family. Old Pete was still prone to wandering, but so far had caused no harm. In fact, his travels had helped introduce them to more neighbors. They were all busy getting ready for the big wedding in December. "Of course, a formal invitation will arrive later, but we hope all of you will be able to attend." That was the furthest thing from Carrie's mind at the moment.

Every day found Carrie getting stronger. Mae and Emma allowed her to help some, but also insisted on daily rest. Winter would be a good time to recuperate, no canning or gardening to worry about. By the middle of November, Emma decided Carrie did not need her any longer. "But," she emphasized before leaving, "if you get to feelin' poorly, I'm willin' and able to be fetched back again." Carrie thanked and hugged her. As she watched Ray help Emma into the wagon, she smiled. Carrie once again had her house and her children to herself.

* * * * * * *

Thanksgiving came and went with little fanfare. The invitation to Olive's wedding arrived and J.W. announced that the family would attend. "It's been a long time since the Sparlings have been together." Carrie wanted to add, "That was your doing sir," but she held her tongue. She asked Mae if she would like to invite Bert to come along, but Mae said the time was not right. The boys were not thrilled at the thought of going to a wedding and used chores as an excuse. As it turned out, only J.W., Carrie, and Mae went to Brown City for the nuptials. It was a huge affair. About 200 people attended. William was there with his daughter Miriam who was to be a bridesmaid. If Mae felt left out, she hid it well. Ellen had remained home with Mother Sparling. Big Pete came, but his Mary's twelfth pregnancy kept her in Bad Axe. There were many Sparlings gathered, but many new faces as well. It felt good to be with everyone, but it couldn't compare to the old Fourth of July parties.

By doubling up, a room was provided so J.W. and Carrie could spend the night. They graciously accepted and hid their discomfort. Mae slept with cousin Laura. Afterward, the ride home was quiet, each deep in thought. Mae was remembering all the pomp and circumstance involved in such a large wedding and doubted she would ever experience the same excitement. J.W.'s thoughts went to his father. Little Pete's boys, Harvey and Norman, kept close to him the entire time. When J.W. tried to talk to him, Old Pete thought he was his brother Christopher, not his son. It had been a hard thing to see. Carrie thought about all the changes that had taken place the past year, mostly about the changes in her marriage and how she felt about her husband since he had returned from Canada.

When they reached home there was a letter for Carrie. It had arrived shortly after they left for the wedding and it was from Carrie's aunt in northern Michigan.

> Dear Carrie,
>
> I am sorry to be the bearer of sad news. Your father passed in late November. We think it was his heart. He had been chopping wood and just fell over. There is no need for you to come now, perhaps in the spring. Your mother is not aware of his death. She is aware of very little now. She is physically sound but there are some failings. My sons are a great help to us ladies and I want to assure you that we are as well as can be.
>
> Again, I am very sorry you have to learn of this by letter. Hopefully, we will see you come spring.
>
> Lovingly yours,
> Aunt Freda

Carrie took the letter to her chair. She hadn't seen her parents in years. Not since they last moved. The train could have taken her there many times, but she always found excuses and now it was too late. Pa gone for good, and Ma as good as dead. She thought back through 1907. So many people had left her. But 1908 was around the corner and it would be better. It had to be.

Chapter 19

In 1908 the Nobel Peace Prizes were announced. Gabriel Lippman was recognized for his method of color photography, and Rudolf Eucken for his philosophic writings. The prize for physiology went to Elie Metchnikoff and Paul Erlich for their work on immunization. Erlich would go on, in 1910, to discover Salvarsan, an arsenic based remedy for syphilis which led to the coining of a new phrase—the magic bullet.

In other news, Austria annexed Bosnia and Herzegovina, William Taft became President of the United States, and two Henrys made the news. Houdini for his milk can escape, and Ford for introducing the Model T automobile. Closer to home, Ubly residents approved raising money for a water tower and the village opened its first public library.

* * * * * * *

As the new year dawned, Carrie hoped 1908 would bring her a new beginning. However some things would not change. A snowstorm in mid-January brought a deep chill to an even colder household. Carrie, feeling so good after surgery, wondered if she and J.W. would draw closer, but that was not to be. She understood his concern about his father, but she had concerns as well. Her pa had died and her mother was in the same condition as Old Pete. But life did go on and you couldn't sit and stew over things beyond your control. At least she wouldn't.

J.W. remained cross a good deal of the time. He found fault with little things, nothing seemed to satisfy him, and it affected the entire family. The boys began grumbling amongst themselves and Mae became moody. Carrie hoped it was just winter doldrums but felt it was too early to mix up her spring tonic. Her family hated the taste, but Carrie, following years of tradition, mixed up a brew every spring.

She also took to her chair every chance she got, and looked forward to Dr. MacGregor's calls. He came once a week to check on her. She had recovered from the surgery, but her eyes continued to be irritated and sore. MacGregor told her they were inflamed from a condition she could neither pronounce nor remember. It was hard for Carrie to keep from rubbing them, especially at day's end. She was to tell him if it worsened.

The doctor also warned her that while she was feeling good as far as the female situation was concerned, she could expect possible flare-ups in the future. "You need to let me know if there are any changes and keep me informed," he stressed. Two dollars and fifty cents, as always, found its way from her hand into his pocket.

* * * * * * *

February brought a blizzard to rival all others. Called "the storm king", it raged for four days and nights. Ten-foot drifts formed, leaving the entire Thumb snowbound. Trains became stuck, mail delivery ceased, and many doctors who set out on house calls were turned back by their exhausted horses. The boys could not run their milk route; it was all they could to do keep a path shoveled or tamped down from house to barn.

Carrie's pa had always said the thicker the onionskin, the colder the winter. She didn't remember if onionskins had been thicker than usual, but she did know they were into a very hard winter. She and Mae kept busy with sewing and mending. J.W. and the boys took care of the milking and used the time to repair tools and implements. Eight days passed before life returned to normal. When mail resumed, there was a package for Peter. He said it contained medicine for his pimples. There was also a valentine for Mae from Bert. Carrie could not tell if her daughter was pleased or not, and warned the boys that teasing was not allowed.

Finally, one day when the men were all out of the house, Carrie spoke to her daughter. "Mae, you've been so good to help me and I appreciate the sacrifices you've made. But you can see how strong I am now, and I feel fine. What I'm trying to say is, if you're delaying any plans for your future because of me, there is no need. Bert seems very nice." Mae barely smiled. "Ma, if it happens, then it happens. Everyone knows I haven't been beset by suitors like Uncle Pete's girls. Bert is nice and well, we'll just see. This is leap year you know, the girls can ask the guys." Then she winked at her mother and the conversation ended.

Carrie knew then that her daughter would be fine whatever the future held. She wished she could have the same ease of mind over Young Pete. He was just not himself, but perhaps her spring tonic would cure his ills and perk him up. February was drawing to a close and it would soon be one year since J.W. had left for Canada. He had said he was home to stay but she wondered. Even though he remained distant, she really didn't want him to leave her again. Carrie decided she needed some time with Violet, so one morning in early March the women chatted over tea and bread.

The winter storms had kept them apart and they had much catching up to do. Both were looking forward to spring and putting out gardens. They exchanged family updates. Violet's girls were doing fine, but Carrie expressed her concerns regarding Young Pete. Violet had heard the worries before. Carrie put her teacup down. "He always gets his chores done, but something just isn't right with him. He seems tired, but still goes into town and stays until the wee hours. Albert is having stomach trouble again and sometimes the pains travel to his sides and back. Scyrel makes it clearer every day that he hates farming. You know, I think it's time for my tonic. Maybe that will set my children back on solid ground again." Carrie did not mention J.W. and Violet did not ask.

* * * * * * *

March brought blue skies, melting snow, and small shoots of green from the earth. It also brought disease. The Sparlings managed to escape a small outbreak of smallpox, but they did not avoid the grippe. Carrie dosed her family with home remedies, which included her foul tasting tonic. When they complained, she reminded them, "If it tastes good, it won't work." By the time they called Dr. MacGregor, most of the symptoms were gone, with the exception of Albert's pains. A milk diet was prescribed, $2.50 was exchanged, and the doctor left.

One day as Carrie was taking some warm milk up to Albert's room, she heard J.W.'s voice coming from Young Pete's room. She stopped, quietly approached the closed door, and listened. "Peter," she heard J.W. say. "I've been thinking about going to Canada again. You cannot believe how pretty it is up there. This Thumb is getting more crowded every day. Up there a man can come and go as he pleases. I'm thinking maybe you should come along." Carrie was stunned and she held her breath to keep from making any noise—J.W. was still talking. "The other boys can make do without us. I haven't decided for sure yet, but you give it some thought. Once I'm feeling better, we can talk again and maybe make some plans."

Carrie didn't linger at the door to hear Peter's response; she didn't want to be caught when J.W. left the room. She numbly took the milk to Albert and then found her chair. Could she have misunderstood? No. She knew what she had heard. He had said he was home to stay but was now considering another trip, with Young Pete. This couldn't be allowed to happen, but she had not been able to stop it before. She left the chair, but this time without any resolution. Carrie went to the kitchen to check the stove. Supper would be soup, bread, and another dose of tonic.

* * * * * * *

Everyone welcomed April. It had been a harsh winter and the coming of spring improved the family's mood, except for Carrie. If she was away from the house, she couldn't wait to be home to see if her husband and oldest son were still there. If she was home, she remained tense until they appeared at the dinner table. She didn't really believe they would leave without telling her, but just couldn't ease her mind about it. Then she remembered

J.W. saying he couldn't leave until he felt better and she smiled. The grippe had lowered his resistance and while he had improved some, he was not back to normal.

Carrie reread Aunt Freda's letter suggesting Carrie come to visit her in the spring. There was no way she could do that now. If she didn't want her family to leave her, how could she justify leaving them? And her ma would probably not even know she had been there. Besides, spring brought house cleaning, gardening, and myriad chores that could not be postponed. No, Carrie would not be making the trip. She would send a note.

* * * * * * *

Dr. MacGregor sat at his desk working on his patients' files when his wife told him he had a visitor. He went to the back room office and was surprised to see J.W. sitting there. "Mr. Sparling," the doctor asked, "what brings you here on a beautiful spring day? Is your wife all right?" The question puzzled J.W. Why ask about her? Anyone could see she was better. He rubbed his beard thoughtfully while staring at the doctor. After an uncomfortable silence, he cleared his throat. "No Doc, my wife is fine. I happened to be in Ubly and thought I'd see if you were in. No need for you to come out to the house if I'm in town anyway, right?

"The thing is, this grippe just won't let go of me completely. I took the medicine you gave me, but I just can't get back to full strength. And I get a funny feeling like, you know, when your foot falls asleep. It feels like that, but on my hands and feet both—like I'm being pricked by thorns or needles. Got some pain on my left side too. Probably nothing and I wouldn't usually bother over such aches and pains." He leaned forward and met MacGregor's gaze. "No one knows and I want to keep it that way. But I'm thinking of another trip to Canada and I can't take on a trip like that while I feel like this."

The doctor seemed lost in thought. He could certainly treat the grippe, but his thoughts were of Carrie. He knew from before how J.W.'s departure had grieved her. She had made such progress since her surgery and he would hate to see her have a relapse. He suddenly realized J.W. was staring at him and quickly returned to the present. After checking pulse and temperature, he gave J.W. more medicine. "Give these powders a week, and if you see no change, let me know."

As J.W. left the office, the doctor noticed him dragging his right leg. "Mr. Sparling," asked MacGregor, "how long has your leg bothered you?"

"Oh, I don't know," he replied. "Guess it just came on gradual, it seems to have a mind of its own now and then. I probably just sat too long."

"Let me know how it goes after about a week," MacGregor said. "And if you decide to go up north, I'll be glad to come out and help the boys."

"Thanks," J.W. answered tersely. "But I wouldn't be going if I didn't think they could handle it all by themselves. By the way, I don't know what my wife usually pays you. Can you put this visit to account and settle later?" Dr. MacGregor said it would be fine, but privately thought if all those on account ever paid up, he'd be doing really well. He had hoped by now to have a nice amount in the bank, but as it was he could barely make ends meet. He promised himself that one day it would be different.

* * * * * * *

The week passed with no word from the Sparlings, so Dr. MacGregor planned to stop by to check on them in a few days. Meanwhile, he saw Carrie in church on Easter Sunday and asked about J.W. She told the doctor that her husband went to church in Tyre. "I mean about his health," he clarified. Carrie seemed confused. "Oh, he's about the same I guess," she replied.

"Well," continued MacGregor, "I'll be out early next week to check." Carrie's answer seemed strange and as MacGregor walked home with his wife, he remarked, "Mrs. Sparling didn't seem too concerned about J.W. Perhaps she didn't understand what I meant. She must know he isn't feeling well."

The next Tuesday Dr. MacGregor appeared at the farm. It was mid-afternoon and he found J.W. sitting on the porch drinking lemonade. He didn't get up as MacGregor approached. "Mr. Sparling," the doctor began. "I haven't heard from you and wondered how you're getting on."

J.W. took another sip before speaking. "I don't guess I'm much better, could even be worse."

Dr. MacGregor could see that his patient did not look as well as he had the week before. "If you think the medicine has helped at all, I could get you a stronger dose," the doctor suggested. J.W. sighed, "Hard to tell if it's helped, but right now I'd have to say no. I'll try the stronger stuff, but I can't abide any more of that durned tonic Carrie keeps giving me. If it was going to work, it should have happened by now.

"My pa was laid up for a long while one spring when I was young. He came out of it and I expect I will too. Just wish it wouldn't take so long." He put his glass down and lowered his voice. "And you needn't worry about coming out to help the boys. I won't be going to Canada this year."

Dr. MacGregor took that as his invitation to leave. He reached into his bag and handed the farmer a bottle. "This is a stronger dose of what you've been taking—won't hurt to give it a try." As he stepped off the porch steps, he heard

Carrie's voice at the door. "I didn't know you were here, Dr. MacGregor. Won't you have a cup of coffee, or I could brew some tea."

The doctor smiled. "It sounds good, but I must be on my way. Two other families are expecting me."

J.W. looked at his wife. "Have you got any money for the doc? I saw him a week ago and got caught short of cash. I wouldn't want to be beholden to anybody."

The look on Carrie's face showed her surprise. She had not known her husband had been to see MacGregor. "Of course," she stammered, "just give me a moment." She disappeared into the house and returned with a note for five dollars. Dr. MacGregor took the money, thanked her, and quickly left.

* * * * * * *

Time passed, and Dr. MacGregor again heard nothing from the Sparlings. He decided to wait a while longer before going back to the farm. He had detected a coolness between J.W. and Carrie on his last visit.

Carrie telephoned the doctor in mid-May. "Dr. MacGregor," she said quietly, "J.W. has taken to his bed and can't seem to get up by himself. He wouldn't let me call before, but now he asks for you to come."

When MacGregor arrived, Carrie met him at the door. "I've tried everything I know, but he's getting worse." She ushered him into the bedroom. The doctor removed his jacket and rolled up his sleeves. "Well now Mr. Sparling, I understand you are having some trouble getting out of bed. Is there anything else bothering you?" J.W.'s face showed worry and he grimaced. "I got an awful gut ache and I've been vomiting."

"Have you been taking the medicine I left?" the doctor asked.

In a weak voice J.W. answered, "I took the pills but you can see for yourself they didn't help. What's next Doc? I'm too young to lay in bed day and night."

"Well," the doctor suggested, "let's have another look and maybe we can see what the problem is."

The examination revealed an inflamed mouth, swollen ankles, and brown spots on J.W's palms. "Is your throat sore?" asked MacGregor. Another grimace from the patient. "Yeah, it hurts but I figured it was from all the throwing up I did."

"Tell you what," the doctor continued. "I can get something else from the druggist. I don't usually carry it, as it is costly. But if he has it in stock I'll be back with it tomorrow. Time we tried something new." Carrie followed him as he left the sickroom. "Dr. MacGregor," she asked. "What's wrong with him?" The doctor paused before answering. "I have a couple of ideas, but need to do some further checking before I know for sure. But Carrie, you've got to take care of yourself. It won't help anyone if you get sick again." She managed a slight smile and he reached out and put his hands on her shoulders.

Mae entered the kitchen planning to tell Carrie the onions and radishes were planted, but the words stuck in her throat. The doctor looked at her. "Mae, I've been telling your mother she needs to take better care of herself." He removed his hands. "I'm sure you would agree."

Mae recovered her voice. "Dr. MacGregor, were you here to see my father? Do you know what ails him?" The doctor gave the same response he had given to Carrie only a moment before. Carrie looked flushed and slumped into a chair. She reached into her pocket for her notepad and wrote the doctor a bearer note for $2.50. He took the note and left.

She then looked at her daughter. "Mae, I think I'll just sit a spell and then we can get at those onions."

Before Mae could tell her ma the planting was done, Carrie rose from the kitchen table and went into the side bedroom where her rocking chair waited. She shut the door. Mae knew her mother would be deep in thought for a while and that was fine. Mae had reflecting of her own to do. She checked her pa who was sleeping, and then went to the front porch. She could see the dust from the doctor's buggy. The doctor was doing his own thinking. He had a lot on his mind.

When MacGregor reached home, he called a colleague, Dr. Conboy. After giving a general description of J.W.'s condition, he asked Conboy to study on it. When Dr. Conboy offered to go out to the farmhouse himself, MacGregor sounded relieved and accepted the offer. He then went to the druggist. Vannest didn't have the medicine the doctor wanted but said he would order it. For now, MacGregor and J.W. could only wait.

The next morning, Dr. Conboy went to MacGregor's and together they drove to the Sparlings. On the way, Dr. Conboy spoke. "I've been thinking about the symptoms you described, Robert. It sounds like it could be neuritis to me."

MacGregor nodded in agreement. "I was thinking along the same lines. Or it could be creeping paralysis. He just cannot make his legs work."

Dr. Conboy rubbed his chin. "But what would cause the neuritis, if that is what he has?"

MacGregor paused before answering. "Daniel, it could be several things. This is only a suggestion, but I've even wondered about syphilis." The look on Conboy's face told MacGregor he had better do some explaining. "I have only heard rumors, but it's a possibility. Be prepared for a coolness as well. Mr. and Mrs. Sparling don't talk much, at least not to each other."

When they reached the farm, Mae and Carrie were working in the garden and the boys were busy with haying. Mae came up to the buggy. "Ma says to go on in and we'll join you soon. Looks like rain and we have a bit more garden to get in." It did look as if the skies could open up at any moment. Dr. MacGregor led Conboy into the house to J.W.'s sick bed. MacGregor spoke first. "J.W., I believe two heads are better than one so I hope you don't mind that I brought Dr. Conboy along."

"Good to see you again John," said Dr. Conboy. "Sure wish it were under different circumstances."

"Not as much as I do," J.W. said in a faint voice.

J.W. struggled to raise himself with his arms. "Sorry I can't get up proper, Daniel." Conboy saw beads of sweat forming on J.W.'s face from the effort to sit up. "Dr. MacGregor says your legs don't want to work," he said. J.W. nodded and turned his head. His chin quivered.

Dr. Conboy examined J.W. but there were few changes from the day before. The mouth seemed improved but the gut ache remained. "I think you have neuritis," offered MacGregor. "Would you agree, Dr. Conboy?"

Conboy hesitated before answering. "It certainly is a possibility."

J.W. tried to shift his position on the bed. "Well I hope the two of you can come up with a cure," he said, his frustration showing. "I got fields to plant." His voice remained weak and Conboy told him to rest.

The doctors left the room and sat at the kitchen table. "What have you given him so far Robert?" asked Conboy. MacGregor replied, "I gave him some magnesium and quinine, in two doses. The stronger one has made no difference yet. I'm considering nux vomica to stimulate the man." Conboy agreed with possible neuritis, but asked about the syphilis. Dr. MacGregor answered quickly. "That is only a consideration right now Daniel. I can't go on rumors I heard, but it's something to think about, privately."

Carrie's entrance ended any more talk of syphilis. She wiped her hands on her apron. "Sorry I didn't come to meet you, but you didn't need me to examine my husband." She looked toward the bedroom and quietly asked, "Have you seen J.W. already?" The doctors exchanged looks and finally MacGregor spoke. "Mrs. Sparling, we think your husband has neuritis and maybe a type of paralysis. Vannest is ordering a new medicine which should be in soon. For now, keep giving him the quinine." She nodded and went to the cupboard for her notebook. When Dr. Conboy saw what she was doing, he protested. "Oh, no, Mrs. Sparling. This visit was strictly voluntary and I cannot accept any payment." She didn't argue and neither did Dr. MacGregor as he pocketed his note.

After the doctors left, Carrie helped Mae finish the planting and suggested they get some water out to the boys. Carrie filled her bucket and looked up to see her daughter staring down the road. "Mae, what are you waiting on? The boys must be parched by now." Mae shook off her daydream and took cold spring water to Albert and Scyrel in the field west of the farm. Carrie went to the north field where Peter and Ray were working.

* * * * * * *

What Mae had been looking for arrived after the women were both gone. Bert Hurford rode into the yard. He looked around and saw that nobody was about. He hesitated but then proceeded with the task that had brought him here. He tied his horse at the trough, squared his shoulders, and entered the house. Bert set a cake he had carried in on the kitchen table and then turned to the bedroom door, which was ajar. He politely knocked on the wall beside it. J.W. looked toward the sound and Bert tried to hide his shock at the appearance of the once strong man. "Mr. Sparling," he began. "I've come to see you, can you take some company for a while?"

"Sure," came the weak reply. "Come on in. You can grab a chair from the kitchen if you like. May as well be comfortable and then you won't have to look down on me. This is an odd time for you to be this far from home on a good work day."

In a shaky voice Bert answered. "Oh I've been working since sun up, but I got something on my mind that needs saying. Probably not a good time with you feeling so poorly, but it's real important to me.

"See, it's like this," Bert began. "My pa sold me his south farm over in Bingham Township, south of Ubly. I mean he sold me forty acres of it, and gave me eighty more. There's a nice house on it and the land is real good. A man could make a living off that farm if he was of a mind to."

Even though he felt rough, J.W. knew what was coming. He wondered if he should speak and relieve the boy of his nervousness or just let him rattle on. He decided to have some fun. "Why that's mighty good of your pa," he said. "That's what my pa did for Little Pete and me. William didn't want to farm, but Little Pete and me? Why, we were real happy to have our own land. What crops you planning to put in? You got good strong horses? A farm has to have good strong horses and then you got to treat them right. Yup, good horses are mighty critical to having—"

Bert interrupted. This was not going as he had planned. "Mr. Sparling, what I'm trying to say is, I want Mae for my wife and I've come to ask your blessing. I'll take real good care of her Mr. Sparling, and I love her. I haven't asked her properly yet, but I am led to believe she'll say yes." He heaved a huge sigh. It was out and he had done what he came for.

J.W. smiled and then became serious. "Son, you know marriage is for a long time. It can be a very long time. You're awful young yet. You sure you want to settle down?"

"Yes sir," Bert replied anxiously. "My folks asked me the same thing. I couldn't be more sure. And I'll be a good husband to your daughter. You needn't worry over that."

J.W. was tiring. "Well I have no objections, and if you want my blessing, you got it. Have you talked to Mae's mother yet?"

Bert's voice grew steadier. "No sir, I wanted to see you first, but I'll be sure to speak to her. You think she'll be all right with it?"

"Hard to say," answered J.W. "She won't like Mae leaving her but it sounds like you'll be fairly close by. And she knows a woman wants and needs her own place—same as a man. You might get a chance to ask pretty soon, I hear voices outside."

Bert heard them too. "Guess I've stayed long enough. I hope you're back on your feet real soon, Mr. Sparling 'cause we're having a real good spring. Thank you Mr. Sparling, thank you very much."

He left the bedroom and entered the kitchen where he saw Carrie staring at the cake. He looked at Mae briefly and nodded. Then he addressed Carrie. "Mrs. Sparling, Ma thought your hands were pretty full now and she sent this cake. It's yellow, hope you like it."

Carrie smiled. "Why that's very thoughtful Bert. Please thank her for me, for all of us." She sensed the cake was not the only reason for this visit. "Did you look in on J.W.?"

"Yes ma'am," he replied softly. "Sure is hard to see him laid up like he is, and I hope he'll be up and around real soon. Has to be hard for him, and you too." Bert started toward the door. "Guess I better get home. Ma says no hurry on returning the cake pan." Carrie thought it funny that these two believed they were keeping a secret from her, but she played along.

"Mae, why don't you see Bert to his horse? I need to check on your pa and then we can start supper. The boys will be hungry." She watched as the young couple walked slowly to Bert's horse. Carrie sensed changes again in her home. She fixed tea for J.W. as she tried to recall her own courtship. Those were happy times; what had happened to change them? Carrie shook the thoughts from her head and took the tea into the bedroom. It gave her great comfort to know J.W. would not be going to Canada.

* * * * * * *

Sunday brought visitors. Word had spread that J.W. was confined to bed. Violet and Ed Styles came after church and Violet brought a loaf of bread, as always. They didn't stay long but while there, J.W. asked Ed to help him sit up. Ed brought a stuffed chair from the parlor to the bedroom and helped J.W. into it. Ed was amazed at how weak the man had become. J.W. said it felt wonderful to sit up again, so the chair remained. After the Styles left, Reverend and Mrs. Mackersie arrived. They brought a book for J.W. to read. Ubly's first public library had just opened and Reverend Mackersie proudly reported he had been the first person to check out a book. Not wanting to tire J.W., the Mackersies left, but not before the minister offered prayer for healing.

Brother William and Big Pete got there about two o'clock in the afternoon. J.W. was thrilled to see them and assured both, after offers of help, that the boys were doing just fine with all of the farm work. William said Little Pete had wanted to come, but the last note Ellen had received from Mary stated that he was busier than ever. Old Pete's condition remained the same. And Mother Sparling? "She must have a good constitution," William remarked. "There is no other way to explain why she's still living."

Big Pete said his family was well, but little Orin, born last February, had not been a healthy baby and Mary was concerned. They had already buried two babies and the sadness had taken its toll. Hopefully the return of warm weather would bring the little one around. Big Pete added, "Uncle William in Canada isn't well. In fact, Uncle John and Uncle Chris are going over there next week. Too bad Old Pete can't join them, but it's doubtful he would even know who they are."

Before leaving, Big Pete helped his cousin back into bed. J.W. had been grateful for all the company; a welcome change from the ordinary. However, he was spent by all the commotion. He took the medicine Carrie brought, ate a few bites of roast beef, and settled down for the night. Sleep came quickly and he dreamed of years gone by; fishing with Big Pete, rough housing with his brothers, and his mother's sugar cookies.

* * * * * * *

The last week of May brought no change to the Sparlings. Dr. MacGregor came out twice to see J.W. He knew the prognosis was not good, but kept an optimistic attitude in front of the family. The weather warmed, but the house still carried a chill if J.W. and Carrie were in the same room. The boys took turns helping their pa from bed to chair and back again. One day when Peter was helping him, J.W. remarked, "Looks like Canada is off for this year. I haven't forgotten about it though. I just know you would love it up there."

Peter, always a person of few words, replied, "Yeah Pa. Maybe next year."

Huron County Tribune ad from March 1908

Chapter 20

Bert came to the farm on Decoration Day and he and Mae went to Ubly. The boys worked until ten o'clock in the morning, cleaned up, and headed for town. Ray would be marching and playing with the band; practice had begun in early April. Albert offered to stay with his pa, but J.W. insisted he go to town and enjoy the festivities. Carrie took her husband a plate of food and then went to the garden to thin radishes. When she came back, she noticed J.W. had eaten about half his food and fallen asleep.

She took his plate to the kitchen and went to the orchard. She sat by the little cross that marked her baby's grave. It needed painting. Fourteen years of weather had battered the small wooden frame. She mentally added it to her list of things to do. Little Edward deserved better. Then her thoughts went to Ubly. The parade would still be large, but nowadays fewer veterans took part. The new fire department planned to march and Carrie smiled as she pictured Dr. MacGregor among them.

As she re-entered the house, the telephone rang. It was her brother-in-law, William. His uncle, for whom he was named, had died. "Will you please pass the news on to J.W.?" he asked. Carrie had only met J.W.'s uncle one time, many years ago, at a Fourth of July gathering. Now he was gone. Death always came in threes and she wondered who would be next.

A letter arrived the first week of June. Aunt Freda wrote to tell Carrie that Isabelle had passed.

> Your mother died in her sleep and we buried her next to your pa in the town cemetery. It was for the best. She was a lost soul for so many years. We even had to pull the shades before sunset. If the sun happened to go down in a spectacular display, she would become agitated and mumble the word fire repeatedly. But now she is at rest.
>
> I received your kind letter after your pa died but there's no need to thank me for anything. I took your folks in because I wanted to.
>
> And I understand why you couldn't come in the spring. I've been in touch with your sisters. Cora came up after your pa died, but I don't expect any of you girls now. Please don't take that in a wrong way. You would be more than welcome. It's just such a long trip and, while I'd love to see you, there's nothing you can do.

Carrie took the letter to her mother's chair. Somehow she felt very close to her at this moment. Perhaps Isabelle was looking down at her and trying to relay a message that she was healed; that the mental and emotional scars had been removed and death had brought victory. Suddenly the arms of the rocking chair became her mother's arms, hugging her just as they had done so very long ago. She felt guilty for all the bad thoughts she had harbored. Carrie was sorry her children never knew the Isabelle she had known, and sorrier yet that Isabelle had never known her grandchildren. And finally, it occurred to Carrie something she should have realized all along. Her mother had not left her on purpose. It was a sickness that had taken her away. So many mixed emotions coursed through Carrie that she thought her mind would snap. She rocked harder and harder, and then release came in the form of sobs. Carrie had not cried in a long time, but now she let the tears flow freely. She cried for her folks. She cried for so many lost years. And then she cried for herself.

* * * * * * *

The following Monday Carrie prepared for washday. Mae, who had been out very late the night before, came into the kitchen and asked her mother to sit down. Carrie hesitated. She had a busy day ahead of her and it held no time for sitting idle. But the look on her daughter's face convinced her to pull out a chair. "Ma," she began. "I want you to know that Bert and I are going to be married. I joked about a leap year event, but he asked me on Decoration Day. He's been dropping hints and I knew he talked to Pa, so it wasn't a big surprise. He has Pa's blessing and I hope we have yours too." Carrie thought back to the day Bert brought the cake. She had been right. He must have told J.W. then. Of course, J.W. had said nothing to her, as usual. She pushed those thoughts away, smiled, and said, "Of course you have my blessing.

"Well, there is so much to do. There are plans to make and invitations to send out. We'll make you a new dress and we need to put together a list of things you'll need to set up housekeeping and—"

Mae broke in. "Ma, listen to me. We're getting married this Wednesday. Reverend Kinney in Tyre has agreed to marry us. I know it's a bad time with Pa sick, but neither of us want anything fancy."

Mae knew her parents could never give her as lavish a wedding as her cousin had last year. She smiled at her mother. "We just want to be married." Carrie paused before answering. She remembered her own excitement at marrying without all the fuss and feathers. How could she deny this simple request after all Mae had done for her?

She rose and went to her daughter with open arms. "Now Mae, don't you give us a thought. There's not much more you can do for your pa, and I'll be just fine. Now, what can I do to help? My gracious! That is the day after tomorrow! Get all your clothes down here. You won't start wedded life with dirty laundry. I wish I had my mother's wedding dress. You know it survived the fire of '71, but I think Cora or Lucy took it last time my folks moved. It just dawned on me, where will you live?"

Mae hugged Carrie and told her all that Bert had told J.W. "We'll be less than ten miles away, not so far when you think about it. The house has some furniture from Bert's Grandma Hurford. I'm going over tomorrow to be sure it is clean." Carrie's mind raced. What could she give Mae for a wedding gift? Her mother gave her the chair, but no! She could not part with that. She thought while she washed the clothes. She thought while she hung them to dry. She thought as she scrubbed the porch with the wash water. And by the time she was removing clothes from the line, a plan had formed. Carrie would be very busy the next two days.

Mae left early the next day for what would soon be her new home. Carrie informed the boys of the wedding and told them she had several errands for them. She then made four telephone calls—to Violet, Sam Soule, Bert's parents, and Emma Faupel. She cleaned the parlor, dining room, and kitchen, and gave her husband his meals and medications.

There had been no change for the better since J.W. first took to his bed. The doctor came out once a week, but he sounded less positive each time. He appeared hopeful in front of J.W., but when he talked to the family privately, his tone was guarded.

When Carrie took J.W. his milk toast that Tuesday, she asked if Mae had told him the big news. "Oh, I heard bits and pieces yesterday when you two were talking. It's time she was married and in her own place. Tomorrow, huh? Reckon she don't want a big wedding like Olive had."

Carrie replied, "No, guess not. But I'm fixin' to have a small celebration right here after the ceremony. Not much else we can do on such short notice. J.W., it's a nice day. Do you want the boys to help you to the front porch?"

"No," he whispered. "I'm kind of sleepy." J.W. had not said so many words to Carrie in ages. It must have worn him out she thought, with a touch of sarcasm.

J.W. slept and Carrie went back to work. She mixed up a cake and ironed while it baked. She didn't count the number of times she went to the cellar, but her legs told her it was a lot. Mae arrived home in time for supper and had to answer numerous questions from her brothers. She also had to endure some good-natured teasing as well. It was quite the happy meal, and they even heard J.W. chuckle from his bed. After all were asleep—Carrie had laid down the law, no prowling tonight—she iced the cake which had been hidden in the parlor, and then sought sleep for herself.

* * * * * * *

June 10, 1908 dawned beautifully and the house became a flurry of activity. Mae had gathered all her belongings and was primping for her wedding day. She promised Carrie that she and Bert would come back to the farm and load his wagon with her things after the service. They had planned to have it done ahead of time, but Mae agreed it could be done afterward just as easily. Bert arrived early, thinking he needed extra time to load the wagon. When Mae told him about the change in plans, he suggested they leave early for Tyre. "It's a pretty day and we can just walk about town before going to the preacher."

As soon as the boys' chores were done, they carried out the assigned tasks related to Carrie's previous telephone calls. Ray went to Violet's house and returned with a huge bundle of plants and ferns. He also brought back a loaf of bread wrapped in a new tea towel, tied up with a pretty pink ribbon. Scyrel and Albert went to Sam Soule's store and came home bearing two new bushel baskets and a small parcel of lemons. Peter put out fresh water and oats. Bert's parents had agreed to come, and their horse would need to be fed and watered. Then he went to Emma's to borrow the wheelchair her late husband had used. When he finished, he helped J.W. into the chair and moved him from the bedroom to the parlor. J.W. didn't put up a fuss. What good would it do? His legs didn't work, so he had no choice but to stay where he was put. Finally, Carrie made the boys clean up, an unheard of request in the middle of a summer workday.

When Bert and the new Mrs. Hurford drove into the yard after the ceremony, they knew something was different. Bert recognized his folks' buggy right off. He helped his bride from the wagon and Ray met them. "I'll take care of the horses, you are expected in the parlor. And Ma says to use the front door!" The couple beamed as they entered the room. There were Bert's parents, Ed and Cecelia Hurford, and beside them sat J.W., in the wheelchair with a blanket over his legs. The boys stood around awkwardly and Carrie grinned through a teary face. A place had been saved for them on the sofa. Mae kissed her folks and then went to the Hurfords. They welcomed her into their family with more kisses and hugs. Mae's brothers had never kissed her, but they stiffly gave her a peck on the cheek and shook Bert's hand.

Carrie announced that refreshments were waiting in the dining room and led Mae and Bert to the place of honor. There, in the middle of the table, sat a beautiful cake surrounded by lovely ferns, and a vase of peonies adorned each end. Everyone else filed in and Peter pushed J.W. into his assigned place. Mae could not tell if her father was happy about it or not, but at least he was out of that dark bedroom. Everyone took a seat and Carrie brought in lemonade. She cut and served the cake and happy chatter filled the room.

Yet another surprise appeared with the arrival of Russell Watkins, a photographer from Bad Axe. Carrie had arranged to have a picture of the newlyweds and her other children taken while they were all together and, more importantly, dressed up.

Too soon the little party ended. Mae and Bert were understandably anxious to be on their way. Cecelia offered to help clean up, but Carrie politely said no. She would need something to keep her busy when her daughter left.

Scyrel   *Young Pete*   *Mae*   *Albert*   *Ray*

The boys helped carry Mae's things to the wagon and then Carrie, with help from Ray, brought out a final surprise. He carried a new bushel basket lined with a beautiful tablecloth Carrie had cross-stitched the previous winter. It contained a large variety of canned goods, all those trips to the cellar. On top sat the wrapped loaf of bread from Violet. A second basket held new pots and pans, a skillet, and four new dishes. Carrie hoped other essentials would be provided as people learned of the wedding. It was customary to visit relatives the first week of marriage and those visits always resulted in a gift, or the promise of one.

The bride and groom left, followed by Bert's parents. The boys were eager to get back into regular clothes even if it meant doing chores. But first, they helped their father back into bed. J.W. had not been used to such excitement and was clearly fatigued.

Carrie was now alone and the tiredness caused by the hectic preparations began to set in. Supper would be an easy meal of beef and gravy over bread. Meanwhile, she cleared the dining room table and started washing dishes. She knew she would miss Mae. Not only for sharing the workload, but also for female companionship. With Ellen and both Marys gone, Carrie realized how much she missed having another woman nearby. But she still had Violet and looked forward to seeing her again.

Since J.W. had taken to his bed, it had been harder for the women to get together. School would close Friday for the summer and perhaps she could get a neighbor to sit with J.W. There was usually a young girl around who needed extra money. She would think about it, but enough thinking for today. After supper, she took J.W.'s medicine to him with a glass of lemonade and bid everyone good night. The boys would probably head for town soon. They had been whispering and exchanging winks at the supper table. It could be that a shivaree was in the works.

* * * * * * *

Carrie slept well and woke feeling refreshed. After breakfast, she worked in the garden and finished cleaning up from the wedding reception. Emma had told her to keep the wheelchair, so there were no errands for the boys outside their usual chores. She heard buggy wheels in the yard and was thrilled to see Violet step out and tether her horse. The women exchanged a warm embrace and Violet said she simply must hear all about the surprise party. Carrie brewed tea while Violet looked in on J.W. He looked very thin and haggard, but managed to pull himself to a near sitting position. They shared small talk and Violet said she hoped he would be up and about real soon. J.W. nodded faintly in agreement.

She returned to the kitchen and listened, over tea and leftover cake, to the account of the wedding party. Carrie thanked her for the flowers, ferns, and bread. "Mae was very touched with your kindnesses, and the tea towel is beautiful." The women shared updates of family health and events, but Carrie chose not to use this time to unburden herself of anything personal, since J.W. was within earshot. When it was time to leave, Carrie walked with Violet to the waiting horse.

Violet put her hand on Carrie's shoulder. "Carrie, how are you really doing? It doesn't appear that J.W. is improving. What does Dr. MacGregor have to say?" Carrie looked around; no one else was near. "The doctor will be here tomorrow, but right now he seems to be at a loss. He keeps giving J.W. new medicines to try, and I've tried my own remedies, but I don't think Dr. MacGregor holds out much hope. I haven't said anything to the boys yet, but it's obvious their pa is failing. J.W. was pleasant to everyone yesterday, but when they had all gone, his silence and crossness returned. I must be used to it because it just doesn't bother me any more." She saw Scyrel coming toward them and abruptly changed the subject. "Here comes Scyrel. The boys take turns helping with their pa." The young man nodded to the women and went into the house. Violet climbed into her buggy and Carrie turned to follow her son.

The next day, as usual, Dr. MacGregor spent about half an hour with J.W. The only change from the week before was J.W.'s attitude. He had become resigned to his condition. The old demands of "you got to fix me up, Doc" were no longer heard. MacGregor tried to raise his hopes with talk of the farm. "Such a grand farm you have, Mr. Sparling. Your hard work has made it a good, productive operation. I saw a wheelchair in the kitchen. Would you like to use it for some fresh air?" He stopped when he saw the scowl on his patient's face.

"I reckon you mean well," J.W. muttered. "But I'll not be sitting outside in that contraption for anyone passing by to look at and pity. Your pills and powders ain't working, so why would I take your advice now? My legs are no better and now my hands are failing me. The gut ache stays with me and I get itchy all over." J.W. turned his face to the window and whispered, almost to himself, "Maybe it's just my time to die."

Dr. MacGregor did not press the wheelchair idea. "J.W., I understand your frustration. Is there anything at all you would like me to do before I leave?" J.W. just shook his head.

MacGregor partly closed the door as he left the room. There stood Carrie, with his fee in hand. She looked so small and vulnerable, and he could see the effect J.W.'s caustic words had on her. She had become used to her husband's outbursts, but now she hurt for the physician. She walked out the side door with the doctor. "I'm sure he didn't mean to go on so," she apologized.

The doctor spoke in a very soothing voice. "Carrie, don't you fret about my feelings. I've heard much worse from the sick beds of other men. How are you feeling? How are your eyes?" She told him she felt fine, although it wasn't the entire truth. When he left, she thought about lashing out at her husband for his rudeness, but when she reached the door, she saw that J. W. was asleep. She closed the door and went to her chair.

* * * * * * *

The next ten days brought high temperatures and the third death. Her sister-in-law Ellen called late on the twenty-second. Big Pete and Mary would be burying another child. But it wasn't the sickly infant, Orin. Little three year old Mary had died. They didn't know the cause of death, but the unbearable heat was suspected. "She just took sick and died," Ellen said. Carrie felt an ache in her heart. If she lived closer, she could help in some way. Or was help fruitless in such a situation?

Chapter 21

July was hotter still, and the abundant strawberries began to taper off. Mae came out the first Wednesday of the month to help make jam. She knew her pa had not gotten any better but it shocked her when Carrie had to stop work to feed him dinner. His hands were now numb, and he could not hold a fork or spoon. When asked, Carrie told her daughter that she or the boys had been feeding him for about a week and that the doctor came out more often. J.W. was now nearly paralyzed from the neck down.

When Dr. MacGregor arrived the next Sunday, it was apparent to all that J.W. would not recover and few words were spoken. MacGregor brought more medicine and Carrie promised she would get it down him. "How is the rest of the family doing, Carrie?" he asked. "We're getting by," she answered. "Anna Pieruski helps me. And the boys are handling the farm work pretty good. I hired the Brethren preacher, Henry Bacon, to lend a hand. He's a good worker and everyone knows a preacher can always use extra money."

Carrie no longer questioned the doctor about her husband's health or his prognosis. She just handed him his money and thanked him for coming.

* * * * * * *

The following weekend many visitors came to see J.W., and each went away sensing the end was near. John Sparling, Old Pete's brother, came to see his nephew on Saturday and Big Pete was with him. The men didn't remain long, as talking seemed to tire J.W. When they tried to say goodbye with a customary handshake, they found themselves holding a limp hand. Big Pete thought he saw a tear escape his cousin's eye as they prepared to leave. Both John and Big Pete told Carrie to call them if she needed anything. She knew they meant every word even though Big Pete was still grieving over his daughter. Carrie wondered if she should ask Uncle John about buying a plot at the cemetery in Tyre. She decided to wait.

Mae's in-laws came shortly after the men left. Cecelia Hurford brought supper for the family and Ed tried to talk with J.W. about weather and crops. Ed hid his concern, but was shocked to see how the man had failed since he last saw him, only three weeks ago at Bert and Mae's wedding. J.W. could no longer sit up and his words were nearly inaudible. Ed wanted to wipe the drool coming from J.W.'s mouth, but knew it would be embarrassing. He stood and told J.W. to rest, adding that he could be proud of his sons and the way they were handling the farm. Carrie entered the bedroom with medicine and Ed Hurford said goodbye.

The Styles arrived as the Hurfords were leaving. Violet put a loaf of bread on the table and went with her husband into the sick room where they found J.W. sleeping. They tiptoed quietly back to the kitchen, but not before Violet wiped J.W.'s chin with a corner of the sheet.

They had only been gone ten minutes when Dr. MacGregor drove into the yard. He went into the bedroom and gently felt J.W.'s pulse, trying not to wake him. When he left the room, he saw Carrie sitting in a rocking chair in the other bedroom. He stood at the door and told her they needed to talk. Carrie told him to come in which he did, closing the door behind him. He didn't want J.W. to wake and hear the conversation he was about to have. "Carrie," he began. "I believe J.W. should go to the hospital now. I can make arrangements for him to go to London, but it will cost."

Carrie nodded and replied, "I can get the money Monday. If you would take care of everything else, I'd be most grateful."

Reverend Bacon was coming from the barn and saw the doctor enter the house. He decided to wait on the side porch. Today was payday—Carrie always settled accounts on Saturday. The windows were open and he heard voices, but no clear words. When he heard a door close, he assumed the doctor had finished and he went into the kitchen, finding it empty. The door to J.W.'s room was ajar and the other bedroom door was shut. He thought it odd and hoped that Mrs. Sparling was not sick now as well.

In a few moments, the doctor emerged from the closed-door room and seemed taken aback by Henry Bacon's presence. A few seconds later, Carrie came from the same room and Henry was relieved to see that she looked healthy. She reached into a cupboard and took out an envelope for Reverend Bacon. He thanked her and went on his way; he had a sermon to finalize.

When the boys came in for supper, Carrie quietly told them what Dr. MacGregor had suggested. They were not surprised and even wondered to themselves why their pa had not been taken there before now. Peter and Albert went in to check on him. Scyrel brought in a load of wood for the stove and Ray made sure buckets of water were handy. They didn't know what the others were planning, but were certain the plans didn't involve sitting at home; it was the Fourth of July. There hadn't been a family event for a couple of years now and the boys wanted to take part in the festivities in town. Ray would be performing with the band at the Independence Day concert. Carrie set out the supper that Cecelia had brought and then fixed a plate for her husband. She didn't hear the hushed conversation at the kitchen table. Albert said Pa wanted to see them, pointing to Ray and Scyrel. Peter had a look of unease but said nothing. "Don't leave the house tonight until you've gone in to see Pa," insisted Albert. They finished supper in relative silence. Carrie returned to the table and ate a few bites of chicken pie, but hardly tasted it. She had to make some plans and telephone calls.

Peter and Albert took turns cleaning up and then refilled the buckets for their younger brothers. Carrie, giving them privacy for Saturday night baths in the kitchen, sat on the front porch snapping green beans. Scyrel and Ray entered J.W.'s room and he motioned for them to come closer. They could see the pain in his eyes. In a weak voice he mumbled, "Boys, I'm not going to get better and. . . ." J.W. labored for breath. "Like I told your brothers, take care of each other and do whatever you need to do to keep the farm going." Ray told his father to rest, but J.W. shook his head. After coughing up some blood, he continued. "I want you to know how proud I am of all of you." J.W. grimaced as pain attacked his stomach. "Albert tells me this is the Fourth of July. Didn't we have some good times years back?" Without waiting for a reply, he added, "Now you two git. Go out and celebrate." J.W. gasped for breath. "Tell your ma I need something for this gut ache."

The boys left, Carrie brought medicine to her husband, and the Sparling house became very quiet.

* * * * * * *

Carrie didn't go to church Sunday. Both Reverend Bacon and Reverend Mackersie visited after services and had prayer with J.W. Mae and Bert came out for the day. Dr. MacGregor and his wife stopped by and Ida put a rhubarb pie on the table as her husband went into the sick room. He had told Carrie he would explain to J.W. about going to the hospital. If there had been any concern as to how the patient would take the news, it was needless. After MacGregor told him they were making plans to take him to London, J.W. only nodded. The doctor went into the kitchen. "Mrs. Sparling, the hospital is ready for your husband. Can you have him at the train station early Tuesday morning?" Carrie assured him they would be there.

"I called J.W.'s cousin, Big Pete," she said. "The boys felt it would be good if he went with you to the hospital. They'll get the wagon cleaned and make it comfortable for the trip to Tyre." She thanked Ida for the pie and the MacGregors left. They had been gone about an hour when William and Ellen drove in. Ellen brought canned pork loin, a cabbage salad, and a wedding present for Mae and Bert. The women talked while William visited with his brother. When he left the sick room, his eyes were teary and he couldn't speak. He immediately went out into the yard and the women gave him time to recover before joining him. William blew his nose and cleared his throat before speaking.

"Little Pete wanted to come, but Pa has become too much for the boys to handle alone. He sends his regrets." Carrie told them of the planned trip to the hospital and promised to keep them informed. Bert went home alone. Chores wouldn't wait and Mae wanted to stay and help Carrie get things ready for Tuesday.

* * * * * * *

Monday was hectic. Fortunately, no visitors came to call and the family was able to get everything ready for the next day without interruption. Carrie went to the bank to get money for the trip, and came home to help Mae with the washing. Peter and Albert took care of the milk route while Scyrel and Ray finished cutting hay in the west field. After supper, the boys cleaned out the wagon. The busy day helped keep their minds from the sobering reason for their labors. By day's end, the preparations were complete and the family could rest, or try to.

The heat of the July day extended into the night and sleep was fitful. Heat lightning lit the sky, but no rain fell. Mae and Carrie took turns sitting with J.W., wiping his face with cool cloths. It brought minimal relief from the heat, but none for the pain. Morning broke but the heat continued. After a quick breakfast, Peter brought a cot into J.W.'s room. Carrie laid fresh linens on it and the boys helped her get clean clothes on their pa. They moved him onto the cot and carried it to the wagon. Albert had hitched Maude and Della, and the horses stood waiting to transport their cargo. Peter drove the team and Carrie sat beside him. Mae and Albert rode in the back to keep the cot steady, and Scyrel and Ray followed on horseback.

When they arrived in Tyre, Big Pete met them and Dr. MacGregor arrived shortly after. Peter bought the tickets and the boys carried J.W. from the wagon to the train. Mae kissed her father and then quickly turned away so he could not see her cry. The boys went to him one by one. Peter busied himself by checking the cot even though there was nothing wrong with it. "Pa," he said. "I never gave you an answer on Canada, but as soon as you're fixed up, we can start planning." He patted his father's shoulder and left. Albert told J.W. not to worry about the farm. "We'll take good care of it while you're away." He had to clear his throat often to prevent sobs from escaping. Ray fixed the pillow on the cot and said, "Once you're home, maybe we could dust off the accordion and you and me could play some music." Seventeen year old Scyrel had no words. He knew if he tried to speak, tears would fall. But he was not too embarrassed to lean down and kiss his father good-bye.

The conductor called all aboard and everyone watched as Carrie approached the cot. Bit Pete held out his arm for her, but she politely refused it. There were no words, no embraces, and no tears. Husband and wife stared at each other. It only lasted for a moment, but it seemed a lifetime. No one would ever know the thoughts each harbored. And then J.W. closed his eyes, grimaced in pain, and turned his head.

Big Pete again reached for Carrie's arm and this time she took it. He walked her to her waiting children and then boarded the train with Dr. MacGregor. The family watched the train leave the station and stood together until it was out of sight. No one spoke on the ride home. Bert met them at the farm and Mae went home with him. She had offered to stay, but Carrie assured her there was nothing to do. The boys saw to the horses and wagon, and then busied themselves with routine chores. Carrie began to strip J.W.'s bed, but suddenly stopped. It could wait. She went to her chair.

On July eighth, Sam Soule rode into the yard. It wasn't unusual for him to make deliveries, but Carrie had not placed an order. He climbed down from his wagon and brought a piece of paper to her. It was a telegram.

> John Wesley Sparling departed this earth at two o'clock on the morning of July eighth. Arrival at Tyre expected late today.

Carrie's hands shook as she reread the message. Sam pulled out a kitchen chair and helped her into it. He saw no tears and thought she must be in shock. "Mrs. Sparling, can I get you anything?" She shook her head and Sam let her sit quietly another moment. Then he continued. "I took the liberty of calling Reverend Mackersie and he's on his way. He will go to Mae and Bert's first. Where are the boys? Can I get them for you?" No answer was necessary, as Albert had just entered the room. One look told him the story. "Albert," Carrie said softly. "Please get your brothers, your pa has passed."

The rest of the day was a blur. Mae and Bert arrived the same time as Reverend Mackersie who comforted the family as best he could. Since J.W. had not attended his church, he didn't want to assume control. He would just offer comfort until Reverend Bacon arrived to set up funeral arrangements. Word spread quickly and the house was soon awash with neighbors. They brought food, condolences, and offers of help. Carrie asked Reverend Mackersie to call J.W.'s brothers and Mae gave him the telephone numbers. Violet appeared and took over the task of setting out the food that was coming in. She also made a list of what was brought, as she knew Carrie would want to thank people later. The boys seemed at a loss as to what they should be doing, but Mae used work as therapy for her grief. She laundered the bedding Carrie had left the day before and reminded the boys to bring in wood and water. She tidied the house and tried to get her mother to eat something.

Reverend Bacon arrived and he and Carrie went into the parlor to discuss the funeral arrangements in private. She insisted Mae and the boys be part of the procedure, and they were summoned. Carrie didn't want to use the church and her children agreed that their father would rather be buried from the home. But they soon realized their house could not accommodate all who would attend and decided on visitation at the home, to be followed by a small service at the Brethren Church in Tyre, close to the cemetery. After the burial, there would be another gathering at the farm.

When the subject of burial was broached, Carrie said she would have to talk to Uncle John. She recalled that Decoration Day conversation when J.W. had expressed a desire to use the small cemetery his uncle had donated to the community. Reverend Bacon asked Carrie if J.W. had a good suit of clothes. "When your husband's body arrives, it will be taken to Mr. McKay, the undertaker. I can take J.W.'s suit to McKay and he will have everything he needs before the viewing."

The plans were finalized and the preacher again offered prayer before leaving. One by one, the children left the room. Carrie sat a few moments longer and when she rose, Violet appeared in the doorway. The women embraced. Violet could feel the tension in her friend slowly give way to near collapse, and helped Carrie to the sofa. They sat together for nearly an hour. Carrie wanted to talk, but the words just would not come.

* * * * * *

Carrie had been on the giving end of other bereavements. She had taken food and offered assistance, but never did she realize how invaluable these small acts of kindness were. During the rest of the afternoon, and most of Thursday, women came in to clean the house, prepare meals, and set the kitchen right afterward. Uncle John had readily agreed to have his nephew interred at Tyre and said he would see to those preparations himself. He also promised to fulfill a second request for Carrie.

Neighbor men turned the hay that had been cut just last Monday. The boys still did the milking; they needed something to do. J.W.'s room was transformed from a dark sickroom into a sunny, clean guest room—Cecelia Hurford's doing. No need for painful reminders.

Big Pete and Mary arrived Thursday afternoon. This gentle giant was deeply affected by the death of his cousin. Having recently been through a death, he knew Carrie would need support when J.W.'s body was brought to the house. The parlor had been prepared for the casket and when it arrived, Carrie leaned heavily on Big Pete as she drew near. J.W. looked good, better than he had in a long time. She stood at his side for a few moments but remained silent and dry-eyed. Big Pete gave her arm to Albert and Peter reached for the other one. Scyrel, Ray, Mae, and Bert joined them. Mae sobbed softly and the boys dabbed at their eyes with their handkerchiefs.

The visitation on Friday brought a steady stream of relatives, friends, and neighbors who came to pay their respects. Most had known J.W. all his life and were grieved and somewhat surprised by his death. Until late spring, he had been the picture of health. Doctors Griffin, Conboy, and MacGregor also joined the assembly. When MacGregor approached Carrie, he apologized for not bringing her husband back alive. "But," he added, "there is no more pain and suffering." Carrie didn't speak, but nodded gratefully.

Among the mourners were many Sparlings. Carrie could not help but remember her first encounter with this family. So many Peters, Georges, Williams, and Marys. Now she could keep them straight, but it had seemed an insurmountable task that Fourth of July twenty-six years ago.

The day was tiring for all the family and they slept soundly that night. Bert's parents volunteered to do his chores, so he and Mae spent the night in Mae's old room. Carrie woke early and prepared breakfast for everyone. She had greatly appreciated all the help that had been pouring in from the community, but a quiet meal alone with her children warmed her heart. Mr. McKay came for the casket about ten o'clock. Everyone said a private farewell to father and husband, and then John Wesley Sparling left his farm and family for the last time.

* * * * * *

A few white puffy clouds floated through a deep blue sky, and a gentle breeze carried the scent of newly mown hay, flowers, and earth. Food started arriving shortly after breakfast and Carrie was not sure where to put it all. But ladies from Ubly Presbyterian came as the family left for the church. They took care of the food and prepared refreshments to have after the service.

The church filled to overflowing. A brief service heard many kind words spoken about the deceased, but Carrie heard very little of it. Among the mourners sat Carrie's sister, Cora. They had not been in touch since Christmas. Carrie didn't know how her sister had learned of the death, but was pleased to see her there. Perhaps she could talk Cora into remaining for a while afterward.

After the service, the assembly followed the casket to the cemetery across the road. Uncle John had been true to his word. The graveyard looked fresh and clean and yes, there was her second request. Only then did Carrie shed her first tears. There beside her husband's prepared grave stood another one, a smaller one. Uncle John had seen to it that her unnamed baby would no longer rest in the orchard, but by his father. She would make sure that little Edward had a stone as well. Carrie and her children stood together as Reverend Bacon spoke a few more words. Then Peter and Albert escorted their mother to the buggy.

News of a gathering at the farm had spread and many other buggies followed Carrie's. There were so many that the west field, now empty of hay, was used as a parking area. Tables had been set outside and a caravan of women, coming from the kitchen, carried food to them. Dr. MacGregor's wife seemed to be in charge and another lady, unknown to Carrie, helped Ida.

Carrie saw Old Pete in a chair by the well; he had not been at the church or cemetery. Grandsons Joseph, Herbert, and Harvey stood by him in case he decided to travel. It proved unnecessary because the old man just sat quietly. He had aged greatly since Carrie had last seen him. Mother Sparling was too ill to attend, but a kind neighbor of William's had offered to stay with her so the family could be there together. J.W.'s Uncles John, Christopher, and Thomas found their way to Old Pete. It was hoped that seeing his brothers would bring Old Pete into the present time. It didn't, and he wasn't even aware that he was at a son's funeral.

Mingling, story telling, remembering, and even laughter was interspersed amid the sorrow of the occasion. It took some doing, but Reverend Mackersie finally got everyone's attention and said grace. Dishes heaped with food covered the tables. In the middle of them all sat a plate of sugar cookies. Ellen had used Mother Sparling's recipe and brought the sweets that had been so loved by J.W. It was almost like the old Fourth of July celebrations except it occurred one week later and the reason for the gathering was not lost on anyone.

The afternoon waned and people prepared to leave. They again paid their respects to Carrie and offered help in the days to come. Dishes were claimed, the wooden tables were folded for transport back to the schoolhouse, and the yard took on its old appearance. Little Pete had taken his father in a buggy to the old homestead. Old Pete looked, for a moment, as if he remembered, but then suddenly any cognizant thoughts were gone; replaced with the now familiar vacant stare. Ed and Violet left, but Violet assured Carrie she would be back. Carrie looked around at the empty yard that had been so full only moments before. Now only a few people remained.

Ida MacGregor and another woman came from the side yard. They had been hanging wet dishtowels on the line. Ida brought the woman to Carrie. "Carrie," Ida began. "I'd like you to meet Jennie Boomhower. Her husband is president of Ubly village. Perhaps you've heard his name, Xenophon Boomhower."

Jennie smiled, "It isn't a name you could easily forget. Actually, my husband is relinquishing his position of president. His law practice is growing and he doesn't feel he can do justice to both. Mrs. Sparling, I didn't know your husband, but I want you to know how very sorry I am for your loss." She pressed Carrie's hand between hers. "Now if you'll excuse me, I want to check the kitchen once more."

She left and Ida spoke. "Jennie has been a tremendous help. Our husbands have become great friends. He does have an unusual name, but they call him Zen. I believe he has political ambitions and you may hear that name again." Ida realized she was rambling and changed the subject. "There is leftover food in the kitchen. If any dishes were left, please let me know and I'll see they are returned to their owners. If you need anything else, please call."

Carrie managed a smile. "Ida, you've done so much already. How can I ever thank you?"

Ida shrugged. "Others brought the food, I only set it out."

There had been so many people that afternoon. Carrie had acknowledged everyone but felt she had visited with none. Close family left last. Little Pete and Mary decided to go back to Brown City for Old Pete's sake. There had been so much excitement they felt he would do better in his own bed. William and Ellen returned to Bad Axe, as did Big Pete and Mary. They gave hugs of farewell before leaving. These cousins, so accustomed to grief themselves, were wonderful comfort. Carrie watched as the last buggy faded into the distance.

As she turned back toward the house, she saw Mae and Cora on the front porch. "How good of Mae," thought Carrie, "Cora probably feels I have ignored her." She joined them and learned that her sister had agreed to stay on an extra day or two. Mae also offered to stay, but Carrie said that her place was with her husband. The boys, changed into work clothes, went to work. Peter and Albert headed for the barn while Ray and Scyrel went to bring in the cows. Bert brought his buggy around and Mae climbed in beside him. Carrie handed her a basket of food. It barely made a dent in the leftovers, but four hungry boys would change that.

Carrie and Cora sat again on the porch remembering people and events from their childhood. The fires of '71 and '81 had been a huge part of their youth, but they passed over those memories for happier ones. Cora talked about the first time she ever saw J.W. "He was walking you back to our wagon. Do you remember? You have been a very lucky woman, Carrie. Marrying him must have been the best thing you ever did. It's a shame he was taken from you." Carrie didn't respond but she had a strange smile on her face and changed the subject. "Do you have any news of Lucy?"

* * * * * *

Carrie woke to the sound of a gentle rain falling on the roof. She knew she should go to church, but decided against it. She was very tired and surely people would understand. Her eyes burned; she would have to call Dr. MacGregor. Cora kept the breakfast conversation lively by talking to her nephews, four young men she hardly knew. She entertained them with stories of some of their mother's exploits as a child. Stories that Carrie had never shared greatly amused her sons. It reassured them to know their mother had not always been so proper.

The boys also avoided church. They milked the cows, but rain prevented any other work. J.W. had never liked them to work on Sunday anyway. Cora and Carrie spent much of the day visiting on the covered front porch. Carrie made a list of things to do and people to thank. There was still a lot of leftover food, so Carrie didn't have to cook; it truly was a day of rest.

The women decided to go into Tyre on Monday. Carrie needed garden seed and stationery for the thank you notes. While there, Cora made arrangements for her train trip back to Flint. The sisters had enjoyed catching up, but both realized they were running out of things to say. Cora jokingly reminded Carrie of what their pa used to say. "Fish and company both go bad after three days." The next morning, Cora bid the boys good-bye and Carrie took her to the station for an early departure. As the women parted, they promised to keep in touch more often. Cora extended an invitation to Carrie. "I'd love to have you spend time with me, under pleasanter circumstances. My door is always open to you." Carrie thanked her and said she would be busy with the farm and her children. "But you never know," she added. "I could surprise you one of these days."

When Carrie arrived home, Dr. MacGregor was waiting for her. He had brought the death certificate, giving cause of death as diffusing myelitis, or a spreading inflammation of the spinal cord. No mention was made of any other disease. She asked if he would look at her eyes. He obliged and could tell they were irritated, although he knew it had not been from crying. Carrie had been quite unmoved throughout J.W.'s funeral, and even his illness.

The doctor gave her some salve and reminded her to avoid straining them. She made no promises and turned to a different thought. "I really appreciated what your wife did last Saturday. And she introduced me to Jennie Boom-something. She said you're good friends with her husband."

"Oh yes," he replied, "Zen Boomhower. He and his wife came from Indiana, and Ubly has welcomed both of us outsiders with open arms." He laughed. "Him an up and coming lawyer and me, a simple country doctor. An odd pairing, but yes, we are becoming the best of friends."

Carrie huffed. "I don't know why that is odd. He couldn't possibly be any finer a man than yourself." MacGregor thanked her for the compliment and also for the money she pressed into his hand.

* * * * * *

It didn't take Carrie long to resume her old routine. The farm had already been deeded to her, and money from an insurance policy on J.W. would soon arrive. By the time she used it to pay down the notes and mortgage, there would be little left. Anyone who thought her husband was a prosperous farmer didn't know about all the notes they owed. It would be a good feeling to pay off some of the debts. They were in the same situation as many other farmers. You spent money to make money and hoped for good stock, good weather, good crops, and good help.

The boys also went back into their old habits. Peter still loved to carouse at night. He had just turned twenty-three and showed no signs of settling down. He sometimes complained of sore joints, but arthritis ran in the family. And he continued to buy creams for his pimples. If Vannest didn't have what he wanted at the drug store, he asked Dr. MacGregor. At times he sent away for patent medicines, but nothing he tried seemed to work and his handsome face remained pocked.

Albert was also concerned with his complexion, but not to the same degree. He could always be talked into a ball game, but had to be prodded to do chores. Ray was happy to be back at band practice. When he blew that horn, he could forget unpleasant times. Scyrel did his work without complaint, but always looked for a reason to go to the general store in Tyre. Mae began settling into her new role. She and Bert had been busy during her father's illness and death. Now she could find her own rhythm and routine as a new wife.

Chapter 22

Even though the August heat set records, enough rain fell to ensure that crops and garden thrived. There would hopefully be good yields. More notes could be paid and the cellar replenished. On Wednesday, August nineteenth, everyone worked extra hard and most farmers put in longer than usual hours because tomorrow was Caledonian Day, an annual Scottish celebration. Always well attended, it took place in Ubly with a great variety of events. You could watch a trapeze act, listen to John Jordan sing, laugh at the comic reading by a Miss Waterworth, and clap your hands as the Irish reel was performed by a talented dance troupe. If you wanted to do more than observe, there were athletic contests—everything from races to jumps and vaults to shot throws. Port Austin, to the north, brought its ball team to play against Ubly. The town reveled in a day that differed so from their usual labors.

The Ubly Concert Band gave two performances, which is why Carrie attended. She rode with Ed and Violet. The women had resumed their weekly visits and Carrie had accepted her friend's offer to accompany them to the big event. Aletha, now thirteen, and five year old Marie bent Carrie's

Ray Sparling (second row from top and third from left) in Ubly Concert Band

ears all the way to town. They told her about their dolls and a new puppy. Both were anxious for school to begin in just a few weeks.

Everyone enjoyed the festivities and it somehow made it easier the next day to do the milking, the cooking, the harvesting, and the weeding.

* * * * * *

Dr. MacGregor now came out to the farm once or twice a week. If no one was ailing, he found the boys and asked if they needed help. He always kept a pair of overalls in his buggy and they had been put to use more than once. He helped a cow with a difficult birth, and he helped at threshing time. The boys wondered why he had become a doctor since he appeared to like farming so much.

September was like all Septembers. The days were long, but the shelves in the cellar were filling up. Anna Pieruski helped Carrie if Mae was unable.

Violet and Carrie continued their regular visits. If Violet mentioned J.W., Carrie found a way to change the subject. On one visit in the autumn of 1908, Violet said her daughters were down with colds. "You know how it is when the days are warm and the nights are cool." Carrie paused and then asked, "What did the doctor say?"

"Doctor?" questioned Violet. "I didn't see a need to call him out for a cold."

"Oh Violet," replied Carrie, "maybe I'm too cautious, but Dr. MacGregor comes out to the farm quite often. I'm fully capable of treating my boys, and I do. I just feel better if the doctor sees them as well. He's such a wonderful man and I trust him completely. You know, he has even helped with some of the boys' work. Don't see how he finds the time, but he does."

For the next five minutes, Carrie spoke of nothing but Dr. MacGregor. If Violet found it strange that Carrie went on and on about Dr. MacGregor, yet didn't talk about her recently deceased husband, she kept it to herself. After all, women in mourning did not all act alike.

* * * * * *

October provided more diversions from everyday life. County fairs were eagerly anticipated as a time to present the fruits of your summer labors. On display were cattle, poultry, skillfully crafted harnesses, as well as art exhibits and fancy sewing work. It also provided a time to visit with other fairgoers and sample great varieties of food. Ray played with the band at both the Cass City and Huron County fairs.

Coming elections also drew interest. Dr. MacGregor's name appeared on the ballot for coroner, Zen Boomhower put his hat into the ring for prosecuting attorney, and W. H. Taft ran for President of the United States of America. All three won.

* * * * * *

On a cold New Year's Eve, Carrie sat in her chair reflecting on the past year. It had brought many changes—births, deaths, and marriages. But some things remained constant. Her boys were still under her roof. She wondered about the future but knew she could deal with whatever came her way. She rose from the chair and went to bed. Tomorrow was another day. In fact, tomorrow was another year.

Chapter 23

A very cold January brought on sickness. The boys all had colds or coughs, and Carrie called Dr. MacGregor when Albert's stomach trouble flared up. Carrie tried home remedies on herself and the boys, but still wanted the doctor's counsel. Her eyes continued to be irritated and sore. One day, after MacGregor had finished treating Carrie's eyes, he reminded her that the meager rays from the coal oil lamp did not give enough light for nighttime work that required good eyesight. "You really must do mending and sewing during the daytime," he argued. She half promised and then brought up an awkward subject.

"Doctor," she began, "I've always settled accounts with you each time you're here, but circumstances are now such that I have no choice but to pay with notes only. The crop yield was not what we had expected. I'll keep records of what I owe and the boys can bring cream, milk, and eggs to Ida to pay down the debt."

"Mrs. Sparling. Carrie," replied the doctor. "I know you'll be fair with me. Why, notes are what I'm used to from most everyone around here anyway. And Ida will appreciate the fresh foods." He took her hands in his. "Now, is there anything else I can do while I'm here?"

Carrie said no and reluctantly pulled her hands away to write the note. The doctor took it, made out as payable to bearer, and went to his sleigh. He understood Carrie's situation and would deal with it. But he preferred to get cash. Sometimes he felt that he spent as much time collecting from notes as he did doctoring. His dreams of a lucrative practice were still only dreams.

* * * * * *

February came and went with nothing extraordinary to recall its presence. Violet and Carrie met once a week and Dr. MacGregor called at the Sparling farm at least that often. Carrie called him early in March about Albert. "He's always been good at getting out of work," she explained. "But this time I believe his hurting is for real. He won't talk much to me, so I don't know how to treat him."

The doctor agreed to come as soon as he could. When he arrived, Carrie told him that Albert was upstairs. He followed her to Albert's room, but the boy insisted that his mother leave the room. After the examination, Dr. MacGregor found Carrie in the kitchen with a puzzled look on her face. "It's a hernia, Carrie, and it appears he has had it for some time. He just felt uncomfortable talking about it to a woman, even though that woman was his own mother." Carrie was relieved to learn the cause for secrecy, but troubled over the diagnosis.

"Oh Robert," she cried, "can he wear a belt or something for it?" This was an awkward conversation at best. "He can," answered MacGregor. "But it won't cure the problem. I've explained corrective surgery to him and it's something he will have to consider for himself. I strongly recommend it, and I know a very good physician in Detroit who does this procedure. If you wish, I can make some inquiries for you while he is deciding."

Carrie stumbled for words. "He's twenty-one years old and I guess he should be the one to decide. You seem confident in this doctor in Detroit, and I'm confident in you. I'll talk to him and encourage him to have the surgery. Do you know how long it would take? And what would it cost?"

Dr. MacGregor thought for a moment. "He would be in Detroit about two weeks, and when he gets home he would have to work back into his old routine very gradually. The other boys would have to carry his load for some time. As to cost, I'll have to find that out and get back to you."

Carrie didn't like the idea of her son having surgery, but she also knew he had been bothered for some time. She felt guilty because she had been quite harsh lately when prodding him to do his chores. Poor Albert had been shirking his duties for a good reason. It was nearly spring and not a good time to be laid up, but they could manage.

"Well," she sighed, "please get all the information and I'll speak to Albert, and the other boys as well." She gave the doctor a note and he left. She then went up to her son. Embarrassed or not, they needed to talk. She told him to remain in bed and get his thinking done. When the boys came in for dinner, she explained Albert's condition and told them what the doctor had advised.

"It wouldn't hurt if you assured him that you can handle his load," she urged. "It could also help him make the decision."

The boys recalled what their pa had said before he died. They were to look out for each other. That memory meant there would be no cause for indecision and they promised they would talk to their brother.

Chapter 24

March twenty-ninth began cold and blustery. Carrie and Young Pete drove Albert to Tyre to catch the train. Dr. MacGregor met them there to accompany Albert to Detroit for the hernia surgery. As the train pulled away, Peter stood by his mother. Carrie noticed her son was having a good day. Lately he had been having spells of forgetfulness. He would leave a room only to return wondering why he left in the first place. He went into town for pimple medicine the week before and came home without it.

She remembered overhearing J.W. talking to Young Pete about Canada and wondered if her son had further thoughts about it. She could not come right out and ask. After all, she had been listening at a closed door. But there was no need to fret about something that might never happen. And if it did, she would deal with it then. She and her son discussed how chores would be done with one less hand. Ray would help with the milk route and, if need be, they could hire a local man for the farm work.

After they reached home Carrie immediately began to churn butter. Scyrel could take it, along with the milk and cream, to Ida MacGregor. She intended to pay down her debt as soon as possible. Dr. MacGregor had said he would need fifty dollars to transport and tend to Albert. The surgeon and hospital bill would be close to two hundred dollars. She had given MacGregor a note for his services and borrowed the two hundred from the bank in Ubly for Albert's surgery.

* * * * * *

The doctor returned from Detroit on April first and telephoned Carrie to tell her Albert was mending nicely. "The operation went well and the surgeon said it was fortunate we decided on this course of action now. Had we waited much longer, recovery would have been an even more lengthy process. And Ida sends her thanks for the foods Scyrel brought. That was very thoughtful." Carrie did not remind him that the food had been intended to pay down her debt.

Albert returned home April twelfth. He had lost weight and looked a bit peaked, but that was to be expected. Carrie could restore the lost pounds with good home cooking. J.W.'s sick room, turned guest room, was once again a sick room. It meant fewer steps for both him and Carrie. Plus, he would not feel so isolated from everyone else. It was good to have him home where he belonged. Scyrel took special interest in Albert and the surgery. He also wanted to know what Detroit was like. Poor Scyrel, he was just not cut out to be a farmer.

* * * * * *

April remained cool—cool enough to butcher a hog. Dr. MacGregor assisted and Carrie made sure he got some of the fruits of his labor. Mae came not only to help prepare a big dinner for the men, but also to cut and grind the meat and render the lard. The day required hard work from everyone, but the thought of many good meals made their efforts worthwhile. They could almost taste the roasts, chops, summer sausage, liverwurst, and headcheese. Albert watched from the side porch. Most of his strength had returned, but he wasn't quite up to butchering.

When Dr. MacGregor prepared to leave, Carrie thanked him for his help. He had seemed distant and distracted all day, and she inquired about his welfare. The doctor smiled. "I'm fine, Carrie. I just have a few things on my mind right now." Carrie would not be put off. "Now see here Robert. If you need the help of this family for anything, do not hesitate to ask. You've been such a source of support to all of us and we'd be honored to return the favor." She had called him Robert on purpose. He looked at her a long time and opened his mouth to speak. But then he shook his head, mounted his horse, and rode off.

Carrie went into the house and called Ida. "Ida, I just wanted you to know your husband is on his way home. I don't mean to pry, but he looked so tired, even before the butchering began. Am I out of place to ask about his health?" "No Carrie, you aren't out of place," replied Ida MacGregor. "He doesn't always share his concerns with me so I really don't know. Mr. Leach from the bank came to call two days ago, and Robert has seemed different ever since. I'm sure it's nothing, but I appreciate your concern." There was a pause and she quietly added, "Maybe we should keep this talk to ourselves."

Carrie forgot the episode until the doctor came to the farm at the end of April. He checked Albert's dressing and stitches and then looked at Carrie's eyes. As she wrote his note he spoke. "Mrs. Sparling, you asked a while back about my welfare and I never gave you an answer. Now I will give that answer and also ask a favor, though it's something I really don't want to do. I'm afraid my bank account is in dire straits. I've tried to collect money owed me, but haven't been able to gather enough to satisfy outstanding debts which are long overdue. You cannot imagine how this pains me, but I must ask if you could see fit to loan me one hundred dollars for a three-month period. If it isn't possible, I will understand."

Carrie always assumed the doctor to be in good shape financially and his request surprised her. She only knew a few doctors, but never thought about them needing financial assistance. In fact, Dr. Herrington in Bad Axe owned an automobile. She looked at Dr. MacGregor and remembered they were due a milk check the next day. "I'll have one of the boys bring it to your office tomorrow afternoon," she said. "And instead of being a loan, why don't you just credit it to our account?"

She took his hand in hers and continued. "I'm glad I could help." An uncomfortable silence followed. They sat facing each other. Finally, the doctor pulled his hands away. Another silence. "Robert, have I made you uncomfortable?" She smiled. "You may find it hard to be on the receiving end, but please believe me. It feels very good to be on the giving end for a change."

Carrie watched from the window as Dr. MacGregor went to his buggy. She continued to watch until he faded into the distance. It did feel good to give.

Chapter 25

Albert grew stronger every day and the doctor said he could begin light work. Heavy lifting would have to wait a while longer. Carrie did her spring housecleaning. She always felt good after everything had been aired, washed, painted, repaired, scrubbed, or brushed. And she loved it when windows could be opened to let the old stale winter air escape. Of course, open windows also allowed dust from the roads to find its way back inside. She got her garden ready to plant and made sure she had seed, canning equipment, and Paris Green. The boys worked to prepare fields for planting, fixed broken fences, and checked on all the machinery that would soon be put to use. Every day saw the Sparlings hard at work, but no one minded. They were relieved to know winter had passed.

Though busy, Carrie took part of a day off to go see Violet. The women tried to maintain weekly visits, but when the growing season arrived they often found it impossible to get away. Right after she fed dinner to the boys, she went to see her friend. Violet had been thinking of Carrie, and welcomed her with a warm hug. Violet's daughters were happy to see Carrie as well. They proudly showed her their nearly finished needlework, and Marie told Carrie all about school. As anxious as both girls had been last fall to begin school, they were now counting the days until it ended for the summer. Their happy chatter reminded Carrie of her childrens' school days; days that had passed so quickly. Violet let the girls rattle on a few minutes and then a barely perceptible clearing of her throat told them it was now grown-up time. Aletha and Marie gathered up their doilies and left the room.

Violet brewed a pot of tea and the ladies sat and chatted at the kitchen table. They saw each other at church, but those conversations were limited to general health and weather. "Violet, your girls are so sweet," remarked Carrie. "But then I suppose they take after their mother." Before Violet could respond, Carrie continued. "Boys aren't usually sweet, you know. My boys are good, but I don't think they'd like it if I said they were sweet." Violet smiled and asked about them. She knew that, to Carrie, these four young men would always be her boys. "Well," began Carrie, "Young Pete still causes me concern. He always does a full day's work, but has a lot of pain in his bones and he's losing his hair. Sometimes, he has spells and can't remember what happened. I think he's just too tired. And, he cannot seem to rid himself of those pimples. He's almost twenty-four years old and you would think his complexion would have cleared by now. I guess the bone pain must be arthritis—it runs in my family. I've discussed it with Dr. MacGregor but he thinks it will all work out in a year or so. J.W. would scold me for worrying."

She paused for just a second or two and then continued. "Albert is recovering wonderfully from his surgery. He'll soon be back to full trot. He still has that nervous stomach, but the other pain is thankfully gone. I guess I'll be back to prodding him to work again before long. Ray loves being in the band. I said boys aren't sweet, but Ray comes close. I can't explain it, but he always has just the right words or hugs when I need them most. Scyrel really pitched in when Albert was laid up. Oh, all the boys did. But Scyrel seemed to miss him the most while he was in Detroit. And he asked so many questions. You know how quiet Albert is. Well Scyrel just peppered him with questions about the surgery. Overall the boys are doing all right. Mae is coming out next week. We'll go to the cemetery and make sure the Sparling plot is presentable. Uncle John takes good care of it, but we want to do our part." She caught her breath. "My goodness Violet, you asked a simple question and I have bent your ears. You can tell I don't have anyone to really talk to at home."

Violet smiled. This visit was like the others. Carrie talked and Violet listened. "Carrie," she said. "My ears are just fine and I love hearing about the boys and Mae. But how is your own health?"

Carrie told her about her eyes, a condition not unknown to Violet. "Dr. MacGregor comes out to check them often and I try to avoid straining, but I suppose it's just something I will learn to live with. Other than that, I am fine." The friends then talked about garden plans and shared a couple of new recipes. There were a few more discussions, mostly about the health and well being of neighbors. Carrie had learned early in their friendship that Violet refused to take part in gossip. Soon they were talked out and it was nearly suppertime. All the way home Carrie thought how lucky she was to have such a good friend.

* * * * * *

Mae arrived the next week as planned. She had dinner with the family and then the women went to Tyre. The cemetery looked nice, but Carrie knew they would find a few weeds. They brought two buckets of flowers and carried them to the graves. Carrie had ordered the headstones and this was the first time she had seen them. There was a large one for J.W. and a smaller one for her young son, dead now nearly sixteen years. Mae pulled weeds and smoothed the grass where they put the flowers. "Ma, the stones look real nice. They did a fine job and I like the open Bible on top of Pa's." She shook her head. "It's hard to believe he's been gone nearly a year now." Carrie nodded, but her interest was directed toward the small stone. "Did you see what I had them put on your brother's marker?" Mae went to Carrie and knelt down beside her to read:

Our loved one has gone before, to meet us on the other shore.

Tombstones of John Wesley Sparling and baby who died (smaller one to left)

Carrie obviously still carried an ache for the child who had lived only three weeks. "It's real pretty Ma," she acknowledged. They transferred the flowers from the bucket into a pair of two-quart sealers, which would be retrieved later. Mother and daughter then left the quiet little cemetery and went home.

The next day was Decoration Day. Ray marched with the band in Ubly, and Albert and Scyrel went fishing after chores. After he did the milk route, Peter went into Bad Axe. Carrie did not go back to the cemetery. Even though it was much smaller than the one in Ubly, she knew folks would be there to pay respects. She just didn't feel she could bear any more well meant words about J.W. She walked about the yard, through the garden, and then did the un-heard-of. She took a nap in the middle of the day—in her chair.

* * * * * *

June began on a very chilly note, but the garden had to be planted so Carrie put on J.W.'s old coveralls and a heavy sweater before going out to drop seeds into the freshly turned soil. She worked all morning, but stopped at noon. The boys, busy planting corn, would be famished. She had put a roast in the oven earlier, and added vegetables halfway through the cooking time. That, plus bread made yesterday and fresh rhubarb pie, ought to satisfy their appetites. It would be ready as soon as they appeared. She had no sooner set the table than she heard the sound of the boys' horses.

Just as the family sat down to eat, Dr. MacGregor drove his buggy into the yard. Carrie went out to meet him and invited him to share their meal. He apologized for coming at dinnertime. "I lost track of time, but can come back later." Carrie would have none of that. She insisted he join them, assuring him there was plenty of food. He finally agreed and said he wanted to check Albert afterward. Conversation was sparse at first—could those boys eat—but as they got their fill, he asked how the planting was progressing. They told him that all was going well. When he asked about any health problems, they answered that they were fine. But he thought Peter looked uncomfortable. Carrie removed the plates and took them to the kitchen. She was cutting pie and didn't hear the doctor when he asked if the boys had any insurance.

They looked puzzled and assured him that they were in good health. "But don't you see," he pointed out. "This is just the time to get insurance. Your pa was insured, and I know young men want their families to be taken care of should anything happen. You are all fit and strong, but you share the duties of the man of the house since your pa passed on. You need to think of your mother and the future." He smiled at them. "Anyway, it's been on my mind and I just thought I would mention it."

The appearance of pie ended the conversation. The doctor devoured his but the boys, stone faced, just picked at theirs. Carrie assumed they were full and said nothing. Finally the boys stood, stretched, and returned to the fields. Albert remained behind long enough for Dr. MacGregor to examine him and hear the words "You are fully recovered young man."

Carrie stopped washing dishes to talk to the doctor. Relieved to hear the news about Albert, she then mentioned Young Pete and her concerns over him. "I can't force him to have a check-up Carrie," MacGregor stated. "I'm sure if he has a problem, he'll come to me. No need to worry that pretty head over what is probably nothing." Carrie felt a blush creep up into her cheeks. The doctor smiled. "I should be going." And yet he lingered. Carrie suddenly remembered to write him a note. After all, he had examined her son, and dinner had never been suggested as a credit. As he left he could see the boys, deep in conversation, as they readied the horses for an afternoon's work.

* * * * * *

Three weeks later, when the doctor appeared for his regular visit to the Sparling farm, Peter met him at the hitching post. "Doc," he said. "We've been thinking about what you said, about the insurance. And we decided it's a good idea, but don't know how to go about it." The doctor patted the young man on the shoulder. "I am very impressed that you boys, I mean men, have come to this decision. I know Sun Life Assurance costs less than others. And my father is an agent for the company in Canada. I can talk to him and see if he could write policies here in America. That is, if you would like me to." Peter shook his head in agreement. "That would be a big help. Just let us know what we have to do." The doctor pondered for a moment. "You would all have to be examined, but I could do that. And then there would be papers to sign. I'll look into it as soon as I get home. It's a wise thing you are doing." The doctor watched as Peter returned to the barn. Was he limping?

Carrie was at the side door. She had seen the doctor arrive and watched as he talked to her son. She was curious and said so. MacGregor responded. "Carrie, your boys have decided to get life insurance." Carrie went to the kitchen table and sat down. MacGregor grabbed a chair and pulled it next to hers. "Think about it. This would require all of them to be examined, including Peter."

Carrie rubbed her temples. It took some time before she spoke again. "You're right, Robert. It's a good idea."

MacGregor nodded. "Now, let me see your eyes."

As soon as Dr. MacGregor arrived home, he put in a telephone call to his father. Alexander MacGregor arrived in Ubly on the twenty-eighth of June and his son met him at the station. The elder MacGregor did not know of the previous conversation his son had had with the boys, but said it was possible to insure them and he had brought all the necessary paperwork. The next day the four young Sparling men came to the doctor's office for their physical evaluations. Ray arrived first. He said he felt fine and the examination proved him right. Albert and Scyrel came in together. Since MacGregor had been treating Albert regularly, the exam took little time. Scyrel insisted that Albert remain during his checkup. MacGregor thought that odd until he discovered the boy had a hernia. That explained all the questions the eighteen year old had been asking. Scyrel wondered if it would prevent him from getting the policy. "No," answered the doctor. "It isn't bad enough yet for surgery and otherwise you are a healthy young man. I do believe though you should be wearing a truss. It will be uncomfortable at first, but without it you will be going to Detroit just like your brother." Scyrel agreed and the two brothers left.

Peter arrived about an hour later, clearly uneasy. The doctor observed that his general health seemed good, and urged the young man to confide any concerns he may have. Peter hesitated, and then began to speak. "Doc, I don't know what's wrong. My back hurts, and so do my legs. My hair's falling out, and I get real bad headaches. I'm always tired and sometimes I forget things. And because of my pimples, nice girls don't pay attention to me. I keep putting stuff on my face for them, but they just come back."

The doctor leaned forward. "Peter, you seem to be in good shape physically, but I thought I noticed you limping last week. I know your job is hard and most farmers have aches and pains. As to the hair loss, I'm afraid you just might be one of those men who go bald early in life. Your tiredness could be alleviated if you got more sleep. It worries your mother that you're out late most every night. I realize you're at an age when you want to have fun, but your health is more important. I can give you some medicine to ease the bone pain and headaches. As far as the pimples, why not stop all your self-remedies for a while and see what happens. More sleep would probably help the forgetfulness. I'm going to pronounce you fit so you can get the insurance because the problems you mentioned can be treated. You just have to take better care of yourself. Is there anything else on your mind?"

Peter looked at the floor. He didn't know how much he could trust the doctor. That girl in Bad Axe (not one of the nice ones) had told him she was sick and couldn't see him anymore. When pressed, she had started to cry and ordered him to leave. He knew about some sexual diseases. Bad blood is what they called one of them. But he hadn't seen her in weeks. He would just do what the doctor had advised. No need to bring up the other matter. "No Doc," he replied. "I promise to do what you say. Can I have that medicine now? I got a headache coming on strong."

* * * * * *

On July 1, 1909, Peter, Albert, Ray, and Scyrel Sparling were each issued a Sun Life Assurance policy with a one thousand dollar benefit. When asked later by Carrie, Dr. MacGregor told her the boys all passed the examinations. "Peter has promised to take better care of himself so you can rest your mind on that."

It appeared that Peter did indeed follow the doctor's orders. He only stayed out late on Saturday night and assured his mother he was sleeping like a log. His face started to clear up and he seemed to be happier than he had been in ages. Even his brothers commented on the change. Of course, there could be another reason for his staying home and sleeping so well. It was a bumper crop year and the boys put in long exhausting days. They had also begun working for neighbors who had no sons. Two dollars a day was good money and the four took turns hiring themselves out. Carrie stayed busy with house and garden, but often did the milking so the boys would not be interrupted. When Sundays came around, the family enjoyed a day of rest. They even skipped church the first two weeks of August. Services were cancelled while Reverend Mackersie took a vacation. The Sparlings could have attended elsewhere, but they didn't.

* * * * * *

The summer was not all work. Fred Wurm, a neighbor, planned a picnic for the Ubly youth at his farm in August. Scyrel and Ray planned to attend, but Albert's stomach flared up and he went to bed. Peter, thinking himself too old for the event, stayed home. His staying home made Carrie curious and she found Peter on the front porch after supper. She knew her son well enough to sense something was on his mind, but did not push. Finally he began what had been a well-rehearsed speech. "Ma," he declared. "I got something I need to talk about. I need to get this out, so please don't say anything until I'm done. I've been feeling so good lately and have even saved up some money." He drew a deep breath. "You never knew this, but before Pa died he suggested he and I go up to Canada for a bit. Course, he got sick and we couldn't go. Well I've been thinking on it a lot, and I hope to go up there early next spring. It wouldn't be the same without Pa, but I could see where he had visited before." Peter paused. "I really miss him Ma, and I just wanted you to know what I'm planning. The other boys could handle things until I got back. I have the money for the trip and Sam Soule got me some train schedules. I want you to understand how important this is to me. I want your approval, but I intend to go, no matter."

Carrie felt as if she had been slapped. How could he think about Canada? His place was here, where it had always been. Her plans for him were to find a nice girl and get married. She would give him land for a house near this one. Words stuck in her throat. She couldn't acknowledge knowing about the conversation between him and J.W. Carrie had assumed that when J.W. died, the travel plans also died. Peter stared at her, waiting for her to speak. She finally found her voice. "Son, you are of an age to make decisions, so I can't stop you. But neither can I give you my blessing. You say you feel good now. What if you took sick up there all alone? What if one of us here at home took sick, or worse? Spring is a long way off and it's much too early to be planning anything so far down the road. You need to give it more thought and then I expect you'll agree with me. Your place is here." Peter kissed her on the forehead and a huge smile spread across his face. "I just wanted you to know. Like you say, it's a long way off."

127

He stepped off the porch and added, "Maybe I'll go over to that picnic after all." Carrie sat stunned. He hadn't even argued. His mind was set and he had dismissed her opinion as irrelevant. For the first time she saw her son as a man. He was near the age of J.W. when they had married. Had he grown up without her knowing it? There was a lot of time before spring. Things could change.

Chapter 26

August weather smiled on the Thumb. Gentle rains fell at the right time and warm sunny days blessed the crops. On a quiet night it was said you could hear the corn grow. Caledonian Day came and went. The attendance broke a record, and it was estimated that nearly four thousand people descended on Ubly for the celebration. Ray again played with the band, and this year Professor Jeremy regaled the crowd with a balloon ascension.

Carrie helped the women from church and they raised over twenty-seven dollars from the food they served. That would buy a lot of new things the church needed. She and Violet had worked side by side so conversation was limited to words that could be heard by anyone. Violet sensed Carrie was upset, but she would have to wait for a better time to learn the reason. School started in a week; she would call upon her friend then.

On a cloudy cool day near the end of August, Violet drove her buggy into Carrie's yard. She brought her usual loaf of bread and the friends sat down at the kitchen table. They talked some of the money they had raised during Caledonian Day and options for its use. Mention was made of Reverend Mackersie's vacation. He had never been gone so long before and they were glad he had returned. Violet finally brought an end to the small talk. "Carrie, are you all right? You seemed on edge last week. I hope you aren't ill."

Carrie hesitated. "Violet, if I start talking, I'll start crying and I may not be able to stop. But I only have you and Dr. MacGregor to confide in. Since you asked first, I'm afraid it is your ears that will get bent. You know how concerned I am about Young Pete. He has informed me that he plans to follow his pa's route to Canada come spring." Tears welled up in her eyes and spilled down her cheeks. "I just don't think I could stand it if he really went. He's been so sickly, and has never been far from home. I guess he must have a lot of J.W. in him. Oh Violet, what am I to do?"

Violet took a sip of her tea. "Carrie, I only have daughters, and wouldn't even pretend to know how to raise sons. I know you want him to settle down so maybe this trip could be a good thing. He's never been far from home, as you say. Perhaps if he were to see and experience other people and places, he would realize how much he has right here. It might just be the very thing he needs to do so he can settle down. This is probably not what you want to hear, but I really don't see how you could keep him from going. You have raised a fine young man, and you need to trust him to remember that upbringing and make wise decisions on his own. If you can somehow accept all of this, it will be a lot easier if or when it happens." Carrie wiped her eyes with her apron. "Yes, and spring is a long way off. He could change his mind by then." She reached across the table for Violet's hands. "What ever would I do without you?"

"We help each other, Carrie. That's what friends are for," replied Violet, not certain her friend had heard a word she had said.

* * * * * *

Dr. MacGregor came out to the farm the first of September to check Carrie's eyes; there was no change. He asked about the boys. "They don't seem to have any complaints. Peter's complexion is clearing up and he seems to be doing much better," she replied. "He's thinking about a trip to Canada, but I don't really think he'll see it through." The doctor barely heard her and Carrie sensed his mind was elsewhere. She asked about his family.

"Everyone is doing as well as can be expected," he said. "I'm looking to move you know."

Carrie gasped. "But I thought you were happy here."

His puzzled face changed to a smile. "I meant to a different house, not a different town. The children are growing and Ida deserves a larger kitchen. If I had a separate room for my office, Douglas could have his own room. Dr. Griffin's place would be perfect, but he won't sell."

"That's ridiculous Robert," sighed a relieved Carrie. "He doesn't even live there. It's been empty a good while and probably needs work. Did he give a reason?"

Dr. MacGregor paused and then admitted, "Carrie, my credit is not the best and I guess that worries him. I'm sorry. I shouldn't be telling you this, but you are more than a patient to me." He cleared his throat. "Where are the boys? I'd like to see them before I leave. And I'm glad to hear Peter is better. If we could just get your eyes taken care of, I would be a satisfied doctor. Oh, before I forget. I will be gone this weekend. We're going to the State Fair with the Boomhowers. Dr. Holdship will be available in my place."

Carrie told him where to find the boys and wrote him a note to pay for his visit. As she watched him leave, she felt a mix of emotions. While happy he felt comfortable enough to confide in her, she was saddened to learn of his financial woes. It just wasn't fair. A good physician and fine man like Robert MacGregor should not have such worries. She took her thoughts to her chair.

The doctor found Peter and Scyrel first, and the change in Peter amazed him. The boy still walked with a slight limp, but his overall appearance and attitude had greatly improved. He could tell that Scyrel was trying to avoid him as he carried a pail of water to his horse. The reason for his evasion became clear when he saw the young lad wince as he lifted the pail. "Scyrel, are you wearing the truss?" asked the doctor. Scyrel's eyes looked to the ground and he shook his head. "How bad is it?" asked MacGregor.

Scyrel tried to sound reassuring. "Some days are worse than others, but I'll be all right."

The words did not convince the doctor, but he didn't push. "Just remember what I said. If it gets real bad it can be fixed. Your brother is a good example. Speaking of Albert, where is he?"

Peter spoke up. "Ray is working at Lorkowski's place and Albert had to run into Tyre." Saying he would catch them another time, MacGregor left them to their work and went on to his next call.

Carrie had spent nearly an hour in the rocking chair and when she rose she had a plan. That evening at supper she shared her thoughts with her family. "I will take out a loan to buy the Griffin place if you are willing to do the repairs. Dr. MacGregor has been more than a doctor to us and it would be wonderful if we could help him now. He could deduct rent from our account and if he ever moved, why we would have a nice piece of property in town."

Albert spoke first. "Can we afford it, Ma? I hear it needs a lot of work and that will take money."

Carrie smiled. "I'll see to the money part. I just need to know if you are willing to fix it up. I think it would be a good investment."

"Yeah Ma," Peter replied. "We can fix it up." His mind was on Canada and he would agree to almost anything to keep Carrie happy. Albert, Ray, and Scyrel followed Peter's lead and voiced their approval.

And so it happened that Carrie purchased Dr. Griffin's place for eighteen hundred dollars. It would be an investment for her boys, a place for Robert MacGregor to live and work, and his payments would either pay the mortgage or be taken out of her account. Albert was right; the buildings needed a lot of work, but slowly the house, barn, and stable became usable again. Carrie invited the MacGregors to Sunday dinner when the work was completed. After the meal of chicken and dumplings, Carrie coyly said she had a favor to ask. "As an investment, the boys and I bought Doc Griffin's place and repairs have made it like new. We want to be sure it stays that way. I heard you need more space and this place would certainly give you that. What I'm asking is, would you be interested in renting it from us? The payments would be twenty-five dollars a month. Or you could subtract what you owe me from what I owe you."

Dr. MacGregor smiled, but Ida was clearly shocked. When she recovered, she cried, "Carrie, this is incredible! We had hoped to buy that place ourselves. It would be an answer to prayer. What a wonderful coincidence!"

Robert and Carrie exchanged a brief glance. Carrie would never tell Ida about the previous conversation she had had with her husband. Robert finally spoke. "Of course we'll rent this house, and bless you Carrie, and you boys as well." The four boys agreed to help transport the heavy pieces of furniture and by the end of October Dr. MacGregor and family were moved and settled.

However, the move took its toll on Scyrel and he was Dr. MacGregor's first office visit in the new place. "Doc, I can't take the pain any more. Albert said the surgery fixed him up good. Can you do the same for me?"

The doctor remarked it was a wise decision and said he would make the necessary arrangements. "Does your mother know?" he asked.

"Yeah," Scyrel answered. "She saw me in a lot of pain so I told her. And Ma said she could get a loan at the Minden bank to pay off the loan for Albert's surgery as well as pay for mine. I reckon the costs will be about the same?" Both Carrie and Scyrel had been too distracted to remember that the doctor's bill would equal two months' rent.

Scyrel looked forward to being pain free, but was also a bit anxious. Albert knew exactly how he felt and volunteered, "Hey little brother, I have some money saved up. How 'bout I go with you and the doc down to Detroit? I think Peter and Ray can handle things for a couple days while I'm gone. Most of the beans are in. The apples are sorted in the cellar and the potatoes are dug. What do you say?" Scyrel readily agreed, pleased that his brother would accompany him on the trip. And he was doubly pleased to know he would be unavailable for the grueling sugar beet harvest.

* * * * * *

The first week of November found Dr. MacGregor in Detroit with Albert and Scyrel Sparling. Surgery went well and Scyrel expected to return home on the fifteenth. At the farm, the cellar nearly burst with all manner of food. Apples had been plentiful and they now rested downstairs. Some were in apple butter, some were stacked for eating, and some were in the vinegar crock. Farm life had a definite pattern, and Carrie never failed to be thrilled at the sight of her full cellar. She decided to take a jar of plum jam to Violet.

Violet welcomed her friend and noticed Carrie seemed happier than she'd been in some time. She inquired about Scyrel, and Carrie said she expected him home the next week. Violet did not ask about Peter, as she didn't want to put a damper on Carrie's good mood. "Did you know the MacGregors have moved into the Griffin place?" Carrie asked. "I do hate to see a nice home sit empty, don't you? Just between us, the boys and I own the place and Robert will rent it from us. He's been so good to all of us and I was very glad to do something for him. And his family of course. He confides in me you know. Such a wonderful man and Ida MacGregor is a lucky woman."

Violet smiled. "I think they are both very lucky." She did not repeat the things she had accidentally heard in town. Violet would not take part in gossip. But she would find a way to talk plainly to Carrie if she ever felt the rumors might have some basis. For now she changed the subject. "I know you had your hands full getting Scyrel ready, but we missed you at the manse last week. Mrs. Mackersie had such a nice luncheon spread for the ladies who served dinner on Caledonian Day. She felt it was the least she could do before they left."

Carrie looked bewildered. "Leaving?" she asked. "They just had a vacation."

"Oh dear," Violet replied. "I forgot you haven't been to preaching lately. Reverend Mackersie has accepted another appointment and his last sermon will be at the end of the month."

Carrie looked confused. "I had no idea. We've been so busy fixing the Griffin place, bringing in crops, and getting Scyrel to Detroit. Where are they going? Who will take his place?" Violet looked up from her knitting and answered. "I understand he is going to a church in Canada and a Reverend Bradfield will take his place."

"More change," muttered Carrie. "Why can't people just be content where they are?"

* * * * * *

Scyrel arrived home on schedule full of chatter about the sights he had seen from the train. "Detroit's a huge city. I'd love to go back again now that I'm healthy. Maybe Sam will send me down for supplies some time." For the moment he was just happy and content to be home. He had been assured that any remaining pain was from the operation and would ease day by day.

Mae and Bert joined the family on the twenty-fifth for Thanksgiving dinner of roast turkey, mashed potatoes and gravy, hubbard squash, celery and apple salad, fresh rolls with butter, molded spinach, oysters, and mince and sweet potato pies. Mae caught her mother looking at her tummy more than once.

Carrie invited the Mackersies to dinner on the twenty-ninth, the day after his last sermon in Ubly. Their house was full of packing boxes and Mrs. Mackersie greatly appreciated not having to cook. When asked, they said they knew little about Reverend Bradfield but were certain he was a good man. Carrie gave them two jars of strawberry jam and a small basket of apples before they left.

* * * * * *

The family spent Christmas quietly at home. They had decorated a tree in the parlor and Mae helped Carrie prepare a lovely Christmas dinner. They had roast goose with all the trimmings. While they worked, Mae told Carrie there was something she and Bert wanted to talk to her about after the holidays. Carrie wondered if she was going to become a grandmother. Gifts were exchanged, nuts were cracked, and the only work done was the daily milking and dishwashing. In a few days a new year would dawn. Carrie, as always, wondered what it might bring.

Chapter 27

Early in the new year of 1910 Bert and Mae arrived by sleigh at the Sparling farm. Bert saw to the horse and then joined his wife in the kitchen. Carrie had a fresh pot of coffee ready and they discussed the weather, seemingly uncomfortable about getting to the point of their visit. Finally Mae spoke. "Ma, we want to give you first notice." Carrie beamed, expecting a happy announcement. "We have decided that neither of us want to continue farming. Bert has several friends in Port Huron and they tell him jobs are plentiful there. We've given the farm a year-and-a-half, so this isn't a spur of the moment decision. Bert's folks don't want to buy the farm back; what they have now is getting to be too much for them. So we thought of the boys. It won't be long before they will be needing land of their own. We wondered if you would be interested in buying it?"

Carrie's beam disappeared. She had suspected Bert was not the farmer his father was. More than once Ed Hurford had done chores for him while Bert and Mae visited friends in Port Huron. Still, this was a shock. Bert sensed her surprise and quickly added, "We don't need an answer right off, just wanted you to have first notice. Think it over and take your time. I don't even have a job yet."

Carrie hid her disappointment. "You've caught me by surprise, but I'll think about it. This is so sudden. Are you sure you want to do this? It's a big step if you have any doubts at all. Port Huron is over sixty miles from here. I would hardly ever see you."

Mae stood and went to her mother. "Ma, we are very sure about this. And when Bert gets a city job he won't need help with chores. I could bring the train and see you about as often as I do now. I could even stay a few days and help during busy times. We won't move until the farm has sold. It would be too hard for Bert to look for a job until then. Ma, this is something we both want and we know exactly what we are doing."

Carrie sighed. "Well, you seem to have your minds settled on this. Let me think on it and I'll give you an answer as soon as I can. Course, I have to talk to the boys. It would double their workload. They've gone to the poultry show in Bad Axe and won't be home until after supper. Bert, what do your folks say about this?" Bert shook his head. "Mother says to do what we think is right, but my father is sore. It bothers him that the farm won't be in the family any more. I hope he will come to understand that I can't stay and be miserable just to keep it a Hurford farm."

Carrie knew all farmers got frustrated with farming; killing frosts, hailstorms, chasing cows, cold winters, and poor yields. But she never heard one say his life was miserable. She changed the subject. "I hadn't planned a big dinner with the boys gone, but I can put something together if you can stay to eat." They agreed to stay and shared leftover roast beef and gravy over day-old bread. When they left, both Mae and Bert gave Carrie a warm hug and Mae added, "Thanks for listening and not being angry." They left, and Carrie was alone. There was mending to do, but she took time for her chair. "Looks like I might be gaining a farm instead of a grandchild," she thought.

When the boys came home, she told them the news. None seemed surprised that Bert wanted off the farm and said they would agree to whatever she thought best. Without saying it out loud, Carrie Sparling decided to buy the Hurford farm.

* * * * * *

When February arrived Carrie owned two farms, and the boys owned a second insurance policy with the Gleaners, a fraternal organization concerned with good works in the community. They were no longer bothered with the idea of life insurance and when offered an attractive policy, the boys joined. Except for Peter. He said he would think on it, but privately had made up his mind. Why put money into another insurance policy when it could be put toward a trip to Canada? The return of good health the past few months had convinced him that he was completely well and he soon resumed old habits.

It began slowly, but before long he frequented old haunts and was occasionally at the barn in the morning milking cows, having just arrived home. Carrie noticed, but didn't say anything. Canada had not been mentioned and if he was happy doing what he was doing, maybe it would never come up again.

Peter's return to good health was short-lived. Soon headaches returned along with a stiff neck. His limp became worse and he was often seen tottering like a drunk. His concentration waned. It was not unusual for him to be given a task and then forget what it was. His legs often felt weak, but his pride would not allow him to use a cane. Carrie didn't know how much longer she could pretend to ignore his condition. An event in late February distracted her.

* * * * * *

The call came on the twenty-fifth. Grandfather, Old Pete, had died early that morning. Although sad, Carrie knew it was the best thing for him and those who had to care for him. But she also remembered the good old days when he was sound in mind, vibrant in spirit, and healthy in body. She called Big Pete to learn who would be going to the funeral. He and Mary planned to attend, and Old Pete's brothers would also be there. William and daughter Martha were going, but Ellen had to remain home with Mother Sparling. How sad she could not see her husband of fifty-four years one more time. When Big Pete asked Carrie if she planned to go, she paused. "Young Pete is doing poorly now and we certainly can't all go. I'll talk to the children. Someone will definitely be there to represent our family."

Word got around, as it always does in a small community. Violet arrived at Carrie's early on the twenty-sixth, offering help with the farm work so the family could attend the service. "Naturally you would think of such a thing," Carrie remarked. "But it has been arranged. Albert is going with Mae and Bert, but Young Pete is ailing again and I need to stay close."

Violet did not need to be told about Peter. She had been to market Wednesday last and had seen for herself. When she spoke to him his eyes were runny and he talked a blue streak. She had not even been sure he knew who she was. Albert had appeared suddenly at his side, said a quick hello, and then guided his brother back toward their wagon. No, Violet did not need to be told. She didn't stay long, but made Carrie promise to ask for help if need be. "We'll be fine," said Carrie confidently. "And I don't think I'll be worrying about Canada any more." Violet thought it a strange remark considering the circumstances.

* * * * * *

Dr. MacGregor continued his weekly visits to the farm. He arrived one windy March day and noticed a threshing machine by the barn. He stopped to watch the Sparling boys and their neighbors busy at work before going into the house.

After seeing no change in Carrie's eyes, he told her he wanted to try a different medicine. He washed his hands and asked about the boys. As usual, Young Pete was Carrie's main concern. "Do you think he would stop threshing beans long enough for me to check him?" the doctor asked. She shook her head. "I don't think he would take kindly to it, you know, with all those men there and him being singled out. Maybe I can convince him to come into town and see you at your office."

She had really wanted to sit down and discuss farm plans with the doctor. He was so easy to talk to and very knowledgeable. He had become a great advisor. But she would soon have threshers to feed. She wrote the doctor a note and he observed her making a notation on the pad of paper she kept with the notes. He thought it interesting; was it just her own reminder or did she not trust him? He had to admit he had not paid rent, and made a mental note to see if he had credited her account for it, as well as the surgery on Scyrel.

* * * * * *

Six hungry men sat at the table; Carrie's sons and the two owners of the threshing machine, Henry and Mose Schlegel. All paid Carrie a high compliment; they ate in silence. When she finally heard some chatter, she knew they were getting full and would soon be ready for dessert. As she served the apple cobbler, Mose Schlegel spoke. "Mrs. Sparling, I think you outdid yourself. That was one fine meal." Murmurs of agreement went around the table. Mose continued. "You have a fine farm here, but then I'm not telling you what you don't already know. I have an offer for you, but please don't answer right off. Your forty acres that border my farm? I'd sure like to buy it from you. I wouldn't bring it up like this, except it's only your family and mine sitting here. I can give you one thousand dollars cash money and I hope you'll consider it."

The offer took Carrie by surprise. Why sell good farmland? "Well Mr. Schlegel, I'll think it over and let you know." He thanked her and joined the others as they headed back to work.

As she cleared the table and washed dishes, she thought it over. This could be a very advantageous deal for the family. Those forty acres were the furthest east of her farm and, with the boys soon to be busy in fields here and at Ubly to the west, it would mean less travel to and from the fields. Plus, the money could be put to good use. She made up her mind to sell, but would not approach Mose until after speaking with the boys. She wanted them to feel they had a part in the transaction. Perhaps she should also talk to Robert. That opportunity presented itself the next day.

MacGregor had new eye drops for Carrie. "This is strong stuff Carrie," he warned. "It's called Atropine and I don't want you to ever dose yourself. I will come out every other day to drop your eyes and hopefully we'll notice a big difference soon. It's something you will have to take for a long time, but if it helps I think you'll agree it is worthwhile."

She agreed to try the new treatment and as he administered the drops, she spoke. "I'd like your advice on some business, Robert." She explained the proposal offered by Mose Schlegel.

"Well Carrie," observed MacGregor, "that land is the furthest from your home. If the price is good, it certainly would be a time saver for the boys. Do you want me to handle it for you?"

"Thank you Robert," she answered. "That is very sweet of you. You've helped with so many things that J.W. would have taken care of, and I appreciate your offer. But I can manage this on my own." Carrie hoped she was right about that and changed the subject. "Has Young Pete been in to see you?"

"Not yet, Carrie," MacGregor said. "Give it time. Men usually balk at seeing a physician. Is he close by now?"

As Carrie wrote the usual note, she replied, "I believe he is in the barn, but I'm not sure." MacGregor pocketed the note. "I'll just go out there and see." He turned to her, cupped her cheek in his hand, and looked into her face. "How do your eyes feel?" he asked.

The gesture caught her off guard and she briefly struggled for words. "When you first put the drops in, there was a slight stinging, but that's gone," she stammered. "I'm not sure if they feel different or not."

The doctor removed his hand and reached for the door handle. "It's probably a bit soon to notice any difference. I'll be back day after tomorrow, but if you need me before that, don't hesitate to telephone." She nodded, still feeling the warmth of his hand. As he opened the door, he saw the notepad again. He had not checked his records.

* * * * * *

He found Peter alone in the straw covered barn trying to scoop manure into a wheelbarrow. MacGregor could not help but notice the boy's lack of coordination. Peter saw the doctor approach and tried to make light of it. "Looks like I'll have to clean the floor next, huh?"

MacGregor smiled and watched where he stepped. "How are you feeling, Peter? You still doing better?"

Peter responded, "Oh, I'm fair. You know, good days and bad. I got no complaints. Ma is pushing that darn spring tonic again, but I reckon the tonic I really need is up in Canada." The next pitchfork load missed the barrow completely and splashed too close for comfort.

The doctor, not dressed for barn work, decided to go. "I'll leave you to your chores, but remember. You can't get to Canada if you're sick."

True to his word, the doctor came to the Sparling farm every other day. He dropped Carrie's eyes, pocketed the notes, and always casually looked about for the notepad.

Chapter 28

Easter that year fell on March twenty-seventh. Carrie insisted the boys attend services with her. Peter's one-time dedication to church attendance had dropped off considerably. Mae and Bert joined the family at church and again at the farm for Easter dinner. They enjoyed baked ham, sweet potatoes, green beans, sauerkraut salad, deviled eggs, mustard pickles, and rolls with butter. Lemon layer cake topped off the meal.

Bert announced that he had accepted a job offer in Port Huron and they planned to be resettled by the first of May. The response was bittersweet. The boys would not admit to missing their sister, and Carrie knew she would have to bid farewell to her only daughter. But the look of happiness that radiated from the young couple pushed those thoughts aside.

One week later, Carrie went to the Citizen's Bank in Ubly. She deposited one thousand dollars from Mose Schlegel, along with a note for two hundred more. Dr. MacGregor had suggested she hold out for fifteen hundred dollars and, after further negotiations, twelve hundred was agreed upon. The remainder of April was bustling. Carrie inventoried canning equipment, fed hay pressers, had the garden plowed, planted early garden, and helped Mae pack for the move to Port Huron.

The day after they finished packing, Violet showed up at the farm with a loaf of bread. She could tell Carrie had been crying and when she entered the kitchen, Carrie tried to speak. However, words were replaced with sobs and Violet held her friend for a moment. Then she pulled back, put her hands on Carrie's shoulders and said, "Now Carrie. Get it all out. You'll feel better, and then you can be happy for your daughter. I saw her in town a few days ago and she was beaming."

Carrie wiped her eyes with her apron, hiccupped, and then smiled. "Violet you must have an extra sense. You're always here when I need you."

Violet, sensing a change of mood, laughed. "Well I hope you remember everything I just said so you can repeat it back to me when Aletha or Marie leaves home."

Violet noticed Carrie rubbing her eyes and asked, "Your eyes are so red Carrie. Is it from the crying or are they still troubling you?"

"Oh, it must be from crying," Carrie replied. "Dr. MacGregor comes by every other day to put drops in them and I think I am beginning to notice a difference."

Violet put her hand to her mouth. "My goodness that must cost a lot of money. Can't you put the drops in yourself, or have the boys help?" Carrie looked surprised. "Gracious no. These drops are strong medicine and should only be given by a doctor. Robert made sure I understood that."

Violet didn't want to hear more about Dr. MacGregor and asked about the boys. "Albert and Scyrel are fully recovered from their surgeries," Carrie reported. "Ray has band practice nearly every night now. They'll give a concert next month to raise money for new uniforms, and Mr. Slack wants everything to go perfectly. He drives the boys hard, but they all love him. Young Pete hasn't mentioned Canada, I think his health is failing again. I've tried all the remedies I know, but they just don't seem to help. I went to Sam Soule last week and ordered some medical journals. Hopefully I can understand them and perhaps I'll find something that hasn't been tried."

The journals arrived the middle of May. One was *Aikens Home Nursing* and the other, *A Compend of Materia Medica*. Carrie learned, to her surprise, that many ailments could be treated with arsenic. Anemia, weak heart, chronic skin diseases, arthritis, diarrhea, and other ailments were listed, as well as instructions for safe dosages.

Carrie's eyes improved, but Dr. MacGregor insisted on continued treatments every other day. The boys checked all the farm equipment and Carrie planted more early garden. She also purchased two more horses to be kept at the Ubly farm. Days were full, but not hectic. It felt like the lull before the storm. A busy summer was just around the corner.

* * * * * *

A few days before Decoration Day, Carrie asked the boys to go over to the cemetery and make certain the graves of their father and brother were presentable. Peter had gone ahead of the others and Albert and Scyrel planned to join him after running the milk route. Ray filled the wood box and patched the fence around the barnyard. Carrie checked Ray's good suit for the upcoming band concert.

About noon Scyrel and Albert came racing into the yard in a cloud of dust. Scyrel drove the wagon and Albert held tightly to Peter in the back. Carrie rushed to find out what was wrong. Peter had a wild appearance and his brothers looked very concerned. They helped him to the ground, but Albert never released his grip on his brother. Peter babbled about Bad Axe, church, and chickens, making no sense whatsoever. Seeing Ray come around the corner, Albert barked orders. "Ray, see to the horses. Ma, call the doc. Scyrel, help me get him inside." The urgency in his voice compelled them to act quickly without question.

When they got Peter to his room, they sat him on the bed. He had quit his babbling and looked around quizzically. Slowly, he began to relax. His

142

shoulders hunched, his fists uncurled, and he began to cry. Carrie felt at a loss, but sat on the bed and put her arm around him. He leaned into her and she stroked his head. Then she asked the boys to go downstairs and watch for the doctor. "Just let us be for a bit," she whispered. After some hesitation, the boys did as asked.

It took an hour for Dr. MacGregor to get the message and another hour for him to reach the farm. He hurried into the kitchen with his bag about two o'clock in the afternoon. Albert indicated he should go upstairs immediately.

MacGregor found Carrie and Peter sitting on the bed. Carrie appeared bewildered and when Peter looked up, his eyes were glassy and sweat ran down his face. MacGregor addressed the young man. "Peter, do you know who I am?" When the lad nodded, the doctor continued. "Can you tell me how you feel? Do you have any pain?" Peter moaned an answer. "It's my back. My back hurts something awful." Dr. MacGregor reached into his bag. "I'm going to give you something for the pain and it will make you sleepy. Do you understand?" Again Peter nodded. Robert and Carrie helped the young man to his feet. Carrie pulled back the covers and they eased him into the bed. Carrie removed his shoes and covered him. She sat beside him on the bed and wiped his brow with the apron she had removed. The medicine took effect quickly and Peter was soon asleep. Dr. MacGregor motioned for Carrie to accompany him down to the kitchen. She hesitated at first, but when her son began to snore she stood and preceded the doctor down the stairs.

The boys sat at the table anxiously waiting for the doctor's report. "He's sleeping right now," reported MacGregor. "Can someone tell me what happened?"

Albert and Scyrel paused and then Albert said, "He just acted crazy. Scyrel and I got to the cemetery to help him with the cleanup, but when we got there a bunch of folks were just standing on the road. All of a sudden we saw Peter pacing back and forth right at the entrance. He was screaming for everyone to git. A man we don't know shouted, 'That crazy coot won't let anyone in.' Uncle John came up then and told us to get Pete home.

"When we tried, he picked up a big limb and waved it around as if he would use it on us. While he was looking at us, two of the men went through the ditch on the far side, came up behind him, and knocked him down. We tried to talk to him, but he kept saying, 'don't let them hurt me.' We got the branch away from him and Uncle John helped get him into the wagon. People were staring and whispering, so we tied his horse to the back of the wagon and lit out fast for home. Once we got him in the wagon he didn't fight any more. Don't know how long he'd been like that. Guess he wore himself out. That's all we know."

No one spoke for a few moments. "Did he say anything while coming home?" asked Carrie. "He moaned some, but that was all," offered Scyrel. They all then looked to the doctor. "I can't say much until I examine him," the doctor declared. "He'll probably sleep a long time now. I have some other patients to see but I'll be back in a few hours. If he should wake and get riled again, try to keep him in the house. My other calls don't have telephones, but if you need me right away here is where I'll be." He quickly wrote a list of the afternoon calls and the boys said they knew where those people lived.

The doctor had no sooner departed than Uncle John drove in. He came into the kitchen shouting. "What in blazes is wrong with that lad? He's got all of Tyre upset." His manner was gruff and Carrie struggled for words.

Finally, Ray spoke. "Uncle John, we don't know what's wrong. The doc gave him something for pain and he's sleeping. Dr. MacGregor will examine him after he wakes up."

Carrie, collecting her thoughts, added, "Gracious, I have no idea why he acted as he did. He's never done anything like this before."

An exchange of glances between Albert and Scyrel did not escape Uncle John's attention. "Speak up boys," he demanded. "Has this happened before?"

Albert paused and then answered. "Kinda, but not so bad as this." When he saw Carrie ready to question, he added, "Ma, he's been having spells a couple of months now. He always comes out of them, so we promised him we wouldn't tell you. We gave Pa our word to watch out for each other and that's what we were trying to do."

Silence fell over the kitchen. Finally Uncle John broke it. "I got to get back to the cemetery. Need to see if he did any damage and try to calm the folks down." Carrie stood. "I'll send the boys along to help. They still need to tend our plot. Thank you Uncle John for your help, but I feel certain Dr. MacGregor will have him back on his feet in no time. I'm sorry he upset the whole town."

Uncle John softened. "Maybe I was a bit harsh. But he was acting real scary and folks just reacted. You are well liked by everyone around here. It'll blow over in no time."

He left and Carrie quickly addressed her sons before they could escape. "I want to know everything, so you'd best start talking. How could you not come to me if he was carrying on so? What else has he been doing? Has the whole town seen these spells?"

Albert answered, "Ma, we were in a bad place. He made us promise not to tell you, said you would try to keep him from going to Canada if you knew. Besides, it was never this bad. He mostly loses his balance, and when he talks he doesn't make sense. His back and neck hurt and he gets sad real easy. I've been sticking close to him, especially in town. And no, I don't think the whole town has noticed." Albert stopped. His brother had lost enough dignity already and he would not add to it by telling about the instances when Peter had wet himself.

Carrie could plainly see her boys were concerned. "At least I know now," she said. "But Canada? Did he tell you he's going? I thought that foolishness was behind him. He can't leave home sick. You can see that for yourselves."

This time Scyrel spoke. "Ma, he planned to go last March, but started ailing again. Said he didn't feel right leaving us in the summer with all the work. We told him we could handle the work if he was fixin' to go. We've hired extra hands before. He really wants to do this Ma, and it would make him real happy if you would go along with it."

Carrie was too overwhelmed to talk any further. She told them they best get over to Tyre so folks could see that the whole family wasn't daft. "Besides, Uncle John is probably expecting you."

Albert stood and spoke firmly. "I'm staying here in case he wakes up and needs me. I got work in the barn and it doesn't take all of us to clean the grave lot."

Carrie couldn't argue with his logic, and she didn't. Albert's assertive attitude surprised her. Ray and Scyrel left the house and Carrie checked on Peter. He was sleeping soundly. She closed his door and went to her chair. "Well," she said to herself, "first Mae and now Young Pete. Everyone is telling me if I want my children to be happy, I have to let them go. Doesn't anybody care about my happiness?" She began to rock and then saw one of the medical journals. She picked it up, read a little, and then became lost in thought.

* * * * * *

An hour later, Carrie resumed her housework. Ray's suit was ready for the concert. She stirred the potato and ham casserole in the oven and set the table for supper. It was quiet upstairs, but every now and then she went to look in on Peter. She wished Robert would return. The boys came back from Tyre and helped Albert with the milking. The family had just finished supper when the doctor returned. He asked about the patient and was told that Peter was still sleeping.

MacGregor took his bag up the stairs. It didn't appear as though the lad had moved an inch. When the door fully opened, the squeak that was on the rainy day chore list caused Peter to stir. Carrie and the boys entered the room behind the doctor and Carrie immediately went to the bed. The linens were soaked, as were his clothes. She spoke, to no one in particular, "Must have had a fever break." Peter heard the voice and opened his eyes. He seemed puzzled at the room full of people. Then a look of recall passed over his face and he hung his head. He didn't know all he had done this time and would talk to Albert alone later. But obviously the doctor and his mother now knew about his problems. Dr. MacGregor eased the awkward situation. "Peter, you had us worried. How is your back?"

"Can't tell until I sit up," he answered weakly. "How long have I been asleep? I need to get to my chores." Carrie told him he had slept nearly five hours and Albert assured him that chores were done.

Dr. MacGregor looked at Carrie. "I need to examine this young man so I'll ask you and the boys to wait downstairs."

Carrie agreed, but said he needed to get out of those wet clothes. "Just put them by the door. You have clean, dry ones in the dresser Young Pete."

Suddenly Peter's voice became strong. "Ma, I'm not Young Pete any more. That's a baby name and I hate it when you call me that! I'm just Peter from now on. Please!"

Again the doctor took control before it could get any more uncomfortable. "Everyone out. Peter, let me help you stand. Your mother is right. Let's get those wet things off." Wet linens were added to the pile of wet and dirty clothes. Peter got out a clean set of clothing, but MacGregor said he wanted to examine him before he got dressed. Peter was uneasy in his nakedness, but he knew an examination was long overdue. Dr. MacGregor immediately noticed Peter's skin. "How long have you had this rash?" he asked.

Peter gulped an answer. "I had it awhile now, just figured I got dust or bits of straw in my clothes from working and expected it would go away. Hey Doc, I just noticed. My back don't hurt. That's good, huh?"

"I gave you some strong medicine," the doctor replied. "But it's bound to wear off. I'll leave more in case the pain comes back." The uncomfortable feeling intensified as the doctor examined Peter's groin. "Peter, how long have you had these warts?" Dr. MacGregor was very somber and Peter began to speak, slowly at first. And then the words came tumbling out. It was as if a dam had burst and he could hardly talk fast enough.

He said he had a sore on his privates a while back but it went away, and he wasn't worried about it until a short time ago. He told the doctor about the girl in Bad Axe. "Doc, I'm not dumb. I know a person can get real sick from, well, you know. They call it bad blood. Gosh Doc, I can't have that! I'm going to Canada."

Dr. MacGregor could see Peter was becoming very agitated. "Now Peter calm down. We don't know for sure if you have syphilis, that's the real name. But there are treatments for it—if you have it. These spells you get, how often do they occur? Do you remember them afterward?"

"I get them every now and then, but never counted them. What I don't remember, Albert tells me. I always know by the way he acts that I've had another one. He's kept it secret, but I'll let him know he can talk to you about them. What do we do now?"

"Well," began MacGregor, "let me finish this examination and then I'll have to study some of my medical books at home. You aren't a little boy so I'll tell you straight. Right now my diagnosis would be syphilis. But let me do some reading and, like I said, if you do have it, we can treat it. I'll go down and talk to your family. We won't mention syphilis just yet, but if you have it, they can't be spared from learning about it."

* * * * * *

Carrie could barely make her feet descend the stairs. She had gone downstairs with the boys and assured them everything was under control. Albert went to the barn and Ray, late for band practice, headed for Ubly. Scyrel went to Tyre. The store was closed but Sam was probably still there and Scyrel needed someone to talk to. When they were all gone, Carrie tiptoed back upstairs just in time to hear the word syphilis. She stayed at the closed door and when it became apparent the examination was ending, she quickly and quietly slipped back down the stairs.

When Dr. MacGregor came into the kitchen, Carrie sat at the table holding her head in her hands. He came up behind her and put his hands on her shoulders. Her right hand reached back to his. She could not reveal what she had overheard. MacGregor squeezed her hand. "I don't think there is any need to worry about him tonight. He seems to have exhausted all his energy at the cemetery." He paused for a moment and then said he would see her in the morning. She nodded and very quietly thanked him.

As he steered his horse toward Ubly, he talked to himself. "This could get very bad for everyone. Maybe I should get a second opinion." Dr. MacGregor was very tired. Too tired to realize Carrie had not given him a note for his services.

* * * * * *

Early Friday morning, Dr. MacGregor arrived at the Sparling farm. Albert and Ray were on the milk route, and Scyrel was hitching his horse to a wagon. The doctor approached him and asked how the night had passed. "We all slept, I guess. But nobody seems to have much energy today. Peter's in the kitchen with Ma and they're expecting you. Do you know what's ailing him?"

The doctor helped Scyrel finish the hitching but ignored the question. "I better go see my patient." He found Peter at the table drinking coffee, and

Carrie at the dry sink washing dishes. "Good morning," MacGregor said. "Scyrel tells me you passed a quiet night. That's good. Sleep is a medicine all to itself you know. Carrie, let me tend your eyes and then Peter and I can go into the next room. I need to re-examine you, young man."

Carrie wiped her hands on her apron, sat in the chair, and tilted her head back. After the drops were administered, he ushered Peter into the room that had been J.W.'s sick room. As MacGregor closed the door, Peter began to disrobe. "No need for that," whispered the doctor. "I just wanted to talk to you privately. Peter, with what you told me, plus your symptoms, I'm almost one hundred percent certain you have the bad blood, as you called it. I don't know how advanced it is, but we can start treatment right away. You know you have to stay away from girls for now don't you?"

"Yeah," Peter replied. "I know. Do we have to tell Ma and my brothers?"

"Peter," the doctor answered, "they have to know sometime because they'll have to protect themselves. You don't want to pass this on to them, and it might help if you didn't have to carry the burden by yourself. But you're old enough to make the decision." Peter thought a moment. "If I don't tell them now, what will you say is wrong with me? They'll want to know."

The doctor had an answer ready. "I've thought about that. Your back pain could be from lifting, and the spell could be caused by too much sun. It's been mighty hot for May. Let me know what you decide. You know my feelings on this though, and if you get sicker they will have to be told immediately."

Peter looked as if he were going to cry. "I can't ask you to lie Doc. Since they have to know sometime, it might as well be now. I can tell my brothers, but it would be awful hard to tell Ma."

Dr. MacGregor got out some medicine. "If you want me to tell her, I will. It's good they are told now. You've made the right decision." Dr. MacGregor removed a bottle of pills from his bag. "I'm going to leave these tablets. Take two at breakfast and again at supper. I'm here every other day for your mother, and next time I come I'll bring another medicine. It's more potent and I need to be the one who doses you. I know you have work to do so I'll try to come about noon. That way I'll be sure to find you. Do you have any questions?"

Peter thought for a moment. "How long until I'm better? Do you think I'll be able to go to Canada?" The doctor looked seriously at the young man. "Peter, I'm not going to make any promises. Right now you just concentrate on taking the medicine. I'm going to tell your mother to wash your clothes separately and to have you use a separate drinking glass. No more sharing the dipper at the well. I understand Albert sticks pretty close to you, and that's

148

good. You need someone nearby in case there are any more spells. If you have any more questions, I'll be back day after tomorrow. Your back should feel better, but I'll leave more pain medicine with your mother just in case."

Peter left the room and quickly passed Carrie on his way to the barn; he needed to find his brothers. Dr. MacGregor came into the kitchen. "Have a seat Carrie," he said. She obliged and started to speak when he interrupted her. "Carrie, let me talk first. I don't know how much you heard outside the door yesterday." Carrie feigned ignorance, but MacGregor continued. "Dear lady, my ears are very good. Anyway, I'm thinking you already know what I'm going to say. It appears that Peter's carousing has caught up to him. I'm treating your son for syphilis and there are things you must do to help."

Even though she had heard that word yesterday, it suddenly became more real and much more frightening. She began to cry. "Oh Robert. I was listening at the door but just hoped what I heard wasn't true." She wiped her eyes and then stiffened. "J.W. always took Young Pete's side. He kept saying 'boys will be boys' over and over. I wonder what he would say now!"

Dr. MacGregor reached for her hand. "Carrie, getting angry at the past won't help. She nodded and the doctor continued. "There are precautions you must take to protect yourself and your other sons." He then told her about the laundry and drinking vessels. "Peter is going to tell his brothers and by dinnertime everyone will know. It may be awkward at first, but it's best that you all know the truth. I told him I couldn't promise anything. But if you follow my instructions, we can hope for the best."

There was really nothing more to say. He stood and Carrie wrote him a note. "Thank you Robert. What would we do without you?" He pocketed the note as Carrie reached for her tablet. After he left, she took the medical journals to her chair.

* * * * * *

Carrie debated long and hard about going to the cemetery on Decoration Day. None of the boys wanted to go, as it had only been a few days since the incident with Peter. But Carrie had another son to think about. So she picked some wildflowers, hitched Queenie to the buggy, and drove to Tyre. Several people were milling about, many more than she had anticipated. Ubly usually drew the larger crowds. She didn't know what to expect but was not surprised when people avoided her. Carrie made her way to the Sparling plot not looking to her right or left, but sensing eyes boring into her back. She could not hear whispers, but imagined them. She stood at J.W.'s grave for a moment and then moved to little Edward's marker. She bent down to lay flowers by his stone and when she rose, an arm wrapped around her.

Violet! Who else always knew exactly what she needed? The tears began to flow, not just for Edward but also for Peter. Violet offered a handkerchief to Carrie with her free hand and just stood quietly beside her friend until the tears were spent. After a few moments, Carrie indicated she was ready to leave and Violet walked with her. One by one, others who had avoided her made their way to the two women. Conversations were brief and topics were limited to weather, spring, and gardens. But the impasse was broken, thanks to Violet. She had not only helped Carrie, but also the others who had not known how to approach Peter's mother. Very few people possessed the keen insight of Violet Styles.

*　*　*　*　*　*

June started out cool, but Carrie planted the rest of her garden anyway. The ground was warm enough for even the tenderest seeds. Dr. MacGregor came every other day to treat both Carrie and Peter. She washed clothes separately, as instructed, and everyone knew which glass belonged to Peter. Carrie found a canteen in the attic and Peter filled it with water to use when he worked in the fields. His back still hurt and he continued to limp. His brothers tactfully added some of his chores to their own. If Albert and Peter disappeared, the family knew it was most probably another spell and they continued on as if nothing was amiss. Carrie bought lemons from Sam but didn't save them for special occasions. She treated Peter often to her delicious lemonade, served in his own special glass.

Chapter 29

A tremendous hailstorm brought work to a halt on the seventeenth. Everyone welcomed the respite, but worried about damage to crops. When the angry black sky finally cleared, Carrie checked her garden and was relieved to see that it had survived. The boys inspected the Tyre fields and reported only minor problems. They planned to check the Ubly farm the next day. That night they ate a hearty supper of bean soup and dumplings. Carrie always made more than enough. She simmered it on a back burner of the stove nearly all day. Scyrel ate any leftovers the next morning. He sprinkled cinnamon on his and ate it for breakfast, one of his favorites.

As planned, Peter and Albert rode over to the west farm and were pleased to find that the storm had missed Ubly completely. When they returned, Peter retched and sank into a lounge in the yard. Albert got him some water and went into the kitchen to find Carrie. "Ma," he reported, "the crops weren't damaged, but Peter's sick. He vomited twice over there and drank all his canteen of water. I'm going to get him some more."

"Wait," Carrie insisted. "Let me bring him some lemonade. It will help get the bad taste out of his mouth." Peter drank the lemonade and agreed to quit work for the day. He didn't argue, as that would have taken energy he didn't have. When told of the vomiting, Dr. MacGregor said it was nothing to be alarmed about.

* * * * * *

June turned into July and the sun beat down for days on end. Peter's condition worsened and he grew weaker each day. Independence Day arrived and departed with little fanfare. Ray played with the band, but didn't stay for the fireworks. Albert remained at his brother's side when he wasn't working. Peter faithfully took the medicine from Dr. MacGregor, but it soon became obvious that it was not helping. Mae arrived on the eighteenth of July to help Carrie.

The boys, minus Peter, had been working the oats at the west farm for two days and Mae decided to carry their dinner to them. She had taken the news of Peter's illness hard, and was glad for the opportunity to go to the other farm. His gaunt appearance had been a shock and she had cried all the way to Ubly. She set the meal in what once had been her kitchen and the boys had just finished strawberry pie when the telephone rang. It was Ida MacGregor. "I don't want to alarm you, but I think you should come home. Your brother is very sick." Mae quickly told her brothers and they all left immediately.

Mae expected Dr. MacGregor to be at the farm, but it surprised her that his wife was with him. When the four siblings arrived, Peter was again on the yard lounge. Albert reached him first.

"You picked a good day to stay out of work, that oat dust is fierce," he tried to joke.

Peter weakly replied, "I got to tell you. I'd trade oat dust for how I feel right now. How come you're here during the middle of the day?"

Albert searched for words and Ray, who had just joined them, lied. "You know Albert, he'll do anything to get out of work. Actually, we were at a stopping point, and decided to come home and see if the oats here are ready. Looks like you drew a crowd Peter."

Peter nodded and winced with pain before speaking again. "Are Scyrel and Mae with you?"

"Yeah. Scyrel is tending the horses and Mae is taking some dishes into the house. Can I get you anything?"

Peter clutched his stomach and groaned. "No, you can see by the bucket nothing stays down."

Albert and Ray had smelled the bucket before they saw it but tried to pretend it wasn't there. Now that it had been mentioned, Albert told Ray to take it to the outhouse and empty it. Peter was spent from what little talking he had done, so Albert suggested he close his eyes and get some rest. "I'll be here if you need me," he promised.

Just then Mae approached with more lemonade. "Ma says for you to drink this. Doc is bringing you another powder and this will help get it down."

Peter grimaced. "I don't see any sense in more medicine." But Mae was insistent. "It can't hurt, can it?"

Just then Dr. MacGregor came to the lounge and offered the medicine to Peter. Too weak to put up a fight, he swallowed the powders and drank the lemonade. "I can't promise to keep it down," he mumbled.

Scyrel finished with the horses and came over to the lounge. "Passed Lorkowski on the way here and he asked about you. How are you doing?" Peter shook his head and Albert nodded a dismissal to those hovering. As Peter closed his eyes, Albert pulled up a chair and sat by his brother.

Dr. MacGregor and his wife prepared to leave. "Mrs. Sparling," began the doctor, "we made plans to dine with the Boomhowers tonight, but if you need me, here is his telephone number. Unless I hear from you I'll be out day after tomorrow. I'm going to ask Dr. Conboy to examine Peter so don't be surprised if he shows up. Keep the medicine going. He's in no condition to work, but I think he realizes that for himself." Mae watched as the doctor dropped Carrie's eyes. "Dr. MacGregor, I'll be here a few days," she remarked. "Couldn't I put the drops in Ma's eyes?"

MacGregor quickly replied, "These are very powerful drops and can only be given by a physician. You will better help your mother by just being here." Mae thought about arguing, but the look on her mother's face told her not to.

The doctor closed the bottle, nodded to the women, and left with Ida. Violet, who had been washing dishes, heard every word but said nothing. Carrie stood to help with the dishes and Violet said, "Please rest Carrie. Let the drops work. Besides, I'm almost finished. Is there anything else I can do while I am here?"

Carrie sighed. "No. I don't know what I would have done if you hadn't been here when Peter started vomiting. I knew Robert was due any moment but, as always, you were here when needed." Violet smiled. "Now Carrie, I had to be in Tyre and only stopped by on my way home. And I know that you'd do the same for me." As she reached the door with the wet dishtowels, Mae joined her and offered to hang the linens to dry.

Carrie stayed in the kitchen chair as her daughter and friend walked out together. "And thanks for the bread," she called after them.

Violet and Mae stood in the yard. Ray and Scyrel were in the distance working on the barn door. Albert still sat beside Peter. "I heard about the situation at the cemetery," Mae said quietly. "I'm so far from home now, and I must tell you it gives me great comfort to know you are near."

Violet put her arm around the young girl. "Mae, your mother supported me when my son died. Because she'd been through it herself, she was a greater help than anyone will ever know." Mae's sudden hug startled her, but she hugged her in return. "It's very good of Bert to understand your need to be here. Please give him my best when you see him." Mae promised, and went to the clothesline as Violet went to her buggy.

When she returned to the kitchen, she voiced her appreciation for Mrs. Styles. "Mae," replied Carrie. "Violet is my dearest and closest friend. I can confide to her my deepest feelings and I know she will lock them away. I only hope you find such a friend. Did you look in on Young Pete?"

Mae nodded. "Yes, he's fast asleep and Albert is with him." Mae chewed at her lip and took a deep breath. The tone of her voice changed. "Ma, I know Dr. MacGregor has been good to the family but would it really be so awful if someone else looked at Peter? You've seen Peter every day and maybe didn't notice the change. But I have to tell you when I first got here and saw him I was shocked at how poorly he looks."

"Mae," Carrie said in a firm voice. "Dr. MacGregor is a fine man and a very good physician. I have complete trust in him. Besides, you heard him say Dr. Conboy is coming out. I would appreciate it if you didn't bring this up again." She noticed the hurt on her daughter's face. "We're all on edge, Mae. Please understand. Robert is trying everything he knows to make your brother better and I will not dismiss him just because Young Pete is not responding. Forgive me if I sound harsh. This is all so difficult and I'm very glad you're here."

Mae put her arm around her mother's shoulder. "We'll get through this Ma." And she made a note to herself never to doubt MacGregor in front of her mother again.

* * * * * *

Dr. Conboy stopped by the farm the next morning. He found Peter in the spare bedroom, the one his father had used. The doctor pulled a chair to the bed. "Peter, Dr. MacGregor asked me to have a look at you. Tell me exactly how you feel son."

Peter squinted through watery eyes. "My back and neck hurt, but the pain in my gut is the worst. My feet feel like they're being pricked." Peter wiped at his eyes with the sheet. "My throat is raw from puking. And I can't do anything without getting tired." He wiped his eyes again. Peter didn't know if Conboy had been told about the bad blood and decided he wouldn't mention it.

Dr. Conboy pushed the chair back and stood. "I'm going to examine you. We need to get you back on your feet again." He took Peter's temperature and checked his pulse. After a closer examination, Dr. Conboy found no visible cause for the patient's condition although it was obvious the young man was very ill.

Meanwhile, in his office, Dr. MacGregor was reading a medical book about the secondary stage of syphilis—the stage when external signs of the disease temporarily subside.

* * * * * *

By Friday July twenty-second, Peter was confined either to his bed or the lounge in the yard. Ray and Albert handled the milk route and Carrie hired a neighbor, Steve Berry, to help in the fields. Mae planned to go home on the weekend, but today was special. It was Peter's birthday. He'd turned twenty-five years old. Carrie was making his favorite dessert, lemon meringue pie. Peter had trouble keeping anything in his stomach, but she hoped the pie would stay down. When the men came in for dinner, Albert helped his brother to the table. He thought it would do him good to sit up, if only for a few moments. Dr. MacGregor would soon arrive with more medicine and probably stay for dinner. Since he came about noon every day to treat both Carrie and Peter, he usually accepted the offer to join them at the table. Today was no different.

Everyone partook of the boiled ham except Peter. Carrie fixed him milk toast, which he had requested. When she served the pie they all wished Peter a happy birthday. He managed only a few bites. Albert, seeing his discomfort, suggested he might want to lie down again. Peter indicated he would rather be outside and was helped to the lounge. The other boys and Steve finished their pie and went back to the fields. As they passed the lounge, Albert told them he would be out later.

Mae saw the doctor open his bag to drop her mother's eyes. She went to the pump for water to start the dishes.

"Carrie," suggested MacGregor. "I think it would be a good idea for Peter to go to the hospital. I can make all the arrangements like before." If Carrie was upset she didn't show it. "I believe you're right Robert. I know you've done your best, but if you think he should go, I agree. Let me know the cost and I will go to the bank Monday morning." The doctor touched her shoulder and said he would take care of it. He removed his hand and turned to see Mae watching from the doorway.

"Mae," said Carrie. "My eyes are still blurry. Would you please write a note for Dr. MacGregor? I can sign it, but if you do the rest I'd be grateful." Mae obliged and the doctor took the note. He took Peter's glass as he left. He still needed to administer that medicine.

Carrie joined Mae in the kitchen. "I guess you heard that Young Pete is going to the hospital."

"Yes Ma," she replied. "I heard. Not a very happy birthday is it?"

* * * * * *

Arrangements were made, and Peter left with Dr. MacGregor on the twenty- seventh of July for London, Ontario. He seemed anxious to go and even tried to joke. "Well it's not the part of Canada I wanted to see, but it's a start."

* * * * * *

Peter Willard Sparling died July twenty-ninth at the age of twenty-five years and one week. Cause of death was attributed to pneumococcus septice-mia, bacteria in the lungs. Reverend Bradfield led the service at the cemetery and he assured those gathered that Peter's suffering had ended and that he had been welcomed into eternity by both his earthly and heavenly fathers.

Chapter 30

J.W.'s insurance policy had been straightforward and named Carrie as his beneficiary. But Peter's policy named his estate as beneficiary. This meant that the insurance settlement would have to go through probate court at Sandusky, the county seat. Robert MacGregor and Albert accompanied Carrie to court along with Sam Soule who acted as a witness. Once there, the doctor was appointed administrator and the paperwork began.

Carrie became frustrated when she learned it might take several weeks before settlement could be made. Dr. MacGregor also seemed upset and mentioned to Carrie that they would have to check the policies of the other boys. "I was sure they listed you as beneficiary," he said. "We may have to get additional papers to amend the policies."

Seeing how this had affected his mother, Albert spoke up. "We'll take care of it Ma. But I don't see any rush."

MacGregor responded quickly. "But don't you see, now is the time to make the changes, while this is all still fresh in our minds. Then we can forget about it."

On August eighteenth, the Sun Assurance policies of Albert, Ray, and Scyrel Sparling were amended by a Special Appropriation of Policy to appoint their mother, Carrie Sparling, as sole beneficiary of their policies. Upon further checking, they discovered that the Gleaner policies had been made out to show Carrie as beneficiary so no special amendments for those policies were necessary.

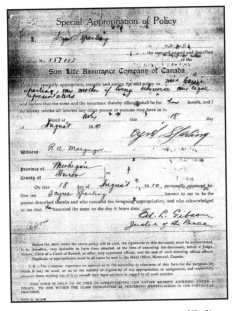

Scyrel's Special Appropriation of Policy

One week later Dr. MacGregor came to the farm, as usual, to treat Carrie's eyes. She wrote his note and said, "Robert I've been neglectful. You graciously stepped in as administrator for Young Pete and I feel you should be paid for that service. The extra responsibility has taken time away from your practice. I spoke to Sam and he said such payments are usually between ten and fifteen dollars, so I am signing this note for seventeen dollars and fifty cents. It should cover this house call and your services at Sandusky. If you think it should be more, please let me know."

The doctor shook his head. "But Carrie, I volunteered to do this as a friend." Carrie responded firmly. "Well, the note is made out and I'll not take it back." Carrie's daily visits to the cemetery tapered off and then stopped. On the last visit, she stopped at Peter's grave and spoke to the mound of dirt. "Your pain and troubles are gone Peter, and for that I am grateful." As she turned to leave she thought, "I guess Young Pete won't be leaving me now."

* * * * *

The August garden needed attention and Carrie had a cellar to fill. She stayed busy from early morning until late at night. Threshers had to be fed, and garden produce had to be canned. She often hired the Pieruski girl to help, as Mae could not be with her all the time.

Working two farms and running the milk route proved to be very taxing for the Sparlings. All the boys missed Peter, but Albert seemed to take it the hardest. A plan was forming in Carrie's mind. She took it to her chair whenever possible. One rainy day in late August she went to Violet's and shared her ideas. As always, Violet listened but said little.

Later, Carrie spoke to Dr. MacGregor. He had dosed her eyes and she informed him of her decision. When he suggested she might have trouble convincing the boys, she smiled. "I can take care of my boys, Robert."

On a late August evening, Carrie gathered her sons around the dining room table and revealed the plan. "I've thought about this for a very long time. Hear me out and you can have your say later. I am leaving this house and moving to the west farm." There was shock on her sons' faces, but she continued. "This farm is where you were born and where you grew up. I know you have many good memories of it, but lately any memories have been sour. We need a change and moving to the other farm will help us all. I'm not selling this place. It will always be a Sparling farm. I'll keep some dishes here and even a couple of beds. But I intend to be settled at the other farm by the end of next month."

Albert spoke first. "It appears you've already decided so I'll not try to change your mind. I admit it's hard seeing Peter's empty room when I go to bed. But if you were fixin' to sell this place, I'd put up a fight." Ray couldn't believe that his mother would leave this farm. She had been so upset when Little Pete, William, and the rest moved away. But, ever the peacemaker, he said, "As long as we still own this land, it doesn't matter to me which house we live in. But I'm not sure I can ever call the west farm home."

Scyrel scowled. It would mean living seven and a half miles from Tyre, Sam, and the store. He stood and looked at Carrie. "Looks like I am outvoted," he declared. He pushed back his chair, stood up, and stormed out of the room. Carrie had expected resistance, but Scyrel's reaction had caught her off guard. But she expected he would come around sooner or later.

* * * * *

The move should have waited until crops and garden were stripped, but Carrie was insistent. She hired extra help to sow wheat and pull the beans. The beets looked good but would not be harvested until much later. The milk route continued but Albert entertained the thought, privately, of giving it up. Mae came for a few days and the women moved dishes, cookware, canned goods, and linens. By nightfall everyone was exhausted, but they were slowly making progress.

September was also fair time, and Albert went to both the Elkton and Huron County Fairs at least one night each. Ray did not relinquish band practice or concerts, and Scyrel never missed a chance to stop by the Tyre store. The boys were young and healthy, or mostly healthy. Albert had a spell of vomiting during mid-September. He blamed it on something he ate. Mae suggested the boys were working too hard, but Carrie didn't let up. "I have strong sons, Mae. Everyone knows Albert is very clever when it comes to getting out of work."

By the thirtieth of September the move to the new house was nearly complete. Robert MacGregor, Ed Styles, and Sam Soule all brought wagons to the farm. Albert and Scyrel loaded them and when they reached the west farm, Ray and Steve Berry unloaded them. Mae had returned to Port Huron so Carrie hired Anna Pieruski to help feed everyone. They devoured fried chicken, mounds of mashed potatoes, fresh green beans, peach cobbler, and fresh bread that Violet had sent with Ed. Lemonade slaked their thirst and the men rested about an hour before going back for another load. Carrie left Anna to clean up so she could take food to Albert and Scyrel. By late afternoon they were done. Carrie, as promised, left enough in the east farmhouse so it could be used for sleeping or eating. The next day the boys herded six very confused cows to their new home, and Carrie drove a wagonload of caged chickens to their new coop.

The Sparlings took advantage of rest on the Sabbath. The move had been completed in accordance with Carrie's timetable, but Scyrel had not come around as she had predicted. He did the work expected of him but remained sullen and withdrawn. Carrie let it pass. She had worked everyone very hard and they were all tired. She would continue the routine they were accustomed to and expected Scyrel's temperament would change. She would not mollycoddle her youngest child; there was too much work to be done before winter.

Chapter 31

E lection time rolled around and Dr. MacGregor decided not to run again for coroner. It was a known fact that the county paid its employees very small salaries. Besides, his practice continued to grow and he had become Bingham Township Health Officer. His good friend Zen Boomhower wanted to remain in public office and his re-election was a certainty. It was expected Republican Donald McAulay would become the next county sheriff, but Carrie cared little for politics of the day. Something that did catch her attention was news of a fire in Ubly.

It brought back many images. It had been over twenty-nine years since the fire of '81, but Carrie still had vivid memories of it. Determined firefighters and a fortunate wind kept destruction in Ubly to only three buildings. Dr. MacGregor joined other volunteers in battling the blaze and he gave Carrie a full description of the inferno the next day. When she went to Ubly days later, she could still smell the smoke. Other recollections filled her mind when she looked at the calendar, October nineteenth. Had J.W. lived, they would have been married twenty-eight years. Two dates, and both brought memories of anguish and pain.

More troubling news arrived when smallpox struck Saginaw, to the west. Several citizens fled to Bad Axe and it was feared they would bring the dreaded disease into the Thumb. Stringent precautions were observed. Every person leaving Saginaw was fumigated and vaccinated. Those who refused were detained in quarantine for three days. Officials stayed on top of the situation and most of the Thumb was spared. Dr. MacGregor, as health officer, spent long hours vaccinating his patients, but made certain his trips to the farm continued with uninterrupted regularity. Since Peter's death it wasn't necessary to come at noon, but habit prevailed. He was more often than not at the dinner table offering advice and suggestions to the young Sparling men. Though he had never farmed himself, he gave his opinion freely and often on when to cut, when to plant, when to thresh, and when to butcher.

After dinner when the boys left the table for chores, he would drop Carrie's eyes and listen to her concerns. Scyrel had replaced Young Pete as her number one worry. "Scyrel is young, and the move affected him more than his brothers," MacGregor tried to assure her. "Give him time and he'll be his old self again."

Carrie always felt better after talking to Robert, but she still took problems to her rocking chair. She and Violet now met infrequently, but Carrie hoped the slower winter months would bring them together again on a more regular basis. The fact that she now lived further from her best friend and confidante was the only negative aspect regarding the move as far as Carrie was concerned.

* * * * *

Elections held in early November produced no surprises. A Dr. Charles Morden took MacGregor's place as county coroner. That same month Carrie resumed attendance at the First Presbyterian Church in Ubly.

* * * * *

Mae and Bert spent most of Thanksgiving Day with the Hurfords, but stopped by the Sparlings later on their way home. Strong tension in the air made the visit quite unpleasant. Mae could not find an opportune time to ask either her mother or brothers the cause of the obvious strain, so she and Bert left after a very short stay, using Bert's job as an excuse. Had Mae been able to speak privately with any of her family, she would have learned the disquiet had several roots.

The first friction came about when Carrie found J.W.'s accordion in Ray's room. He had surreptitiously moved it from the attic at Tyre to his room in Ubly. He thought he had hidden it well, but apparently not well enough.

Tyre General Store

Carrie was adamant. The accordion would not be allowed in this house. Ray agreed to take it back to Tyre. He had sensed she might be sensitive to its presence, but her hostile reaction surprised him. Shortly after that, Albert

162

announced that they were giving up the milk route. Such a decision made no sense to Carrie. She knew Albert missed Peter, but he had two other brothers who could help and she felt giving up the milk route would cause a needless loss of extra income. Scyrel, emboldened by his brothers' actions, stated his intention to work for Sam at the store in Tyre. Carrie quickly formed a sound argument against this plan. "We're at least seven miles from Tyre. How can you do farm chores and still work at the store? Think about it, there just isn't enough time in one day." She thought she had him there but his reply sent her mind reeling.

"I love store work and I hate farming! Ma, I already talked to Sam. He needs my help and has given me a room over the store. I won't be going back and forth every day. I start in January."

It was almost more than Carrie could bear. She prepared the traditional Thanksgiving meal, but ate very little. Though Carrie's appetite had vanished, her sons' had not, and there were few leftovers. After dinner, Carrie cleared the table methodically and quietly and the boys found work in the barn, or so they said. They came back into the house when Mae and Bert arrived. Everyone felt the tension but small talk filled the gaps until the Hurfords departed. Carrie then went to her chair and the boys let her be.

Albert ordered Ray to take the accordion back to Tyre immediately. "Scyrel and I will do the milking," he said. Ray readily agreed. Unknown to anyone, he had been teaching himself to play and hoped one day to be as good as his pa. He should have realized it was foolish to bring the instrument to the west farm, but it had a comforting effect on him. He didn't think his mother knew how much he and his brothers missed their father. "Oh well," he thought, "this will be better. I can play to my heart's content at the empty farmhouse." When he returned, the milking was done, the kitchen table was bare, and Carrie's bedroom door was shut. The boys would have to fend for themselves for supper.

* * * * *

Friday morning seemed normal. Carrie prepared a huge breakfast of fried potatoes, slabs of bacon, biscuits with jam, and scrambled eggs. She made no mention of the previous day and acted as if it had never happened. The boys didn't know whether to be relieved or concerned, but they took the optimistic approach and silently thanked the chair. Albert and Ray did the milk route— only one more month of that. Scyrel brought wood and water into the house.

Dr. MacGregor arrived as usual, and when they sat down to eat Carrie spoke nonstop. "Robert you are going to see some changes around here. I guess my boys have minds of their own and they've made some big decisions without my knowledge. Their milk route is to be given to the Knectel boys, and Scyrel has chosen to live in Tyre and become a storekeeper. I must say I was taken by surprise when I first heard. But what can I do? Albert, pass the meat to the doctor. Looks like I'll be hiring men come spring. Two farms and only two farmers. Yes, extra help will be necessary. Save room Robert, I have apple pie for dessert. Oh, did you know that Ray has taken to the accordion now? I'm not sure why. The band only has horns, but so be it." The doctor could not get a word in. He looked at the boys but it was apparent that they were as puzzled as he. Had their mother accepted the new arrangements, or was she being sarcastic? When they finished eating, the boys left the house, eager to talk with each other about what they had just witnessed.

Dr. MacGregor treated Carrie's eyes. "All right Carrie, the boys are gone. I can't believe you are happy with these changes. I know you too well. Do you want to talk about it?"

Carrie sighed, "Of course I'm not happy, and I don't understand their new attitudes. It almost seems that they are all against me."

"Would you like me to talk to them?" MacGregor asked.

Carrie shook her head. "Not yet, Robert." She wrote a note for the house call but the doctor noticed she did not reach for her own account tablet. Truth was, Carrie had searched for it, but it could not be found. It must have been misplaced during the move. She felt it wasn't necessary to get a new one because the old one would appear one of these days. Besides, if you could not trust your own doctor, whom could you trust?

Chapter 32

The bitter cold that settled over the region in December held the promise of killing off the few stubborn pockets of smallpox that remained. Drummers were especially affected, not because they had the disease, but because it was feared they might carry it. Some businesses carried signs barring these traveling salesmen from entering their stores altogether. The Sparlings remained healthy except for Albert's occasional stomach flare-ups.

* * * * *

Christmas fell on a Sunday. Carrie had been busy shopping and planning a huge feast. Bert and Mae were coming and Carrie was determined to give her family the best day she could possibly manage. She rose early to fix a breakfast of sausage and pancakes. The goose cooked in the oven while the entire family, at Carrie's insistence, attended church. When they arrived home the men tended the horses and Mae helped Carrie set out dinner. Sweet potatoes, rolls and butter, glazed carrots, green beans, corn oysters, cranberry relish, celery, and cabbage slaw joined the goose at a very full table. Dessert consisted of pumpkin pie, mincemeat pie, and applesauce cake. Mae brought sugar cookies; she had gotten her Grandmother Sparling's recipe from Aunt Ellen.

A festive atmosphere, unlike that on Thanksgiving, found everyone relaxed and happy. Laughter filled the air and when they could eat no more, Carrie and Mae cleared the table and washed the dishes. Then they began to open the presents. Carrie received a fancy apron, new handkerchiefs, a pair of kid gloves, and an afghan—Mae's handiwork. Mae opened a hand mirror, perfume, and a new shirtwaist. Bert got a box of cigars (even though Carrie banned their use indoors), a deck of playing cards, and a new cap. The boys expected the usual presents and were not disappointed. They each unwrapped socks, a sweater, and new overalls. Then Carrie pulled out her surprise.

Each boy had one more gift that had been hidden under her bed. Albert received a framed photograph of Peter. Carrie had gone to Watkins Photography in Bad Axe. Mr. Watkins still had the negatives from the picture he had taken over two years ago. He had been able to isolate Peter and provide a lovely frame for a picture of Peter alone. Albert held it with his left hand while his right hand softly traced Peter's image. Ray opened his gift next. It was a book titled, *How To Play the Accordion*. When he looked at Carrie she explained, "I was wrong to make you take your pa's accordion back to Tyre. I don't want you to feel you have to leave your home to play it. If you still want to keep it here, I would enjoy hearing you practice."

Scyrel hardly knew what to expect when he opened his present. The box contained a new pair of slacks and a shirt. And they were not farm clothes. "If you're going to be a storekeeper, you must look the part," she remarked. Joy and relief spread throughout the parlor. Each boy kissed Carrie, but words were hard to find so great was the surprise. Only Mae noticed that Carrie's face had a knowing, almost calculating smile.

There remained one family custom to make the day complete. The sound of nuts cracking was broken only by small utterances as they passed Christmas cards and letters around the table. It was a very happy day and everyone, in his or her own way, looked forward to the new year.

Chapter 33

Early Monday morning on January second, Scyrel packed a grip with enough clothes for a week. He was anxious to be gone and begin work at the store. Carrie told her son she would do his laundry if he brought it home. He had not even considered it, but realized he couldn't ask Sam's wife to wash his dirty clothes. They finally decided that he would come home on Sundays and exchange soiled clothing for clean.

His attitude had greatly improved since Carrie's change of heart. He didn't know why she had decided to support him and wasn't about to question it. Albert and Ray teased their brother about being so gussied up and pretended to slop some manure from their boots onto his clean shoes. After a quick good-bye, Scyrel rode away.

Albert watched until Scyrel was out of sight and headed back to the barn, but Ray lingered. He wondered if his mother might need a shoulder to lean on. She guessed the reason for his hesitation. "I'm fine Ray. Scyrel thinks he wants to be a clerk so I'll let him try. But he'll be back." She smiled and added, "I'm going to Violet's later today. Don't forget I need wood brought in. You'll have to do Scyrel's chores now."

Carrie was pleasantly startled by a hug from her son. "Thanks Ma," was all he said.

Dr. MacGregor arrived at noon and shared a dinner of leftover chicken pie. Albert and Ray would be eating at the Lorkowskis. The hay press was there and the boys were hired to help. They would need to find more such jobs since they were no longer delivering milk and cream to customers. The doctor treated Carrie's eyes and stayed a bit longer. They sat at the kitchen table, drinking coffee. "I suppose Scyrel has left for Tyre," said MacGregor. "How long do you think he'll last? You know, being indoors most of the day. That might be fine in winter, but come spring I reckon he'll miss the smell of turned earth."

Carrie sighed. "I guess we'll have to wait and see. I just told Ray that his brother would be back. I know that as much as I know anything." She wrote MacGregor's note and he started to leave.

"Oh I almost forgot," he said. "Ida and I want to thank you very much for the Christmas gift. That wasn't necessary, but we appreciate it. You're so good to us with fresh cream and eggs, plus a house to live in. When Ida opened your card and the money fell out we were speechless." Carrie stood and faced the doctor. "Robert I only wish it could have been more."

Robert MacGregor put his arms around Carrie Sparling and she put her head on his chest. It only lasted a moment and no words were spoken. Suddenly realizing this was more than a friendly hug, they each took a step back. The silence was broken only by the sound of the door shutting as MacGregor left the house.

* * * * *

Violet expected Carrie and had brewed tea to go with the pound cake she served. The friends had not been able to get together since before the move. Aletha was now a young woman of fifteen, and little Marie would soon turn eight years old. They were at school now, but Carrie hoped they would get home before she had to leave.

Violet looked at her friend. Carrie was glowing. "Carrie, didn't Scyrel leave this morning? I thought you'd be upset, but you look wonderful. Is everything all right?"

Carrie smiled. She could tell Violet anything—almost anything. "I'll not try to fool you Violet. Of course I'm upset that Scyrel has left home. But the more I thought about it, the more I realized he would just have to get this storekeeping out of his system. I don't think he'll last a month. Scyrel will come home. I have no doubt. As for Albert and Ray, they have more time now that the milk route is done so they've hired themselves out to other farmers to replace that lost income. Farming two places will be difficult but we'll get it done. And Robert is always willing to lend a hand. The way his practice is growing I don't know how he does it all. You know how active he is in the church and the village. But he still finds time for his patients. I honestly don't think I could manage without him."

Carrie paused for breath and Violet spoke. "I agree that Dr. MacGregor is a fine man and isn't his wife nice? It is obvious she and her husband are very much in love." Carrie almost felt scolded. But Violet would not do that. Besides, there was no reason to feel guilty. It had only been a hug.

Violet changed the subject. "Did you hear we're getting a new minister? His name is Thomas Hurd and he'll start in March. I'm sure we'll have a welcome dinner for him. May I count on you to help?"

Carrie nodded, but still felt a bit uncomfortable from the remark about the happy MacGregors. She looked out the window and used the darkening sky as a reason to leave. "I think I best get home. I'm so sorry to miss the girls. Please give them my love."

Violet watched until she was just a speck in the distance. "Dear God," she prayed, "keep Carrie in Your care and close any doors she should not enter."

* * * * *

Carrie did not regret the move to the west farm, but she missed being close to the general store in Tyre. Scyrel could bring orders home to her, but it wasn't the same as being there. The store in Ubly had all she needed; it was just a matter of getting used to the change. She found she often felt isolated living over four miles from the nearest town. Tyre had been conveniently located about one mile from the old farm and she hadn't considered the distance when she planned the move. She had always been able to remain up to date with a visit to the general store so she decided to subscribe to the weekly Bad Axe newspaper, *The Huron County Tribune*. It would make her feel connected and help fill the void of not getting the news fresh from the store. She had to buy a magnifying glass as sometimes her eyes misread the small print. It was published every Friday and she enjoyed reading the articles, and sometimes talking back to them. The paper contained many advertisements—everything from clothing to medicines, utensils to buggies, and even automobiles. "An automobile. Imagine!" she thought.

Foods to prepare and ranges on which to prepare them were often on sale. She even saw an ad from a bank promoting something called a checking account. "No thank you, notes are just fine."

There were notices of deaths, and the society columns kept one abreast of who was visiting whom and the like. "My, I didn't realize how often the MacGregors and Boomhowers kept company."

One article especially caught her eye. It was a suggestion to hold a celebration in memory of the Great Fire of '81. "Well I don't need a celebration to make me remember that."

She read an article about a local judge, Watson Beach. "Never heard of him."

Several people were quoted regarding the safety of the county courthouse and all of them agreed it was in need of replacement and not repair. "I suppose we citizens would be expected to pay for that."

Yes, it would be fair to say that Carrie enjoyed reading the newspaper and talking back to it.

One day in late February as she was reading the weekly news, Ray raced into the house calling urgently for her. "Ma I think you best call the doc, Albert has a terrible headache and says he don't feel good." Carrie rose from the parlor chair as Albert appeared, holding his head. His face was puffy and his eyes were almost shut. Carrie helped him to a chair and asked what was wrong. "I don't know Ma," he answered. "But my head feels heavy and my back hurts." Carrie told him to go lie down on her bed, the only first floor bedroom.

She called Dr. MacGregor who had already been there earlier for her eyes. "You just caught me Mrs. Sparling. Ida and I were on our way to Zen and Jennie's. What do you need?" Carrie described Albert's symptoms.

Within the hour, Robert and Ida MacGregor arrived at the farm. The doctor examined Albert and returned to the kitchen. "He'll be fine Mrs. Sparling. It appears to be a kidney infection. I want you to put him on a milk diet. It could get boring for him, but if you have Granula or Postum, that would offer some variety. I told him he must remain on this diet for a week and I'll be back on Monday. I gave him something for the pain, and once he starts this diet the swelling in his face should go down." Carrie wrote his note and the MacGregors left.

Scyrel arrived Sunday as promised and brought parcels for his brothers. Carrie didn't know what they contained, but assumed he used some of his wages to impress them with gifts. He was surprised to learn Albert had been ill, but when told the condition had improved, he quietly breathed a sigh of relief. He did not like the idea of leaving the store and returning to farming. As it turned out, Albert claimed to be completely well and begged to eat some of the chicken and dumplings Carrie had prepared. "You can have a dumpling with milk, but no chicken or gravy," she insisted. "Dr. MacGregor will be here tomorrow and if he takes you off this diet, I'll fix whatever you want."

It would have been more difficult to eat his soggy dumpling had it not been for Scyrel's nonstop description of work at the store. "I've moved up from stocking the shelves and cleaning floors and spittoons, to taking and wrapping orders. Sam even trusts me to be in charge if he has to be out. Ma, you know how Sam always finds lemons for you? Well it seems he knows what everyone wants or needs. And I'm learning that as well. I can tell you what kind of soap the Lorkowskis always buy and it's not the same as what the Schlegels use. Course I hear lots of gossip, but Sam tells me to keep that to myself. He says I have a good head for storekeeping."

Carrie listened to her youngest son and saw the happiness on his face. Could she have been wrong? It was going on two months since he left. "Well," she thought, "wait until spring. He won't like working inside all day when he could be outdoors watching life return to the fields. He'll be back." However, a small cloud of doubt was forming.

* * * * *

Dr. MacGregor came on Monday. He tended Carrie's eyes and then examined Albert who was anxious to be released from his rest, and especially from the milk diet. The doctor seemed pleased with the recovery and told the young man to slowly get back to his usual routine. "But," he warned, "if you start ailing again, get more rest and go back on the diet." Albert thanked him and headed for the barn. Ray had been doing all the chores and now he could take some of that load off his brother. Albert had always found ways to get out of work, but he decided being sick was not the way to do it. It sure felt good to feel good.

Dr. MacGregor accepted coffee from Carrie and drank it as she wrote his note. She looked at the doctor and then averted her eyes. "Robert when Albert got sick I had a terrible feeling that he had what Young Pete had, you know, the bad blood. You said it was contagious and I couldn't help but wonder if all my boys might have caught it. I was careful, like you said with laundry and dishes, but is there any chance it could have happened?"

The doctor put his cup down. "Carrie, there is always a chance. I rarely see Scyrel, but neither Albert nor Ray exhibit the behavior Peter showed. I'm out here enough to keep watch, so don't worry about it. I can treat it if it happens and can catch it early. Peter's condition was advanced. And remember, I listed his cause of death as a lung problem, not the other."

Carrie looked at MacGregor a long time before speaking. "I know that Robert, and I'm grateful. I would hate for the whole Thumb to think poorly of us."

Dr. MacGregor quickly added, "Now don't get me wrong Carrie. I didn't lie on his death certificate. He did have bacteria in him." He looked intently at Carrie. "How are you doing? Any changes in your eyes?"

Carrie blinked. "I think they're about the same. I need a glass to read the newspaper and they still burn some. Guess I just have to get used to it." Not wanting to hurt his feelings, she added, "but they feel so much better after the drops."

"Glad to hear it," the doctor replied. "I'm going to do some more reading. Perhaps the drops need to be administered more often, or there might even be a new medicine we can try." He took her note and stood. Since that hug, both he and Carrie sensed awkwardness when it was time for him to leave. She could not get Violet's comments out of her mind and remained in her chair as he went to the door. She loved Violet dearly, but her friend had a loving husband and she could not possibly know the loneliness Carrie felt.

Not completely reassured by the doctor's words, Carrie spent the next hour in her chair rereading the medical journals she had ordered from Sam last year. Rising with new resolve, she went back to the kitchen. Albert had requested roast beef for supper and she needed to get it started.

Chapter 34

March's reputation for wind was preserved. The chicken coop blew down one day while Dr. MacGregor was at the farm. He quickly changed clothing and helped Albert and Ray chase down the birds and give a temporary fix to the structure. Two chickens had been killed when the coop fell, which solved the problem of what to cook for supper.

Violet called on Carrie after Reverend Bradfield's final sermon to discuss the welcome dinner for Reverend Hurd, set for Saturday the eighteenth. The church had added a new wing so they would not have to borrow the schoolhouse again. Violet recruited Carrie and the boys to assist in both set up and clean up. Several women donated food for the larder in the manse and Carrie provided canned meat and vegetables. She and Violet went over final preparations while they nibbled on lemon cookies. Conversation was limited to the upcoming event with only a few passing comments on family and health. Dr. MacGregor's name did not come up.

Scyrel came in from outside and greeted Mrs. Styles. He said the coop was fixed and he'd be heading back to Tyre. Carrie briefly explained to Violet the wind damage of the previous week. "Your clothes are on your bed," Carrie told him. "But can't you at least stay for supper?"

He hugged Carrie. "Ma, if I stay for supper then you'll want me to stay for something else. I like to get back early so I'm ready for Monday morning." This conversation had been repeated every time Scyrel announced it was time for him to leave.

Violet smiled and spoke. "Scyrel it would seem you've not grown weary of your new job. I heard Sam is most pleased with your work."

Scyrel smiled. "Yes Ma'am. I mean no Ma'am. I'm not tired of it at all."

Violet saw the dismay on Carrie's face and changed the subject. "I hope you can come to our dinner next Saturday. We're all anxious to meet our new minister and want to give him an enthusiastic welcome." Scyrel hesitated. "I'll think about it, but Saturday is mighty busy so I can't promise." He left the women and went to retrieve his clean clothing and leave more parcels on his brothers' beds.

Carrie sighed. "Violet, I really thought he would have come to his senses by now. He doesn't belong in that store any more than I do. He's just a farm boy, and I don't appreciate Sam filling his head with other ideas. It doesn't even seem to bother him that Albert and Ray are doing the work that four boys used to do."

Violet remained silent. What she wanted to say were words Carrie would not want to hear. Scyrel's return to the kitchen saved her from saying anything. She sensed the need for mother and son to have time alone and said she must be going. Carrie packed some bread, jam, and cookies in a bag. It was apparent by looking at Scyrel that Sam's wife fed him to his liking. But Carrie couldn't just let him go back without some home cooking. Scyrel kissed his mother and mounted his horse. Carrie went to her chair.

* * * * *

The dinner for Reverend Hurd celebrated two events. The congregation welcomed the new, young, energetic preacher while initiating the new building addition to the church. After the meal Reverend Hurd went around the room trying to learn names. When he got to Carrie, she introduced Albert and Ray, and told him another son had not been able to attend. He shook hands and began to speak. "Mrs. . . ."

"Sparling," Carrie said. "It will take time for you to put names and faces together. But you're lucky in one sense. Years ago this area was filled with Sparlings. But many have moved away or. . . ." Carrie paused. "Some died."

The new minister nodded sympathetically. "Is your husband here?"

Without hesitation, Carrie answered. "No he has passed, going on three years now." She smiled as she accepted the minister's condolences.

About fifty people attended the dinner and all agreed that if Reverend Hurd was as good in the pulpit as he was out of it, they were very fortunate to have him as their new minister. The evening drew to a close. Women began to gather their dishes, and Albert and Ray folded tables and chairs. Dr. MacGregor helped with the tables and purposely worked alongside Albert to inquire about his health. "I'm fine Doc. Couldn't be better," he replied. Albert really was feeling good and had made plans to do the town after chores. He had tried to talk Ray into going to Bad Axe with him, but Ray had other plans. A few of the band members were getting together to look over some new music.

When the Sparlings arrived home, Carrie unloaded dishes and linens while the boys changed clothes. She wasn't hungry, but knew her sons would be. So she prepared hash and by the time milking was finished, their supper was hot. They ate, and again changed clothing for their evening plans. Carrie was nostalgic as she cleaned up the dishes. She thought back to the dinner, and telling Reverend Hurd about all the Sparlings who had once filled the Thumb. "Well," she thought, "he won't have any trouble remembering the few of us who are left."

* * * * *

174

Dr. MacGregor arrived before noon on Monday. He dropped Carrie's eyes and told her he had ordered a stronger dose of atropine. "Hopefully you'll soon notice a big difference," he stated.

Carrie thanked him and wrote his note. "Robert, we talked before about what Young Pete had and if my other sons could catch it. I know you told me not to fret, but Albert is staying out at night again. Could you talk to him? I think if a man approached him he might pay more attention."

Dr. MacGregor shook his head. "Carrie, he's young and bound to want some fun."

Carrie's eyes teared, and she opened her mouth to speak. Seeing what was coming, the doctor quickly added, "But if I get a chance I'll talk to him." As she wiped an escaping tear, Carrie thanked her doctor.

MacGregor could not stay to eat as he was meeting Zen for lunch at the Ubly Hotel. When he left, Carrie took another load of wet clothes to the clothesline. The bright sun and gentle breezes would dry the laundry in good time. She went back into the house to fix dinner. And since it was the first day of spring, she prepared her dreaded spring tonic. She hoped the pork steaks and mashed potatoes would take the boys' minds off the tonic; how they hated that brew! Both Albert and Ray were served a full glass, but Albert's was a bit stronger, just in case. After dinner the boys went their own ways. Albert helped a neighbor thresh beans and Ray went to Tyre for supplies. He could have gone to Ubly but old habits died hard. Sam was sure to have what they needed and it gave him a chance to see his younger brother.

Carrie washed the dishes and had just begun her third load of laundry when Reverend Hurd rode into the yard. She had not expected him and apologized for her appearance. "There is nothing to apologize for," he assured her. "I only see an industrious woman doing Monday chores. I plan to visit all the church members, but if this is a bad time I can come another day."

Carrie wiped her hands on her apron. "Gracious no. This is a good time. Can I fix you a cup of coffee? It's fresh from dinner." The new minister smiled. "That sounds good," he said. She poured two cups and suggested they go into the parlor, but he assured her the kitchen was fine. "It's so homey and comfortable. In fact it's my favorite room of any house."

They sat at the table and Carrie spoke. "I enjoyed your sermon yesterday. I hope you'll like it here." Reverend Hurd sipped his coffee and responded. "The welcome was wonderful and I believe I will be very happy in Ubly.

"Mrs. Sparling, you told me Saturday that your husband had passed, but I have since learned that your eldest son died last summer. I am so very sorry for your losses. You appear to be a very strong woman, but if you ever feel a need to talk please don't hesitate to call me. God wants us to share each other's sorrows as well as the joys." He took a sip of coffee. "I imagine your sons are all out working now. I met two but you said there was a third."

Carrie poured more coffee. "Yes. Albert is twenty-three years old, and Ray will be twenty-one come Saturday. My youngest, Scyrel, is working at the general store in Tyre but it's only temporary. I also have a daughter, Mae. She is married and lives in Port Huron."

The discussion then went to weather and an appreciation of the arrival of spring. The preacher noticed last Friday's newspaper on the table. "I understand there is much concern about the safety of the courthouse in Bad Axe."

Carrie responded quickly. "That's what they say, but I would hate to see it torn down. It survived the fire of '81. Were you in the Thumb then?"

"No Mrs. Sparling, but I certainly heard about it and can't imagine the horror." Carrie's mind went back to her mother. "Yes. It was a horror and it affected many people for a long time."

The preacher finished his coffee and said he really should be on his way. "It was so nice to visit with you Mrs. Sparling. And thank you for the coffee. I'll let you get back to your laundry, but could we have a word of prayer before I leave?" Carrie nodded and bowed her head. "Dear Lord, I thank you for this beautiful spring day and for your goodness to us all. Bless this house and the nurturing hands of this loving mother as she cares for her children. Keep us all strong for your service. Amen." He reached for the door handle. "Give my regards to your sons. I look forward to talking with them and also meeting Scyrel."

Carrie resumed her washday chores with a lighter heart. "He seems like a very nice man," she thought. "He reminds me some of Reverend Mackersie. And calling on every member. That's a good sign."

Chapter 35

April brought wood buzzers to the Sparling farm, and Carrie hired the Pieruski girl to help feed the hired hands. Anna worked hard, and Carrie remembered how valuable the girl had been when she'd had her private ailments. The two women also began the ritual of spring-cleaning. While dusting underneath Albert's bed, Carrie discovered the opened parcels Scyrel had brought. They contained patent medicine, not gifts as she had thought. When she asked her sons they said it was for pimples, like Peter had used. Carrie suggested they give their faces a rest from shaving by growing beards. "A beard would hide those pimples," she added. But the boys laughed at her. "We're not old men yet Ma."

April also brought election results. The citizens of Huron County, by six hundred votes, said no to a new courthouse. Easter fell on the sixteenth and Carrie attended church alone. Albert remained in bed with stomach pains so Ray did the milking and didn't get cleaned up in time to accompany Carrie to services. Scyrel, due home for dinner and an exchange of clothing, had not yet arrived. Mae and Bert would be spending the holiday at home. Carrie tried to listen to the sermon, but thoughts of her children crowded out Reverend Hurd's message. She and Violet exchanged a few words after church and Violet said she would be over the next day. "We have to get as many visits in as possible before the busy season is upon us," she noted.

When Violet arrived, coffee and cake were set out. Each had mending to do, so they sewed as they chatted. Though cordial, there seemed to be a slight tension in the conversation. If Carrie mentioned "Robert" MacGregor, Violet responded with a casual comment about "Dr." MacGregor. Violet also knew Carrie was upset that Scyrel had not returned home for good and was even more involved in the daily operation of the store. She herself had seen him at work and he had been so happy and helpful.

Violet felt it best not to mention Scyrel so she asked about Albert. "You know he missed church yesterday," replied Carrie. "He stayed in bed most all day with stomach problems. Robert will be here later for my eyes and we also need to go over the plans for the next planting. He'll probably put Albert back on the milk diet."

No sooner was the doctor mentioned than the sound of his buggy was heard. "Goodness," exclaimed Violet. "I've lost track of time and need to get home." Carrie thanked her for the bread, and as Violet gathered her mending she remarked, "I believe bread is my favorite thing to make. I do some of my best thinking while kneading the dough." She greeted Dr. MacGregor on her way out.

Carrie's eyes were treated, and they chatted for a bit while the drops worked. "Albert's stomach is bad again Robert. I've been dosing him, but I'd like you to look at him. He may need the milk diet again. He spent most of yesterday in bed, but managed to do chores this morning. The boys are due in for dinner soon, can you stay?" The Sparlings shared a meal of beef stew with Dr. MacGregor. They discussed the operation of the farm, at least Carrie and MacGregor did. Albert and Ray never complained to their mother, but the two of them had more than one conversation regarding Dr. MacGregor and his advice. They felt they were more than capable of planning for the seasons without his help.

The doctor finished his stew and spoke to Albert. "I understand your stomach has been bothering you again." Albert tried to sound convincing. "I'm all right. It's a lot better than yesterday." The doctor pursued the matter. "Since I'm here, how about if I examine you and maybe we can prevent a relapse." Albert agreed, and the two men went into Carrie's bedroom. The examination showed nothing specific but it gave Dr. MacGregor a chance to talk to the young man privately. "Are you getting enough rest Albert? You know it's very important that you take care of yourself."

Albert smiled. "So Ma told you I go out at night. I thought she might be behind this. Look, I know she doesn't like it, but it's my life. Anyway, now you can report back that you discussed it with me."

If it were not for his charming smile, Dr. MacGregor might have thought Albert was being sarcastic, or even rude. He stood. "Young man, you are correct. It is your life, but don't forget your life affects others. I have some powders I'd like you to try. See if they settle your stomach." He reached into his bag and gave Albert a small bottle. "Put a good pinch of this with hot liquid, like coffee. It will mix easier. Try it once a day and maybe we can eliminate those stomach problems once and for all."

The men left the room and Albert joined his brother outside to check and mend fences. Carrie was writing the doctor's note and looked up. "How is he Robert?" The doctor accepted the note and spoke. "I think he'll be fine. I gave him something for his stomach and also talked to him, like you asked, about his late hours. There's not much else I can do Carrie."

She sighed. "Thank you, I do appreciate all you do for us. J.W. always said to let boys be boys, but Albert should be thinking of settling down soon. We have the two farms and one could be used by him and a bride."

The doctor looked surprised. "Is Albert seeing someone?"

Carrie shook her head. "No one special, but there are plenty of nice girls around. One is bound to catch his eye. Oh my, I've written your note but it doesn't include the medicine. I can write another," she said and reached for her notepad.

Dr. MacGregor put his hand on hers. "Don't worry about that now. You can pay me next time." He left the farm and headed toward Bad Axe. It was a good distance, but he had a very important errand.

* * * * *

"Dr. MacGregor, this is an honor. What can I do for you?" The owner of Yauch Motor Sales anticipated a sale. Robert tried to hide his own excitement. "Mr. Yauch, I saw your ad in the newspaper for a runabout. I am very interested in exchanging my buggy for an automobile that could stand up to many miles and rough roads." Mr. Yauch also tried to hide his excitement. "You are a man of the future Doctor. More and more, people are learning the advantage of owning an automobile. Dr. Herrington has had one for some time now and he says he can call on nearly twice the number of patients as when he used the horse and buggy. Do you have any idea when you might want to make a purchase? I can offer very favorable terms."

"Actually," replied MacGregor, "I was thinking of placing an order in the next week or two. And terms won't be necessary. I plan to pay in cash." The men shook hands and parted—each with a grin on his face.

MacGregor arrived at the Sparlings two days later. He treated Carrie and asked where he could find Albert. She directed him to the pasture where her son was tending to a sick cow. The doctor traded his shoes for boots and helped Albert isolate the ill animal. Once they had her tethered, Albert looked at its mouth. "Hate to pay a vet if I can treat her myself. But I can't see anything wrong, so guess I'll have to get Uncle John." The cow bellowed in protest.

"I forgot your uncle was a veterinarian," MacGregor remarked, wiping his hands on his pants. "I came out to see how you're feeling. Are you taking the medicine I left?"

"Yeah," Albert answered, "but I still have the gut ache. Do you want me to keep taking it?"

MacGregor nodded. "It has only been two days, so I think you should continue for a bit longer. I probably shouldn't ask, but are you getting more rest?"

Albert almost smiled. "If you mean am I staying home at night, then yes. You shouldn't ask." They untied the cow and walked back to the gate together. As MacGregor walked toward his horse, he looked back. "See you Friday, Albert."

* * * * *

On Friday, April twenty-first Albert told the doctor he wasn't going to take the powders any more. The pain remained and now he was sick to his stomach. His eyes itched and he blamed the powders. Dr. MacGregor appeared to be more concerned that Albert was not taking the medicine than he was about the side effects. "Tell you what," he suggested. "Let's try something else." He poured a solution into a small cup and offered it to the young man.

Albert, relieved to be off the powder, swallowed the new potion and groaned. "I don't know which is worse – this or that stuff Ma gives me."

MacGregor smiled. "Albert you know medicines aren't meant to taste good."

On Sunday, Carrie and Ray attended church. Albert, still feeling sick, stayed home, and Scyrel arrived about ten o'clock. He had parcels for his brothers and lemons for Carrie. They sat down to a dinner of ham, sweet potatoes, green beans, and fried apples. Once again, Scyrel talked excitedly about his job. He was so animated that he did not see the frown on Carrie's face. "Gosh," he declared. "I've been working for Sam nearly four months now. The days just fly by." Even though he had been told not to, he shared a few items of gossip; things people would soon learn if they didn't already know. He finally ran out of news and asked about the farm.

"We'll be harrowing and seeding next week," replied Albert. "And a couple of apple trees in the orchard need trimming. Missed some dead branches last January. Going to hire Perry Cole to help. Then Mr. Sadler wants to hire us. Philo Richardson asked first, so we'll either do both or divide it up."

Carrie stood to clear the table. She couldn't listen to another word. Scyrel should be ashamed, off playing storekeeper while his brothers managed two farms and worked for others as well. She asked if they wanted anything else and they all agreed, more lemonade. As she carried their glasses into the kitchen, she made certain Albert's glass went back to him. The other two could be mixed up, but she was treating Albert the same way she had Young Pete. Nobody seemed to notice.

The weather was pleasant and Ray suggested they get up a ball game. There were enough guys in the area, and it was a great way to pass a Sunday afternoon. After a few telephone calls, the game was on. Albert, always ready for play, quit after half an hour saying he felt tough. Carrie spent the afternoon outside mentally laying out the garden. She hoped May would be warm enough for early planting. The sound of chatter told her that the ballgame was over and the boys would be hungry. And Scyrel would be leaving soon.

Ray and Scyrel appeared, laughing, but Albert was not with them. When she asked, Ray shrugged. "I thought he was here. He said he didn't feel good and quit the game."

Scyrel added, "I'll check his room when I get my things." When he returned, he reported Albert was asleep in bed. "Tell him I said good-bye to lazybones." Then he kissed Carrie and left.

Carrie went to check on her now oldest son. She shook him awake and asked what was wrong. "Don't know Ma," he answered in a weak voice. "My legs felt like they were giving out on me so I came in to lie down. How long have I been asleep?"

Carrie thought a moment before answering. "I would guess maybe an hour. Can I get you anything?"

He shook his head. "No, I'll be down in a minute to help with milking." As he tried to stand, Carrie saw how weak he was, and told him to stay put. "I'll help Ray. Dr. MacGregor will be out tomorrow, but I can call him to come out now if you wish."

Albert did lie back down, but told her not to bother the doc. "I'll be all right," he said.

* * * * *

The next day Carrie did laundry and had just finished washing Albert's clothing when the doctor arrived. She told him of Albert's condition the day before and MacGregor said he would check him. As he headed toward the stairs, Carrie stopped him. "He isn't in bed now. Got up early and has been acting normal. I just don't know what to make of it."

The doctor opened his bag for the atropine. "Sounds like it wasn't serious, maybe he just needed rest." He dropped her eyes and added, "Carrie, I have something I must discuss with you and there is no easy way so I'll just have to say it. My bookkeeping is rather poor. In fact Ida says it is horrid. I hate to admit it but I've misplaced many of your notes, and I've been trying to figure out exactly what you owe. You know, visits and medicine. Ida is trying to help, but I just wanted to warn you. I'll be sending you a bill soon and it could be hefty."

"I wish I could be of help Robert," she replied. "I used to keep a record of what I owe, but I guess it got lost in the move. You just figure as close as you can. I know I can trust you."

* * * * *

On Wednesday, just after Dr. MacGregor treated Carrie's eyes, Ray came racing into the house. He and Albert had been working in the orchard and Albert had fallen from a tree. Dr. MacGregor grabbed his bag and followed Ray back to where the boy lay. They helped him sit up and leaned him against the tree from which he had fallen. He grabbed his stomach and kept saying he had a gut ache. By the time Carrie got there, the doctor and Ray had Albert on his feet. With his arms around their shoulders Albert limped back to the house. After a quick examination, Dr. MacGregor stated the boy was going to be fine. "He just had the wind knocked out of him." He gave him something for the stomach pain, which Albert washed down with lemonade in his own glass.

"No more work today Albert," MacGregor stated. "Carrie, you may have to hire some help. I'd like to pitch in, but my schedule this week is really full. I'm on my way to Bad Axe now for an appointment."

Carrie assured him they would be fine. "We can manage Robert. I'll help Ray with the milking, and Big Pete's sons are going to be here tomorrow to harrow the west field. Perry Cole is usually available as well. Don't worry about us." She wrote his note and joked, "should I pin it to your sleeve?"

He smiled and said it wouldn't be necessary. Ray, puzzled over that exchange, shrugged his shoulders and went back to the orchard. Carrie set up the ironing board; the irons would heat while the chicken soup was cooking. Robert MacGregor went north to Bad Axe to see Mr. Yauch.

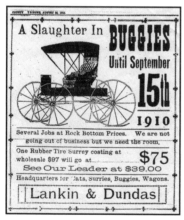

Huron County Tribune

Huron County Tribune

Chapter 36

On Friday, Albert got to the barn late and Ray started to complain about doing the work alone. "Ray," scolded Albert firmly, "if you felt as bad as I do, you'd understand."

"I thought Doc was taking care of you," said Ray, slightly chagrined. "He's always giving you one thing or another."

Albert paused, wondering how much he should say to his brother, and finally decided he had to talk to someone. "The doc and Ma don't know the half of it. They treat my stomach, but don't know about the blood when I go to the privy. Or the sore throat. I'm getting scared Ray. What if I have what killed Peter?"

Ray's eyes opened wide. Albert had had stomach problems all his life, but he never associated these latest spells with what Peter had. "You have to tell the doc, Albert. Or maybe go over to Dr. Conboy's. I can handle the chores."

Albert tried to smile. "You're right. Maybe I'll go see Conboy come Monday. Ma won't like me going to anyone but MacGregor, but she won't have to know. Right?" he asked, looking at Ray for confirmation.

Ray nodded. "Sure, I won't tell her." The brothers went about their work and Ray watched Albert carefully. They should have gone separate directions to get more accomplished, but Ray refused to let his brother out of his sight. The work would get done eventually.

* * * * *

Saturday began as Friday had. The boys worked together and started seeding. Suddenly Albert started vomiting. Ray raced to his brother who was on hands and knees over a pile of greenish yellow vomit. Albert continued to retch even though it appeared his stomach had emptied. Ray helped him into a sitting position and said he was going to have Ma call MacGregor. "Stay here and I'll be back as soon as I can." They were working on the west farm and it didn't take Ray long to reach the house.

"Ma," he yelled. "Call the doctor, Albert is sick something awful." Before Carrie could respond, he was on a horse and riding back to the field. Ray was about the same weight and height as Albert, but it was all he could do to get him on the horse. Albert's legs refused to cooperate and his entire body was limp. Finally, after several efforts, Ray got his brother on the horse and carefully led the animal to the house.

When MacGregor arrived, he found Albert on the lounge in the yard with a bucket beside him. Obviously his stomach had not emptied. Dr. MacGregor immediately gave the young man some bismuth. It worked quickly and Albert soon rested. Carrie then asked Ray what had happened, and he decided to tell his mother and the doctor about the symptoms that Albert had kept from them. Carrie appeared upset and the doctor tried to calm her. "Now that we have all the information, it will be easier to treat him. How long have you known about this Ray?"

The doctor's tone seemed harsh and Ray, feeling undue guilt, blurted out, "Yesterday. He only told me yesterday!"

The doctor sighed. "Well, now it's out. We can't change what was. The bismuth did its job and there's nothing else I can do for him now." Carrie wrote the note and the doctor put it in his bag. "Carrie, Ida is still planning on all of you for dinner after church tomorrow. If you can't make it, we'll understand." Carrie rubbed her eyes. "We'll have to see what morning brings." MacGregor left and Ray went back to seeding. He would have to ask his mother to get in touch with Perry for Monday's work. He couldn't handle everything alone. Carrie found her journals and took them to her chair.

* * * * *

Sunday dawned bright and beautiful and the temperature flirted with seventy degrees. It would be a lovely last day of April. Albert got up early to help with the cows. He claimed to feel better, but his face was pale and he seemed very weak. Carrie decided they would go to church as planned, and it was Albert's turn. The Sparling boys were good, solid citizens, but as is often the case with young men, they tried to avoid church. So Albert and Ray had devised a plan to pacify their mother. They would take turns going to church with her. Ray hitched the buggy while Albert cleaned up and changed clothes. As they left, Carrie reminded him, "Ray, Ida is expecting all of us for Sunday dinner. When Scyrel gets home, you both hightail it over to their house." Ray mumbled an answer. Scyrel could go if he wanted, but Ray didn't feel like it.

After church, Carrie and Albert went to the MacGregors. Scyrel and Ray were nowhere in sight. An embarrassed Carrie told Ida they should not wait. "Perhaps a calf is coming, or a fence could be down. You know there's always something unforeseen happening." She tried to sound carefree, but inside she fumed. She would certainly give her sons a piece of her mind when she got home.

That speech was never delivered. Halfway through the meal, Albert asked to be excused. When Carrie went to check on him, he was in the side yard, vomiting. She went back for the doctor who went to the cabinet to get more bismuth. "I'm so sorry, Ida," Carrie explained. "Albert is ill again and I really need to get him home."

Carrie forced Della into a fast trot and they were soon at the farm. Ray and Scyrel, waiting for their scolding, approached slowly. When they saw their brother, they hastened their steps. Scyrel unhitched the buggy and saw to the horse. Ray helped Albert. He suggested they get him up to his room, but Albert said no. "It's so nice outside, just get me to the lounge." After they got him settled, a bucket was provided and immediately put to use.

Albert looked all around wondering how he could feel so terrible on such a beautiful day. The birds sang as they built their nests. Cows mooed in the pasture. The smells of spring were all about him. No, he should not feel poorly on such a day, but retching soon reminded him otherwise. Carrie sat by her son and kept wet rags on his forehead. Albert said he felt hot and she wiped his arms and face with more damp cloths.

The sound of a buggy caused her to look up. The MacGregors arrived and Ida took leftover food from dinner into the house. The doctor checked Albert's pulse and temperature. Scyrel, not knowing what to do, stared at his brother. Ray suggested they take a walk. The two headed down the road and Scyrel spoke first. "I'm worried that he's really sick."

Ray kicked at a stone. "I know." They took a few more steps in silence and then Ray continued. "I have to tell you, he told me he was afraid he might have what Peter had. I think he's been sicker than any of us knew. I wonder if Doc will want to take him over to London like he did Pa and Peter."

Scyrel stopped walking. "Do you think he's that bad off?" Ray turned to his brother and saw a tear in his eye. "I don't know Scyrel, but he sure ain't good." They walked a few more paces and then turned back toward home. "I'll call Sam and tell him I can't work tomorrow," offered Scyrel. "No," replied his brother. "You go back to Tyre. I can manage. Might need you later, but not yet." Scyrel agreed on two conditions. He would not leave until after milking, and Ray was to call him if the need arose.

When they reached the yard, the MacGregors were leaving. Albert was asleep, but he was tossing and turning, clearly uncomfortable. "I'll call later, Mrs. Sparling," promised MacGregor. "I gave him something to help him sleep and it appears to be working." He looked at Ray and Scyrel. "Your mother needs all the help you can give her." They nodded and then Ray spoke. "Scyrel wants to stay here," he informed them, and Carrie's face brightened. "But I told him to go back to Tyre. I can take care of things here just fine," he lied. Carrie's smile disappeared but she held her tongue.

After the MacGregors were out of sight, Scyrel helped in the barn and then prepared to leave. He went to Carrie who was sitting by Albert. "Guess I'll be on my way," he said. But Carrie did not respond. She acted as if he were not even there. Ray witnessed it. "We'll be all right Scyrel. I'll call if we need help." Carrie looked as if she would speak, but no words came. Scyrel left and Ray offered to sit with his brother. "No Ray," she said. "I don't plan to abandon Albert."

The gentle breeze of the day grew stronger and much colder. Carrie woke Albert and helped him into the house. "You sleep in my bed," she suggested. "No need for climbing stairs." Albert, too weak to argue, agreed. MacGregor telephoned shortly after he got home and Carrie said, "I got him into bed Robert, but he's still vomiting and now has diarrhea." The doctor told her he would be right back. Ray kept busy emptying the bucket or chamber pot; the former was still yellowish green and the latter, bloody.

Dr. MacGregor returned to the farm about seven o'clock that evening. He gave Albert medicine for pain, but could not stop the purging. He remained at the farm until midnight and told the family he would be back at first light. When he left, the air had turned considerably colder. Spring could be fickle. That proved to be an understatement. The entire Thumb awoke to a snowstorm and the temperatures had dropped at least forty degrees.

Carrie told Ray he would have to do the milking alone; she could not leave Albert. The doctor arrived about nine in the morning to find Albert awake and complaining again of a gut ache. When the doctor touched the young man's stomach, he grimaced with pain. Albert then began to rub his legs and feet, saying they were burning and tingly. Mae made her weekly telephone call and Carrie told her of the situation. Mae said she would come immediately, but they convinced her to wait until the snow stopped. She hung up and then called her mother-in-law.

Cecelia Hurford arrived within an hour. In no time word had spread, and other neighbor women joined her. They took over the kitchen and saw to it that Ray and Carrie ate and rested. Laundry tubs were brought in to wash the soiled bedding. The linens couldn't be hung outside so Cecelia draped them on a rack near the wood stove. Albert had been washed and dressed in a clean nightshirt. By the time they left the house looked and smelled much better, and a beef stew simmered on the stove. Ray helped them into their buggies and thanked them repeatedly. Carrie would have added her gratitude, but she had fallen asleep in her rocking chair. Dr. MacGregor, seeing her at rest, bent over Albert and whispered that he would be back. "Try to rest," he told him. On the way out, Ray met him. "He ain't good, is he Doc?" MacGregor did not respond except to say "I'm going to ask Dr. Conboy to come out and examine your brother."

On Tuesday, the second day of May, the temperatures had risen and the melting snow created muddy roads. It slowed MacGregor's journey, but he arrived about nine o'clock again. He went into the house and found Carrie washing breakfast dishes. "Robert I'm so glad you are here. I think Albert is going to be all right. He rested well all night."

When the doctor went into the bedroom he realized Carrie's description of rest was actually a near comatose condition. He examined the patient and when he touched his abdomen, Albert winced and groaned. His lips were swollen and he was slightly jaundiced. His face was puffy and MacGregor asked Carrie if Albert had been urinating. "Now that you mention it, I don't think he has gone since last night."

The doctor didn't try to hide his concern. "Carrie, if he doesn't urinate the poison builds up inside him. Try to get liquids in him and maybe that will force evacuation. I have other calls to make, but Dr. Conboy has agreed to come out later this afternoon. If you need me before that, call Ida. She will know how to reach me."

She began to write a note, but he stopped her. "Don't worry about that right now. Ida is going over my books and we will put together a bill soon. She's convinced me I must be more careful. Several people owe me, but I can't doctor and chase money at the same time." Dr. Robert MacGregor, clearly agitated, declined her offered cup of coffee. "Too many calls to make," he mumbled as he left the farm.

* * * * *

About five o'clock that afternoon, Dr. Conboy and Dr MacGregor arrived in MacGregor's buggy. As the doctors approached the house, they met Carrie taking a load of clothes to the clothesline. "Carrie," Conboy said softly. "Dr. MacGregor tells me your son fell from a tree last week and may have internal injuries." What he did not relate was the remainder of the conversation held during the ride to the farm. Robert MacGregor had hinted strongly that the boy's weakened state was possibly caused by syphilis.

Carrie said she would be back in a moment and continued on to the clothesline while Dr. Conboy went in to see Albert.

The boy's pulse was weak but rapid; his eyes were red and he told Conboy they were sore; that they ached. After he spoke, he asked for water. "I just can't get enough to drink," he added in a faint, hoarse voice. Dr. Conboy lifted Albert's head and brought a water glass to the inflamed lips. He then continued with the examination. Albert flinched and cried out when Conboy barely touched his stomach. Albert drew in sharp breath and asked Conboy how his arms and legs could be numb and yet tingly and sore at the same time. Without waiting for an answer, Albert clutched his stomach and closed his eyes.

Dr. Conboy pulled the blanket up to Albert's chin and motioned for MacGregor to follow him into the kitchen. "I wasn't able to do a thorough examination Robert, but I see no outward signs of syphilis."

"Perhaps symptoms can subside Daniel. I think that fall started this," said MacGregor. "And his vulnerable state won't let him heal. He's going to die, isn't he?" Conboy nodded and neither spoke for a moment.

"Would you tell Carrie, Daniel? You've known the family longer. I just cannot bear to be the one. You could say his body is too tired and weak to fight any more." Dr. Conboy did not appreciate being asked to give Carrie the news. He had made only this one visit to Albert and it made more sense for her to hear it from the attending physician. But he remembered his friendship to the family, especially J.W., and said he would speak to Carrie, who entered the house just as the doctors finished their conversation.

Dr. Conboy cleared his throat. "Carrie, I'm so sorry," he said as he put his arm on her shoulder. "I'm afraid there is nothing we can do." Her knees buckled, and MacGregor caught her before she hit the floor. He helped her to a chair and Dr. Conboy brought her some water. She took one sip and buried her head in her hands. Dr. MacGregor pulled a chair next to hers and sat beside her. Dr. Conboy said he would just get his bag and be on his way. As he re-entered the bedroom, Albert lay very still. He checked for a pulse, nothing in the left wrist. He quickly walked to the other side, but could find no pulse in the right wrist either. He went rapidly back into the kitchen. "You'd better come quickly," he exclaimed. MacGregor and Carrie went into the bedroom while Dr. Conboy made a hypodermic of strychnine and digitalin with water from the stove. He gently nudged Carrie aside and injected the solution into Albert's arm. He checked the heartbeat and it sounded stronger. However, within thirty minutes it again weakened. He looked at MacGregor. "This isn't going to help him and there's nothing more I can do."

MacGregor asked, "What did you give him, Daniel?" Conboy explained the mixture he had given. "I have extra tablets and can leave them with you. I don't see a need for me to stay, but I came in your buggy and I have no way to get home."

MacGregor took the strychnine tablets and went out the door to find Ray. It didn't take long; Ray was pacing by the well. "Ray, your mother needs your help. Dr. Conboy has no way home, and I plan to stay here. You can use my rig or yours, it doesn't matter." He left Ray alone by the well. Ray did not want to be away from his brother. Perry Cole, who had been out to inquire about work, was probably still in the barn. Ray found him and told him to get a fresh horse and hitch it to the buggy. "We need to get Dr.

Conboy home." Cole sensed the urgency. He had been a friend of Albert's for a long time. "I'll take care of it," he replied.

When Dr. Conboy approached the buggy, he saw Ray standing alone by the well and felt tremendous pity. He went to him and put his arm around him. "Ray, you need to be strong now, like your pa used to be. There's no easy way to say this, but you best get Mae and Scyrel home. Your brother is dying."

Ray went into the house. His mother and MacGregor were with Albert. He took one step inside the bedroom door and upon seeing his brother lying so still, began to cry. Carrie motioned for him to come closer and told him to bid his brother good-bye. He got to the bed, but words would not come. He patted his brother's shoulder and left the room.

* * * * *

About ten that night a horse and buggy drove into the yard. Everyone assumed it was Perry Cole. Instead Dr. Corcoran entered the kitchen. Carrie looked confused. "I called him," said MacGregor.

Dr Corcoran examined Albert and agreed the young man was near death. When told about the fall, and suppression of urine, Dr. Corcoran observed, "It could be uremic poisoning, but he is too far gone to treat. I'm so sorry Mrs. Sparling. I wish I could have helped." Carrie nodded numbly.

Ray heard another buggy enter the yard. This time it was Perry Cole and Ray went to help him unhitch. "Can you stay the night Perry? I think we may need you come morning. You can sleep in one of the beds upstairs." Perry agreed, but was not sleepy. Strange things were happening to this family. He sat in the parlor remembering gossip he had heard in town over the past weekend. The talk had come from only a handful of people, but the remarks were troublesome.

Dr. Corcoran left just as Scyrel arrived. Ray met him. "It's bad Scyrel. You better go to him now." Scyrel entered the room, but Albert did not respond. He had been told Albert was comatose, but hearing and seeing were two very different things. He grabbed his brother's hands, but they were cold and limp. Dr. MacGregor sat in a chair by the window and Carrie, in her chair by the bed. It was a bizarre scene. Albert lie dying, but no one did anything. It was as if they were just waiting.

He went back to the kitchen and sat at the table with Ray. Neither spoke for a long time; words seemed futile. Finally Scyrel asked about Mae. "She and Bert will come tomorrow," Ray answered. "Or she might just take the train by herself tonight. Sam will see she gets here." Tiredness soon overtook the brothers and they reluctantly went to bed. As Scyrel fell asleep, he thought this was one heck of a birthday present. Scyrel Sparling had just turned twenty years old.

A few hours into the third of May, before the sun could announce a new day, Albert Wesley Sparling breathed his last. Dr. MacGregor woke Carrie, who had fallen asleep. She looked up and asked, "Is it over Robert?" He nodded and she began to stroke her dead son's brow. MacGregor then went to get the other boys. As he entered the kitchen, he reached into his pocket and withdrew something. He looked at it for a moment, and then threw it into the wood stove. The fire flared as it devoured the new fuel, and the doctor went upstairs. He did not notice Perry Cole standing in the doorway watching.

Chapter 37

The quiet house soon stirred with activity. MacGregor sat with the family around the kitchen table waiting for the undertaker. He had asked their permission to perform a post mortem. "It could pinpoint the problem," he explained.

But Scyrel was adamant. He did not want his brother cut up. That would be bad enough, but if the cutting confirmed bad blood everyone would know. "He's gone Doc. Cutting him up won't change that," he insisted.

Mae and Bert arrived with the sun, having taken the night train to Tyre. Sam brought them to the farm but didn't stay. Mae spent a few moments alone with Albert, and then Dr. MacGregor went in to try to comfort her. "I did all I could Mae. Now I want to do a post mortem to find out what killed him."

Scyrel came up behind them and interrupted, "No need for cutting Mae. I already told the doc no."

The discussion ended, as Hector McKay the undertaker arrived. Dr. MacGregor again gave up the argument and went back to treat Carrie's eyes before he went home. Carrie sighed. "Not today Robert."

Cecelia Hurford came after the doctor and McKay left. She shooed the family into the parlor for their privacy while she went to work in the kitchen. She knew the Sparlings would not admit to hunger, but when the aroma of coffee and bacon escaped the kitchen, the family realized they were indeed hungry. When called to the table they ate in silence, as if feeling guilty for eating while Albert's body lay in the next room.

Slowly, conversation began and Ray tried to relate the events of the previous days to Scyrel and Mae. Mae quickly became confused. "Ray," she noted. "You keep saying this doctor and that doctor. Who all was here?" When he mentioned Conboy and Corcoran in addition to MacGregor, she spoke before she thought. "Well it seems he waited a long time. In fact, too late to call for help." Carrie looked at her scornfully and Mae apologized. "I'm sorry Ma. I didn't mean it bad. I'm just so sad and tired and, how can this be happening?" She began to cry and Bert drew her to his chest.

The table again became quiet until Perry Cole broke the silence as he entered the kitchen. "Mrs. Sparling, the milking is done. I'll be back to take care of the cows this evening, so don't any of you concern yourselves over it."

Reverend Hurd arrived next. He immediately went to Carrie and reached for her hands. "Mrs. Sparling, I am so sorry. I had errands in Bad Axe all day yesterday and just now learned of Albert's death. I would have been here sooner, but I just didn't know. Please tell me what you need."

Carrie looked at the preacher. "Need?" she asked. "Need?" she repeated.

Mae then suggested, "Ma, do you want Reverend Hurd to do the service for Albert?" Carrie shook her head as if to clear it. "Oh yes, the service. Of course." The minister asked if they could go into the parlor where it would be quieter. He knew that the house would soon be filled with relatives, neighbors, and friends; not asking what to do, just doing. Cecelia began to wash the dishes and Violet Styles arrived to help. She would go to her friend later.

Once again the Sparlings, minus one, gathered to prepare for a funeral. After a few minutes of planning, it became apparent that Carrie was near collapse. When the preacher suggested she lie down and rest, she looked at him oddly. "But I can't," she explained. "My son is in my bed."

Scyrel and Ray helped her to an upstairs bedroom away from all the commotion that was occurring now, and that which was yet to come. Mae assumed control and helped plan a short funeral service. Since Reverend Hurd barely knew Albert, Mae and her brothers gave him personal anecdotes of the young man for use in the service.

Just as Reverend Hurd had predicted, the house and yard soon overflowed with visitors. Carrie was in no condition to greet anyone, so Mae took charge of meeting, accepting, and thanking.

★ ★ ★ ★

Dr. MacGregor returned to the farm in the afternoon. Several women were in the kitchen and talk ceased when he entered. He mumbled a greeting and asked about Carrie. "She is overdue to have her eyes treated. Is it all right if I see her?"

Mae answered. "She's upstairs Doctor. If you'll follow me, I'll see if she is awake." Mae turned toward the stairs but not before observing certain looks pass between the women.

When Mae opened the door, MacGregor saw that Carrie was not asleep; she was walking back and forth, frantically, with her arms wrapped about her. When she saw the doctor, she went over to him. "Robert, how good of you to come. I must look a fright. So much noise in my head. I can't rest. How is Ida?"

The doctor and Mae exchanged glances. "Mrs. Sparling, I need to put the drops in your eyes. Remember how we do it?" Carrie nodded and sat on the bed with her head tilted back. He gently applied the medicine to her eyes. "Have you slept Mrs. Sparling?" he asked.

She did not respond and Mae volunteered the answer. "We've tried to make her rest, but she won't give in."

Carrie sat on the bed with her head still back to absorb the drops and the doctor used the opportunity to whisper to Mae. "I have something that will help. Shall I give it to her?"

"By all means," Mae replied. "The arrangements have been made and there's nothing for her to do now." After the sedative was given Carrie began to relax. Mae helped her mother lie down. "Thank you Doctor," Mae said softly. "I'll stay with her now." MacGregor left, closing the door behind him.

Carrie fell asleep quickly, but Mae remained. A short time later there was a light tap on the door. Mae opened it. "Mrs. Styles, Ma is sleeping, but I know she'll want to see you when she wakes up." Violet patted Mae's arm. "That's why I'm here. Your mother isn't the only one who needs rest. They tell me you haven't eaten, and poor Bert is worried about you. Why don't you go get a bite to eat and try to rest? I would be very happy to sit with my friend, just as she once sat with me." Mae could think of no argument and also knew her mother could not be in better hands. She left the room and Violet settled into a chair near the bed.

* * * *

Violet woke to the sound of the rooster crowing. Someone had thoughtfully put a blanket over her. She rubbed her neck and looked over at Carrie. She stood to stretch and Carrie opened her eyes. She sat up quickly. "Violet, what happened? I had a terrible dream that. . . ." A look of realization appeared on her face. "It wasn't a dream was it? Albert is gone. I have to get up. There are so many things to do."

Violet sat on the bed and put her arm around Carrie. "Everything has been taken care of. You can be very proud of Mae." Violet stood. "Shall I get some water so you can freshen up?" Carrie nodded, but when Violet went to the washstand she found fresh water, soap, and a towel. A clean dress had been draped over a trunk. "I think someone beat me to it. Do you want me to stay and help you?"

"No thank you," Carrie replied. "I can manage." She began to wash as Violet left the room.

Carrie appeared in the kitchen later to find Violet at the table. Mae stopped cooking breakfast, went to her mother, and put her arm around her. Carrie looked at the door to her bedroom. It was open. The bed was remade and the curtains were drawn open to allow the sunshine in. Mae anticipated her mother's question.

"Bert's mother, Mrs. Richardson, Mrs. Douglas, and Mrs. Jurges were here until late last night. Albert is in the parlor. Do you want to see him now?"

Carrie took a seat. "I need a few moments. Where are the boys?" she asked.

"Ray is in the barn with Perry Cole," Mae answered. "But Scyrel went back to Tyre." If Carrie thought that odd, she did not show it.

Mae turned to Violet. "Mrs. Styles you must be very tired. Won't you have a bite to eat?"

Violet hesitated. "Are you sure there's nothing else I can do for you?"

Mae shook her head. "You've done so much already, and I'm sure Ma will need you even more after tomorrow. Right, Ma?"

Carrie did not look at Violet. She just stared out the window as if expecting someone. "We'll see," she finally muttered. "Violet can't be here every day you know." Mae looked at her mother. She had never heard her talk so abruptly to Violet. She opened her mouth to speak, but Violet caught her eye and nodded ever so slightly to refrain. Mae would have to learn what Violet already knew. No two people grieved the same.

* * * *

Sam Soule put his arm around Scyrel's shoulders. "Of course I understand. I would think poorly of you if you had decided otherwise. I'll miss you and not just because of the work you do. I'd never try to replace J.W., but I must say you've become like a son to me. And I'll always have a place here for you if circumstances should change."

* * * *

Dr. MacGregor arrived at the farm as Violet prepared to leave. Though he had tended Carrie's eyes the day before, he felt they should be treated again due to the tremendous strain. Carrie's abrupt mood suddenly changed and she said, "Robert, let me walk Violet to her buggy before you drop my eyes. Mae, perhaps you can get the doctor something to eat." Violet quickly finished her coffee and the two women went outside. "Thank you again Violet. We'll have to meet again once all this is behind us."

Violet hugged her. "You are very strong, Carrie, but there is no weakness in admitting you need help."

Carrie smiled. "I know, but one must look on the bright side. Albert missed Young Pete terribly. They're together now, and Scyrel is home where he belongs." Violet did not respond. Perhaps Carrie had not heard Mae say he had gone back to Tyre.

Violet had driven about a mile down the road when she met Scyrel on his horse. He held a large grip and barely nodded a greeting as they passed.

Carrie returned to the kitchen and went to the doctor. "Robert, I've not seen Albert this morning. Would you go with me?" He stood and the two left the kitchen for the parlor. Mae, holding a dishtowel, stared at their backs. When they returned, Scyrel was sitting at the table with Mae. His eyes were red and puffy. Carrie put her arms around him, but he didn't return the embrace. He just sat very still. "Scyrel," she said. "Robert is going to Ubly to pick out a coffin for Albert. Would you like to go with him?"

Scyrel stood. "No, I best find Ray and see what needs doing," he replied before leaving the house.

The doctor treated Carrie's eyes and then went to Ubly. He found Chris Sparling, cousin to the family, and said he needed a favor. Chris and the doctor then went to McKay's and chose a coffin. Hector promised he would get it to the farm right away.

The men parted and MacGregor went to Dr. Corcoran's office. "Sorry to bother you, Sylvester." MacGregor then explained his visit. "Before I sign Albert's death certificate, I want to be sure we agree on the cause of death as acute nephritis. You were the last physician to see him other than myself."

Dr. Corcoran paused before answering. "Robert I only checked his heart and pulse, but from what you had told me prior, I agreed that nephritis might be the cause. Do you now have doubts?" MacGregor responded quickly. "Oh no. It's just that it's best to be certain. So as long as we agree that nephritis killed Albert, I will sign to that effect."

* * * *

After dinner, provided by Reverend Hurd's wife, people began arriving to pay their condolences. Albert lay in a mahogany coffin that was placed on two straight chairs in the parlor and Carrie sat in a chair beside him. Mae remained in the kitchen with Mrs. Hurd. Ray and Scyrel were cleaning up to be with their mother in the parlor. When they reappeared, the minister's wife convinced Mae to join her family.

A steady stream of visitors came to the farm. They conveyed their sympathies to the family, but once outside they talked to each other in hushed tones. John Sparling told Carrie the grave had been dug. She thanked him but didn't sense his coolness. Little Pete and his Mary had few words; they were too bewildered. No one had told them Albert had even been sick so his death came as a great shock. William and Ellen paid their respects and Ellen spoke. "Mother Sparling is so upset. She wonders why she remains on this earth for no apparent purpose while Albert is taken before his time." Big Pete and Mary shared their sorrow with Carrie. Their oldest son George and his bride-to-be Abby stood beside them. Throughout the afternoon, one Sparling after another came to offer comfort. Carrie could not help but think once again that so many Sparlings were together. No one from Carrie's family attended, probably because they did not get word of the passing.

At the cemetery Reverend Hurd provided a very moving service for Albert. When it was done Carrie again thought, "I must order a stone—no, two. But that can wait." Most people had said their good-byes at the cemetery but a few, including Big Pete, came back to the house. The family ate a meal prepared by the churchwomen and, as before, Ida MacGregor and Jennie Boomhower were in charge. By dusk, the family sat alone at the kitchen table. Bert helped with the milking and Mae made a list of people the family needed to thank. She told Carrie that they would stay until Sunday, but Bert simply had to be back at work Monday morning.

* * * *

The next day Dr. MacGregor again called on Chris Sparling for another favor. He explained the insurance delays when Peter had died. "We filed amendments to the policy for Albert, but if they have not yet taken effect, would you speak to your brother Peter and ask if he would be a bondsman for Carrie?"

The request took Chris by surprise. The funeral had been just yesterday and the doctor was already looking into the insurance. He realized MacGregor was waiting for an answer and spoke. "I can talk to my brother of course. Is it urgent? I can help Carrie if she needs money."

The doctor put up his hands. "No, it isn't urgent. It's just that a person tends to put these things off. I told her I would get things started for her. I've already been to see Zen about it. By the way, I passed your Uncle John on my way into Zen's office. Is he always so brusque?" MacGregor got no reply so he continued. "Anyway, I told Zen what I told you. Carrie wants me to be administrator of Albert's estate. Zen gave me the forms to fill out in case the amendments have not yet been applied. We may not need your brother or these forms, but it doesn't hurt to be prepared." Robert MacGregor thanked Chris Sparling and left. Chris sat stunned for a moment and then telephoned his brother, Big Pete.

* * * *

John Sparling had indeed been to see Zen Boomhower. "I can't put my finger on it, but I have a great uneasiness about all these deaths. I'm not making accusations yet but, as prosecutor for the county, I think you need to be very diligent and know that people are talking."

"John, I understand your grief," Zen replied. "But there's not much I can do right now. People are always going to talk, but I can not act on idle gossip."

"Then I intend to do some checking," John huffed. "I'm telling you something is not right." The familiar voice of Dr. MacGregor was heard in the outer office and John left, grunting a gruff hello to Robert as he exited the office.

* * * *

On Sunday, Mae accompanied Carrie to church. She would rather have stayed home with the men, but Carrie insisted on going and Mae did not want her to go alone. After services ended, Carrie accepted more condolences and the women returned to the farm.

Conversation at the dinner table was mainly about the farms. Perry Cole agreed to remain on at least until after planting. Bert, glad to be done with farming, asked, "How long can you keep two farms going?" It was a question on everyone's mind. Carrie answered, at least for herself. "Bert, I've got two strong sons. Perry will help, as will Big Pete's boys."

At that moment Scyrel interrupted. "Ma, we pay Perry but you know George and Roy won't accept any money. We can't keep taking advantage of their good will. I'm here for now but only until everything is settled. Sam said I'm welcome back any time."

It was the most Scyrel had said in days and an uncomfortable silence filled the room. Everyone knew Carrie expected Scyrel to remain on the farm and his statement came as a surprise. Undeterred, Carrie added, "Perhaps we should not be talking about the future just now. We're all tired and sad and saying things we don't really mean." She stood and began to clear the table, indicating the discussion had ended. Mae looked at Scyrel expecting to see remorse for his statement. However, Scyrel's countenance was one of resolve and determination. Ray also noticed the look and secretly wished he could leave with Mae and Bert. It could get very tense in the days to come.

Chapter 38

On Monday May eighth Dr. MacGregor came to the house to treat Carrie's eyes. He arrived near the dinner hour as he had done more often than not. While the drops worked, he told Carrie the insurance filing had been taken care of. "Oh Robert," she exclaimed. "You are a dear. I hadn't even thought of it."

He smiled at her. "I only thought if I could get it started for you it would be one less thing for you to worry about. I brought the papers for you to sign. Remember the amendments we filled out after Peter died? I think they will keep you from going through probate. But just in case, I made inquiries to speed the process." Carrie signed the claim forms and automatically reached for her notepad. "No need for that Carrie," he said. "My accounts are nearly back in order and I hope to send out bills by next week."

Carrie invited the doctor to stay for dinner. "Scyrel has been so sullen and he says he plans to go back to the store in time. Maybe you could persuade him that a man must accept his responsibilities, even if it means changing his own plans."

Robert MacGregor wasn't sure he was the person to convince the lad. Scyrel had been cool ever since he had suggested a post mortem on Albert. "I can't promise anything Carrie," he replied. "But if the situation presents itself, I'll certainly do what I can. He hasn't set a date to leave has he?"

Carrie shook her head. "No but he does sound determined." No sooner had she uttered those words than Ray, Scyrel, and Perry Cole came in from the field and it was obvious any talk of responsibility would not occur today.

* * * *

Two days later MacGregor again arrived at the Sparling's, but not at dinnertime. He had decided to avoid Scyrel when others were around. If he were to approach him it would have to be when he and the young man were alone. As he dosed Carrie's eyes he told her he had talked with his father the day before. "The amendments have been applied and my father said your claim would be processed soon. You could even have a check by month's end."

Before Carrie could respond, Perry rushed into the house calling for her. "You got a real sick calf in the south pasture."

When Carrie said she would be right out, the doctor told her to rest her eyes. "I'll go check, just let me change into boots and overalls."

When he reached the calf it took no examination to know the animal was weakened from the scours. "Get her to the barn Perry. She needs to get out of the elements and into a dry bed of straw. The mother will follow." As soon as Perry picked up the animal it started bawling and, sure enough, the mother joined the procession. Scyrel was just coming out of the barn when the caravan arrived. MacGregor quickly explained the situation and Scyrel begrudgingly thanked him for his help.

Perry had gone back to the pasture and it seemed like a good time to talk to Carrie's youngest. He put his arm around Scyrel's shoulder. "Listen son," he began. He got no further before Scyrel pulled away. Immediately MacGregor realized he should not have called him son. He started over. "Scyrel I hope you're not still upset with me about the post mortem. You'll learn as you become a man that some decisions can be very hard and it's often difficult to know if you've made the right one." He paused but Scyrel remained silent, staring past the doctor. MacGregor continued. "Your mother says you don't plan to stay here on the farm. I hope you know how much she needs you here. And if you don't think of her, what about Ray? Trying to do this by himself is asking too much. Doing the right thing sometimes means doing what you ought and not what you want." Scyrel still did not respond, but MacGregor felt he had said enough for now. He went to his buggy, stripped off the overalls and boots, and headed for Ubly. Carrie had dinner ready by noon and the men devoured roast chicken with noodles and gravy. Perry reported that the sick calf seemed somewhat better, but other than that it was a quiet table.

Carrie wasn't in the mood for conversation either. She had more garden to plant, but decided she needed time alone. As she rocked she thought of Bert's comment about working two farms. Maybe she was pushing her sons too hard. And Scyrel was right about Big Pete's sons. She couldn't accept their charity any longer. If she hired more help, the cost would eat into the profits. But if she asked her sons to work only one farm, the workload would be lightened and hopefully their attitudes as well, especially Scyrel's. There would be no question as to which farm to sell. Any nostalgia for the place in Sanilac County was gone, and she refused to even think back to the days when Old Pete, Little Pete, and William all lived within shouting distance. If they didn't care about family, neither would she. Besides, she refused to live so close to Tyre, Sam, and the general store.

* * * *

On Monday the fifteenth, Carrie was coming from the clothesline when MacGregor arrived. He dropped her eyes and accepted a cup of coffee.

Carrie asked if he had the bill made up yet. "Actually," he replied. "I have it with me. It reads as a bill for services rendered in April, but it also includes medicines and some unpaid notes from February and March. Carrie the amount is quite steep, but it doesn't have to be paid all at one time. I promise to do better with my accounting in the future."

Carrie took the envelope and put it, unopened, in her apron pocket. "Robert, it's all right." She smoothed her dress, tucked a stray hair behind her ear and looked at him pointedly. "Everything is all right."

Robert MacGregor took her hand and looked around to make sure they were still alone. "I talked to Scyrel last week, but I'm not positive it helped. Hopefully I planted a seed of responsibility in his head. How is he acting?" Carrie sighed. "He's very quiet and seems so sad. I've decided to sell the east farm in hopes that a lighter workload will change things. But I haven't told the boys yet. I need to work out some details in my mind." She went to the stove for more coffee. "Before I forget, my eyes feel much better on the days you treat them but by the next day they are bad again."

He smiled. "Carrie, that's easy to fix. I can put drops in every day, make it part of my daily schedule. If you want them done on Sunday, I'll do that too." Carrie heated his coffee and said, "That won't be necessary. I do very little on the Sabbath, so there is little strain." Dr. MacGregor finished his coffee and left. Carrie continued with the laundry and began to prepare the noon meal.

After washing the dinner dishes, Carrie decided to rest before finishing the laundry. She had a lot on her mind and she took thoughts of Scyrel and of selling the farm to her chair. As soon as she sat down she heard a crinkling sound. It was the doctor's bill in her pocket. She took it from her apron and opened the envelope. The bill read, "For services rendered in April," just as he had said, $963. She stared at the bill. It would be months before the crops came in. She wished she had found her account book. Carrie rubbed her eyes and looked again. It read the same. She began to rock. He had said some of the debt went back to previous months. And there was the medicine for Albert and her eyes. She had been too busy to pay attention to details.

Carrie stopped rocking. "Besides," she told herself, "Robert wouldn't do that to me." She sat still for a moment. Then she put the paper back into the envelope and began to rock again. Carrie would pay the bill but probably not at one time. For now she would keep this to herself. Maybe it was a sign that selling the east farm was the right thing to do.

* * * *

True to his word, Dr. MacGregor arrived every day and treated Carrie's eyes. She went about her normal routine; house cleaning, cooking, and gardening. She hadn't seen Violet since Albert's funeral so it was a pleasant surprise when her friend drove her buggy into the yard on a rainy Wednesday afternoon. Violet entered the kitchen and produced a loaf of bread from under her wet shawl. "This lovely rain kept me out of the garden," she declared. "So I decided to take the afternoon off to visit. How are you doing Carrie?"

Carrie took the bread and put the kettle on for tea. "Violet," she said, "it's wonderful to see you. I've been thinking about you. Did you bring mending? Seems as though I never get caught up on that task."

Violet responded by pulling socks and shirts from a large bag. "I am almost taking the afternoon off," she laughed.

After idle chitchat about gardens and weather, Carrie looked at her friend. "Violet you're a godsend today. I don't want to sound unappreciative, but I really expected to see more friends and neighbors after Albert passed. Folks were so good about that after Young Pete died. I suppose everyone is busy but it wouldn't take a lot of time to just drop by." She paused. "You must think badly of me."

Violet hesitated a bit too long and that gave Carrie concern when she was hoping for reassurance. Violet finally spoke. "As you say, this is a busy time." She then looked down and tried to concentrate on a sock hole.

Carrie wasn't fooled. "Violet, I consider you to be my best friend and if there is more to be said, you should know you can be open and honest with me."

Violet put down the sock and stared at Carrie until both became uncomfortable. At last, she reached across the table and took Carrie's hands in hers. "Carrie you are also my best friend, and that is why I must say some things that you won't want to hear. I wouldn't hurt you for the world, but I also don't want others to hurt you. There are things you need to be aware of. I don't have to tell you about the gossip mill in a small town. That mill is up and running strong lately." Carrie looked confused and Violet continued. "Carrie, people are saying things. Things that are not good." Carrie still looked confused. "Listen," she continued. "There's no nice way to say what is being rumored so I'll just have out with it. Some folks are suspicious about Albert's death. They say he was too young and too healthy to die like he did. Some are complaining that Dr. Herrington was not called in by Dr. MacGregor for consultation in his case." Carrie looked as if she would interrupt, but Violet did not let her. "Carrie, you need to hear me out. I should have brought this to your attention earlier, but I held off thinking the talk was due to the shock of his death. I thought that in time it would pass. But the talk is getting stronger and much more open. I'm sure you would notice if you went into town."

Carrie would be quiet no longer. "What do you mean suspicious?" Privately she wondered if word of bad blood had gotten out, but didn't say it aloud. "Just what are people saying Violet? I have to know."

Violet drew a deep breath. How she hated to be the one to repeat these stories. But better her than someone else. "People are wondering if Albert did not die from natural causes." She paused to let that sink in and Carrie stood.

"I don't understand. The death certificate said how he died. How do they think he died? Are they doctors? What gives them the right to say such things?" Carrie stopped talking and looked at Violet, suddenly realizing. "So that's why people haven't been coming by." She took a deep breath. "I guess I won't be relying on friends for support. Thank goodness I still have family."

Violet looked at Carrie. "Your Uncle John is among those who are airing their suspicions. And he is becoming quite vocal."

Carrie slumped back into her chair. Her mind was racing, but words were slow in forming. Finally she spoke. "Is there more?" Violet nodded. "Carrie, people are wondering why Dr. MacGregor is here so often." She exhaled slowly. This was not easy. "They think there is more going on than is normal between a doctor and his patient." Carrie swallowed and stared blankly out the window.

Violet stood and went to Carrie and put her arm around her. "You still have many friends. Many who aren't a part of this. I only told you as a friend who cares about you and does not want to see you hurt."

Carrie pulled away from Violet's arm and turned to face her. "And what do you say Violet? What do you think?"

Violet had gone too far to back down now. "I think people are cruel Carrie. I don't think they realize the harm they cause and I think you should try to ignore them, as I do. I think when you go into town, be it Ubly or Tyre, you should hold your head high. I think that will help put these gossipers out of business."

Carrie snorted. "You think that will do it?"

Violet hesitated, but only for a second. "That and one other thing. Have Dr. MacGregor teach you or the boys how to put the drops in your eyes. Then he wouldn't have to be here so often." Violet released a huge breath; it was out.

Carrie took a sip of tea and picked up an overall for mending. "I guess I should thank you for being so honest. I'm stunned by all of this and will have to give it very serious consideration. I will also speak to Robert about my eyes, but he told me before that these drops are very strong and should only be given by a physician." Her voice suddenly became more agitated and her stitching more frenzied. "Dr. Herrington couldn't have saved Young Pete. Why do folks think he could have saved Albert? I will not live my life according to what others think is proper. And I will hold my head high in town. You can count on that." There were many more things she wanted to say, but decided to hold her tongue for now. After a short silence she added, "Ed must wonder what happened to you, time does get away from a person. Thank you for the bread."

Violet knew she was being dismissed. She gathered her mending, took her cup to the dry sink behind Carrie, and put her hands on Carrie's shoulders. She squeezed them gently. Carrie did not respond nor did she stand or walk with Violet to the door. Violet tried to be understanding as she realized what a huge burden she had placed upon her friend. "Will you be all right Carrie?" she asked.

Carrie looked straight ahead. "I'll be fine Violet. Thank you again for the bread." Violet left the house wondering if she had done the right thing.

Carrie tried to absorb everything as she rocked. She even wondered if Violet believed some of these things. After all, Violet had suggested Robert not come to the house so often. "Easy for her," Carrie thought angrily. "She has a loving husband at her side." The rain had strengthened and darkened the skies. The day had grown dark and dreary inside and out. She rocked and thought. Her chair, which had helped her on so many previous occasions, did not help today. In fact its squeak sounded almost accusing. She left the chair and returned to the kitchen. The boys would be in for supper soon. Soup and Violet's bread would have to suffice. She wasn't hungry and would not sit at the table with them. With everything that had happened she did not need to observe Scyrel's moodiness tonight.

The next day broke with abundant sunshine and it did wonders for Carrie's attitude. Robert would be out soon. She would ask again about putting the drops in herself, even though she already knew the answer. She wondered if Robert was aware of the gossip. Carrie decided to go on with her life as if Violet's words had never been uttered. There were things that needed doing; one farm to sell, and one to run. There was a garden to tend and boys to take care of. Carrie would rise to the tasks ahead and woe to anyone who got in her way.

Chapter 39

Carrie's first outing since Violet's visit fell on Decoration Day. She watched Ray march with the band at Ubly and then drove Hannah to the cemetery at Tyre to put flowers on the Sparling plot. The earth over Albert's grave had not yet fallen, and it reminded her that he and Young Pete still had no headstones. "Later," she said to herself. As before, only a few people gathered in Tyre and only polite conversations took place. Thankfully, Uncle John was not there; that would have been awkward. The day was pleasant enough and Carrie drove home with a lightened heart.

* * * *

On June first Dr. MacGregor arrived early to treat Carrie. Scyrel avoided these visits and the doctor had decided he would no longer speak to him of responsibility. He mentally washed his hands of the lad where that topic was concerned. Carrie wrote his note and again apologized that the larger bill had not yet been paid. MacGregor told her not to fret over it. "Most of this is my fault. I know you'll pay when you are able." As he left the farm and headed for Bad Axe, he repeated those words and smiled. He had not told Carrie, but his father had called the day before and said the Sun Life Assurance draft was ready for mailing. When Dr. MacGregor walked into the automobile dealership, Mr. Yauch met him at the door. MacGregor smiled and said, "I'm ready to place that order now John."

* * * *

The following Wednesday, Dr. MacGregor arrived at the farm obviously in a very good mood. After treating Carrie's eyes and accepting a note along with a cup of coffee, he handed her a piece of paper; a check from Sun Life in the amount of one thousand dollars made payable to Carrie Sparling. "Oh Robert," she cried. "I won't have to go through probate. And this came so quickly. How can I thank you?" She continued to stare at the paper so long that MacGregor had cause for concern. It disappeared, however, when she looked up and exclaimed, "I can pay your bill now!"

He successfully hid the relief in his voice when he answered. "Well that is up to you of course. Remember, I told you it didn't have to be paid all at once." Carrie smiled. "Take the check Robert. I'll be getting another from the Gleaners soon."

She endorsed the check and handed it back to the doctor. Dr. MacGregor finished his coffee and tore up the note she had just written. He leaned over and gave Carrie a peck on the cheek. "You are a dear lady." Carrie had no words, but after he left she gently caressed the cheek that his lips had touched.

* * * *

Carrie, free of medical debt, decided to talk to the boys that evening. She had two people in mind that might want to buy the east farm. It was time to move ahead.

Robert took the endorsed check to the Hubbard Bank in Bad Axe. He then went to the automobile dealership. John Yauch accepted $684, and told him the car would be in before the end of the month.

* * * *

The meeting with the boys had been bumpy. They were stunned to learn their mother had given the Sun Life insurance check to the doctor. Carrie tried to explain how so many medical bills had piled up and reminded them they had been too concerned over Albert's sickness and death to realize MacGregor's care came with a price. Ray asked if the bill had given any credit for house rent owed by the doctor. It was a question that caught Carrie off guard. She recovered quickly and told him that Robert MacGregor was an honorable man and, while the bill was not itemized, she felt certain the proper adjustments had been made. There was nothing the boys could do and news of selling the east farm took their minds off the insurance check. They were relieved to have less work, but privately wished she were selling the west farm.

* * * *

The east farm did not sell as quickly as Carrie had hoped and Scyrel and Ray were hard pressed to work both places. Perry Cole and Will Smith were hired to help. Carrie didn't push her sons, and when they wanted to go into town to let off steam, she remained silent. She had grown accustomed to Scyrel's surliness, but Ray surprised her. Ray who always seemed to know when she needed support; this same Ray now appeared guarded around her. She did not know how, or even if, she should approach him. Perhaps the boys had been bothered by the same stories Violet had heard. Perhaps her sons were just tired, and deservedly so —unless. Dear God, she could hardly bear the thought. Was bad blood running through her family? She would have to talk to Robert. For now she dug out the medical journals and studied them anew in her chair.

* * * *

206

Carrie saw Violet only at church now and their short conversations were pleasant enough. There had never been harsh words between them. It just seemed as if an unwritten edict had determined they needed time apart. And of course they were busy. Garden planting was nearly finished, but strawberries were coming on strong. One chore from the past was now history. The Paris Green worked so well on the potatoes that hand picking the nasty bugs off the plants was no longer necessary. Carrie still took great pride in having a cellar full of canned goods. She had never been able to adjust from a family of seven to three, and still planted and canned much more than was needed. It never went to waste. Mae always took some home and Reverend Hurd and his family were most grateful for her gifts of food.

June saw Sunday school picnics, school graduations, baseball games, band concerts, and popular variety shows called Chautauquas. There was something for everyone, but Carrie could not interest herself in any of it. She held her head high when in town not knowing if the idle chatter had ceased. She didn't avoid public gatherings. She was just more comfortable at home in her chair.

* * * *

Dr. MacGregor drove his buggy into the yard on the twenty-sixth of June. He treated Carrie's eyes and enjoyed fresh strawberry jam on biscuits. There was a jar for him to take home to Ida. He seemed to be in no great hurry so she decided to ask him, again, about the bad blood. "Robert, both Ray and Scyrel are just not themselves. I took all precautions, but is it possible?" She couldn't finish; she just could not say those words aloud. He knew what she was asking, but as before, he could not give a definite answer. Neither boy had been to see him with any complaints, so an unplanned physical examination was out of the question. He asked if they were still using patent medicines for their complexions. She nodded. "Scyrel always finds an excuse to go to Tyre for supplies. Maybe once or twice a month he brings small parcels home. When I ask, he says it is personal but I'm sure he and Ray use it for pimples. Why?"

MacGregor licked a bit of jam off his finger. "Well," he explained. "I can give them something that will work as well, or even better. And it does wonders for a poor complexion. You can never be sure about patent medicines. I'll bring some out tomorrow. If they're curious, you can say it's a free sample of a new drug that helps prevent blemishes. Patent medicine for pimples is usually applied directly to the skin. My medicine is in liquid form and works from the inside out."

Carrie looked confused. "But Robert, what about the other?" The doctor thought for a moment. "I hope by giving them a free sample I can regain their trust. If there are any problems, then they will come to me. I really don't think you have to worry about syphilis, but if it comes to that I'll treat them vigorously. There's really nothing more I can do at this point." Carrie knew he was right, but he had not given her the assurance she had hoped for. As he pocketed her note he added, "I'll be here early tomorrow to take care of your eyes, and I also plan to return in the afternoon." Carrie, always happy to see this man, asked why. The doctor grinned. "That, dear lady, will be known tomorrow. Thanks for the jam."

* * * *

The next morning Dr. MacGregor made a very early visit to the farm. He left a bottle, unmarked except for the directions to take one teaspoon daily for complexion. He treated Carrie's eyes and said he would be back after dinner. The boys came in for breakfast after milking and were curious. "Was that the doc who just left?" asked Ray. "Yes," replied Carrie. "He brought by a sample of a new medicine for pimples and thought you two might want to try it." Scyrel and Ray looked at each other and then at Carrie. "You mean there's no charge?" scoffed Scyrel. Carrie ignored the sarcasm. "Dr. MacGregor has been very kind to this family. He knows you're always putting stuff on your face. As a physician he is offering something safer than those patent medicines and I, for one, appreciate it." The boys didn't argue. They sat down to sausage, pancakes, fried eggs, and biscuits. Scyrel reported they would be working at the Tyre farm. "Do you need anything from the store?" he asked.

"See if he has any lemons," Carrie answered. "If he doesn't, ask him to order some for me. It's almost the Fourth of July."

The boys left the house and Carrie cleared the table. The irons on the stove were hot enough for her to begin pressing clothes. While doing so, she found missing buttons and small tears. It prolonged ironing time, but reminded her of happy times mending clothes with Violet. Perhaps she should call on her friend. It had been a month since the two women had spent any time together. They could certainly have a friendly conversation without the mention of Robert or town gossip. Yes, she would make time to go see her friend.

Carrie was deep in thought at the ironing board when a loud, blaring noise caused her to jump and nearly drop the iron on her foot. Then it blared again! The loud noise came closer and it seemed to come from the side yard. She hurriedly put the iron back on the stove and looked out the kitchen window. She could scarcely believe her eyes.

There in her yard was an automobile with Robert and Ida MacGregor inside. She quickly smoothed her hair and wiped her face with her apron. The door slammed behind her as she approached the belching, noisy machine. The doctor reached down and squeezed the horn. That was the noise she had heard. He then jumped out of the quivering beast and told her to get in. When she hesitated, he helped her into the rumble seat before she could react. And the next thing she knew they were flying out of the yard and onto the road. Conversation was impossible so she just hung on for dear life behind the deliriously happy couple in front of her. They showed no fear, but Carrie was terrified. She had seen automobiles before, but had never even entertained the thought of riding in one. The doctor turned right at the next road, went a mile and turned right again. After two more right turns at mile markings, they approached the farm. Carrie's eyes were full of dust and her hair had blown out of its bun. She looked a fright, but her only concern was to put her feet on solid ground.

When Robert stopped the automobile it shuddered to a standstill. He and Ida both turned to look at her. "What do you think Mrs. Sparling?" he asked. And then he laughed, heartier than she had ever heard before. Ida was a bit more composed. "Robert, I think we've given Carrie quite a start. You better help her out so we can explain."

Carrie was visibly shaken and Dr. MacGregor helped her into the house. Ida followed and the three sat down at the kitchen table. "Has the cat got your tongue?" the doctor asked.

Carrie stammered. "I – well – surprise – when?" were the only words she could summon. He laughed again and Ida spoke. "Robert, you best explain, and quickly."

MacGregor sighed. "I never meant to alarm you Mrs. Sparling. I—we wanted you to be among the first to see our brand new automobile. We just picked it up today. Isn't it a beauty? And what a difference this will make in my practice! No horse to tend and I can see almost twice as many patients as before."

"And you Mrs. Sparling," offered Ida, "This is all possible because of you." Confusion again crossed Carrie's brow. "Your generous gift," continued Ida. "Robert told me you insisted on giving him the amount necessary to buy this automobile. We will never be able to thank you enough." Carrie started to explain that a thank you was not mandatory when a person paid a bill, but the words came out all wrong. Her struggle for words was misconstrued by the MacGregors as excitement from the ride. Ida spoke again. "Are you all right? We were so excited ourselves that we wanted to share it with you. I think we should let Carrie catch her breath Robert. Besides, we must get home. Bonnie and Douglas only know we went to Bad Axe to bring home a surprise." She looked again carefully at Carrie. "Are you certain you are all right?"

Carrie forced the words out. "Yes I'm fine. Of course I was taken by surprise just to see that machine come into my yard. And then to actually ride in it, well it was just such a. . . .a. . .. But no, I'm fine. I would offer you something to eat or drink but. . . ."

Ida laughed. "Oh no, we couldn't. We really must get home to show the children." MacGregor said he first needed to wash out Carrie's eyes, as the road dust would not be good for them. "Would you mind getting my bag, Ida?" As soon as his wife was gone Robert spoke quickly to Carrie. "Ida does get confused at times Carrie. She knows full well your check was not a gift. She just didn't expect the bill to be paid in full, and so promptly. Let's just humor her for now. She has had to scrape by so often over the years as I was building my practice and she will—" He was interrupted by the footsteps of his wife as she brought the bag into the kitchen. Dr. MacGregor washed Carrie's eyes and gave her a little wink, unseen by his wife, as he followed Ida out the door to their new possession. Carrie watched and listened. She saw Robert help his wife into the automobile, and heard their happy, excited prattle. Then the vehicle once again came to life and the MacGregors drove away.

Carrie sat down, but was not comfortable so she stood. She walked over to the ironing board and then back to the window. The MacGregors were out of sight and she could not remember when she had last seen a couple so totally happy, even giddy! Suddenly her loneliness seemed all the more intense.

She went to the mirror over the dry sink and gasped. Her face was covered with dirt except for the funny lines down each cheek from the eye washing. And her hair! She didn't know if a comb would stand a chance in the tangled mop. She sat down again, completely bewildered. She had to get control of herself and her emotions; there would be time to think about a plan later. Yes, later! She could not afford to sit now and pity herself.

Time was getting away from her. The ironing waited and dinner had not been started. No matter how she tried to think about the tasks at hand, her mind kept returning to the happy MacGregors. She went to the cellar for a jar of beef and came back up with a jar of jam. When she returned for the meat, she forgot to bring carrots to add to the stew. Her loosened hair kept falling in her eyes, which reminded her of the ride in the automobile. Her hair fought the comb and a babushka settled the argument. She finally got the stew assembled and went back to the ironing board where she had been when the MacGregors had driven into the yard. Mending would have to wait. Carrie went through the motions; iron, fold, stack, put away, set the table, bring in water. And by the time Ray and Scyrel returned from the east farm, a delicious aroma filled the kitchen.

She was about to ask them if they wanted supper before or after milking, but they clearly had something on their minds. "Ma," began Ray. "You won't believe what we heard at Sam's. Ken Jurges heard it from Harry Pangborn who got it from Bud Schelling. He said Doc MacGregor bought an automobile! Can you believe it? Don't that beat all?" Scyrel put a bag of lemons on the cupboard. "Do you think it's true Ma?" he asked.

Carrie looked at her sons. No need to deceive, she was certain neighbors had seen her on the ride. She paused and then spoke. "Well I guess it must be so. Either that or I just had a crazy dream about riding in it."

Ray let out a slow whistle. "You mean it's true and you rode in it?"

Carrie managed a smile. "Dr. MacGregor and his wife were kind enough to drive here on their way—"

Ray interrupted. "You actually rode in it? What was it like?"

It was one of those rare moments in the life of any parent. She, their mother, was actually interesting to the boys beyond clean laundry and good food. And, if only for a short time, they were in a good mood. She smiled and remarked, "It went much too fast for my liking and a person gets so dirty and rumpled. I suppose it would be fine for some, but I'll stick with Hannah." The boys continued to pepper her with questions until she finally admitted that her eyes had remained closed, due to fear or grit, through most of the ordeal. Seeing they would get no more from her, they went to bring in the cows for milking.

After supper, Carrie again took a comb to her hair. She sat in the chair and painstakingly removed the snarls and tangles. As she worked, she thought. Her boys had been so talkative and excited about the automobile, such a refreshing change from their recent sourness. But she knew it wouldn't last. And then what? Scyrel was determined to become a storekeeper and Ray's only outside interest was the band. And she was still not sure about their physical health. Robert had told her not to worry. Robert. Her thoughts went back to him. Robert. Laughing with his wife, winking at his patient. What did it all mean? Did it even mean anything?

Chapter 40

July arrived with a vengeance. The first three days were unbearably hot and ninety plus degrees in the shade made it inescapable. On Monday evening a storm to the north dropped temperatures by ten degrees and the Fourth of July festivities drew great crowds. Mae and Bert had arrived the night before, the first they had been home since Albert's death. Mae helped Carrie with dinner; fried chicken, potato salad, green beans, biscuits, and strawberry shortcake for dessert. And of course, fresh lemonade. It was a small gathering compared to the celebrations of past years, but Carrie did not dwell on the old days. Doing so was futile.

After dinner Mae and Bert went to visit his parents before returning to Port Huron. Scyrel and Ray headed for Bad Axe to watch a baseball game between that city and rival Harbor Beach. Carrie had planned to work in the garden, but decided it was too hot. So she took her mending to the front porch. Carrie could still see the strange look on Mae's face when she had asked if she thought her brothers looked sickly. Mae almost looked frightened when she answered. "Ma, Scyrel looks fine to me. Ray may be a bit peaked, but this heat wears on a body something awful. Why? Did they say they are sick?"

"No," Carrie replied. "But I sometimes worry about them, you know, Young Pete and Albert both died so young." She had quickly changed the subject, but the look on her daughter's face came back to her now.

Scyrel and Ray ran into cousins George, Roy, and Joseph at the ball game. In fact, there were several Sparlings watching the contest. Uncle John approached the boys halfway through the game and asked after their health. They replied that except for the heat all was well. "I understand your mother is selling the farm over at Tyre," he commented. "Any prospective buyers yet?"

Ray responded that he was aware of two possibilities. "I heard Ma and Dr. MacGregor talking about it."

It did not take great insight to recognize that bringing the name MacGregor into the conversation had a palling effect. Uncle John shook his head and asked, "Is he still coming out to the house all the time?"

This time Scyrel spoke. "Yeah, he has to treat Ma's eyes. Says only a doctor can do it."

Uncle John weighed his words carefully. "Say, have you boys ever thought about going to Canada, like your pa? Two of my sons are there now and they love it. I know J.W. enjoyed it too. It would be a great adventure for the both of you."

Any excitement on their part was short-lived. "Don't see as we can do that, Uncle John." Ray declared. "Who would run the farm? Besides, we haven't got the money for such a trip."

Uncle John would not be put off. "Well don't dismiss it entirely. Give it some thought and start saving your money. You never know what the future might bring." He patted each boy on the shoulder and added, "Tell your mother I said hello." Uncle John left the boys with new thoughts. Scyrel and Ray looked at each other, but no words were exchanged. Talking with their uncle had dampened their enthusiasm for the remainder of the game. They continued to watch, but in silence. Canada, Pa, MacGregor; the words sent a mix of emotions through the young men. Without admitting it to each other, both felt a sense of unease for the present as well as the future. The ride home was very quiet.

* * * *

The following Friday found MacGregor at the farm for his daily visit. "Are the boys taking the medicine I left?" he asked. "I can get more if they need it." Carrie, her head still tilted back, answered, "I don't know. I left it on the table for them, but it has disappeared and I really don't know if they used any or not." "No matter," he replied. "I'll bring another bottle out tomorrow, just in case. Ida and I are taking the children on an automobile trip beginning next Monday and I want all loose ends tied up before we leave. Dr. Holdship has agreed to come out to see to your eyes in my absence."

The news took Carrie by surprise. She had become accustomed to these daily visits and even looked forward to them. She had never thought of his not being there and silently cursed the automobile. She managed a smile and asked, "Where are you going?"

The doctor answered while putting her note in his pocket. "We're going over to Canada to see family, and then my brother and sister-in-law will drive us north into New York. We'll be gone a couple of weeks I imagine. I don't want you to worry. You'll be in good hands with Dr. Holdship."

After he left, she sat at the table letting the drops work. She knew Doc Holdship was more than competent, but he wasn't Robert. She shook off the thought and went to the garden; beans, tomatoes, and weeds all needed picking.

When the doctor arrived the next morning, Carrie greeted him in a freshly washed dress with a matching ribbon encircling the bun in her clean hair. And she smelled of lavender water. After he treated her eyes, Carrie wrote his note and reached into her apron. She withdrew twenty dollars and handed it to him. "What's this for?" the surprised doctor asked. She gave a small laugh. "I want you to use it for something special while you're gone. Something to remind you of us poor folks you are leaving at home." She smiled coyly. Was she actually flirting? "Just have a good time and return safely to us," she said. And then, as if an afterthought, she asked for his brother's address in Canada.

He reached into his bag. "Funny you should ask. I had already written it out for you in case you would need to reach me."

* * * *

Carrie went to the Ubly bank Monday morning. She made a withdrawal and then headed for the MacGregors, but she was too late; the family was already gone. While in town, she stopped at Dr. Holdship's office. As long as she was there he could administer the eye drops and save time and travel out to the farm. They exchanged pleasantries and she decided that if he was part of the gossip brigade, he hid it well. In fact nobody in town seemed to be shunning her. It made her think of visiting Violet, but she decided to wait a bit longer. Carrie tried to continue with everyday chores but was restless and often found herself thinking about Robert and Ida. She wanted them to have a good time. Just not too good. The next day she took the withdrawal to the post office.

* * * *

One morning, in the middle of the month, Carrie asked the boys about the medicine from Dr. MacGregor. "He brought out another bottle before he left on his trip because the first one had disappeared. He wondered if you have been using it."

Ray said he had taken it for a few days, but quit as it gave him a funny feeling. She looked at Scyrel. "I only use what I get through the mail. It works good enough and I don't have any of the after-effects MacGregor mentioned. I can take care of myself Ma." She didn't want to fight with her sons, but their attitude toward Robert made her very cross.

"For the life of me I do not understand your obvious dislike for Dr. MacGregor. He has been here for us in sickness as well as health. He helps us with farm problems and even rolls up his sleeves for dirty work. He has butchered a hog, fixed a corncrib, and helped deliver a stubborn calf. You should be grateful to him."

The boys didn't want a fight either. Where the doctor was concerned, their mother was narrow-minded. "Maybe when he helps, we get the feeling that nobody thinks we can run this farm on our own. We can you know!" Scyrel insisted. Ray just shrugged, said he had to be excused, and headed for the privy.

"Is your brother all right?" asked Carrie.

"It's just a stomach thing. It'll pass," said Scyrel snickering at his little joke.

Carrie did not find it amusing. "I'll fix up some tonic. That'll set him back on his feet."

The next time Dr. Holdship came to treat Carrie's eyes, she asked if he knew when Dr. MacGregor would return. He quietly replied, "When he gets here, I reckon."

* * * *

Dr. MacGregor and family arrived at his brother John's house in London on the twenty-fifth of July, and they talked about the trip for hours. Traveling by automobile, seeing new countryside, not being called out in the middle of the night; it had been a wonderful vacation. The next morning John MacGregor was going through the accumulated mail. "You have something here from Ubly, Robert." Robert MacGregor took the envelope and opened it. Two fifty-dollar bills were enclosed. There was no note, but the return address was Carrie Sparling, Ubly Michigan, U.S.A. "What is it Robert?" asked his wife.

He looked startled as he spoke. "Mrs. Sparling has sent us one hundred dollars."

"What on earth for?" Ida asked. "Aren't we square on billing?"

Dr. MacGregor looked at his wife. "I thought so, but I'll double check when we get home. I can always credit it to her account."

* * * *

Carrie decided not to attend church the last Sunday of the month. So she missed seeing Robert and family who had arrived home the night before. On Monday the thirty-first she was pleasantly surprised when he appeared in his automobile. As he put the drops in her eyes, he told her of the wonderful things they had seen and done. "Did you receive the money I sent?" she asked. He hesitated and then, remembering, answered. "Yes I did. But I don't think you owe me any money right now." She smiled. "Well, I wasn't sure and decided to send it just in case. I thought it might come in handy on the trip."

Dr. MacGregor spoke. "Actually, we didn't receive it until we returned to my brother's home, but what a sweet thought. I'll check the books again. If you don't owe anything I can give it back or just credit your account."

She smiled again. "You can just apply it to my credit. I used to keep a running account of my own, but it got lost during the move. I never started another one because I feel if you cannot trust your own doctor, who can you trust?" MacGregor made a mental note to check his books, and changed the subject by asking how the boys were.

Carrie sighed. "Ray gets tired easily so I've been giving him my tonic. Scyrel is going strong, day and night. Makes me think of Young Pete out carousing. I feel I should say something to him, but I don't want cross words between us again. Oh, I did ask the boys about the medicine you left here. Ray took some, but Scyrel sticks to the patent stuff he orders from Tyre. I put the new bottle over by the dry sink, but I don't think it's been used." She paused, looked down, and then up into the doctor's face. "I can't tell you how happy I am to know you are back. Dr. Holdship is a fine person but I'm very glad you're home again."

Chapter 41

A beautiful, soaking rain fell the first day of August. Farmers were thrilled, not for a day off but because the corn and oats had been showing stress from the hot, dry, July winds. Carrie told the boys at breakfast that they would be having company. Their cousin Elwood was going to bring his new bride Marie to visit for a day or two. Ray looked at Scyrel with a teasing smile. "Where will you go visiting with your sweetie?" he asked his brother. His answer was a hard kick to the shin under the table. Carrie did not bite at the tempting bait. So Scyrel had a girlfriend. That would explain his absence every night after chores. It could also mean much more. The east farm had not sold and it would be a wonderful place for Scyrel to take a new bride. But then her mood darkened. If he had bad blood, it would ruin everything.

The boys finished eating and left the house, Ray limping from his brother's kick. When they reached the barn Scyrel asked him about the medicine MacGregor had left. "You said it made you feel funny, but did it work?"

Ray bent down to rub his shin. "I don't know," he groaned. "I stopped taking it. Why?"

Scyrel paused and pointed to his face. "You can see for yourself," he said. "I'm broken out real bad. Guess I got immune to the patent medicine. Maybe I'll give MacGregor's stuff a try." Ray shrugged his shoulders and opened the barn door. Scyrel headed for the pasture thinking, "Doc said one teaspoon a day, so two should work better and faster."

The following day Scyrel went to the Morrison's farm to help with threshing. It was a most productive day, but the work was very hard. Over three hundred bushels of wheat were threshed that day and each bag, hand carried, held between one and one-and-one-half bushels. For a young man who hated farming, Scyrel threw himself into the work. Morrison paid well. Maybe the money could take him back to Sam's store or even Canada; or it might be spent on a nice young girl. He finished for the day and went home.

His cousin and wife had arrived and he was expected to visit with them, which he did while sipping lemonade. He then excused himself and, after cleaning up, went to Bad Axe. Ray had also been threshing, at the Douglass farm. He was not invited to accompany his brother so he talked with Elwood and then challenged him to a game of checkers before going to bed.

The next day Scyrel continued at the Morrison's and Ray went back to the Douglass farm. The work was hard and dusty. When Scyrel came home that night, Carrie thought he sounded hoarse. She excused herself from Elwood and Marie. "I need to make him some hot stuff for that throat." He drank what Carrie brought him and headed for Bad Axe.

Scyrel and Ray were again hired out on the fourth; Ray for threshing and Scyrel for cutting oats. But the boys, at Carrie's prompting, remained a bit longer at the breakfast table to visit. Elwood and Marie planned to leave right after the meal. Though pleased that the cousins had wanted to spend time with her, Carrie was anxious to get back to her routine. As the newlyweds went to their buggy, Dr. MacGregor drove his automobile into the yard. The departure was delayed as Elwood inspected the machine. When they finally did leave, the doctor treated Carrie's eyes. He noticed the complexion medicine on the dry sink and made a mental note that it had been used.

Ray arrived home first, about five o'clock in the afternoon, and Scyrel came shortly afterward. As they were feeding and watering their horses, Scyrel asked Ray if he would finish the oats for him. "Got a date with Verna?" Ray asked with a wink.

"No. No date. I just don't feel good," he answered. Ray said he would do the oats. "Band practice isn't until eight tonight so I'll have plenty of time."

Carrie, who expected her youngest to once again make tracks for Bad Axe, was surprised when Scyrel announced he was going upstairs to lie down.

She asked if something was wrong and he said, "I bought some oranges off a peddler earlier today and they didn't set right. I just need to rest for a bit." Carrie let it be for a while and decided to check him in an hour or so.

Ray came in at seven o'clock and began to clean up for band practice. He asked about Scyrel. "I checked him an hour ago," she replied. "He told me he vomited twice and thinks he will be feeling better soon without that stuff inside him. But since you are going into Ubly, why don't you stop at Dr. MacGregor's? Tell him Scyrel is doing poorly and would he please come out? I would telephone, but Scyrel might hear me and I think it would upset him even more." Ray agreed, and when he reached Ubly he stopped at MacGregor's. The doctor was finishing a late supper, but said he would be out after he ate.

MacGregor arrived about nine o'clock that night. He found Scyrel walking outside the house wearing nothing but shoes and trousers. "Scyrel your mother sent word that you were doing poorly."

Before the doctor could continue, Scyrel stopped short, put his hands on his hips, and grumbled, "Is that why you're here? Well there's no need to stay. I told Ma what was wrong and it's nothing that requires a doctor." He heard the side door slam and turned to see Carrie on the stoop. "Ma when will you stop treating me like a baby? I told you I wasn't sick, I just felt bad.

And now you've gone and called the doc out here for nothing!" The more he talked, the angrier he became.

Dr. MacGregor quickly intervened. "It's a good thing you're not sick. Makes my job much easier. Tell you what. I'll leave some bismuth for your stomach and calomel to clean you out. You should be back to normal by morning." The doctor reached into his bag and handed two bottles to Scyrel. The young man hesitated and then reluctantly accepted the medicine.

As MacGregor drove away, Carrie and her son had words. Carrie thought Scyrel had been rude, and Scyrel didn't appreciate the doctor being called without his permission. When Ray returned later, he found Scyrel scowling on the couch in the parlor and Carrie in her rocking chair. He slipped away to bed.

* * * *

Early the next morning a call came to Dr. MacGregor. Scyrel was no better, could he come right out? Ida asked if she could accompany him. "Of course," stammered MacGregor, surprised by the request.

Seeing his confusion, she explained, "You might need me." And she quietly added, "It might be good if I was there." Their eyes met for what seemed a long time. MacGregor nodded and opened the door for his wife.

When they reached the farm, the doctor went in to see Scyrel. The young man was much sicker and quite weak. He was still vomiting and the calomel had not yet taken effect. The boy's temperature read 101, and his pulse felt weak but rapid. Because the calomel had not worked, an enema was administered. MacGregor remained with the patient another half hour and then told Carrie he would be back later. She was canning tomatoes and he told her not to bother with a note now.

As he helped Ida into the automobile MacGregor remarked, "I think I should call in another doctor. I don't want to be in this alone." Ida saw the concern in her husband's face. "Who would you call?" He grimaced and answered, "It would have to be Dr. Herrington." When he saw her questioning look he added, "I know, I know. But do you remember the criticism I took after Albert died? Lots of folks wondered why I hadn't called him in for consultation then. And they wondered out loud! It'll have to be Herrington. I'll call him as soon as we get home."

Dr. MacGregor returned to the Sparling farm at seven that night. There had been no change in Scyrel's condition with the exception of an onslaught of diarrhea. He told Carrie that Dr. Herrington would be arriving shortly. "What for?" she asked. "I don't think Scyrel is seriously ill, he just has a touch of stomach trouble. I really wish you hadn't called him, Robert." Dr. MacGregor looked puzzled, but before he could respond another automobile drove into the yard. Dr. Herrington came in the side door, not at all pleased to have been called out on a Saturday night. But he remained courteous and asked to see the patient.

Scyrel had been moved into Carrie's bedroom. Dr. Herrington examined the young man and said, "Sorry chap. I know you're tired of being probed, but we have to get to the bottom of this, don't you agree?" Scyrel nodded. After he finished, he patted Scyrel on the shoulder. "Try to get some rest son," he advised. He then returned to the kitchen where Carrie waited. "I don't think your son is seriously ill Mrs. Sparling, but if you or Dr. MacGregor want me to come out again I shall do so."

He nodded ever so slightly to MacGregor, a nod that indicated he wanted the doctor to come outside. When the two physicians reached Herrington's automobile, they faced each other. "Robert, I found no temperature and his pulse was near one hundred. His abdomen is sore, but given the purges that is understandable. If you want my opinion I would give Wine of Ipecac to clean out anything in his stomach and bowels, and then give a sedative to quiet the diarrhea. I see no reason for my being called out and I don't believe the lad to be all that ill."

MacGregor did his best to remain calm. "You don't understand Will. All the others who died took sick this same way. I'm afraid this boy may succumb as well." Dr. Herrington paused and searched for a reply. "I can't speak for the others. I can only tell you what I saw in Scyrel, and he does not appear to be deathly ill to me."

* * * *

Dr. MacGregor returned early on Sunday the sixth. Scyrel still complained of a terrible gut ache. The vomiting had lingered and it was greenish yellow. MacGregor continued to administer ipecac, bismuth, and calomel, though these medicines were clearly not working. Carrie had been unable to sleep for care of her son. MacGregor told her she must ask neighbors for help, but she refused. Ray also looked haggard. The work at home and Tyre had become too much for Ray alone. He had to refuse neighboring jobs and hired Perry Cole to help him.

Dr. Conboy arrived late on the seventh, having been called by MacGregor. He examined Scyrel and could not help but think back three months before when he had seen the same symptoms in Albert. The vomiting and diarrhea could not be stemmed, and the young man's stomach pain had become severe. His mouth and throat had become inflamed, and his nose and eyes were sore. Conboy checked for appendicitis, but concluded that was not the problem. Nor could he find any other sign of disease in the patient, although MacGregor had suggested pancreatitis. He gestured toward the door and MacGregor followed him into the kitchen, leaving Carrie rocking beside her son.

The doctors conferred. Upon learning which medicines were being given Conboy suggested, "Why not stop all those medications? They don't seem to be working. I'll leave some strychnine powder like I did for. . . ." He paused. "Like I did for Albert. Give him 1/100 of a grain in water three times a day. Maybe that will restore some of his vigor. I'll be back tomorrow afternoon."

When he returned the next day, he again examined Scyrel only to discover that the symptoms remained. He thoroughly checked the patient's eyes and mouth. "Scyrel, are your eyes sore?" he asked. Before the young man could reply, MacGregor spoke. "He has conjunctivitis, Daniel." Conboy's eyes never left Scyrel's face and the patient nodded yes. "Do they itch?" Again, MacGregor quickly spoke as if Scyrel wasn't even there. "What are you looking for?" Conboy remained silent and checked the pulse, which was fast and feeble. Then he left the room. As he reached the kitchen, Dr. MacGregor caught up to him and grabbed his shoulder. As Conboy turned to face his colleague, Dr. MacGregor asked, "Daniel, are you thinking arsenic?" Conboy looked surprised. "Yes, Robert. I am."

"I was thinking the same thing," disclosed MacGregor. "In fact, I wonder now if that's how the others went."

"Others?" questioned Conboy. MacGregor replied. "You know, the rest of the family. And look at Ray. He doesn't appear to be in the best of health."

The side door banged and Carrie came into the house with clothes from the line. "Well Daniel, how is my son?" Dr. Conboy looked at MacGregor and then back to Carrie. "Mrs. Sparling, I believe your son is very ill with some kind of poison in his system." Carrie said nothing for a long time. "I'm not surprised," she finally answered. "He's been threshing, and by the time he gets home he has dust and dirt in his eyes, nose, mouth, and probably his lungs as well."

Daniel Conboy hid his surprise at her reaction. But when he left the farm he went directly to Bad Axe and found Xenophon Boomhower. After the men talked, Zen said if the young man died he would order an investigation. "But," he told Conboy, "let's not have it come to that."

Boomhower called Ida MacGregor. "Ida, this is Zen. Yes, Jennie is fine. We're fine. I wonder if you would tell Robert when he gets home that Dr. Conboy and I would like to speak with him this evening. We'll be around about eight o'clock."

* * * *

That night Ida served coffee to the three gentlemen and then left them to their discussion. Boomhower spoke first. "Robert, Daniel tells me Scyrel Sparling is very ill." Zen became uncomfortable and unbuttoned the top of his shirt. "I'm sure you heard some of the wagging tongues after Albert died. As your friend and also as prosecuting attorney, I must tell you that if the boy dies, I will have to open an investigation."

"That would be a good idea Zen," replied MacGregor. He paused as if searching for the right words. "But why not take some precaution now and hopefully prevent a tragedy?" MacGregor stared at Boomhower, idly twisting his wedding ring. "I can't be there all the time."

The inference was obvious, but no one wanted to point a finger without proof. Finally Zen spoke. "Would Mrs. Sparling agree to a nurse at the house?"

MacGregor said he would have Ida telephone to ask. "If Carrie agrees," added MacGregor, "I know a nurse who used to work at the hospital where my father practiced. I believe she lives in Port Huron now. Her name is Margaret Gibbs."

Zen and Daniel nodded in agreement and Conboy added, "The quicker the better."

Ida MacGregor called Carrie. "Mrs. Sparling, Robert tells me Scyrel is no better and we wondered if you would consent to have a nurse come to the house to help. We both think you are pushing yourself much too hard."

Carrie thought for a moment. "Mae is coming tomorrow, but if Robert thinks it is a good idea, then yes." Ida then made a telephone call to Port Huron. Margaret Gibbs was available and would arrive in Ubly the next day.

The men greeted the news with partial relief. Ida sensed this and suggested, "If you like, I could go to the house and stay until the nurse arrives." The three men readily accepted the offer and the meeting closed.

Later that night, the doctor and his wife arrived at the Sparling farm. MacGregor gave Scyrel a dose of strychnine and then showed both Ida and Carrie how to prepare and administer a second dose later that night. "Mrs. Sparling, Ida is very concerned about your health and has offered to help until the nurse arrives. We hope you can get some needed sleep." If Carrie was suspicious of her overnight guest, it was hidden by extreme fatigue.

* * * *

Early the next morning, Ray met Mae at the train station and the two talked on the way home. "How bad is he?" she asked. "Dear God, it's only been three months since Albert died. What is going on?"

Ray didn't speak for a long time. "I don't know what's happening, Mae. Dr. Herrington and Dr. Conboy have both been out to look at him."

"What about MacGregor?" asked Mae.

Ray shrugged and shook his head. "Oh he's here every day. But three doctors and Scyrel just gets worse." Silence followed, as brother and sister sat deep in thought. Mae looked at her brother. Ray's chin was quivering. She patted his knee.

Ray straightened his shoulders and wiped at his eyes with his shirtsleeve. "Did I tell you a nurse is coming to stay at the house?" he asked. "Ma's acting strange, guess she's tired. I just stay out of everybody's way, except to see Scyrel." He wiped his eyes again and Mae pretended not to notice. "He's in a lot of pain Mae, and he can't talk much. But I think he likes it when I sit with him." Mae assured Ray he was doing the right thing. Ray looked at his sister. "He'll be glad to see you, but don't let on you came because he's sick."

When they reached the farm, Ray saw to the horse and buggy, and Mae walked into the kitchen. She went to Carrie who was washing dishes and gave her a hug. Carrie smiled, but was obviously distracted and she looked more tired than Mae had ever seen. "You might want to go see your brother now," Carrie suggested. "Before doctors start coming out again." Mae gave her mother another hug and went into the bedroom.

When Mae entered the room, Ida MacGregor rose from her chair by the bed. "He's sleeping Mae, and that's good. He'll be happy to see you." She excused herself. "I'll go see if I can help your mother." Mae looked around. The drapes were drawn and the small room was depressing. She looked down at her baby brother. He looked so small and vulnerable. Very quietly she sat down beside him, her mind going many different directions. She forced herself not to cry.

She had been sitting there about an hour when Scyrel began to moan and clutch at his stomach. He opened his eyes and tried to smile at his sister. "Can I get you anything?" she asked. The involuntary response was severe retching followed by vomiting into an already half full pan. She grabbed a cloth and wiped his face when he was done. She also planned to empty the offensive pan as soon as possible.

"Mae," he groaned. "How long you been here?"

She remembered Ray's warning. "I got in this morning. I'm sure Ma's garden could use an extra set of hands. Scyrel, is there anything I can get for you?" she asked again.

"No," he answered weakly. "I don't think so. My gut hurts so bad. Damn, I hurt all over. Wish I could get hold of that peddler who sold me those oranges!"

Mae didn't know what that meant, but an answer was not necessary. Carrie came into the room with milk toast and lemonade. Mae tried to joke. "Gosh Scyrel, you must rate pretty high. Getting lemonade, and not on a holiday."

Carrie put the tray on a table and sat beside the bed. As she lifted the glass to his lips, she said, "The lemonade helps the medicine go down, right?" Scyrel didn't answer. He never took his eyes off Mae.

"Well little brother," Mae remarked. "I'm going to take my things up to my room, but I'll be back so don't try to leave." He smiled and she left the room. As soon as she reached the kitchen, the tears poured. Ida MacGregor went to her and held her tightly.

Chapter 42

Dr. MacGregor arrived with Nurse Gibbs about noon. Ida and Mae had prepared a light lunch, but the nurse insisted on seeing her patient first. She found Scyrel sleeping, closed the bedroom door, and sat at the table with the others. Dr. MacGregor had brought her up to date on the patient during the drive. "I see there is only one bedroom on this floor. Do you have another room nearby where I can sleep?" she asked. Nurse Gibbs took her work very seriously. She had been put in charge and in charge is where she planned to be.

"Why don't we move Scyrel to the parlor and you can use the bedroom," Mae proposed. "We can get a bed from upstairs for my brother and it won't be so dreadfully dark in there."

Dr. MacGregor agreed. "That's a good idea Mae, but the room can't be too bright. His eyes are quite sore. Leave the sheer curtains pulled and it should do quite well. I would stay to help, but really need to get Ida home. I expect she has been up all night." Ida began to protest but she was indeed fatigued and wondered how Carrie had managed for so long.

By one o'clock, Ray and Perry Cole had set up a bed in the parlor and helped move Scyrel into it. Mae stripped his old bedding and immediately set it to soak; it would have to go through at least two washes. She began to clean the bedroom for the nurse and told Ray to empty the foul pan. "And find another one to use while that one is being cleaned." Nurse Gibbs took an immediate liking to Mae. She would be a tremendous help. But she was not certain how much the mother could contribute.

Dr. MacGregor returned to the farm after taking Ida home. Mae was cooking supper while Nurse Gibbs prepared more strychnine. "Where is everyone?" MacGregor asked. Mae noticed an anxious look on his face. "Ma is upstairs in bed and Ray is in the barn," she informed him. Before she'd finished speaking, the doctor headed for the stairs. Seconds later Mae heard her mother's bedroom door open and close.

Dr. Conboy arrived, unannounced, about seven that evening. Mae greeted him and took him to the parlor. Conboy examined Scyrel and found the symptoms were unchanged. He turned to leave the room and saw a curious MacGregor standing in the doorway. "Hello Robert. Our patient says he is feeling somewhat better." He patted Scyrel on the shoulder. "Let's hope this is the turnaround we've been waiting for." He went into the kitchen and MacGregor followed close on his heels. Robert quickly glanced around the room and, being assured they were alone, asked, "What are you doing here Daniel? I didn't expect to see you."

"Zen and I were talking," he replied. Conboy lowered his voice and looked around. "He said it might be good for me to speak frankly to Mrs. Sparling. He thought if I spoke openly enough, and she was the one giving him poison, it would scare her enough to stop."

"Not necessary," reported MacGregor, without hesitation while fumbling through his bag. "I already scared the devil out of her. She's in bed now and near collapse. I give her about four months and she'll be in an asylum." MacGregor smiled at Dr. Conboy. "Sorry you made the trip for nothing."

Dr. Conboy knew he was being dismissed, but would not go easily. "Has the nurse arrived?" he asked. "I thought she would be with the patient." MacGregor didn't know where Nurse Gibbs was, but wanted to satisfy Conboy enough that he would leave. "Yes, she got here about noon. I believe she is indisposed at the moment," and he nodded at the closed bedroom door. "I told her we suspect poison and that she alone is to give him any food, liquid, or medicine—with no exceptions." Conboy nodded. "That's good. Maybe the lad will pull through yet." As he drove home, however, he didn't think the young man's chances were very good.

* * * *

Nurse Gibbs rose early to see her patient. She was a stickler for cleanliness, and insisted sheets and bedclothes be changed daily. Though she had liked Mae immediately, she never left Scyrel alone with anyone. She had been hired to do a job and if, in doing that job, she caused hard feelings, then so be it.

About ten o'clock, an automobile drove into the yard. Big Pete and his brothers, James and Jake, left the vehicle and started toward the house. Word had spread fast of Scyrel's illness and his cousins were very concerned. They had dropped everything when the telephone call came from Ubly. MacGregor met them and gave an overall picture of the young man's status. Jake asked if they could see him. "Your Uncle John is in with him now. We try not to tire the boy, so if you don't mind waiting—"

Big Pete interrupted. "What exactly is wrong with him Doc?" The question was civil, but presented in such a way to make it clear the Sparlings wanted an answer.

"Could be a couple of things," said MacGregor. "Pancreatitis for one, and the boy said he got some bad oranges off a peddler." Seeing the looks on the men's faces, MacGregor knew they would not be put off. But he was not about to inject the word poison into the conversation. "You know we've had both Dr. Conboy and Dr. Herrington in to examine Scyrel. Herrington said it was a bilious attack and not serious." He hoped the name Herrington would have a calming effect on the men. "Actually, the other boy looks sicker than this one." When the men looked around, MacGregor continued. "Ray. He's over at the Tyre farm. Stays to himself most of the time except for milking. And he sits with his brother a couple times each day."

The side door opened and Uncle John stormed out. Dr. MacGregor said the other men could go see Scyrel, but only one at a time. Jake went first and the doctor followed him, to check Scyrel and avoid John Sparling. John waited until MacGregor was in the house and out of earshot. Then he turned to his nephews. "This isn't good. I'm telling you that boy has poison in him. I may only be a vet, but I know poison when I see it." He kicked at the dirt with his boot. "And I'll tell you something else. Every one of them boys was insured and I believe if they hadn't been, they'd all be walking around today."

Uncle John left abruptly, leaving James and Big Pete speechless. They had heard rumors of course, but considered them as only speculation. Never had the hearsay been this open and accusing. Both James and Pete took their turn visiting Scyrel, and the ride home was solemn. They did not expect to see Scyrel Sparling alive again.

When their automobile drove out of sight, Carrie left her chair and came downstairs. She had been sitting by a window that looked down on the side yard. Had only Big Pete been there, she would have come down. But she had heard John Sparling's voice and decided to remain out of sight.

Dr. MacGregor dosed Carrie's eyes and accepted the invitation to stay for dinner. Mae returned from Ubly with the few things the nurse had requested. The doctor left after eating, Carrie did the dishes, and Mae snapped green beans. She had blamed her mother's behavior on being tired. And yet, after a good night's sleep, Carrie still said little and went about her chores as if nothing had changed. Mae found it difficult to know if Carrie was deep in thought or having no thoughts at all. She also thought her mother's feelings could have been hurt. Carrie had taken lemonade in to Scyrel, but the nurse had refused to let him drink it.

Mae smiled when she saw Mrs. Styles appear in her rig. Violet alighted from the buggy and reached back for a large dish and parcel. Mae went out to greet her and help carry the packages. "You couldn't have come at a better time," she said. "Ma will be thrilled to see you."

The women entered the kitchen and Mae immediately sensed tension. But it was short lived, thanks to Violet. She put a chicken casserole on the stove and went to Carrie. Violet drew her friend to her. "I am so sorry about Scyrel. I would have come sooner, but I've been in Minden nursing my mother. I just returned this morning and Ed told me. I've brought supper for you and some, oh dear, where is it?" She looked at Mae. "Oh yes—Mae brought it in—and bread." Mae put the loaf on the table and excused herself. She felt the women needed time alone.

Carrie sighed. "Oh Violet. I behaved rather badly last time we—" Violet interrupted. "Now Carrie. We were both tired and out of sorts that day. We will not think of it again." Carrie was near tears. "I had planned to come visit you, I really did. But time got away from me and now. . . ." Carrie's voice trailed off and she started to cry. "He's very sick. Violet, I haven't done right by my boys." Violet thought the remark odd and tried to reassure her friend. "Carrie, as mothers we all feel we've fallen short at times. You're just tired now and very concerned. You can't blame yourself for any of this."

Carrie dried her tears on her apron and looked at Violet. "You just don't know, you just don't know," she muttered. Violet again put her arms around Carrie. "Let it all out. You'll feel much better if you do." She had meant tears, but Carrie just shook her head and repeated, "You just don't know."

Dr. MacGregor arrived shortly after and he greeted the women on his way into the parlor. He met Mae coming out carrying a pan; the boy was still purging. He talked briefly to the nurse and looked over her notes. "How are you feeling, Scyrel?" he asked. The boy groaned. "Can't get rid of this gut ache and my arms and legs feel like they got pins stuck in them. Can't I have something to eat besides gruel and milk toast? Don't see how a body can get better eating this stuff. I swear I smell chicken."

Dr. MacGregor compromised. "Stay on the diet one more day and then maybe we can allow something more substantial." He knew the boy was dying and should be allowed to eat to his heart's desire. But he could not give the appearance of giving up in front of the patient. "Stick with it one more day, you can do that can't you?" Scyrel turned his face away. MacGregor asked the nurse if she needed anything and then returned to the kitchen.

"I see no change Mrs. Sparling. He's having some numbness in his legs and arms. For now, we will just continue to try to purge him of the—" He stopped and glanced at Violet. "—of whatever infection is inside him. Is Nurse Gibbs meeting with your satisfaction?"

Carrie nodded. "She's helpful, but won't let me give him any lemonade and he does love it so." MacGregor smiled. "I half-promised your son some chicken on Saturday, so maybe he can have some lemonade then." He looked at Violet. "It's good to see you Mrs. Styles. Please give my best to Ed." He left and Violet remained another half hour. She went to see Scyrel before she left, but his eyes were closed. "Tell him I was asking about him," she told Nurse Gibbs.

The nurse joined the dwindling Sparling family for a supper that was eaten in silence. When they finished, Ray did the milking and Mae offered to help him. She had not had any time alone with him since the ride from Ubly. "Scyrel's going to die, isn't he?" she asked as they began the barn chores. Ray took a deep breath and nodded. He looked at his sister. "What were they in to, Mae? Why did they get sick and not me?" She wanted to hug him, but knew it would make him uncomfortable. Didn't he realize how sick he looked?

Ray continued. "You've been gone, but after Albert died there was lots of talk." He lowered his voice. "Some folks are even saying he was poisoned. What will they say if Scyrel dies?"

Mae gasped, "Poison?"

"That's what some are saying," he confirmed. "Ma said if he had any poison in him it was from the threshing dust. But no one else who was threshing with him got sick, just Scyrel." This was more than Mae could take in. Ray was the only one she could talk to and she didn't know what she would do if he took sick. But how could she prevent something from happening when she didn't know what that something was? They finished chores in silence and went back to the house. Carrie put out lemonade for her children and then turned back to the dishes in the dry sink.

When Ray saw Mae reach for her glass he bumped the table hard enough to cause both drinks to tip over. "I'm sorry Ma," he said. "I'll clean it up." Carrie turned at the sound, grabbed the dishrag, and caught most of the drink before it hit the floor. "I'll make some more," she offered. But Ray protested. "No Ma, you're tired." He looked intently at Mae. "Besides, we aren't thirsty." He took the rag from Carrie and continued to clean up as Mae stood by speechless.

* * * *

Ray went into the parlor according to his new routine. He sat with Scyrel and told him about the day. "I saw Sam this morning. Told him you're feeling tough. He says you best get better soon. And to tell you the job is still open. Said he couldn't find anybody as good as you." Scyrel managed a weak smile. "Ray, if you see him again? Tell him I'll be back as soon as I'm on my feet. That is, if I can feel them. I never should have left him in the first place and I wouldn't have except. . . ." He didn't finish but both boys knew what would have been said. Had Albert lived, Scyrel would still be working in Tyre. The talking tired him and Ray knew it was time to go. "See you in the morning," he said, and gently pumped his fist into Scyrel's shoulder. It was as close to a show of affection as the boys would ever share.

That night Carrie sat a long time in her chair listening to the day shut down. An occasional cow lowed in the distance and crickets filled the night with their songs. Beside her lay crumpled up wads of the medical journals she had trusted. Ray paced in the yard trying to tire his mind and body for sleep. Mae tossed and turned with strange thoughts running through her mind before she finally gave in to slumber. The last sound she heard was the nurse getting another glass of milk for her brother.

* * * *

Morning was announced by the rooster, and the house came to life. Scyrel was given his usual breakfast of eggnog and he prayed it would stay down. Mae prepared breakfast for the family and the nurse. She wished the aroma of sausage could be kept from the parlor, but that was impossible. The rest of them needed nourishment for whatever the day might bring.

Dr. MacGregor arrived at ten o'clock and seemed pleased to hear that the patient had not vomited in fourteen hours. That was the good news. The bad news was that he was much weaker and his eyes were still sore and now puffy. He stayed with the young man while Nurse Gibbs freshened up. She had spent the night in a chair by the bed to keep an eye on her patient and to give doses of strychnine at the appointed times. MacGregor's wife planned to come out and relieve her later in the day so Nurse Gibbs could take a much-needed nap.

MacGregor tended Carrie's eyes and had started toward his automobile when Mae caught up to him. "Dr. MacGregor, may I have a word?" she asked.

He smiled at her. "Of course. You want to know about your brother."

Her answer shocked him. "Actually, no. I believe Scyrel is going to die—like Peter and Albert. I'm concerned about Ray. Would you agree that he looks almost as bad as Scyrel?" She did not allow him to answer. "Doctor, I heard about the rumors in town. What do we need to do now to keep Ray healthy?" She had made no accusations, but her words spoke volumes.

Dr. MacGregor knew he had just been given notice that Mae was keenly aware of the circumstances and would do anything necessary to prevent Ray from following his father and brothers to the grave. She had delivered nearly the same speech to her mother over the morning breakfast dishes. Mae had not waited for an answer then and did not wait for an answer now. She had done what she set out to do and returned to the house.

Chapter 43

Scyrel felt encouraged. It was now late afternoon and he still had not vomited. Frequent enemas brought results, and his throat no longer ached from the constant regurgitations. He was certain that the doctor would let him have solid food. When MacGregor came that evening he saw a patient nearing death, but couldn't bring himself to stifle the young man's hopes. He left an order for breakfast, a soft egg. At night the boy was to have chicken broth and crackers. He told the nurse to be generous. "If any pieces of chicken should escape into the broth, just pretend they aren't there." He winked at Scyrel who was trying to smile. The nurse followed the doctor out of the room and asked, "Doctor, do you really think he will recover?" MacGregor sighed. "No. But at this stage, some semi-solid food can't hurt him. By the way, Mrs. Sparling used to receive the Bad Axe newspaper every Friday. If you happen to see it, be sure Scyrel doesn't read it." The day drew to a close and each person in the house retired to their bed or chair listening to a soft, soothing rainfall.

> The Huron County Tribune – Friday August 11, 1911
> "Ubly: Scyrel Sparling is very seriously ill at his home west of town. At present there is but little hope entertained for his recovery."

* * * *

Nurse Gibbs woke suddenly. Scyrel was vomiting green fluid with curds. She washed his face and moved the pan to the edge of the doorway. His face looked grim and she knew he would be disappointed if the awaited egg did not appear. "Don't you worry young man," she said. "I am going to go poach that egg right now. Doctor's orders, right?" She smiled and went to the kitchen. A few minutes later, Ray appeared with the soft egg breakfast. Nurse Gibbs followed right behind him and remained in the sick room while brother fed brother.

"Going to be in the oats today as soon as it dries off," Ray reported. "And did I tell you Belinda dropped her calf during the night? She's a pretty little thing, just like her momma. Well I got to get busy, but I'll be back to see you before band practice tonight. Maybe you can sweet talk Nurse Gibbs into another egg." Again, the very gentle jab of his fist on Scyrel's shoulder.

The egg stayed down for about an hour and the nurse noted it on the chart. The doctor arrived before dinner. He saw to Carrie's eyes and checked his patient. MacGregor looked the worse for wear and admitted privately to the nurse that this case was keeping him up at night. He observed from the chart that the semi-solid food had come up, but still made notations that the broth and crackers were to be given later, no matter what.

It was not known who avoided whom, but the doctor and Mae did not exchange words that day. As he left the house, Carrie gave him a questioning look. He shook his head no. "I'm sorry Carrie."

A young man lay dying while people went about their business as if oblivious to the fact. Both Carrie and Mae looked in on Scyrel, and Mae read to him from a favorite book. But it was the job of the nurse to tend the patient, and daily chores kept mother, sister, and brother from collapsing with grief and frustration. At three o'clock Scyrel retched and the green vomit now contained a blood clot. Nevertheless, he was given broth and crackers for supper.

* * * *

Had the Sparlings lived closer to town, they would have heard the church bells ringing. Robert MacGregor attended services with his family. Zen Boomhower approached the doctor afterward. "Robert," he said, "Will Herrington was asking about Scyrel. He saw the article in the paper and wonders if he might have missed something before. And I—well I encouraged him to go see the boy. I hope that's all right." MacGregor seethed inside but was too tired to argue.

"There's no harm in it, I guess. But I don't see any good in it either. If you think he should come out, then so be it." Zen saw the extreme fatigue in his friend's face and could only imagine the toll this was taking. When MacGregor got home, he immediately telephoned Dr. Conboy. "Daniel, I hate to bother you on the Sabbath, but Herrington is coming out to see Scyrel and I was hoping you would come with him. No, I see no change for the better. He's dying Daniel. For the life of me I do not know what is keeping him alive."

But Scyrel was still alive. He ate an egg on toast (without the milk) for breakfast, followed by a dish of delicious ice cream. His lips were swollen and his throat very sore. The ice cream soothed both. Ray spent time with his brother and then left for Tyre. He had never felt so helpless in his life.

Mae had prepared the noon meal and planned to read to her brother when the dishes were done. She had almost finished when she noticed the bottle over the dry sink. Carrie had told her it was medicine from the doctor for pimples. Having seen that the bottle was less than half full, she had asked Ray about it. "Yeah," he had told her. "We both had some. I didn't take much 'cause it made me feel funny, but Scyrel used it until he got sick." She knew Scyrel was done with it, but what about Ray?

Mae was alone in the kitchen now and she saw no one in the yard. She slipped the bottle into her apron pocket and went to the privy. When she returned, her pocket was empty.

* * * *

Carrie had spent the better part of the day with her son. She had wanted to bring him lemonade, but knew Nurse Gibbs wouldn't allow it. The doctor had agreed to broth and crackers, but changed his mind about the lemonade. Carrie had become frustrated with the nurse. Nurse Gibbs only allowed Carrie to sit with Scyrel by his bed. She no longer felt in control of her own house. Nurse Gibbs had taken over.

Carrie was pulled from her thoughts when she heard MacGregor call her name. "Mrs. Sparling, Dr. Holdship and I need to examine Scyrel. Doctors Herrington and Conboy will be joining us shortly. I just wanted you to be aware." She looked at her son and then at MacGregor before leaving the room.

MacGregor checked Scyrel's pulse and put his stethoscope to the young man's chest. Scyrel's legs thrashed under the sheet and he clutched his stomach. His voice sounded faint and raspy, and tears ran down his cheeks. He grabbed MacGregor's wrist. "Please don't let me die," he begged.

The doctor tried to reassure him. "Scyrel, you're not going to die. Put that thought out of your head." MacGregor patted Scyrel's hand gently and removed it from his wrist. He noticed a strange look on Holdship's face. "Why don't we wait outside William," he suggested.

Shortly after, Herrington and Conboy drove into the yard and the four doctors convened on the lawn. MacGregor and Conboy then walked toward the house ahead of their colleagues, conferring quietly. The other two physicians could not make out their words. Once inside, the doctors stayed with Scyrel about fifteen minutes. Dr. Conboy checked the pulse and it registered one-twenty. He knew death would make its claim before long.

The men left the house and MacGregor spoke. "Dr. Herrington, if this boy dies, and I think we know he will, I would like you to do the post mortem. Daniel, William, I would like you both to be present as well." No commitments were made, but the men shook hands. Conboy and Herrington left for Bad Axe and Holdship rode back to Ubly with MacGregor.

Ray returned from the fields late. Perry Cole had done the milking for him. He went into the parlor to speak to his brother, but the nurse put her finger to her lips. Scyrel was resting and should not be disturbed. He quietly climbed the stairs to bed. All was quiet. His mother and sister were already asleep. Carrie Boddy Sparling had turned forty-six years old that day.

* * * *

Monday morning came and the family found their way to the kitchen to begin their day. Mae prepared breakfast while Ray did the milking. Carrie went to the parlor to sit with her son. Nurse Gibbs was trying to get him to drink some milk. He tried to swallow the liquid, but his tongue was swollen and his body was quivering. The nurse tried to coax Carrie out of the room, but Carrie would not budge. Scyrel once again retched and vomited. Then he fell quiet. Carrie wiped his brow and went to the kitchen. Right after breakfast, Mae's mother-in-law arrived. Cecelia asked about Scyrel. "Not good," Mae replied.

Dr. MacGregor came shortly after ten o'clock. He dosed Carrie's eyes and went to the parlor. One look told him all he needed to know. One of Scyrel's feet stuck out from under the sheet and his toes wiggled involuntarily. He appeared to be sleeping, but his mouth was wide open and occasionally his body jerked. MacGregor knew the end was near. He talked privately to the nurse, gave her a packet of powder, and said, "I'll be back after dinner."

After sitting with his brother, Ray went to the loft in the barn and sobbed as though his heart would break. He tried to focus on work around the farm, but did not plan to be far from the house that day. Mae did laundry and Carrie worked in the garden. Cecelia made herself useful by starting dinner. At noon, Scyrel vomited again and clutched his stomach in agony. Nurse Gibbs prepared the powder from the doctor and helped her patient swallow the morphine. Soon his body appeared to be at rest and his hands fell to his sides; the pain had eased. When MacGregor arrived at two o'clock he gave the nurse more morphine powder. He said he had rounds to make, but would return afterward.

As he left, Reverend Hurd arrived. He prayed with Scyrel, but didn't think the boy had heard him. He then went to the kitchen and offered more prayers with the family. Cecelia Hurford left about 5:30 and Reverend Hurd, sensing the end might be near, sat alone on the front porch.

The Sparlings didn't eat supper. No one felt hungry and the food Cecelia had fixed went uneaten. The family just sat quietly in the parlor. They had felt so helpless when the pains gripped Scyrel, and it now gave them some relief to see son and brother resting. Ray had also grieved, privately, at the loss of dignity to which Scyrel had been subjected. His strong brother had been reduced to a victim of medicines, countless enemas, and self-soiling in less than two weeks.

At six o'clock, Scyrel gasped. Nurse Gibbs immediately went to him. She felt for a pulse; there was none. She looked at the anxious family and said, "He suffers no more." And then, for the first time in days, she left them alone with her patient.

* * *

Nurse Gibbs telephoned MacGregor and then placed a call to the Hurfords, as promised. About seven o'clock that evening, Dr. Holdship came to the farm with MacGregor. The nurse met them at the side door and told them the family was still with the deceased. Dr. MacGregor telephoned Conboy and Herrington. "Scyrel has passed," he told them. "I would appreciate it if you would do the post mortem." The men agreed, but at 9:30 Dr. Herrington telephoned the farm. "Daniel and I have had an emergency come up. Keep the body cool and we will do the post mortem early tomorrow."

MacGregor debated the next course of action. Cecelia and Ed Hurford had arrived during the telephone call, and undertaker McKay shortly after. McKay could have been sent home and asked to return in the morning, but Dr. MacGregor put another plan into action. He asked Dr. Holdship to assist in the autopsy. "I see no reason to wait and make the family suffer any longer than necessary." Nurse Gibbs and Cecelia went into the parlor and gently told the family that the doctors now had work to do. Mae, Carrie, and Cecelia went with the nurse into the kitchen while Ray sat with Reverend Hurd and Ed Hurford in the dining room.

The men set to work. Hector McKay put the body on a cooling board and Dr. Holdship began to cut under the direction of Dr. MacGregor. He first removed an enlarged and crumbling liver. "It appears to be cancer of the liver," MacGregor stated. "Maybe that will stop some of the wagging tongues." He instructed Holdship to take the organ into the dining room to show the men. When the doctors' work was done, McKay took over and finished preparing the body. It was two o'clock in the morning. Doctors MacGregor and Holdship had already gone. MacGregor had taken a two-quart sealer filled with embalming fluid and pieces of Scyrel's liver, spleen, pancreas, and lung. The next morning he deposited them in Dr. Conboy's office.

* * *

On the morning of the fifteenth, neighbors began arriving to pay their respects. There was no viewing that day as Scyrel's body remained on the cooling board in the parlor. A casket would be delivered later that afternoon. Word reached Doctors Conboy and Herrington that the autopsy had been completed.

Boomhower had been serious. An investigation such as Ubly had never before witnessed began. The authorities informed Coroner Morden and he left Bad Axe with Prosecutor Boomhower and Sheriff McAulay to impanel a jury in Ubly. The jury arrived at the farm shortly thereafter, and was duly sworn in upon viewing the body. Dr. Morden placed the remainder of the liver in a crock with more embalming fluid and set September twelfth as the date for inquest, allowing time for the organs to be examined by experts at the University of Michigan at Ann Arbor. When the formalities ended, the jury went home.

Dr. Morden prepared to leave and found MacGregor on the porch staring at the fields. "Robert, do you know where Mrs. Sparling is?" Robert shrugged. "I assume the nurse is with her. She isn't well." Morden didn't know that a nurse had been in attendance, and asked if she had kept a record. MacGregor answered, "Yes. Would you like to see it?" When Morden indicated that he definitely would, MacGregor found it and handed it to the coroner who quickly glanced through it.

"Robert, it says the deceased vomited blood. How did his stomach look?" MacGregor, without hesitation, said the stomach looked good. Morden saw the note about bloody stools and asked about the intestines.

"Intestines looked good Charles," was MacGregor's reply. Dr. Morden was clearly confused. "You mean there was no congestion or inflammation in the linings?" "No," replied MacGregor. "Everything looked good. Puzzling, isn't it?"

* * *

Scyrel's funeral took place at the home. The day had begun with heavy thunderstorms as if the heavens were protesting this life cut short. But by noon the skies had cleared and, as before, women from church arrived to set up tables for food. For Carrie it was all a blur. She saw familiar faces and assumed they were talking to her. But a rumbling noise thundered inside her head and she heard nothing else. She only nodded at the passing sympathizers. As Reverend Hurd delivered the eulogy, she sat to the side with Mae and Ray. Looking over the assembled mourners, she saw Sparlings—Big Pete and Mary, Little Pete and Mary, and William and Ellen. Big Pete's brothers Chris, James, and Jake all sat with their wives. And old Uncle John was behind them. There were many Sparling cousins, but no one from the Boddy family attended. At one time, she would have welcomed this gathering. But now she just felt very alone and wished they would all leave.

When the service ended, Ray helped Carrie into the wagon that carried her son. It was an odd procession from the farm in Ubly to the cemetery in Tyre. People rode in buggies, wagons, automobiles, and a few went by horseback. When they reached the cemetery, many others were already there. Most had not attended the funeral, but had come out of respect. "Or," Carrie thought, "out of morbid curiosity." If there were rumors after Albert's passing, they would only increase now. She determined to continue to hold her head high and let them talk. She knew she couldn't stop them.

Fortunately the service was short, as the day was getting very hot. Carrie glanced down at the broken earth on Albert's grave. Grass had just begun to cover the wound in the ground. She then looked to Peter's mound and baby

Edward's stone. The droning noise in her head grew louder and Carrie's knees buckled. Mae and Ray caught her before she fell and held her between them until the final "amen." As her son and daughter helped her back to the buggy, a sound broke through the noise in her head. The sound of wailing. She looked to her left. The crying came from Sam Soule. Carrie's only thought was, "That's odd. Sam isn't even kin."

When they arrived back at the farm, family and friends helped themselves to a wide assortment of food. Carrie knew she would be sick if she tried to eat. She remained outside for perhaps half an hour and then went into the house and to her bed. She didn't even notice Violet working in the kitchen as she passed through.

* * *

Mae planned to stay the week, but knew after that she had to return to Port Huron. Her life was there. She hated to leave her mother who was near mental, emotional, and physical exhaustion. Even more, she feared leaving Ray. But she remembered Nurse Gibbs had been paid for two weeks service, and Mae was relieved to learn that the nurse had already planned to stay on until the twenty-third.

The parlor was cleaned and returned to its former use.

PORT HURON HOSPITAL

CLINICAL RECORD

Case No. _____ Name _____

Date _____ Day of Disease _____ Room or Ward _____

HOUR	T.	P.	R.	IMMEDIATE ORDERS AND CLINICAL NOTES	DEF. URINE

Nurse Gibbs' records for treating Scyrel from
August 9, 1911, to his death on August 14, 1911

240

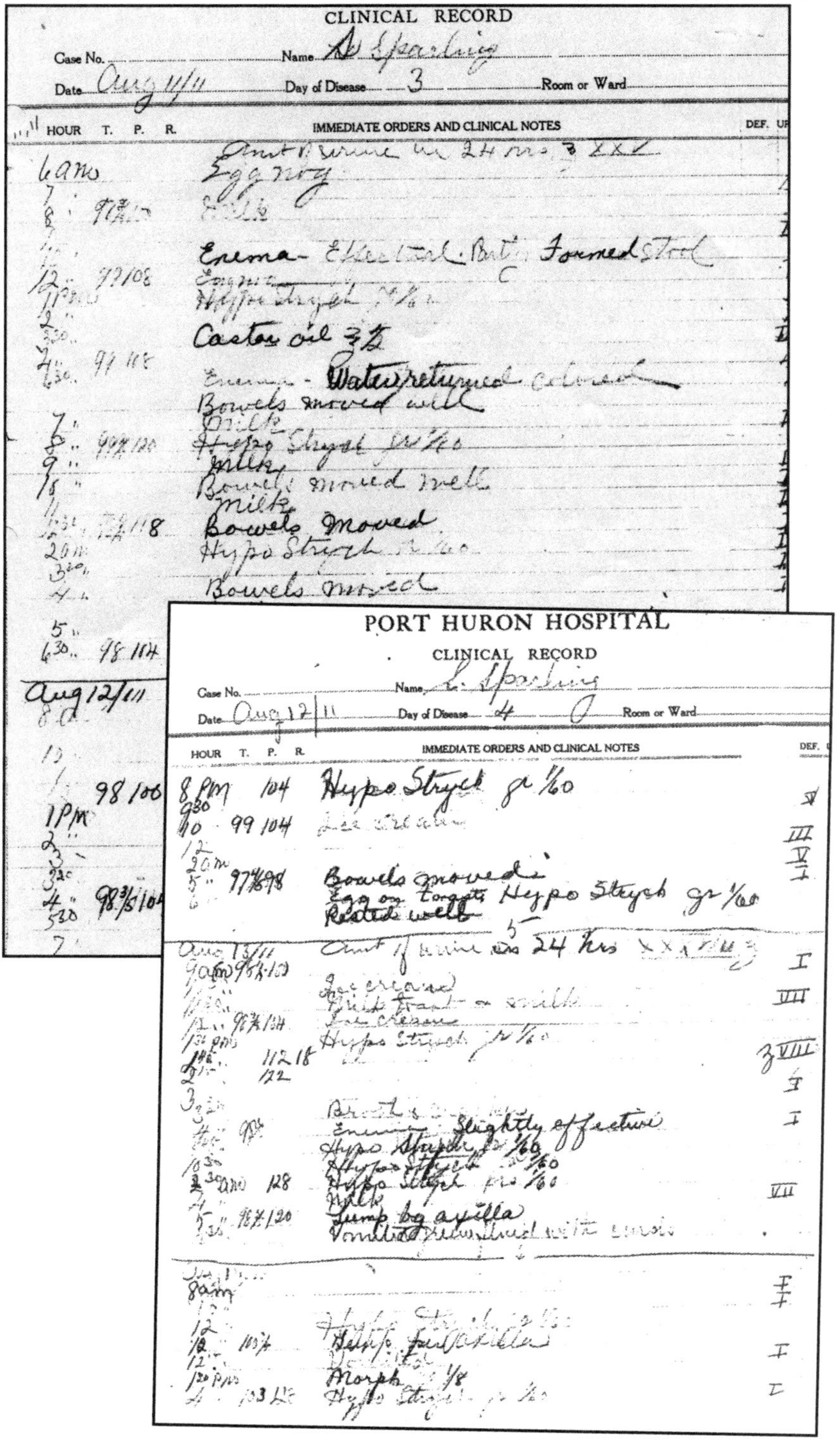
CLINICAL RECORD

Case No. Name S. Sparling

Date Aug 11/11 Day of Disease 3 Room or Ward

HOUR T. P. R. IMMEDIATE ORDERS AND CLINICAL NOTES DEF.

6am Egg nog

Enema - Effectual. Part. Formed stool

Castor oil ʒ ½

Enema - Water returned colored

Bowels moved well

Milk

Hypo Strych gr 1/60

Milk

Bowels moved well

Milk

Bowels moved

Hypo Strych

Bowels moved

6³⁰ 98 104

Aug 12/11

98 100

1 PM

98⅗/104

PORT HURON HOSPITAL

CLINICAL RECORD

Case No. Name S. Sparling

Date Aug 12/11 Day of Disease 4 Room or Ward

HOUR T. P. R. IMMEDIATE ORDERS AND CLINICAL NOTES DEF.

8 PM 104 Hypo Strych gr 1/60

10 99 104 Ice cream

Bowels moved

Egg on toast Hypo Strych gr 1/60

Rested well

Aug 13/11 Amt of urine in 24 hrs

Ice cream

Ice cream

Hypo Strych gr 1/60

Enema Slightly effective

Hypo Strych gr 1/60

Hypo Strych gr 1/60

Hypo Strych gr 1/60

Milk

Lump by axilla

Morph 1/8

Chapter 44

Dr. MacGregor came daily to treat Carrie's eyes although Nurse Gibbs had offered to do it for him. Other than that, there were few callers and the peace and quiet was appreciated. By week's end however, Nurse Gibbs noticed that an unusually high amount of traffic passed the farm. She saw vehicles slow and come to a near stop in front of the house before proceeding. "The town is abuzz over this latest death," Dr. MacGregor explained when she expressed her concern. "The story even made the Detroit newspapers. Mrs. Sparling is in no condition to talk about any of this, especially to strangers. Be sure to shield her from them. I'll mention it to Ray."

Oddly enough, Dr. MacGregor did not heed his own advice. A man who would much later be identified as Tom Phillips, a Detroit newspaper reporter, tried to corner the doctor as he left the barbershop in Ubly. MacGregor lengthened his strides, but the persistent Phillips scurried to keep pace and peppered MacGregor with questions. "Are you shocked by these deaths and, as their physician, do you feel any responsibility?" MacGregor's silence did not deter the reporter. "Doctor, do you know how these men died? Is it true they were poisoned? Who could have done this?" Robert MacGregor continued on, trying to ignore the man. He was only a short distance from his home where he could slam the door on this intruder. Phillips continued, "Is it true that you and Mrs. Sparling are having an affair?" MacGregor stopped walking immediately and glared at the man. "They all had syphilis," he said through clenched teeth.

"What about the poison?" asked Phillips.

"Don't you get it?" the doctor snapped. "It was in the medicine they took for the disease. They all took arsenic." MacGregor had reached his home. He entered and shut the door in Phillips' face. As he watched the man turn and walk away MacGregor felt uneasy. He had just done the very thing he had warned Nurse Gibbs not to do.

* * *

On the twenty-third, as Ray prepared to go to the Cass City Fair, Nurse Gibbs told him that she was leaving on the afternoon train. "I'd better say my good-byes now Ray. I'm sorry to have met you under these circumstances, but I hope you'll feel free to call me should you have a need in the future. Take care of yourself and your mother." Ray hated to see her leave. His mother had become distant, spending more time in the old rocker than ever before, and he had enjoyed the conversations with Nurse Gibbs.

When he returned late that night, he was pleased to see the nurse reading a book by the light of the coal oil lamp in the parlor. She looked up. "I missed my train Ray. So your mother asked me to stay on a while and I have agreed. Guess you'll have to put up with me a bit longer." Ray spent the next hour bending her ear about the fair.

On the twenty-fourth, Violet called on Carrie. She brought bread and mending, but didn't stay long. The nurse remained in the room with them and even though Violet had no words that the nurse should not hear, the situation was very awkward. Carrie looked tired and was quieter than usual. Violet said she would come back another time.

If any good news occurred at this time, it was that the Tyre farm had sold. Carrie had even hinted at selling out completely and moving to Port Huron. Ray didn't know how he felt about that. He was just a farm boy and didn't know how he would fare in the city. By the end of August the Tyre farm was emptied of personal items and that bond was severed. Nurse Gibbs agreed to remain another week even though Carrie's physical health had improved. During that time, Dr. MacGregor received Scyrel's Sun Life Assurance forms from his father and helped Carrie with the paperwork required to file a claim.

By now Nurse Gibbs had already intercepted two reporters who were trying to gain admittance to the house and firmly ordered them off the premises. When Big Pete and his brothers James and Jake appeared, she also gave them a curt dismissal. "Sorry gentlemen," she insisted. "I don't know you and my orders are that Mrs. Sparling is not to be disturbed." The brothers were furious. As they left, Big Pete wondered aloud, "Who gave such orders anyway?"

"I think I can guess," James hinted. The men left, but Big Pete promised himself to try again later. Maybe if he brought Mary things would be different. He knew about the rumors, but Big Pete was a fair man and until evidence was given, he would support his cousin's family.

* * *

Gossip raged in the community, but Dr. MacGregor only noticed a slight change in his practice. There had been no report from Ann Arbor and, without proof, people who had come to depend upon Dr. MacGregor continued to do so.

But one case in particular would come back to haunt him. On the thirtieth of August, Dr. Corcoran called MacGregor for consultation about a case in Tyre. It involved a very sick child. MacGregor suggested that the family, the MacDonalds, hire a nurse as soon as possible. "How quickly can we get one?" Mrs. MacDonald asked.

"It's getting late," MacGregor noted. "I see no way to bring a nurse here before tomorrow."

Mrs. MacDonald persisted. "But doctor, what about the nurse staying at the Sparlings?"

MacGregor shook his head. "No, I'm afraid she is needed there."

The frantic mother would not give in. "But if we could have her for only this one night?"

Again the doctor shook his head. "I'm sorry, but I am now between the devil and the deep and she has to stay there." The statement made no sense to the woman, but MacGregor left before she could say anything else.

* * *

That same day Nurse Gibbs stared out the window. She had nothing to do. She didn't regret her decision to remain with the Sparlings after Scyrel died. In fact she had grown fond of them. But her nursing skills were not being put to use and the monotony of each day was wearing on her.

* * *

On August thirty-first, Dr. MacGregor arrived to treat Carrie's eyes. In Tyre, Suzie MacDonald prepared for her child's funeral.

* * *

On September seventh, Nurse Gibbs left to care for a patient at the McCreary's in Tyre. She felt sympathy for Carrie and all she had been through, but Carrie had grown more and more reclusive. Ray brought her chair back into the parlor and Nurse Gibbs often heard her talking as she rocked. She couldn't make out the words and just let her be. For someone dedicated to nursing, the days at the Sparling farm had become long and tedious. She was excited about a change and felt she would be much more helpful at the McCrearys. One week later, Ray called at that home. "Ma sure misses you," he told the nurse. "Would you be willing to come back when you're done here?"

"Ray, I can't answer that now," she responded. "I know I'll be here at least another week. You may not even need me by then." Ray said he would check in a week. The nurse felt sorry for him. All his brothers gone, and now he lived alone with his mother who was withdrawing from life. But she could not remain purely for sympathy's sake.

* * *

The inquest, set for September twelfth, was delayed until the twelfth of October; the chemists in Ann Arbor needed more time.

Time dragged on. Carrie rarely went into town and only seemed happy when she was in her chair or canning produce from the garden. Ray filled his time after chores with band practice and county fairs. The Huron County Fair was expecting record crowds. They had signed a contract with the Glen Curtis Company to offer flying exhibitions in a biplane. On the twenty-first of September, Carrie asked Ray to go to Tyre and bring Nurse Gibbs back. She had telephoned to say she would spend a few days with them before returning to Port Huron. He didn't have to be asked twice. Ray was happier with her there. Nurse Gibbs went to the Friday night band concert, which made him very proud. Carrie had not attended in months, and he envied other members whose parents were always in the audience. On Sunday, Carrie and Ray took Nurse Gibbs to the train station. She promised to return to be with them during the inquest.

* * *

By October, the gardening was done. Sugar beets would soon be harvested and the busiest days of farm life were coming to an end. It would have been better to be busy now. The inquest loomed before Carrie and Ray, but they did not speak of it. And while they didn't know what to expect, its impending presence weighed heavily upon them. Dr. MacGregor also felt the effects of it. He treated Carrie's eyes daily, but she noticed he did not stay as in times past.

* * *

Dr. MacGregor continued his practice. Elmer Hunter, aged sixty but looking eighty, had been one of MacGregor's first patients. Hunter had just returned from a hospital stay in Detroit. MacGregor called on the gentleman every day even though he knew the man was dying. When he finished his examination of Mr. Hunter on the eleventh of October, he spoke privately to the man's wife and daughter. Ora May, the daughter, was in tears. "My father was always so strong and healthy. Are you saying there is no chance for his recovery?"

"There are worse things than death," MacGregor answered. As he packed up his bag he added quietly, "I will probably be arrested by tomorrow evening and I would willingly exchange places with your father."

246

Chapter 45

On October 12, 1911, Dr. MacGregor testified before a coroner's jury regarding his treatment of the Sparling family and, in particular, the treatment of Scyrel Sparling prior to his death. After listening to the testimony and studying reports from Ann Arbor, the jury found that Scyrel Sparling died from arsenic poison on the fourteenth day of August 1911. The workloads of Prosecutor Boomhower, Coroner Morden, and Sheriff McAulay had just become heavier.

The day after the inquest Dr. MacGregor again called on the Hunters. "Well Elmer, how goes it? Did you get any sleep?" When Mr. Hunter replied in the negative, MacGregor added, "That makes two of us then." Mrs. Hunter asked the doctor how the inquest had gone. "They found arsenic in the liver, but I knew they would," he answered her. "I told Dr. Conboy that before the lad died." Mrs. Hunter looked confused. "That sounds bad, but don't doctors give arsenic as a medicine?" The doctor looked at her a long time before answering. "Yes. But I never gave him any."

* * *

Nurse Gibbs returned to Ubly as promised. When word of arsenic poisoning reached Carrie, the nurse prepared for a collapse. But it never came. Carrie went about her daily chores as if nothing had happened. Mae had also returned for the inquest. Her mother, who insisted on a fall house cleaning, put her to work. Carrie had finally decided to sell out completely and move to Port Huron. She and Ray could live with Mae and Bert until they found a place of their own. Part of the cleaning included setting aside items for an auction. They would not be able to take all their belongings, and money from an auction would bring in extra cash. At first Mae and Nurse Gibbs humored her, but it soon became apparent that Carrie was serious. She actually did intend to leave the area.

Five days later Carrie insisted the house be cleaned again. The women saw the determined look in Carrie's eyes as she frantically scrubbed the same place on the floor over and over. Rather than argue, they cleaned again.

For the second time in a week, Nurse Gibbs found herself on a stool cleaning the top of the cupboard. This time she found something that had not been there before. She pocketed the small jar and decided it was time to visit the sheriff.

* * *

Violet was ashamed that her visits had dropped off and she appeared at the farm a few days after the inquest. She had no idea what she would say, but knew she could no longer avoid seeing her friend. She joined Carrie, Mae, and Nurse Gibbs at the kitchen table, eating bread and drinking tea as if they were all far removed from the events surrounding them. Violet had observed before that Carrie dealt with grief in her own way, but surely the news of arsenic poisoning had reached her ears. She should have been outraged and demanding answers. Instead, she asked Violet if she would come to Port Huron to visit her and joked, "Don't forget to bring bread." She winked at Violet who hesitated and then managed an uncomfortable smile.

When it was time to leave, Mae walked Violet to her buggy. "Mrs. Styles, thank you for coming. Your visits always make Ma feel better. I don't know what to make of it. At times she acts as if nothing has happened. But other times she acts as if she knows exactly what happened."

Violet put her arm around the young woman. "It may just be more than she can handle right now," suggested Violet. "I'm glad you're here and I suppose it's also good that Nurse Gibbs has remained. How is Ray doing?"

Mae paused. "He's very quiet, but then he always was. His health seems a bit better than before. He and Ma are certainly welcome in our home. I just don't know if he can adapt to so many changes. But I'll worry about that when and if it happens."

★ ★ ★

On October twenty-seventh, *The Huron County Tribune* ran the following banner headline:

WHO KILLED SPARLING IS QUESTION OF THE HOUR
That Sparling Family of 4 Were Foully Murdered
Seems No Longer In Doubt

Who killed Scyrel Sparling, his two brothers and father? This is the question the people of Huron County are now asking almost with one voice. It is also the question that Prosecutor Boomhower, Coroner Morden, and Sheriff McAulay are working day and night to solve. The other question of how the Sparlings died appears to have been settled. It is now generally and, in fact, satisfactorily proved that at least Scyrel Sparling, aged 20 years, of near Ubly died last August from arsenical poisoning. The other members of the family, a brother about two months before Scyrel and the father and another brother, within two years before that time died under circumstances and conditions so similar to Scyrel's that there seems little doubt but what the whole (sic) four were poisoned and "killed" in the same manner by the same administration of arsenic.

All sorts of rumors and stories are afloat and the Tribune could this week publish columns of intensely readable matter about the case, but the authorities are hard at work and it wouldn't be right to interfere with their efforts by premature publications however well founded they might be. So far no arrests have been made and probably none will be made until the officers believe they have the case cinched.

That same day, the body of Albert Sparling was exhumed and Dr. Holdship performed a post mortem. He removed the liver, stomach, spleen, and part of the intestines, which Coroner Morden sent to Ann Arbor for analysis. No sooner had Holdship returned home than Dr. MacGregor appeared. "William," he asked. "Did they take up all the bodies?" Dr. Holdship answered, "No, the order only called for Albert's."

MacGregor continued his query, "Do you think they will find arsenic?" Holdship paused before saying, "I would not be surprised if they do."

Robert MacGregor quickly nodded in agreement and threw his hands into the air. "Well I wouldn't be surprised if they found arsenic in all of them. And I would give my left leg to the hip to find out who gave it to them."

* * *

Big Pete and Mary came to see Carrie as October drew to a close. They noticed Nurse Gibbs was still there although neither Carrie nor Ray appeared to be ill. This time the nurse allowed them to stay, but if the conversation leaned toward the death of Scyrel, the inquest, or rumors, she interrupted, insisting this was not the proper time and changed the subject. In a time of darkness and suspicion, their dialogue was limited to small talk.

Carrie told Big Pete that she was selling out and they were having an auction on the fourth of November. "Most everything to be sold is in the barn. If there is anything you want, please take it. I know how close you and J.W. were." Big Pete said he would take a look but pay a fair price, as he did not want something for nothing.

* * *

The day of the auction dawned bright and crisp. Several would-be buyers and some curiosity seekers arrived early. When the actual sale began at ten o'clock, the yard was full. Mae had returned for the event and helped answer any questions about the items. Ray stayed until the bidding began and then he walked up the road and into a sugar beet field. He didn't want anyone to see him cry. Scyrel had not been dead three months and his home was now full of people, many of them strangers, fingering items used by him, his pa, and brothers. Mae and Bert had no room or need for farm equipment. But Ray was deeply hurt to know it would be gone by day's end. He had overheard two men talking about a buggy seat. They allowed as how it wasn't worth much and Ray had wanted to scream at them. His pa had made that seat. Next to the seat was a small milk cart. On those rare occasions when there had been free time he and Scyrel, as little boys, would give each other rides in it. The thought of Belinda and her calf being led to a new home brought another round of tears. He looked around at the fields. They would be plowed and harvested by others while he looked for work in the city, probably an indoor job. He racked his brain. Was there any way he could stay here to live? He knew the answer. It wouldn't be fair to Mae and Ma had already told him he was now the man of the family.

Ray didn't know how far he had walked, but it was dark by the time he got home. The yard looked as empty as his heart felt. When he went into the kitchen Mae went to him and hugged him. She knew what a hard day this had been for him. And she also knew there were many hard days ahead. Carrie sat at the table with a cigar box, counting the money in front of her. "Ray," she exclaimed, "we have over eleven hundred dollars here. That will certainly help us buy a place in Port Huron. I need to find a safe place to keep it until I can get to the bank on Monday." Carrie continued to talk, oblivious to her son's grief.

The next day, Ray took both Nurse Gibbs and Mae to the train station. Both were going home to Port Huron but would be back in a week. Carrie wanted to be moved by Thanksgiving, and there were still a few loose ends to tie up.

* * *

Dr. MacGregor arrived at the farm early Monday morning to drop Carrie's eyes. He was surprised to learn that Nurse Gibbs had gone home but seemed relieved to learn she would return. "I understand the auction went quite well," he stated.

"Yes," Carrie replied, "Mae is coming back with Nurse Gibbs next week and we should be able to prepare for the final move. I was wondering though. . . ." Carrie's voice trailed off and she stared at the floor. "Could you show Mae how to put the drops in my eyes? Someone will have to do it for me until I can find a new doctor."

MacGregor hesitated a moment. "I wouldn't normally agree, but as you say, you must have them. I'll show Mae exactly how to do it when she comes."

Carrie looked at Robert MacGregor a very long time before asking questions long on her mind. "Did they find any bad blood in Scyrel? And Albert, will they find it in him? I couldn't bear it if their memories were tainted. There are enough rumors floating about as it is."

Dr. MacGregor cleared his throat. Everyone thought Carrie had been losing her mind. In fact, he had privately encouraged the nurse to watch for any signs of insanity. But this conversation made it clear that, at least for this moment, she was completely lucid. "I don't think they found syphilis in Scyrel, but if they weren't looking specifically for it, it could be missed. Right now their focus appears to be on the poison." Robert and Carrie looked at each other for several seconds before casting their eyes elsewhere.

"Will you come visit me in Port Huron? You have to go there to cross over into Canada to see your family." She looked down and then quietly added, "I'm going to miss you Robert."

Carrie looked very frail and Dr. MacGregor wanted to take her in his arms. But he thought better of it and just put his hands on her shoulders, "Of course," he replied. "I'll stop by to visit my favorite patient. You can't be completely rid of me you know. And I'm sure Ida would insist on it. She is very fond of you."

At the mention of Ida, Carrie's body stiffened and she pulled away. "Let me get some cash. I don't want to write any more notes than necessary, you understand, with the move and all." He took the money and said he would be back the next day. After he left, she went to her rocker and it was there Ray found her when he came in for dinner.

* * *

Dr. MacGregor returned to Ubly and was in Ed Gibson's barbershop when he met Sheriff McAulay. "How are you doctor?" the sheriff asked.

"As good as can be expected Donald," answered MacGregor. "Have you heard anything from Ann Arbor on Albert?"

The sheriff shook his head. "I haven't heard anything. Maybe Zen has."

MacGregor drew a deep breath and spoke firmly. "I'll tell you right now they will find poison in him. I told Conboy that all along. And if you take up J.W. and Peter, you'll find arsenic in them as well." The barbershop grew quiet. MacGregor rose from the chair and checked his appearance in the mirror.

"What's more, I know a man who can make Mrs. Sparling confess."

McAulay was shocked. "For God's sake, that is what we want. Get busy and find that man!"

MacGregor looked at McAulay. "I only have to peer into a looking glass to find him."

McAulay appeared confused, and then the realization hit him. "Oh my," he exclaimed.

And MacGregor replied, "Exactly" before donning his hat and walking away.

* * *

Mae and Nurse Gibbs arrived on Saturday morning. The day was cold and stormy, and the trip from the station in Tyre to the farm took twice as long as usual. Once home, Ray saw to the horses and was soaked and shivering by the time he reached the house. Carrie had made hot tea for everyone, but didn't notice that no one drank until she first took a sip. She was too busy explaining her plans for the move the following weekend. Mae reached into her pocket and pulled out a letter she had received the day before. "Ma, I think you should read this." Carrie rubbed her eyes and took the piece of paper.

> Mrs. Hurford,
> It has come to my attention that your mother
> and brother are planning a move to another city.
> This is an awkward and unsettled time, and while
> no charges have been made, I must strongly
> encourage you to convince your mother of the
> importance of postponing the move for the present
> time. If you have any questions, please feel free to
> telephone or come by my office. I hope to have
> matters resolved in the near future and beg
> your patience in this situation.
> > Cordially,
> > Xenophon Boomhower
> > Prosecuting Attorney for Huron County

Carrie read the letter twice. She became agitated and excused herself from the table. She took the letter to her chair and Mae explained the contents to the nurse and Ray. When the nurse offered to go in to Carrie, Ray said, "It's best to just let her be."

Part Three
The Thumb Points Fingers

Chapter 46

Wagging tongues were now joined by pointing fingers. The coroner's jury presiding over the inquest into the death of Albert Sparling received the reports from Ann Arbor. They thoroughly examined all aspects of the case, and the official report found that Albert Sparling had also died from arsenic poisoning. The case was not taken lightly. The meeting began November twenty-first and did not end until the early morning hours of November twenty-second. Sheriff McAulay then filed the required complaint against Dr. MacGregor and Nurse Gibbs. Justice James Skinner issued warrants for their arrests.

* * *

"There must be a mistake." Dr. MacGregor wiped his forehead with a handkerchief. "I don't understand, but I suppose I should thank you for letting me know personally." Robert MacGregor hung up the telephone and told Ida he would be back soon and left the house to walk and think.

* * *

Zen put the telephone down. He did not remember doing anything more difficult in his life. To tell someone to prepare to be arrested was hard enough. But the knowledge that he would soon be doing his best to ensure that his friend be tried and convicted for murder was almost impossible to grasp. Jennie looked at her husband. She wanted to comfort him and assure him that he was in the right. But she knew nothing could give him relief from the task that lay ahead. Zen put on his coat and left the house to think while he walked.

* * *

Dr. MacGregor telephoned the Sparling farm and spoke to Nurse Gibbs. Then he sat down with his wife and children to prepare them for a very rough day. At 10:45 that morning, Sheriff McAulay arrived in Ubly at the home of Dr. MacGregor. Accompanying him was the court stenographer, Wilbur Beach. Automobile dealer John Yauch drove the arrestors in one of his cars. After a tearful good-bye, the doctor got into the automobile and the group drove to the Sparling farm.

Having been forewarned that she was also to be arrested, Margaret Gibbs stood, stoically, waiting with a small valise at her side. The automobile drove north to Bad Axe and reached the county jail at noon. When they tried to exit the automobile, a photographer appeared and began taking pictures. It agitated the doctor and nurse, but they were able to thwart the man's attempts by use of his hat and her handkerchief. Sheriff McAulay shouted at the photographer and quickly ushered his prisoners into the jail.

Shortly after the group left the farm, Big Pete and Mary arrived to find Carrie trembling in her rocking chair as Ray stood helplessly by. Mae had left for home only three days ago and he wished she were here now.

Prosecutor Boomhower arrived shortly after and they all went into the kitchen. Zen Boomhower told Carrie she was not under arrest, but in the interest of everyone involved it had been decided that she should remain in the charge of someone who could care for her. The hidden intent was to see if she would let down her guard away from the doctor's control and confide in Big Pete. Big Pete had been approached and agreed to have Carrie move into their home two miles north of Bad Axe. When it appeared she might refuse this suggestion, Boomhower told her she had no choice in the matter. He then left a speechless, weeping Carrie Sparling and returned to Bad Axe. Many long nights and days lay ahead of him.

Mary tried to console Carrie. "You've been under such a strain and it will do you good to be in new surroundings. You can have a nice quiet night here and join us tomorrow." The two ladies then went into the bedroom to gather clothes.

Big Pete spoke to Ray. "Ray, we'd like you to join us as well." Ray's world had been turned upside down and he wanted to lash out. Big Pete was the only one available.

"Is that an order?" he asked.

Big Pete replied, "No Ray. We just thought there's no need for you to stay here alone. When the new owners move in, you'll have to have a place to live for sure." Ray knew Big Pete only wanted to help and he softened his tone.

"No, I'll just stay here for now. I expect Mae will be back as soon as she learns of this. We still have a month before the new folks come and there are things that need doing before then."

He paused and then added, "How long do you think all this will last?"

Big Pete wanted to hug the frightened, bewildered young man, but he opted for a pat on the back. "I wish I knew son. I wish I knew. We'll just have to take each day as the good Lord gives it to us. Call us if you change your mind, or better yet, just saddle your horse and head north. As for your mother, she needs to be at the station by nine o'clock in the morning. Here's her ticket. We'll be there to meet the train and get her safely to our home. Ray," Big Pete emphasized, "be sure she is on that train."

Ray nodded. He knew exactly what his cousin was inferring; his mother did not need the sheriff coming for her like he did the others.

When the women re-entered the kitchen, Mary went to Ray. "Are you going to join us?"

Ray swallowed hard. "No ma'am, but thank you for the offer." Big Pete and Mary said their good-byes. Big Pete carried a large satchel with clothes so Carrie would not be bothered with it on the train. When they were gone, Carrie slumped into a kitchen chair and held her head in her hands. Her body began to convulse with sobs and Ray stood behind her with his hands on her shoulders.

Neither one spoke for a long time. Finally Carrie stood. "We have to telephone Mae. She needs to know. I'm sure she'll come as soon as possible. I did laundry yesterday so you are set for clean clothes. There's canned meat and vegetables in the cellar. I'll get some bread started now. If you need more you'll have to go to the bakery in town. You and Mae help each other. You know all that needs doing before the new people move in. I should be back long before all that, but you can start those jobs now." Carrie needed to be busy and baking the bread helped. Ray called Mae and his sister said she hoped to arrive Friday.

As Carrie punched the bread for a second rise, a buggy drove into the yard. Reverend Hurd came into the kitchen. "Mrs. Sparling," he said. "I heard about Dr. MacGregor and Nurse Gibbs. This is a terrible shock and I just had to come by to see you." Carrie tried to speak, but tears fell and she could not form the words. Ray had seen the preacher arrive and came into the house. "Reverend Hurd, Ma has been told she must—" Ray stopped. "That she needs help now." He continued. "My pa's cousin has opened his home to her and she leaves tomorrow for Bad Axe. She's been through a lot and we think a change will be good for her."

Reverend Hurd understood the words, those spoken as well as those left unsaid. He had heard all the rumors, and while he didn't believe any of them he knew many others did. Therefore, the day's happenings were not a total surprise. "It appears you will be in good hands, Mrs. Sparling," he said. "And you Ray?"

"I'm staying here for now," he replied. "Ma and I will both be fine."

He tried to sound convincing, but didn't think he had fooled the preacher. Reverend Hurd then shared some scriptures and after a short prayer, he left. Ray walked him to his buggy and Carrie went to her rocking chair.

The following morning came in cold and blustery. Neither Ray nor Carrie had slept well and by six o'clock both were dressed and in the kitchen. It was hard for Ray not to automatically head out for milking. Years of doing so had been his habit, but now the cows were gone. Carrie had started to prepare breakfast when the kitchen door opened. The howling wind had prevented Ray and Carrie from hearing the Styles buggy. Violet and Ed came into the kitchen and set to work. Without a word, Violet opened the box Ed carried and removed the packed food. Then she began to cook. Ed started brewing coffee and when Carrie recovered from her surprise, she set the table.

In thirty minutes the four sat down to bacon, sausage, eggs, fried apples, and biscuits. Word always spread fast in a small community, and word that hinted of scandal traveled even faster. Ed broke the awkward silence. "Ray, do you miss your girls?" He was obviously referring to the cows.

Ray tried to smile, "They were part of my daily chores, but I can't say as I miss them on cold days like today."

Ed chuckled. "I know what you mean, indeed I do."

Violet put her fork down. "Carrie, is there anything you need me to do before you leave?" Carrie wiped at her eyes and shook her head. She reached for Violet's hand and Violet squeezed it warmly. "Now," Violet continued, "you finish getting ready. Ed will drive you and Ray to the station. I'm going to stay and take care of these dishes." Carrie had no choice but to obey and within a few minutes she was ready to go.

She hugged Violet as if she didn't want to let go. "I don't know what to say," she whispered. She then looked at the table and smiled. There was Violet's trademark loaf of bread tied with a bright, cheery, yellow ribbon. Another hug and then Carrie went out the door and into a very uncertain future.

* * *

Ray and Ed helped Carrie onto the train. Mother and son had an awkward good-bye before the train pulled out. Ed took Ray home, and what could have been a cold stark kitchen was instead bright and warm, filled with the aroma of beef stew on the back of the stove. "Just stir it now and then," Violet instructed. "You have our number if you need anything." And then they were gone. Ray had a fence to mend, a barn door to tighten, and shed roofing to replace, but he didn't do any of these things. He just went from room to room before falling into his bed crying. Much needed sleep finally overtook him.

* * *

A reporter approached Carrie on the train. She looked at him through red, swollen eyes. When asked for her opinion, she spoke openly. "Until right now I never accepted the fact that my boys may have been murdered. This just reopened their deaths to me and I find myself grieving all over again."

She broke down and the reporter offered his handkerchief. When she recovered, he asked if she thought Dr. MacGregor had been jailed unjustly. Amid crying hiccups, she answered, "I am so completely dumbfounded and stricken by all of these events I don't know what to think. My mind is rocked between doubts and fears. Every mother believes her children to be the best, but mine truly were. God knows I loved them dearly and tried to do my best by them. I cannot imagine anyone so vile as to want to poison my sons."

* * *

At noon on Thursday Big Pete met Carrie at the Bad Axe train station, Ray was blissfully sound asleep, and Dr. MacGregor and Nurse Gibbs appeared before Justice Skinner. The accused each entered a plea of not guilty to the charges against them. The doctor, who appeared worn and weary, was held to the circuit court, without bail. He obtained the services of Bad Axe attorney George Clark, and a hearing was set for December fifth. Nurse Gibbs, charged with being an accessory after the fact, retained the Walsh Brothers law firm from Port Huron. She was also held for examination on December fifth, under bail bond of one thousand dollars. That bail was secured by friends and Nurse Gibbs left Bad Axe for Port Huron on Friday the twenty-fourth of November.

The next day *The Huron County Tribune* gave great praise to the three men instrumental in bringing this case to its present status. "Coroner Morden and Sheriff McAulay have given their time and overtime in assisting the Prosecutor. Young Zen Boomhower, being tasked with a huge case, has handled himself with skill and has given attention to every detail. His duties have been extra difficult, given the fact that the Boomhower and MacGregor families have enjoyed a close friendship over the past years. Nevertheless, he has performed these tasks in such a way that the citizens of this county should take great pride in his devotion to duty."

Mae arrived later that day alone. Bert planned to join her at his parents for Thanksgiving the following Thursday. She purchased a copy of the newspaper and was reading it when Ray appeared at the Ubly train station. There was little conversation on the ride home, but once inside Mae peppered her brother with questions. "Did you have any idea this would happen? How long will she be at Big Pete's? Should we hire an attorney? What are people saying? Ray is it possible. . . . ?" She could not finish that question. It left brother and sister with thoughts that no child should ever be forced to consider.

* * *

On Sunday the topic of Reverend Hurd's sermon was, "Let him that is without sin cast the first stone." He had struggled with the sermon for three days, and strongly encouraged his flock to take the message home and reflect upon it. At the close of the service he asked, "If you have faith in the innocence of Dr. MacGregor please stand and show that sentiment." No one in the congregation remained seated. At one time he had planned to ask the same question regarding Mrs. Sparling. But since she had not been charged with anything, he felt the question would indirectly suggest guilt and did not ask it. When other members of the Sparling clan heard of the sermon, they were very upset as they felt he had taken sides. It was a no-win situation for the minister.

Carrie felt uncomfortable at Big Pete's. Everyone treated her kindly, but she was not allowed to do anything. Mary still had seven children at home, ages nine to twenty-five. And there were bound to be extra men around to feed if the hay pressers or corn shredders were working. Carrie knew full well that extra hands in the kitchen were always welcome, but if she offered her help she was told, "No dear. You need your rest." She was tired of resting so she rose one morning long before daylight and decided to start breakfast. When Mary came into the kitchen a look of horror passed over her face. That was when Carrie Sparling realized the awful truth. Even Big Pete's family were concerned about the rumors. Especially when it came to preparing food.

The next three days, Carrie did little but pace and mutter. Finally Big Pete called Ubly. "Ray, it's Pete. We would like you, Mae, and Bert to join us for Thanksgiving. Your mother is quite restless. We think it would help if she could spend some time with you. I can pick you up at the station, so talk it over and let us know." Ray put the telephone down and relayed the information to his sister. At the same moment each looked into the parlor, and then at each other. "Mae, I'll give Big Pete a call and tell him we're coming, but we won't be using the train."

*Huron County Tribune Headlines
from late 1911 and early 1912*

Chapter 47

Thanksgiving 1911: Zen and Jennie Boomhower enjoyed a feast of roast goose with all the trimmings. Zen did his best to remain off duty and enjoy the time with his family. Sheriff McAulay allowed his deputy to do the same. Mrs. McAulay brought a light snack to her husband and returned home to finalize the main dinner that would be eaten later. The sheriff permitted Dr. MacGregor time out of his cell to visit with his wife, father, and brother. Ida could not bring so much as a piece of pie to him. She visited nearly every day, but never in his cell and she never brought the children as they both felt it would be much too upsetting for them.

The Sparling home north of Bad Axe burst at the seams. In addition to the seven children at home were George's fiancée, Big Pete and Mary's oldest daughter Pearl with husband and daughter, Mary's parents, the Shaws, and of course, Carrie. When Mae and Ray drove into the yard the group totaled eighteen. The two youngest sons, Lee and Mervin, tended the horses for Ray. An older son, Roy, helped bring in Carrie's rocking chair. Mae saw Mary look quizzically at the beat up chair and went to her. "It's a long story, but Ray and I think this will help." She looked around and asked, "Where is she?"

Mary pointed upstairs. "She says she isn't hungry, but I think she just feels very awkward. Maybe you and Ray can change her mind. We didn't tell her you were coming. We wanted it to be a surprise."

Mae and Ray climbed the stairs and knocked lightly at the closed door. There was no response. "Ma it's me, Mae. And Ray is with me. Can we come in?"

The bedsprings creaked, followed by the sound of hurried footsteps. Carrie opened the door and fell into the arms of her children. "Oh what a lovely surprise. Is Bert with you? Have you come to take me home?"

The two children looked at each other and back at their mother. "Not yet Ma, but soon we hope," Mae replied. "Bert is at his folks and sends his best. Mary has cooked a wonderful dinner and everyone wants you to join them at the table. Won't you please come down with us?"

Carrie stiffened slightly and then rubbed her eyes. It was then Mae noticed how sore they looked. "Ma, who is taking care of your eyes?" Carrie wiped them again. "I didn't want to bother anyone, so it just didn't get done."

Mae's heart fell. "Where are the drops? I'll do it right now and then I can show Big Pete's daughter how to do it. Susan is eighteen years old, and I'm sure she is very capable."

The moment the drops hit Carrie's eyes she felt a soothing comfort. She blinked and looked at her children. "You've come all this way. The least I can do is have dinner with you."

The threesome descended the stairs just as Pearl and Mary were ushering everyone into the dining room. After a slight pause, Big Pete went to Carrie. "I knew the smell of good food would bring you down." Everyone began to speak about the delicious aromas and the ice was broken.

When all had eaten their fill, and more, the women began the cleanup. Mary allowed Mae and Carrie to help clear the table and then announced, "Ladies, I have enough help in the kitchen and you only have the afternoon together. Why don't you use this time to visit?"

As soon as Carrie entered the parlor she saw the chair. "Oh," she cried. "Oh my. How? Did you and Ray bring it?" She was already in it when Mae answered. Carrie rocked and then looked at her daughter. "I suppose it's silly, but did I ever tell you the story of this chair? This survivor?"

Mae smiled. "Yes you did, but I'd love to hear it again." Ray joined them and Carrie momentarily forgot the troubles of the present to again recount the two big fires and how the chair had endured.

The afternoon passed too quickly and darkness soon settled in. Mary offered beds for them to stay the night but Ray and his sister declined, explaining the need to continue preparing the house for its new owners. Susan promised to treat Carrie's eyes and Mary handed a basket of leftover turkey and ham to Ray. Carrie had said her farewells in the parlor. There was already a marked change in her and Big Pete thanked them for coming and bringing the chair. "Who could have guessed?" he said as he shrugged his shoulders.

Thanksgiving came to an end. And tomorrow December would arrive.

Chapter 48

Bert helped Ray with the shed roof before returning to Port Huron, alone. The situation at hand was stressful for everyone, and Bert and Mae's marriage had suffered strains from the many separations. Mae planned to stay in Ubly through the seventh of December and then go home to her husband. That would give her ample time to prepare clothes, furniture, kitchenware, and canned goods for the move. Bert's parents had found someone to move the belongings provided they were boxed or crated and ready for transport. Ray had not decided when to leave for Port Huron. A lot depended on the outcome of his mother's stay at Bad Axe. For now he would remain at the farm.

Carrie became comfortable at Big Pete's. At least as comfortable as she could be, given the circumstances. The rocking chair had been a blessing, and Mary no longer found her underfoot. Carrie freely discussed the case, but only in generalities and gave no implications or insight into the mystery.

On December fifth, many buggies and other vehicles arrived in Bad Axe. There had also been an increase in train passengers to the town. The hearings of MacGregor and Gibbs had caused great curiosity and many people hoped to witness the event. They were disappointed to learn the proceedings had been delayed until the thirteenth. Both prosecution and defense agreed to the postponement. The prosecution needed the testimony of the Ann Arbor chemist who was tied up in another case, and the defense was expecting new developments—or so they said. The announcement was made late Monday afternoon and word did not reach the general public before the curiosity seekers began to arrive.

The swell of onlookers raised concern as to where to hold the examination. By expert accounts, the courthouse was considered unsafe and no one wanted to risk a catastrophe by overcrowding. But there were no other options at the present and it was hoped that word of the unsafe courthouse and the upcoming holiday would keep large crowds away.

On the thirteenth of December, the examination of Dr. Robert A. MacGregor in the death of Scyrel Sparling got underway. For whatever reason, the expected large crowds did not materialize and the hearing safely took place in the circuit courtroom before Justice Skinner. Ray was the first person questioned. He was an unwilling witness and his answers were short and often vague. Questioning continued for hours about each sickness, death, insurance, and other matters of a largely factual nature. He was even asked about the use of patent medicine. Ray's testimony gave victory to neither side and he left the courtroom tired and confused.

His ambiguity made him the topic of many whispered conversations. It wasn't clear if Ray was trying to protect his mother or the doctor. Or if his knowledge of all that had occurred over the past years was indeed limited. Perhaps he had selective amnesia, or maybe the horrible events had worn him to a frazzle. As Ray exited the courthouse, Big Pete hurried out after him. "Ray I don't want you to go back to Ubly tonight. They gave you the dickens today. You come home with me. We'll collect your belongings later." Ray was too exhausted to argue, and as they headed north, the chemist from Ann Arbor took the stand.

★ ★ ★

Twenty-six year old Roy Pryer gave a detailed description of the Marsh test he used on the viscera of Scyrel Sparling. That procedure had determined the young man had died of arsenic poisoning. He had also tested the embalming fluid. "Some undertakers use a fluid which contains arsenic and that could affect the outcome of any testing," he explained. He was later asked if he had tested any materials other than the viscera and embalming fluid.

Q. Did you examine a bottle labeled arsenic?
A. No.
Q. Did you examine a bottle labeled strychnine?
A. Yes sir.

At the mention of strychnine, whispers spread through the courtroom. This was something new.

Q. And did you determine if that bottle was correctly labeled?
A. Yes sir. It contained strychnine.

Mr. Pryer was asked a few more questions before being excused. It was too late in the day to continue with more witnesses and court was adjourned for the day.

★ ★ ★

John Sparling had been in court and when he reached home, put in a call to Big Pete. "Has Carrie said anything about a bottle of strychnine at the farm?"
"There's been no mention of it," Big Pete replied. "Why?"
"Apparently one was found out there," John yelled.
Big Pete's shoulders slumped. "Strychnine?" He heard the creak of Carrie's chair as she rocked in the parlor and lowered his voice. "I'll find a way to ask her about it John," he sighed. "But she hasn't told us much so far and I don't

think she'll start now." Big Pete noticed the creaking sound of the rocker had stopped. "By the way, I brought Ray home with me. I'm going to insist he stay with us for a while. I had an uneasy feeling in court this morning and well, I just plan to keep him here."

John was pleased. "Glad to hear it. The boy looks mighty poorly if you ask me."

Big Pete hung up the telephone and found Ray. "Come on young'n, there's work to do." Ray followed Big Pete to the barn. "I'll get set up in here and you go bring in the girls. George and Roy will be pleased as all get out to find the milking is done." When they finished that chore, Big Pete walked slowly to the house and Ray followed, almost like a puppy. Big Pete thought to himself, "I reckon he misses his pa and brothers more than any of us could guess."

"Ray," Big Pete declared, "as long as you are here, I'll be putting you to work. An honest day's work for room and board. How does that sound?"

Ray almost smiled. His pa's cousin was treating him as a grown-up and he liked it. "Sure Big Pete. That's more than fair."

Big Pete stopped and faced the boy. He put his strong arms on Ray's shoulders. "I heard about that patent medicine in court today. You promise that you didn't use it?" Big Pete looked stern. "Be honest with me son."

Ray paused. "Well I did take some stuff Doc brought out for Scyrel and me, for pimples. Made me feel funny and I didn't take it again. I don't know what happened to it. But patent medicine? No sir. I never did take any of that stuff."

Pete smiled. "Glad to hear it son. I don't allow any of that snake oil in my house. Now let's go see what Mary has for supper."

Mary smiled as she watched Ray eat. She didn't know where he was putting it, but he obviously found room. Carrie had had very little appetite since her arrival, but Mary didn't worry over it. Her upbringing held that when you got hungry, you ate. Besides, she had no time to pamper or plead. Carrie had been there three weeks, but it seemed much longer.

After supper Big Pete joined Carrie in the parlor and closed the door behind him. "Carrie," he began, "there's been testimony given about a bottle of poison, strychnine, found at your house. Can you account for it?"

Carrie rocked a moment and then stopped as she spoke. "I never had any strychnine about the house. Doc Conboy had some, but it was in tablets. If they found a bottle of poison in my home it was a put-up job, plain and simple." She was done talking and again commenced to rock.

* * *

Testimony resumed on Friday. The hired girl, Annie Pieruski, testified that at times when Dr. MacGregor came to the house, he and Mrs. Sparling would go into the bedroom and close the door. The defense weakened her testimony with two questions.

Q. Mrs. Pieruski, do you know why the doctor came to the house during the time you were there?
A. He put drops in her eyes, and he also. . . .

Annie blushed and put her head down.

A. And he treated her for something personal.
Q. I see. Now Mrs. Pieruski, if you yourself had this, let's call it a female ailment, and your doctor came to the house, a house with four sons, would you want the bedroom or examining room door shut?
A. (Still blushing). Of course.

Jacob Sparling, brother to Big Pete, recounted his visit to the farm before Scyrel died. He testified that when his Uncle John came out from seeing the patient he was very upset and seemed positive that the boy had been poisoned.

Coroner Morden's testimony was short and used to establish the fact that he had indeed delivered the viscera to Ann Arbor.

After a noon recess, Undertaker Hector McKay took the stand and most of his answers dealt with the post mortem.

Q. Tell us in detail everything that was said and done in that room.
A. After I got Scyrel on the cooling board, the doctors went on with the work of opening up the body.
Q. Tell just what they did please.
A. Dr. Holdship took the knife and used it himself. I held the light and Dr. MacGregor looked on and told us what to do. Told Holdship what organs to take out. They took out the spleen, the liver, and part of a lung. I believe they also took a kidney, but can't be sure. When they came to the liver, it was spotted or broke on one side, kind of raw looking. Dr. MacGregor said, "Here's the trouble." They put it on a plate and took it into the dining room to show the people there what the trouble was. I think Ed Hurford and Reverend Hurd were in the dining room. Maybe Ray too. Dr. MacGregor called it liver trouble. Or cancer of the liver.

They went back to the parlor then and Dr. Holdship cut a small piece off it, about an inch square, and put it in a two-quart sealer with some embalming fluid on it. He added a piece of the lung and spleen, I think. Then they left and I did my job.

When asked to describe the liver, he answered, "It looked raw and the shiny coating was gone. Part was honeycombed so you could run your finger through it. It seemed rotten."

Q. Did both doctors agree that the liver was cancerous in nature?
A. Yes sir.

Sheriff McAulay gave the final deposition. He also spoke about a bottle of strychnine but otherwise, his testimony related to conversations he had with Dr. MacGregor, including statements about arsenic and a looking glass.

Big Pete attended the afternoon session, and a reporter stopped him as he exited the courthouse. When asked about Mrs. Sparling's condition and the report of poison found, he replied, "Mrs. Sparling has been at my home for three weeks. She has made no statement that would implicate any other party, and says she still finds it hard to believe her sons were poisoned. As far as the mysterious bottle of poison, she said she owned no such bottle. If one was found, she—well let's just say it makes her suspicious."

Chapter 49

Reports of the court hearings caught the attention of people far and wide. And while Ray was giving his first day of testimony, the bodies of his father and oldest brother were being exhumed. When asked, the officials stated, "The bodies were exhumed to satisfy an imperative demand from the citizenry. Heart, liver, stomach, spleen, and kidney were removed from very well preserved cadavers, and these viscera are to be taken to Ann Arbor for examination."

* * *

Big Pete's uneasy feeling was accounted for on Saturday the sixteenth of December when he received a telephone call. He found Ray and took him into the parlor where they joined Carrie. He cleared his throat. "Carrie, I just heard from town. The sheriff is on his way and you are to be arrested. You know I will help you any way I can, but for now there is nothing we can do to stop it."

Carrie stopped rocking for a moment. "Will you let Mae know?" she asked.

"Mary is telephoning her right now," he replied. Carrie drew a deep breath. "I suppose I need to pack a few things." Ray stood silently with tears in his eyes.

Big Pete broke in. "For God's sake Carrie. It's either you or the doctor that did this. You better tell all you know, and soon."

Carrie gave a weak smile. "I've already told all I know. If anyone poisoned my boys it must have been the doctor, although I am not accusing anybody." She left the room and climbed the stairs to the bedroom she had been using.

About thirty minutes later, the sheriff drove into the yard. Big Pete's son Roy met him and offered to tend the horses, but McAulay declined. "We won't be here very long," he told him. Then he went to the house, apologized for the intrusion, and read the warrant to Carrie, charging her with the murder of her son.

She remained dry-eyed, but sniffles and sobs were heard coming from Ray and her cousins. "I'm ready to go Sheriff, but you must know this. I have told all there is to tell. I am completely free from guilt. I loved my boys and would never ever cause any harm to come to them." Mary helped her with her coat and Carrie went to the waiting buggy followed by McAulay, Big Pete, and his family.

Just before the sheriff slapped the reins to his team, Susan came running from the house carrying a small bottle. "Sheriff these are eye drops for cousin Carrie. She needs them every day. Please be sure someone does this for her." McAulay pocketed the medicine and said he would see to it.

As they left the farmyard, Roy nudged his father and Big Pete went over to Ray who was doing his best to hold back tears. "Let's have us a walk son," he said, and the two headed for a cold, bare orchard.

* * *

Big Pete and Ray met the mid-morning train to Bad Axe. When Mae arrived, they filled her in on details not covered by the telephone call of the day before. Immediately the group headed for the jail while church bells chimed in the distance. Thankfully, Carrie was brought to them in a visiting area and her children did not have to see her behind bars. Mae hugged her mother and asked about her eyes. "Sheriff McAulay's wife puts the drops in for me," she replied. Though left unsaid, it was obvious to everyone that somewhere in the confines of this building was the same doctor who had treated those sore eyes for years. Carrie looked pleadingly at her daughter. "Mae, I did nothing wrong. Now they say that Nurse Gibbs found a bottle of strychnine at the house. I thought she stayed on as our friend. Seems she had another reason. And when she couldn't find anything then they had to. . . ." She couldn't finish. Mae again held her mother and gave her a handkerchief. The room remained quiet for a few moments until Sheriff McAulay interrupted to announce the time for visiting had ended.

As they left the jail a reporter approached Mae and asked for a comment. Mae bristled and stepped between Big Pete and Ray. The three then went by buggy to Big Pete's home where Mary had Sunday dinner waiting. When dishes were done, Mary handed Mae a stack of letters from friends and relatives. They had been sent to Carrie during her stay there.

From Violet:
> My dear friend, I miss our mending chats and hope to come see you in Bad Axe before you leave for Port Huron.

From Reverend Hurd:
> Be strong Mrs. Sparling. And may God's peace, which passeth all understanding, envelop you and give you comfort.

From the Hurfords:
> Ed and I checked the farm the other day. Your children have left everything in excellent condition for the new owners.

From sister Cora:
> Carrie dear, we are all so saddened that tragedy upon tragedy has befallen you. Remember you are always welcome in our home.

From Little Pete:
> We are stunned by these injustices, but relieved to know you are with Big Pete and his family.

As the day drew to a close, Mae's Uncle William arrived. He had invited her to stay with him and his family in Bad Axe. It was closer to both the courthouse and jail. Mae hugged Ray and left with her uncle.

* * *

On Monday morning, Carrie appeared before Justice Skinner for arraignment and pleaded not guilty. She had obtained the services of attorney Paul Woodworth who asked for a hearing. It was set for the twenty-eighth of December. There were intimations that Carrie's defense would be to plead insanity. However, those close to her and those who had spoken with her felt insanity would be very hard to prove.

Huron County Tribune
Headlines from
December 1911 and January 1912

Chapter 50

The last two weeks of 1911 passed with great activity in the Thumb. Most of the populace busied themselves with Christmas shopping and baking. Schools presented long-rehearsed programs. A charity ball was held to benefit the hospital. And Bad Axe merchants were pleased with the trade they experienced. For many, there was relief that all the work involved in the holiday was nearly done. Others however experienced a different and deeper meaning of the holiday and vowed to never complain or take it for granted again.

Ida MacGregor visited her husband every day. She remained positive and confident during these visits, but once home her demeanor dissolved into uncertainty and fear. Mae also visited the jail daily to see her mother. Uncle William offered to drive her, but she preferred the walk. "I do my best thinking then," she explained. She treated Carrie's eyes if Mrs. McAulay had not yet been there, and mother and daughter tried to have normal conversations. The farmhouse in Ubly was now empty, and Bert reported everything had arrived safely in Port Huron.

Ray called on his mother every other day and each visit revealed a stronger, more assured young man. Living at Big Pete's seemed to have a most beneficial effect on his health and well being. If Carrie noticed she made no mention, but Mae was thrilled with his appearance. Privately she felt confident he had been saved from the fate of their father and brothers. As was bound to happen, Ida and Mae arrived at the jail together the Friday before Christmas. The women nodded at each other, but words were not spoken. It was just too awkward given the fact both were visiting accused murderers. Alleged murderers who had acted together in conspiracy, according to some.

* * *

Christmas Day, 1911

William and Ellen opened gifts right after breakfast. Mae bought a three-pound box of Virginia peanuts for the family and a new bed jacket for Grandmother Mary. She visited her mother once dishes were done, and then took the train to Ubly. Bert met her there and they drove to his parents for the Hurford celebration. She had given Ray a new shirt the day before, and accepted talcum powder from him. She never knew Ray to shop before and made a mental note to thank Mary for the prompting.

Big Pete and family waited until evening to open presents. They were pleased with the box of ribbon candy from Ray and he was equally happy with their gift of boots for farm work. He spent the afternoon with Carrie. Carrie cried after both her children had left. She had not been able to purchase so much as a package of raisins for them. They had assured her it didn't matter but, as a mother, she could not be convinced.

Carrie also had some surprise visitors that day. Little Pete and his Mary had arrived in Bad Axe on Christmas Eve. They visited with Carrie for thirty minutes of awkward conversation. Mary admired the new shawl Carrie had received from Mae, but didn't see the new handkerchiefs from Ray. Those had already been put to use.

Handkerchiefs were also a welcome gift for Dr. MacGregor. Few things were allowed into the jail, but the sheriff examined these packages and gave consent. Ida also gave her husband a book about courage. He regretted that he had nothing for her or the children, but she assured him Bonnie and Douglas had been amply gifted by his parents. As for herself, she needed nothing more than the love he had given her over the years. "Besides," she added, "once you are free we'll have a belated celebration."

* * *

Two days after Christmas Carrie received another visitor. Violet was inwardly shaking as she entered the jail. Ed had been very upset that she even wanted to enter that building. Carrie was brought to the visiting area and the two women hugged for a very long time. Words were hard to come by, but Violet felt her presence was enough. She had not been allowed to bring any bread to her friend, but that was a blessing. It would have made light of serious circumstances. After a while Carrie began to sob. And then, for the first time withholding nothing from her friend, Carrie unburdened her soul. When half an hour had passed, the sheriff told Mrs. Styles it was time to leave. As she left the jail, Violet's face was filled with shock and disbelief.

On the twenty-eighth, as agreed upon, Carrie Sparling came into Justice Skinner's court with her lawyer at her side. Once again Mr. Pryer from Ann Arbor was unavailable and the hearing was delayed until January tenth. Carrie returned to her cell having said absolutely nothing.

Chapter 51

Bitter cold broke records as 1912 began, and for ten straight days the night temperatures never rose to zero. A blizzard didn't help the situation. Train travel was delayed, and Carrie's examination had to be held in Justice Skinner's office due to a lack of heat in the circuit courtroom. After the previous postponement Mae had returned to Port Huron, but she was back on the tenth to help Ray support their mother. He was also there to be questioned.

Coroner Morden and undertaker McKay had already taken the stand. Nothing new was learned, as the questions were basically a repeat of those asked at MacGregor's hearing. Dr. Morden stated again the procedure by which viscera from Scyrel had been handled. Attorney Woodworth made no cross-examination, and asked Hector McKay only a few questions after his testimony. Ray was being sworn in when Mr. Pryer from Ann Arbor arrived late, due to the weather.

A short recess allowed Boomhower to meet with Pryer after which he approached the judge to ask for an adjournment. The judge allowed it, and a new date of January nineteenth was scheduled. Mae tried not to show her frustration. The trips back and forth were not the issue; it was the cancellations, rescheduling, and the effect they had on her mother. She could not stay there another nine days to wait for the next hearing and made plans to go home.

Rumors flowed regarding the sudden adjournment. While Boomhower said it was due to new evidence, two other possibilities were talked about among court employees. Some theorized there had been an incomplete examination of Scyrel's liver. Another supposition was that Dr. Vaughn, head of the Hygiene Department at Ann Arbor, needed to know specific, detailed, symptoms of Scyrel's illness to give a positive cause of death.

These postponements were certainly necessary for a fair trial, and attorneys on both sides welcomed the extra time to prepare their cases. But to those languishing behind bars, the delays brought depression and anxiety.

That week of delay passed slowly. Ray visited his mother regularly and continued to gain strength and self-assurance. Big Pete and William also called on her, but it was Mary and Ellen whose visits were most appreciated. The ladies knew what a woman in jail might need. They brought personal items not stocked in jails. Few women had ever been behind these Huron County bars.

When the nineteenth finally arrived, Mae sat behind Carrie as witnesses were called. Ray joined her after giving vague testimony similar to what he had given at MacGregor's hearing. Big Pete was called and his testimony centered on the visit he had made to the farm in October. "Any time Mrs. Sparling and I began to talk about the deaths, Nurse Gibbs would interrupt, saying, 'Mrs. Sparling, you know you are forbidden to talk'." Under cross-examination by Attorney Woodworth, Big Pete stated that he planned to stick by Mrs. Sparling as far as was right.

Sheriff McAulay testified about the bottle of strychnine found by the nurse and then Dr. Conboy took the stand. When asked his opinion as to the cause of Scyrel's death, he stated, "My diagnosis was and is poisoning by arsenic."

Under cross-examination he was asked, "If you suspected arsenic, did you ever mention it to the mother?"

Conboy repeated earlier testimony. "I said it appeared the boy had some poison in him and she agreed with me. She said it was probably caused by dust from threshing."

The last witness came as a surprise to Carrie. Louisa Richardson, a neighbor, took the stand and recalled a conversation she had with Mrs. Sparling after Albert died. "We were talking about insurance and I told Mrs. Sparling that life insurance might come in handy," she testified.

Boomhower asked for Carrie's reply. "Why," began Mrs. Richardson, "she said she was thinking of taking out more insurance and that she felt the worst was yet to come." Carrie vaguely remembered talking about insurance to Louisa, but could not recall saying anything about the worst to come. Her attorney, Mr. Woodworth, took some of the sting off Mrs. Richardson's remarks by asking how the Sparling family got along. "They were very kind to each other," she replied. "It was a very happy home."

* * *

At that point Xenophon Boomhower asked Justice Skinner that Carrie Sparling be held over to circuit court for trial. "This case should be thrashed out in court," he argued. Paul Woodworth gave strong argument against such action and Carrie's hopes were raised when she heard him say, "The place for this to be thrashed out is here and now. To be a beneficiary of an insurance policy is not a crime. I see no significance in the conversation these two women had. It was simply the talk of a woman mourning the death of her child. I ask that Mrs. Sparling be discharged."

Justice Skinner took very little time to announce his decision. "I find evidence that a crime has been committed. There is probable cause to believe her guilty as charged and I will bind her over to circuit court." Ray put his head down, Mae wept, but Carrie just sat stone-faced. She was allowed only a moment with her children before being whisked back to her cell.

Mr. Woodworth spoke to Mae and Ray to assure them he would do all in his power to get their mother released. When Mae asked if she should return to Port Huron, he suggested she stay in Bad Axe for the next few days. Big Pete and Ray drove Mae to Uncle William's. There was no talking among them except when Mae alighted from the buggy. Big Pete tried to be reassuring. "Mr. Woodworth is a good man, Mae. I know he will do everything he can to make things right." He didn't mention he had had a conversation with the lawyer before the hearing regarding possible bond. He didn't want their hopes to be raised and dashed once again.

Dr. MacGregor, who began his time in jail strong and optimistic, had slowly grown weaker and full of doubt. Even though Ida visited every day and his father once a week, the time in jail had taken a toll on the doctor. Many thought it ironic. Two people who had lived miles apart and yet managed daily visits were now only yards apart but never together.

* * *

On Monday, January twenty-second, Dr. Robert A. MacGregor was awarded bail by Judge Watson Beach of the circuit court. Prosecutor Boomhower had told the judge he was not ready for trial, and MacGregor's attorneys, Joe Walsh and George Clark, immediately asked that their client be granted bail. It was set at fifteen thousand dollars. The next day bondsmen were secured, and that afternoon Dr. MacGregor left the county jail. He took his first breath of fresh air in sixty-two days, and boarded the 3:12 p.m. train for Ubly. While waiting for the train, Attorney Clark had asked, "Robert, do you know your friends actually pledged ten thousand dollars more than what was needed? Seventeen men all contributed to your cause and I do believe had we needed more, we could have obtained it easily."

When MacGregor walked into his house and the arms of his family he was pale and thin, but his spirits were high. In fact he received four professional calls that afternoon and resumed his practice at once.

The terms of MacGregor's bail stated that he reappear in court on January thirtieth to hear a motion that his trial go over to the April term of the court. His troubles were not over, but the relief and joy he felt with this new freedom overshadowed that for now. Prosecutor Boomhower gave a statement to the press that the case against Dr. MacGregor would be pursued with renewed vigor come April. He also announced that an eminent criminal lawyer, Ernest Snow, would be brought in from Saginaw to assist him.

While MacGregor had boarded his train, Carrie Sparling was being arraigned. She entered a plea of not guilty and her attorney made a motion for bail, which was granted by Judge Beach. Big Pete Sparling and his eldest son, George, secured the declared amount of ten thousand dollars. Mae, who had gone to court with her mother, now understood why the attorney had suggested she remain in town. She thanked Big Pete and George repeatedly, and then mother and daughter walked to William and Ellen's house. Carrie refused the offer of a ride. She wanted to feel the brisk winter air on her face. Ray joined them for dinner but decided he would stay with Big Pete a while longer. George was soon to be married and Big Pete could use his help.

After supper Ellen showed Carrie to her room. Carrie looked around and quietly, but firmly, announced, "I think I would just as soon stay in jail. My life is ruined. But I will fight the charge to clear my name for the sake of my children."

Mae and Carrie took the Thursday morning train to Port Huron. When they arrived, several reporters were waiting. Carrie took one look and began to shake. Bert, showing unusual spunk, successfully thwarted any attempts to speak to his wife or mother-in-law. The Port Huron newspaper had been very aggressive in its coverage of events in the Thumb, and Bert knew it would continue. But for now they felt they had won a small victory and continued on to their house alone.

Carrie had never been to the Hurford home. The house was cramped with furnishings from the farm, but once she and Ray had their own home that problem would be solved. Mae opened a curtain showing her mother an ample back yard. "Bert said he'll find a good spot for you to have a garden. He knows how much you enjoy working in the soil." A tear tried to escape Carrie's eye, but she brushed it away.

Then Mae opened the door to Carrie's bedroom. There by a window sat the rocking chair. Mae smiled, "Big Pete crated it up and sent it here last week." Carrie clutched the bodice of her dress and went to the chair. She stroked the back before sitting down. Carrie caressed the arms of the chair and began to rock. Mae watched her mother for a moment before leaving, closing the door behind her.

* * *

Dr. MacGregor appeared in court on the thirtieth to hear both attorneys agree to a trial date in March. He then returned home and continued his medical practice. A few patients had left him for other physicians, but he had all the work he could handle. He could never erase the thought of what loomed ahead, but doctoring kept him busy and got him through each day.

On January 31, 1912, the coroner's jury met in Sanilac County after results were received from Ann Arbor. The report indicated that John Wesley Sparling and young Peter Sparling had no sign of organic disease to cause death. They also found no arsenic, but the bodies did have appreciable amounts of strychnine. It was decided no further action would be taken at this time, but the results were sent to Prosecutor Boomhower. After all, a bottle of strychnine had been found at the Sparling farm.

January of 1912 came to an end with no newsworthy events. Carrie Sparling remained in Port Huron under bail provided by her husband's cousins. Dr. MacGregor remained in Ubly under bail provided by friends and neighbors. Nurse Gibbs lived as before, with her sister in Port Huron. Attorneys Boomhower, Snow, Clark, Walsh, and Woodworth all began to prepare for the task ahead. The stage was being set.

Part Four
The Trial

Chapter 52

The calendar for the March term of the circuit court began Monday, March twenty-fifth, the day Ray Sparling quietly turned twenty-two. Newspaper headlines announced the courthouse had been deemed unsafe for the magnitude of the trial. Judge Beach had ordered props placed so as to support dangerous portions of some walls. During the reinforcing, more defects were discovered and the judge immediately issued a statement that the MacGregor trial would be held in Tribune Hall, located upstairs in the Huron County newspaper building.

His order was followed. Beach had never been considered the most preeminent jurist, but he always enjoyed the unswerving confidence of the people. They did not regard him as infallible, but believed wholeheartedly that whatever action he took was as right as humanly possible. If some didn't agree with his decisions, they never disputed his reputation for fairness. He was fair, but also stern, and his demeanor gave witness to all that he was in charge of his courtroom.

Attorneys for both sides continued to work tirelessly. Defense Attorney George Clark, though much thinner and tired-looking, appeared confident. He'd spent months studying the case from all angles with special emphasis on the medical and scientific aspects. His assistant, Captain Joseph Walsh of Port Huron, was considered a most able lawyer, but did not exhibit the same air of assurance as Clark.

Zen Boomhower had also pored over each part of the case. This would be his first major trial and he wanted no stone left unturned. He knew it would be difficult, but had no intention of letting his friendship with the accused interfere with his pursuit of justice. His assistant, Ernest Snow, seemed to garner the most attention. His extreme self-confidence gave many to believe him arrogant and overbearing. But those close to him knew Snow to be a person dedicated to his profession.

Carrie's attorney, Paul Woodworth of Bad Axe, prepared for his client's upcoming trial, but since no date had been set, he remained quietly in the background.

The case opened on Tuesday, April second, with jury selection. By Thursday, not a single juror had been selected from a pool of fifty. On Friday, Snow grilled possible juror Alfred Avery who became impatient. Avery suddenly blurted out, in front of everyone, that he thought MacGregor guilty. Clark leaped to his feet in protest and Avery was excused.

Clark then asked that the other jurors be excused as well due to possible prejudice following Avery's remark. Judge Beach refused that request.

On Saturday the sixth, the trial was halted. Attorney Clark put forth a new strategy to replace the jury pool by disputing the manner of jury selection. Each township should have submitted names for jury selection based on a percentage of its population. These figures were greatly skewed. Some had submitted too many names while others, not enough. It was only a technicality but, as Clark pointed out, still a matter of law. Judge Beach adjourned court to consider the motion.

The following Monday, the judge announced his decision. Lists with excessive names would be pared down, and those with insufficient names were to be discharged. He ordered new panels be obtained. Thus, twenty-five possible jurors were dismissed without ever being questioned. He adjourned court to Wednesday and Sheriff McAulay, with a force of deputies, scurried around the county in rigs, automobiles, and by train to subpoena new jury lists from those townships that had been discharged.

George Clark had won a partial victory. Though he had requested all possible jurors be removed, the actions to replace deficient lists worked in his favor. Of the original slate, only three jurors remained in the box.

A reporter later asked the attorney why he had not requested a change of venue. Clark answered that he had considered it, but when it became apparent a new jury panel would soon be selected, he didn't believe it would be approved.

Two headlines filled the front page of the April nineteenth issue of the Huron County Tribune. First was the report of a tragedy on the high seas. The Titanic, mightiest of ocean liners, had struck an iceberg and sunk, causing great loss of life. The second headline was news that the trial of Robert A. MacGregor was again adjourned, until April twenty-second. This postponement was caused by the illness of defense attorney George Clark. It was learned he had valiantly worked for his client despite a month long battle with malaria and fever. Dr. Herrington, on the previous Saturday, had ordered Mr. Clark to bed. It was then discovered the patient had developed typhoid fever and was to be admitted to the hospital. Clark would not be able to work on this case for at least two months. His assistant, Captain Joseph Walsh, asked for a continuation to the June term. Judge Beach labored over his decision, but he felt a responsibility to expedite a trial that had already had a number of delays and denied the request.

On Monday, April twenty-second, Judge Beach compromised slightly and adjourned the trial to May first to give Walsh extra time to prepare since he was now the head defense lawyer. Paul Woodworth, attorney for Carrie, would be his assistant. No one voiced discontent, or even surprise, that Carrie's lawyer would also be assisting in MacGregor's defense.

When the latest delay was announced, a sitting jury still had not been impaneled. Over one hundred possible jurors had been examined and excused. Some were dismissed because they were not citizens, some were over the established age limit, and some had shared their firm opinion as to guilt or innocence. One person was excused in absentia. He had been dead for over a year.

On May first, jury selection resumed and to the relief of all, a jury was secured. The following men were sent home to prepare for a possible long absence:

William Zeigler	Martin Sturm
Robert Bowman	Charles McDonald
Julius Armbruster	Henry Binder
Arthur Cooley	William Bannock
James Edwards	Henry Islee
William Keeler	Frank Peterson

These gentlemen would be sequestered at the Steadman Hotel during the trial that was now set to begin Monday, May sixth.

* * *

Ray thanked the Sparlings for their kindnesses. "I'll sure miss your good cooking Mary," he remarked. He then held out a hand to shake good-bye to Big Pete. The older man took his hand and drew the boy to him. "I understand your decision to be with your ma now," he acknowledged, "just know our home is always open to you. I think the girls might miss you." Ray boarded the train for Port Huron. He carried one satchel, his horn, and J.W.'s accordion.

Jury and two officials in the MacGregor Trial in Bad Axe

Xenophon A.
Boomhower
Prosecuting Attorney

Ernest A. Snow
Assistant to the
Prosecuting Attorney

Captain Joseph Walsh
Defense Attorney for
MacGregor

Paul Woodworth
Assistant to
Walsh

Judge Watson Beach

Sheriff Donald G. McAulay

Chapter 53

The trial finally began but, surprisingly, only a handful of people attended, many of them women. Suggestions that some testimony could be lurid did not discourage the fairer sex from attending. In fact, some speculated it might have even drawn them there.

Prosecutor Boomhower began the proceedings with his opening statement. "The crime of which the defendant is charged, is the murder of Scyrel Sparling by arsenic poison, administered on or about August fourth, 1911 and of which he died, August fourteenth, 1911. We expect to show that when arsenic is taken into the system it is rapidly eliminated, and after a period of from ten to twenty days, none will be left in the system. In this case we shall show you that every symptom manifested by Scyrel Sparling between the fourth and fourteenth of August was a symptom of arsenic poisoning. We will show you, by experts, that even after that period, arsenic was found in his liver. We shall go further and show you by Dr. Warthin of the University of Michigan, that Scyrel Sparling did not die from any disease.

"We shall show you that on August second, 1911, Scyrel Sparling was engaged in threshing at a farm in Bingham Township and was apparently in the best of health. That night he came home and the next day again worked on that farm. On the morning of the fourth, we will show you that he was not feeling very well. We shall show you by the defendant's own words that he attended Scyrel from then on. We shall show you that although on the fifth the boy did not appear to be very ill, the doctor was greatly alarmed about him, and that Dr. Herrington of Bad Axe was called. Evidence will be introduced to show that when the Bad Axe doctor came, he did not think that the boy was in a serious condition, but the defendant declared that he would not live and that his brother Ray would also die. On the seventh of the month Dr. Conboy, of Bad Axe, was called. The latter on his visit told Mrs. Sparling to stop giving the medicine to the boy and that he would come again the next day."

Boomhower continued to relate the events chronologically for the jury and then proceeded to give hints at what was to come. "We shall go back into 1908 and show the relationship existing between Mrs. Sparling and Dr. MacGregor even before the death of John Wesley Sparling, the woman's husband. We shall show that he had her under his control; that he practically ran the business of the Sparling farm after John Wesley Sparling's death." Boomhower went on to include information regarding the insurance policies and how one of them allowed the defendant to purchase a new automobile with cash money. He concluded with the following: "It will be shown to you that the motive for this crime was not only to secure insurance money, but also to secure the property on which the doctor lives, by means of the control he had over Mrs. Sparling. We shall show that he tried in various ways to throw suspicion off himself, and we will show that the whole affair was a conspiracy with the objective to divide the spoils."

Hector McKay was the prosecution's first witness.

QBoomhower. Mr. McKay, please tell us how you are connected with this case.

A. I am an undertaker in Ubly and was called to the Sparling home after Scyrel Sparling died.

QB. Were you present during the post mortem done by Doctors MacGregor and Holdship?

A. Yes sir.

QB. Mr. McKay, did the doctors remove the liver of the deceased?

A. Yes, right after they removed the spleen.

QB. And was anything said at that time?

A. Dr. Holdship took the liver out and laid it on Scyrel's breast. Dr. MacGregor pointed to it and said, "Here is what killed the boy, cancer of the liver."

QB. What did Dr. Holdship say?

A. He agreed with MacGregor.

QB. What about the stomach and intestines?

A. They were not removed.

QB. Was anything said about them?

A. Dr. Holdship picked them up and asked Dr. MacGregor whether he should take them out.

QB. What did MacGregor say?

A. He said, "They look good to me."

Boomhower, relieved to finally begin the trial, sat down and Joseph Walsh stood for cross-examination. He privately hoped he was prepared to defend his client without the help of George Clark.

QWalsh. Mr. McKay, you have been an undertaker for some time now, is that correct?

A. Yes sir.

QW. Have you ever seen a cancerous liver before?

A. I'm not a doctor, but I've seen some pretty bad livers.

QW. You stated that both doctors agreed the liver was cancerous. Did you agree with them?

A. As I said before, I am not a doctor. But that liver looked real bad. It was spotty and one side was broken off. It didn't have the normal shiny coating. It looked raw and there were ulcers on it. There were sores and part of it looked like a honeycomb.

QW. After the liver was removed, what was done with it?

A. They put it on a plate and took it to the dining room.

QW. Why did they do that?

A. To show people that the liver caused Scyrel to die.

QW. What people?

A. Reverend Hurd was there. And Ed Hurford. I think Ray might have been with them too.

QW. Now Mr. McKay, you described the liver to this court. Do you suppose the doctors, seeing the friable nature of the organ, could easily claim cancer to be the cause?

A. I suppose so.

QW. What was done with the organs that were removed?

A. A good chunk of the liver, maybe three to five pounds, was put in a crock. A small piece was put in a two-quart sealer along with the spleen. I covered both with Red Falcon embalming solution.

QW. What happened to these containers?

A. MacGregor took the sealer with him.

QW. And the crock?

A. It stayed in the parlor. When I finished with the body, I straightened the room, covered the crock, and put it under the cooling board.

Hector McKay was excused and, due to the lateness of the day, court was adjourned until the next day. Robert MacGregor spoke with his attorneys and looked at Zen before leaving. He could not catch his old friend's eye and didn't know what he would have done had he been able.

Dr. Daniel Conboy took the witness stand Tuesday morning and Attorney Snow conducted the interrogation.

QSnow. Dr. Conboy, how did you come to be involved in Scyrel Sparling's treatment?

A. I was called to the Sparling home by Dr. MacGregor on August seventh.

QS. What was Scyrel's condition when you arrived on the seventh?

A. He had pain in his abdomen and his mouth was inflamed. His pulse was running near one hundred and he was very weak.

QS. Did you examine him for disease?

A. Yes I did.

QS. And what did you find?

A. I found no infectious disease in the lad.

QS. Did you suggest any treatment at that time?

A. Yes, I gave the opinion that all medicines should be discontinued for the present. That is, all medicines he had been taking. I left some strychnine tablets for them to administer so the family would not feel that nothing was being done for their loved one.

QS. But Dr. Conboy, isn't strychnine a poison?

A. Only when overdosed. In small, controlled amounts, it acts as a tonic, a stimulant to the heart muscles.

QS. Did you have occasion to speak to the boy's mother?

A. Yes. I said her son was very ill with some kind of poison in his system.

QS. What was her response?

A. She thought a moment and then agreed with me. Said he'd come home, after threshing, covered with dust and she wouldn't be surprised if his whole system was poisoned.

QS. When you left the sick room did anything unusual occur?

A. Dr. MacGregor followed me out of the room and asked, "What are you thinking, are you thinking arsenic?"

QS. What did you say?

A. I said that I was.

QS. And what, if anything, did MacGregor say?

A. He said, "That is odd. I was thinking of the same thing."

QS. Did he say anything else?

A. Yes, he told me he believed the others had died in the same way.

"Objection," cried Joseph Walsh. "I move that last answer be stricken from the record." Judge Beach denied the motion saying, "I will permit mention of the deaths of other family members."

QS. What else did he say at that time?

A. He said he thought Ray would die too.

Another objection by Walsh was likewise denied. He shook his head and sat down. Robert MacGregor closed his eyes briefly and then stared at the table in front of him.

QS. What was the condition of Scyrel on August eighth?

A. There was no change. Dr. MacGregor told me the only medicine given was my tablets. He also said he gave the lad an enema.

QS. Did you examine the boy yourself?

A. No. Dr. MacGregor told me the boy had tenesmus, the urge to urinate or defecate without result. I took his word for it and didn't bother the young man with further probing.

QS. When you left the farm, what did you do?

A. I went to see Zen Boomhower.

QS. Did you discuss Scyrel Sparling with him?

A. Yes. Zen, Mr. Boomhower, said if the boy died he would order a post mortem.

QS. What happened then?

Conboy repeated the sequence of events that led up to the hiring of Nurse Gibbs.

QS. Did Mr. Boomhower say anything at that time as to his suspicions that Mrs. Sparling was poisoning her son?

A. Not in so many words. We had no proof, so words were carefully chosen. The subject of the conversation was that the boy was being poisoned and needed to be watched closely.

QS. Did Dr. MacGregor state any suspicions he had regarding the mother being responsible for the poison?

A. He appeared to put the blame on her. I don't know how to explain it. He didn't say anything for a fact. He just spoke underhandedly.

Joseph Walsh leaped to his feet and objected to the word underhandedly. The judge sustained the objection and the word was stricken from the record.

Dr. Conboy then rephrased his statement saying that Dr. MacGregor hinted about Mrs. Sparling, but never made any actual accusation. The court called a recess for dinner and Officer Joseph Murray escorted the jury to the Steadman. Court resumed at one o'clock.

QS. Dr. Conboy, when did you next go out to the Sparling farm?

A. I went back the next day, August ninth.

QS. And were you called out there by Dr. MacGregor?

A. No, Prosecutor Boomhower suggested I go.

QS. Did he say why?

A. He wanted me to talk to Mrs. Sparling.

QS. How did the doctor react to your appearance?

A. He seemed surprised. When I told him I was going to try to scare Mrs. Sparling so she wouldn't give any more poison. . . .

He looked at Joseph Walsh who was rising to his feet.

A. . . . . if she was doing so.

Walsh sat down.

QS. Did the defendant respond?

A. Dr. MacGregor told me he had already seen to that.

QS. Did you examine Scyrel?

A. Yes. He was about the same except his eyes looked some better. He told me his hands and legs felt tingly.

QS. Dr. Conboy, what do you think caused the death of Scyrel Sparling?

Joseph Walsh objected to the question but Judge Beach said the question was crucial. He ordered a brief recess while Officer Murray took the jury for a short walk. Walsh and Snow argued the question's admittance. "Dr. Conboy had no proof at that time," began Walsh. "And his answer would only be speculation."

Attorney Snow made his argument. "Dr. Conboy saw the boy three times before he died," he said. "And he certainly has an educated opinion as to cause of death."

Judge Beach again stated that the question was crucial and he would allow it. The jury returned and questioning continued. Snow looked at Walsh with a slight smile and began.

QS. Dr. Conboy, I ask you again. In your opinion, what caused the death of Scyrel Sparling?

A. I believe he died of arsenic poisoning.

QS. Dr. Conboy, you saw the patient on three successive days. Did you see him again before he died?

A. Yes, Dr. MacGregor called me and asked me to come out to the farm. He said I could ride with Dr. Herrington who had also been called.

QS. What day was this?

A. It was August thirteenth, a Sunday.

QS. And did you go?
A. Yes. Dr. Herrington and I arrived about four in the afternoon. Dr. Holdship was there and he and Dr. Herrington walked toward the house together.
QS. Did you walk with them?
A. I was with Dr. MacGregor. He came over to me as soon as we arrived.
QS. Did he say anything to you?
A. Yes, but it was hard to hear him.
QS. What do you mean?
A. He talked very low and very quiet. He wondered if Dr. Herrington knew about the arsenic.
QS. And did he?
A. No. Dr. Herrington had only been told that poison was suspected.
QS. Was there any further discussion?
A. No, I felt uncomfortable talking in whispers. Besides we had reached the house.
QS. What was your diagnosis when you saw Scyrel on that day?
A. I knew the young man was near death. In fact, he died the next day.

Attorney Snow asked Dr. Conboy to testify as to the symptoms of arsenic poisoning. "There is vomiting and purging," he explained. "Pain travels across the abdomen. The lining of the throat, mouth, and nostrils become inflamed or congested. Nerves are later affected and the patient experiences tingling and numbness in the limbs. Paralysis can follow. Pulse is weak, feeble, and slow or it can be rapid, weak, and fast. There is hardly any fever to speak of."

QS. Dr. Conboy, in a post mortem if you lifted the stomach say, three inches from the body cavity, could you distinguish its condition?
A. Not in regard to inflammation, no.
QS. Are you saying that if inflammation of the stomach occurs, it is observed on the inside?
A. Yes, in the stomach lining.
QS. And what would you expect to see?
A. If a person died from arsenic poisoning, the lining of the stomach would be red and congested.
QS. When did you next see the defendant?
A. He came to my office the day after Scyrel died and brought the two-quart sealer with the liver, spleen, and so forth.

QS. Was anyone else there?

A. Yes, Dr. Herrington.

QS. What conversation took place at that time?

A. Dr. Herrington asked about the stomach and intestines.

QS. How did the defendant answer?

A. He said they were all right.

QS. Anything else?

A. Dr. Herrington asked if they had cut into those organs during the post mortem and Dr. MacGregor said that they had been opened.

At this point Dr. MacGregor became agitated and nudged Walsh's arm. He whispered furiously to him. Judge Beach asked if there was a problem and Walsh said no as he calmed his client.

QS. Dr. Conboy, you described the symptoms of arsenic poisoning to this court. Would you agree that the other deceased members of the Sparling family exhibited these same symptoms?

Before Dr. Conboy could answer, Joseph Walsh burst from his seat. "Your Honor, I must vigorously object to bringing other family members into this trial."

Judge Beach asked all attorneys to come before him. He then adjourned court until Wednesday and the hall was emptied of jury, witnesses, defendant, and observers.

Ernest Snow spoke first. "Your Honor, we feel we are not only correct, but impelled to bring up the case of Albert Sparling while Dr. Conboy is on the stand. He observed symptoms in both patients and can give vital information as to the cause for both their deaths. It will show conspiracy."

Judge Beach asked, "And how can you tie Dr. MacGregor to the death of Albert during a trial for the murder of Scyrel?" Snow responded. "We will show, your Honor, that the defendant's intent was to eliminate the heirs to the Sparling estate. He was already living in a house purchased for the boys. As long as those boys were alive, he could not expect to own the property outright." Judge Beach looked over his spectacles at Snow. "And can you prove intent?" he asked. Snow was quick to respond. "We will show the court Dr. MacGregor's patterns. He became a close advisor, a confidant to Mrs. Sparling. She was under his spell. When Albert died, he was insured for two thousand dollars and we will show that the defendant and Mrs. Sparling divided that money between them."

Walsh interrupted. "Your Honor, Mr. Snow has really stretched this case into fantasy. How can he possibly read the mind and intent of a person he barely knows?

We are here to learn who caused Scyrel Sparling's death. If Albert's demise can be brought under this umbrella, where will it end? Will my Aunt Sadie's death also be opened up for the jury and court observers? Court is here to provide and share proofs. There is no proof available as to my client's intent to own a property." Judge Beach then addressed Zen Boomhower. "Do you have any proof as to the cause of Albert Sparling's death?" Boomhower answered. "Only the circumstances concerning his death. We intend to show what was said and done in regard to the illness and treatment of Albert, and remarks made by the defendant himself." Judge Beach took the arguments to his chambers alone.

After careful consideration, Judge Beach told the attorneys that while arsenic was agreed upon as cause of death for Scyrel, there had been no proof given of criminal intent, and the question of mistake or accident had not been eliminated. "The case as it now stands," he stated, "has shown little to no testimony of any crime committed by Dr. MacGregor. Without proof of a crime, testimony regarding the death of Albert could prejudice the jury. If further testimony shows criminal intent by way of autopsy, incidents, and or circumstances on the part of Dr. MacGregor, I shall consider allowing Dr. Conboy's testimony to include the death of Albert Sparling. But not now."

After Judge Beach handed down his decision on the matter, Snow asked if the witness, Dr. Conboy, could be withdrawn and recalled at a later time. Joseph Walsh protested that he had the right to cross-examine the doctor as far as he had testified. But Snow insisted that he did not want any cross-examination to take place until he was done completely with the witness. "We have been told by the court that our next line of questions for this witness must wait for further information. When we have finished, Mr. Walsh, he will be all yours."

Walsh was not satisfied. "Your Honor, I must take exception if I am not allowed to cross-examine this witness here and now as to what he has just testified."

By this time both Snow and Walsh were red-faced and shouting. Judge Beach ordered them to stop at once and Snow responded, "Your Honor, I was only trying to straighten Walsh out."

Walsh shouted, "If he wants to straighten me out, he need only name the time and place!"

Judge Beach pounded his gavel. "Gentlemen, this court is closed for today. I have ruled on your concerns and the matter is ended. I suggest you both retire to a good meal and a sound night's sleep. We have a long way to go and I'll not have my court interrupted by your childish behaviors." Privately, the judge wondered how fisticuffs would have turned out. Walsh was an ex-college athlete and Snow, a six-footer of powerful proportions.

Chapter 54

On Wednesday morning, Judge Beach announced to the court that Dr. Conboy's testimony and cross-examination would continue at a later date. He then asked the prosecution to proceed and Dr. Herrington took the stand. The doctor told the court he had called upon Scyrel Sparling twice. The first time he observed no indication of illness other than an upset stomach. "However," he testified, "Dr. MacGregor told me all the other Sparlings had been taken the same way, and he expected Ray to also succumb. The second time I saw the boy it was obvious that nothing could be done to save him." Walsh then began his cross-examination.

QWalsh. Dr. Herrington, you said the boy did not seem all that ill when you first examined him?
A. Yes.
QW. Do you now have any concerns that you may have missed something important?
A. Mr. Walsh, physicians are always troubled when someone we have been treating dies. However, I stand by my original opinion. When I first saw Scyrel Sparling on August fifth, he showed none of the symptoms I saw the day before he died.

Dr. Herrington was excused and Joseph Walsh hoped his disappointment did not show. He had wanted Herrington to admit that doctors, including himself, could make mistakes. He got that, but not in the way he wanted. Herrington had come across as humble, not arrogant. Dr. MacGregor looked confused; he did not understand why his attorney had excused Herrington immediately after a potentially damaging statement.

Ernest Snow, however, was pleased with Herrington's last statement and noticed the jury had been listening very carefully. He hesitated a moment to let it sink in before calling Dr. Holdship to the stand.

QSnow. Dr. Holdship, you performed the post mortem on Scyrel Sparling, is that correct?
A. Yes sir. Under the direction of Dr. MacGregor.
QS. You heard Mr. McKay testify that you agreed with the defendant's cause of death?
A. Yes sir. I heard that.

QS. Is it true?

A. Sort of.

QS. What does 'sort of' mean?

A. Dr. MacGregor is a more experienced physician, and he was county coroner for a time. If he looked at the liver and diagnosed cancer, who was I to argue?

QS. Do you still believe that liver was cancerous?

A. In light of all that has happened, I would say definitely not.

QS. When the defendant said you did not need to cut into the stomach or intestines, were you also bowing to the perceived impression of his superiority?

A. Excuse me?

QS. Why didn't you open the stomach and intestines?

A. I was told it wasn't necessary.

A very confident Ernest Snow thanked the doctor and sat down as a very nervous Joseph Walsh approached.

QWalsh. Dr. Holdship, did you know at the time of the post mortem how to identify cancer of the liver?

A. No sir. It has been my understanding that an ordinary examination of an organ will not reveal cause of death. It must be ascertained by a person specializing in the field of pathology.

QW. And yet you agreed with Dr. MacGregor, took the liver into the dining room, and pronounced cancer is what took the boy.

A. Yes. At that time I agreed with Dr. MacGregor.

QW. When you finished the post mortem, did you state the cause of death?

A. Did I?

QW. That was the question.

A. I just agreed with Dr. MacGregor.

QW. I didn't ask you about agreeing. I asked if you stated the cause of death.

A. Yes, I made a statement.

QW. Did you speak the truth?

A. I don't think so.

QW. Were you stating an untruth at that time?

A. No sir.

QW. Let me understand. You stated the truth at that time as you believed it?

A. It was a mistake.

QW. Did you state the truth as you believed it at the time?
A. Yes.
QW. So at that time you believed the cause of death to be cancer of the liver.
A. Well, I don't know.

Mr. Snow stood and addressed the bench. "Your Honor, I insist this witness be treated fairly. He has answered the question, more than once." Judge Beach replied, "I agree Mr. Walsh. The question was to what Dr. Holdship believed and he has answered." Walsh tried to argue, "But your Honor, I asked him if his belief was—" Judge Beach did not let him finish. "He said he didn't know. Proceed Mr. Walsh."

QW. Dr. Holdship, let's make this easy on everyone. On the night you conducted the post mortem, did you or did you not believe the liver to be cancerous?
A. I can't say. I am not a pathologist.
QW. I will try again. I am not asking you if you are a pathologist. I am not asking if you have since learned you were right or wrong. Did you, on that night, state that you believed Scyrel Sparling died of liver cancer?
A. I stated that he died from liver cancer, yes.
QW. Thank you, Dr. Holdship.

Judge Beach called for a dinner recess and a frustrated Walsh and a bedraggled Dr. Holdship each drew a long sigh. As Holdship left the stand, Dr. MacGregor looked at him, but the former colleague would not meet his gaze as he scurried out of the courtroom. After Holdship passed, MacGregor saw Boomhower looking at him, but when their eyes met Zen turned away. MacGregor looked down at the table; it could not avoid him.

That same day, in Port Huron, Bert Hurford came home for dinner. Mae greeted him with a huge hug and motioned for him to follow her. She led him to the window overlooking the back yard. Carrie was busy cleaning off the garden space he had dug. "This is the first she has been outdoors," Mae said. "It's also the longest she has been away from that old chair. Perhaps she has turned a corner." Bert was not convinced, but kept his doubt to himself. He knew the trial was in the early stages. He smiled. "Let's hope so Mae. Still, we need to keep newspapers and reporters away from your mother."

Chapter 55

Afternoon court resumed with Coroner Morden on the stand, questioned by Attorney Snow.

QSnow. Dr. Morden, as I understand it you had planned to perform the post mortem on young Scyrel, correct?

A. That is correct.

QS. But we know now that you did not. Can you explain?

A. An emergency came up and I told Dr. MacGregor I would be out first thing in the morning to conduct the autopsy.

QS. And did you go out there the next morning?

A. No, I had another emergency and did not finish until almost noon.

QS. Dr. Morden, when did you actually reach the farm?

A. I was getting ready to go when Dr. MacGregor came up to me in Bad Axe and told me the post mortem was already done.

QS. Were you surprised, maybe even angry?

A. I wasn't angry but yes, I was surprised. I asked about the viscera and he told me what had been done with it. Then I went to Ubly.

QS. What was the purpose in that, if the procedure was already done?

A. I was going to impanel a jury in Ubly to prepare for an inquest.

QS. And did you?

A. Yes, I went with Mr. Boomhower and Sheriff McAulay.

QS. Who was at the farm when you arrived?

A. Some neighbors and I assume Mrs. Sparling was there, although I didn't see her.

QS. Was the defendant there?

A. Yes, he must have left Bad Axe about the same time we did. He asked if I had any objections to his being there and I told him I didn't.

QS. I understand the nurse had kept an account of the boy's illness. Did you see that record?

A. Yes, and it was troubling.

QS. How so?

A. I noticed that the patient had vomited blood and I asked Dr. MacGregor if he had opened the stomach to account for it.

QS. And his reply?

A. He said that he had and it looked normal.

QS. Was there anything else troublesome?

A. Yes, the record showed that Scyrel had bloody stools. Again I asked the doctor if he had opened the intestines. He said he had and they looked fine.

QS. Dr. Morden, what would bloody vomit and bloody stools indicate to a physician?

A. It would indicate irritation, congestion, and possible laceration.

QS. And would this be visible from the outside?

A. Absolutely not. Those organs would have to be cut into.

QS. And did the defendant tell you he had done that?

A. Yes he did.

QS. Dr. Morden, when you viewed the body at the house could you have opened the stomach and intestines?

A. Sure.

QS. Then why didn't you?

A. Because I'd just been told it had already been done.

Attorney Snow said he was done with the witness. Judge Beach addressed Attorney Walsh. "It's getting late. Would you prefer to cross-examine this witness in the morning?" Joseph Walsh smiled and said, "No your Honor." He approached Dr. Morden. "I won't need much time."

QWalsh. Dr. Morden, have you ever had reason to question Dr. MacGregor's capabilities, honesty, or ethics?

A. No sir.

QW. Dr. Morden, I have a copy of Dr. MacGregor's testimony from the inquest of October twelfth, 1911. Do you recognize this as being the authentic testimony given on that day?

A. Yes I do.

QW. And Doctor, would you please tell the court who signed this document on page fourteen.

A. Dr. MacGregor did.

QW. Ah, but there is another signature as well. Would you please read the area I have circled to this court?

A. Subscribed and sworn to before me this twelfth day of October 1911. C.B. Morden, Coroner. Yes, I signed it.

QW. Now Dr. Morden, please turn back to page thirteen and read the testimony I have circled.

Question by Morden – In what condition were the other organs of the body, the stomach?

Answer by MacGregor – As far as I could see it looked normal.

Question by Morden – You looked at the intestines?

Answer by MacGregor – Yes, sir.

Question by Morden – How did they look?

Answer by MacGregor – They looked normal too.

Question by Morden – Did Dr. Holdship open up the stomach to see if there were any lesions in it?

There was a hesitation from Dr. Morden, and Attorney Walsh encouraged him to continue reading. Morden looked at Boomhower and Snow and then read on, quietly.

Answer by MacGregor – If he did, I did not see him.

Walsh pretended he could not hear and asked the witness to speak up. Morden begrudgingly repeated the statement. Attorney Walsh, clearly pleased, remarked, "Well Doctor, it seems you were indeed told by Dr. MacGregor that the stomach was not opened. I have no further questions."

Judge Beach asked, "Any redirect?"

Ernest Snow stood. "I have just one your Honor."

QSnow. Dr. Morden, do you still maintain that regardless of his previous testimony, the defendant told you person-to-person that he did open the stomach and intestines?

A. Yes sir, that is what I recall.

Court adjourned for the day.

Chapter 56

On Thursday, Alexander MacGregor was in court and, for the first time, Ida MacGregor appeared. They sat behind Dr. MacGregor and his attorney. Big Pete and Ray Sparling also sat together and when Ray was called to the stand, people noticed a difference. He looked stronger and much healthier than before. Snow was anxious to question Ray and, with a confident smile, began.

QSnow. Ray, where are you now living?
A. In Port Huron.
QS. Do you know the defendant's attorney, Mr. Walsh?
A. Well I been to his office with Ma.
QS. Did you discuss this case?
A. Not really. We had to sign more papers about the sale of the farm.

Attorney Snow continued to hammer the same questions at Ray. How well did he know and how often did he visit Mr. Walsh. Finally Walsh objected. "Your Honor, the witness has already answered. There is no point in these questions." Without hesitation, Snow glared at Walsh and replied, "I'm wondering why Mrs. Sparling went to the defendant's attorney." Snow looked at MacGregor and then back at the judge. "My questions are necessary for the purpose of showing a conspiracy between the defendant in this case and Mrs. Sparling."

Several eyes in the hall turned to look at Ida MacGregor who leaned forward and put her hand on her husband's shoulder. He reached back and held her hand. Walsh erupted as he leaped to his feet. "I take exception to that, a very improper remark!" Judge Beach pounded his gavel. "It may be answered, but let the jury know this. It may be answered to show the attitude of the witness and not, I repeat not, to lend credence to a possible conspiracy."

Snow willingly gave up that path of questioning and moved on to Dr. MacGregor's treatment of the family. He had successfully planted the conspiracy theory.

QS. Did Dr. MacGregor give your family medicine?
A. Of course.
QS. Do you know what kind of medicine?
A. Sometimes he gave us medicine for pimples.

QS. Pimples? Did he give Scyrel pimple medicine before he died?
A. I don't know.
QS. Was the defendant your family's main physician?
A. Yes.
QS. How was Scyrel's health before he died?
A. He was sick.
QS. I mean before he took sick. Did he like to mix it up with others? Was he strong?
A. Sure.

Snow spent a long time drawing from Ray a timetable of when and where Scyrel got sick, and a few jurors had to stifle yawns.

QS. Ray, when the defendant came to see your brother did he bring any medicine?
A. I don't know.
QS. Were you concerned about your brother?
A. Of course I was.
QS. But you say you don't know if the defendant gave him any medicine?
A. I didn't see any.
QS. How often did the defendant come to your house?
A. Whenever anybody was sick.
QS. Did he come when nobody was sick?
A. He came to treat Ma's eyes.

Snow tried not to show his frustration. His hopes had been to show, through Ray, that not all the Sparling family trusted Dr. MacGregor. He walked away from the witness and went to his table.

Ray sat expectantly, his legs jiggling under the table. He was trying so hard to do the right thing, but had no one to guide or direct him. He just wanted this to be over and done.

Snow took a deep breath and again approached the witness stand.

QS. Ray, was the defendant at your house every other day during your brother's illness?
A. I suppose so. He was trying to help.
QS. And did he help him?
A. I don't know.

QS. Let me put it another way. Did your brother die after the doctor treated him?

Walsh stood "Your Honor, I object to the suggestion in that question." The judge agreed and ordered Snow to rephrase.

QS. Did your brother die?
A. Yes.
QS. Ray let's go back to before Scyrel died. Did you help fix up the house where the defendant lives?
A. Sure, we all helped.
QS. Did you think the house was a gift to him?
A. I don't know.
QS. Didn't your mother buy it as an investment for you boys?
A. I don't know.
QS. Has the defendant ever paid rent while he has lived there?
A. I don't know.
QS. Ray, there are certainly a lot of things you don't know. Let's go back a bit more. All you boys carried life insurance?
A. Yes.
QS. What companies did you use?
A. Sun and Gleaners.
QS. Why did you take out life insurance? You all were healthy farm boys, weren't you?
A. Thought it was a good idea, that's all.
QS. Who helped you with the Sun insurance?
A. Dr. MacGregor. He said his father could give us a good deal and it wouldn't cost a lot of money.
QS. Who examined you for that insurance?
A. Dr. MacGregor.
QS. And did he say you were all healthy?
A. Sure.
QS. Ray, did any of your brothers have hernia surgery?
A. Yes, both Albert and Scyrel.
QS. Do you know how much the operations cost?
A. We got a mortgage for two hundred dollars when Albert went. He was first. When Scyrel went, we got another mortgage for seven hundred dollars. It paid off the first mortgage and also Scyrel's operation.
QS. Did your mother pay the defendant to go with them?
A. Yes, fifty dollars each time.

QS. Now go back to the time after Albert died. An insurance check from Sun Life Assurance came to your mother, is that correct?

A. Yes.

QS. What was the amount of the check?

A. One thousand dollars.

QS. And what did she do with that money?

A. Ma gave it to Dr. MacGregor.

QS. Why?

A. Because we owed him.

QS. Did your mother give the defendant more money after that?

A. I guess if we owed it, she did.

QS. Ray, who was the insurance check made out to?

A. Ma.

QS. Not Albert's estate?

A. No, she had trouble getting Peter's insurance, so they filled out some papers so she could get the insurance money without going through court.

QS. Who is 'they'?

A. Dr. MacGregor helped Ma.

QS. Ray, did you boys have a milk route?

A. Yes.

QS. Did you ever take cream to the defendant's house? I mean to where he lived?

A. Sometimes.

QS. Didn't you take some every day?

A. No sir.

QS. Did the defendant pay you for it?

A. I don't know.

Ernest Snow, thoroughly dissatisfied with Ray, gave up and took his seat. Judge Beach called a recess for dinner and, as before, the jurors followed Officer Murray to the Steadman Hotel.

Big Pete watched the jury leave. He was torn as to what to do. He had vowed to stick by Carrie, which is why he helped provide her bond. But Ray's testimony had done nothing to implicate the doctor and that caused Big Pete to rethink his position. He finally made a decision, a very difficult one.

He quickly made his way to Attorneys Walsh and Woodworth and motioned for Ray to join them. "Ray, I know this has been very hard for you. But did you hear yourself on the stand? It sounded like you were helping

MacGregor. If the doctor didn't give the arsenic, that leaves only one possibility." He tried to catch Ray's eye, but the boy's head was down. He turned to the attorneys. "Mr. Walsh, Mr. Woodworth, I'm afraid George and I can't stay on Carrie's bond any longer. I'm sorry. I supported her a long time, but things look different now."

Walsh and Woodworth could see that Big Pete's mind was set and began to explain the procedures that would release him from Carrie's bond. Ray was stunned. And hurt. He went to a back corner of the courtroom and tried to eat the lunch he had brought. He had never felt more alone in his life.

In the afternoon, Ray was again on the stand for cross-examination. His uneaten lunch remained in the corner and Big Pete was gone.

QWalsh. Ray, did you and I meet before this trial?
A. Yes.
QW. Why was that?
A. There were more papers to sign about selling the farm. Seems there was always more papers to sign.

Two jurors and several observers nodded in the affirmative.

QW. Did we discuss this case at that time?
A. I only remember signing papers.
QW. How long has Dr. MacGregor treated your family?
A. I don't know, maybe five or six years.
QW. Were you or any of your family unhappy with his care?
A. Not that I know of.
QW. You were asked about the doctor giving you or your brothers medicine.
A. I answered that.
QW. Yes you did. If Dr. MacGregor had given medicine to your family, would that be unusual?
A. No, that's what doctors do.
QW. Do you think Dr. MacGregor did everything possible to save Scyrel's life?
A. I don't know. Why wouldn't he?
QW. Indeed, indeed. Ray, you helped fix up the house Dr. MacGregor lives in. Does that seem wrong to you?
A. No. He needed a place to live and we had an empty house.
QW. That is a very generous attitude. About the life insurance for you healthy boys. Were you the only healthy boys in Huron County to carry life insurance?
A. I don't think so. Lots of my friends have it.

QW. So you don't think there is anything wrong with having life insurance.
A. No. If something happens. . . .

He hesitated and his voice began to tremble.

A. . . . . that money would help keep my pa's farm going.
QW. Why did Dr. MacGregor go with Albert and Scyrel for their hernia surgeries?
A. I don't know. We didn't have a pa and they were embarrassed about it in front of Ma.
QW. Bear with me young man. We all know this entire ordeal has been very hard on you. But these are important questions and I am almost done.
The insurance from Albert, did it bother you when your mother gave it to Dr. MacGregor?
A. No. Like I said. We always pay our bills.
QW. Did it seem wrong after Peter's death to change the beneficiary on the policies?
A. No. Ma had to go to court and do more paperwork to get the money from Peter's policy. That money was supposed to help with the farm, but if you can't get it, where's the help?

There were more understanding nods from the jurors.

QW. Ray, for some reason Mr. Snow was very interested that you may have given free cream to Dr. MacGregor's family. Was that a strange thing to do?
A. I hope not, 'cause we give some to the preacher and the schoolteacher too.

Walsh smiled and a few snickers were heard from the spectators.

QW. Ray, when Scyrel died what did Dr. MacGregor say was the cause of death?
A. It was a disease, but I don't remember the name.
QW. Had you ever heard the word before?
A. No.
QW. Did he ever say cancer?
A. No, I would remember that.
QW. Would you remember if he said syphilis?

Ray bristled and clenched his fists.

A. No. Scyrel never had that!

QW. Ray, let's talk about Nurse Gibbs. Was she helpful to your family?

A. Yeah, Ma was tired from taking care of Scyrel and everything else.

QW. Everything else?

A. You know, what mothers do.

QW. Nurse Gibbs stayed with you after Scyrel died. Whose idea was that?

A. We all wanted her to stay. She was a big help to Ma.

QW. So, she remained with your family out of friendship?

A. Yes.

The hour was late and Attorney Walsh headed for his chair. "Your Honor, I have no—, excuse me, I do have one more question for this witness." He turned back quickly to face the young man. "Ray, where at the farm did your family keep strychnine?" The question was so unexpected that no one could miss the total shock on Ray's face. Ray firmly replied, "We don't have a place. I mean, we never had it on the farm." Walsh winced before he could stop himself. He had taken a chance. He had gambled on Ray blurting out an answer that would implicate his mother and remove suspicion from his client. It had not worked.

When the judge asked Snow and Boomhower if they had any redirect, they smiled broadly and said no, in unison.

Thursday had been an emotionally draining day. The prosecution took dinner together to go over notes on Friday's coming testimonies. Attorneys Walsh and Woodworth not only had to prepare for the next day, but also had to deal with Big Pete's request to be taken off Carrie's bond and find new securers for that bond.

Ida MacGregor had been stoic throughout the day and even though innuendos of improper conduct had stung, she gave her husband a warm and loving smile as she and Robert's father left Tribune Hall.

No one seemed to notice a young man walking with head down toward the train station. Ray was on his way to Ubly to stay with Bert's parents. It was just too far to keep traveling back and forth between Port Huron and Bad Axe.

* * *

Court on Friday was very different from the day before. The testimony consisted mainly of numerous scientific and medical terms, and while attorneys on both sides tried to keep it on a level for laymen, they did not always succeed. Roy Pryer explained the Marsh test, which was applied to Scyrel's liver. His conclusion was arsenic poisoning. Dr. Warthin, Head of Pathology at the University of Michigan, presented his study, which was twofold. First, he carefully examined the viscera for infectious disease and told the court none was found. Next, he explained the necessity to know symptoms in order to make a positive diagnosis. When he was asked for his medical opinion as to what could cause the deterioration of the tested organs he replied, "arsenic poisoning."

QSnow. Professor Warthin, is arsenic a cumulative poison?
A. It is not. It is quickly secreted from the body.
QS. Is it possible that a lethal dose of arsenic could enter the human body and also be eliminated before death?
A. Yes.
QS. How long can a person live before all arsenic leaves the body?
A. It varies by dosage and patient.
QS. Professor, how is arsenic eliminated?
A. Through urine, through the intestines, or it could be vomited out. It could also pass through mucous membranes.
QS. If a person was given arsenic and died ten days later with only a trace of arsenic found in his organs, what would that indicate?
A. If the patient had symptoms of arsenic poisoning and even a trace of arsenic was found, it would prove to me that patient died of arsenic poison.
QS. Professor, did you find any sign of cancer or syphilis in Scyrel Sparling?
A. None.

Snow had no further questions and Walsh approached the witness.

QWalsh. You mentioned ways that arsenic is secreted, and you stated that it is secreted quickly. But if you did not know the symptoms and found no arsenic, how could you still diagnose arsenic poisoning?

At this point, Dr. Warthin went into a technical description of what arsenic does to organs of the body. Very few people in court had a remote idea of what he was saying and Walsh was sorry he had brought it up. Joseph Walsh had no further questions, but Ernest Snow had one redirect.

QSnow. Professor, if a person had been given a lethal dose of arsenic and then been subjected to repeated enemas, would that increase the elimination of the poison?
A. Certainly.

Chapter 57

The weekend meant different things to all involved in the trial. Judge Beach needed to clear his head before he had to rule on the admissibility of testimony concerning Albert's death in two days. He went to visit the widow of a dear friend. Rudolph Papst and Watson Beach had remained close friends since serving together in the Tenth Michigan regiment during the Civil War. Captain Papst, known as the man who named Bad Axe, had died the previous January, but the trial had prevented Watson from paying his respects as well as he would have liked.

Attorneys Snow and Boomhower felt optimistic about the case. They spent a few hours tying up loose ends and took most of the weekend off.

Attorneys Walsh and Woodworth were not as fortunate and worked both Saturday and Sunday, mostly with Dr. MacGregor, in preparation for his upcoming testimony. Dr. MacGregor was exhausted after the weekend sessions. They gave him very little time to spend with Ida and the children.

Big Pete and his brother James went to Port Austin. A fire had consumed several buildings there the week prior and a Mr. Wallace had asked the brothers for advice. His house and barn were among seven others lost in the blaze. The Sparling brothers' reputation for rebuilding after the fire of '81 had spread far and wide.

While still at Mae's in-laws, Ray received a telephone call from Attorney Walsh. Carrie would have to appear in person regarding the new bond. He took the train to Port Huron and arrived at Mae and Bert's house Sunday afternoon. He found his mother checking the strawberries she had planted the day before. She greeted her son but didn't mention the trial. Somehow, he would have to make Carrie understand why she had to go to Bad Axe. She didn't know that Big Pete had withdrawn her bond. She didn't know the seriousness of all that was happening. In fact, she did not seem to be aware of anything except the strawberries.

* * *

On Monday morning, Attorney Snow called Elwood Sparling who testified as to Scyrel's general health in early August. "We were spending a few days with the Sparlings. Scyrel had been threshing on the third and when he returned Carrie fixed what she called 'hot stuff', because she thought he sounded hoarse."

QSnow. Did she offer the hot stuff to anyone else?
A. No sir.

QS. Did you see the defendant at the house during your visit?

A. Yes, Dr. MacGregor was there the mornings of the third and fourth.

Snow turned the witness over to Walsh.

QWalsh. Mr. Sparling, you said Scyrel appeared healthy?

A. Yes sir.

QW. Do you know what was in the so-called hot stuff?

A. No sir.

QW. Did you see Dr. MacGregor give any medicine or substance to Scyrel Sparling?

A. No sir. He was treating Carrie's eyes.

Boomhower next called Henry Bacon to the stand. He asked the preacher to recall an incident in 1908. The incident Henry had forgotten until being prepared for court now had the attention of everyone in the room. Bacon told Boomhower he had gone into the Sparling house to collect his pay. Upon entering the kitchen he discovered J.W. was sick in one bedroom and Mrs. Sparling and Dr. MacGregor were together in the other bedroom. And the door was nearly shut. A few gasps from the courtroom were heard, and MacGregor had a puzzled look on his face. Reverend Bacon, feeling he had given important testimony, was pleased with himself as Walsh approached for cross-examination.

QWalsh. Reverend Bacon, is your memory so good that you can swear to something that occurred almost four years ago?

A. Yes sir, it is. I thought it odd then and that's why I recall it now.

QW. Has your wife ever been ill?

A. A few times.

QW. Did you call a doctor for her?

A. When she needed one, of course.

QW. Having said that, do you still think it odd that a doctor and a patient were in a room together?

A. I know what you're getting at, but Mrs. Sparling did not seem ill at the time.

QW. Are you a physician as well as a minister?

A. No, but—

Walsh interrupted and thanked the preacher, saying he had no further questions.

Anna Pieruski was called and testified to being at the Sparling farm when the doctor and Mrs. Sparling were behind a closed bedroom door. As in the December hearing, she admitted that Mrs. Sparling was being treated for a private, female condition and was entitled to her privacy.

Neighbor Dale Morrison was called next to testify as to Scyrel's good health prior to August fourth. "He had been helping me at threshing and let me tell you, he was a strong young man," said Morrison.

Chester Kell, a neighbor of the Sparlings, was sworn in just before dinner.

QBoomhower. Where do you live Mr. Kell?
A. I'm a neighbor to Mrs. Sparling. At least I was until they sold.
QB. Did you ever see the defendant at their farm?
A. I sure did.
QB. How could you know this?
A. Well, my place is on higher ground.
QB. Did Dr. MacGregor come often?
A. At least three times a week for a while, and then it was every day.
QB. Who was sick all those times?
A. I don't know as anyone was sick every time.

Boomhower thanked Mr. Kell and took his seat as Attorney Walsh approached the witness with a quizzical look.

QWalsh. Mr. Kell, what is your occupation?
A. I'm a farmer and have been all my life.
QW. Are you in good health?
A. You bet. I can put in a day's work just like when I was younger.
QW. Does the farm keep you busy?
A. Are you kidding? Farmers are always busy.
QW. Then perhaps you can explain to the court your ability to plow, plant, harvest, buzz wood, press hay, thresh oats, shred corn, milk cows, feed horses, mend equipment, and still keep a close watch on your neighbor as to who comes and goes? I doubt you have an answer, and I have no more questions.

Mr. Kell pulled at his collar and tried to explain, but the judge told him he was excused. He left the stand scowling at Joseph Walsh, who smiled back. Judge Beach sensed a growing tension and called for a long noon recess. Sam Soule took the stand in the afternoon.

QBoomhower. Mr. Soule, how well did you know Scyrel Sparling?

A. I knew him quite well, especially after he came to work for me.

QB. How did that come about?

A. Well I liked all the boys. But Scyrel just kinda grabbed at my heart, especially after J.W. passed. He came to the store every chance he got and, in January of last year, I asked if he would like to work for me. I would never pull him off the farm, but it was winter and he didn't have as many chores.

QB. Was he a good worker?

A. My yes. He took to storekeeping right off and even gave me a few good pointers about selling.

QB. If he liked it so well, why did he leave?

A. When his brother Albert died, Scyrel said he had to go home to help his other brother Ray. Was down to just the two of them by then.

QB. Was he upset about leaving?

A. He was real sad, but he felt he had to go. I told him. . . .

Sam paused and cleared a lump from his throat.

A. I told him the job was his any time he wanted it back.

No one quite understood the relevance of Sam's testimony until he exploded. "And I'll tell you this. If Albert hadn't died, Scyrel would still be in my store and we wouldn't all be sitting here today!"

Attorney Walsh carefully picked his words during the cross-examination. The emotion of this witness had spread throughout the hall.

QW. Mr. Soule, would you like a moment to collect yourself?

A. No. I'm fine.

QW. Did Scyrel's mother ask him to come home?

A. Not that I know of.

QW. Did Dr. MacGregor suggest he return?

A. Not that I know of.

QW. So Scyrel returned to the farm of his own free will?

A. Yes, that's the kind of lad he was.

Attorney Walsh said he had no more questions of the witness.

Robert MacGregor was relieved. He remembered the conversations when he had tried to impress upon Scyrel the importance of duty and doing what was right. Apparently Scyrel had kept those talks to himself.

Chapter 58

O n Tuesday, the judge addressed the attorneys in his chambers. "I previously denied any testimony regarding the illness and death of Albert Sparling. I also ruled against suggestions of conspiracy being brought to the jury at that time. In light of the testimony already given, I now overturn those decisions because of new information presented in court. One, medical experts have stated that Scyrel Sparling was poisoned. Since Dr. Conboy examined both Albert and Scyrel, he may give his medical opinion. Two, Albert's autopsy indicates arsenic poisoning as well. This lends credence to a conspiracy. And lastly, Dr. MacGregor visited the Sparlings on a regular basis and he was given money from Albert's insurance, another suggestion of conspiracy. Mr. Boomhower, if you wish to continue Dr. Conboy's testimony this afternoon, it will be allowed."

Joseph Walsh, not pleased with the ruling, sighed. He had expected it.

* * *

Dr. Conboy again took the stand in the afternoon.

QSnow. Doctor, when you were here last I asked you if any other member of the Sparling family exhibited the same symptoms as Scyrel. You may now answer that question.

A. I can only speak regarding Albert.

QS. You examined Albert during his last illness?

A. Yes, I was called to the home by Dr. MacGregor on the second day of May. Albert was very ill and it was difficult to find a pulse. I left some strychnine tablets in hopes they would stimulate the boy. Privately, I felt there was little hope for his recovery.

QS. Would you describe for the court his symptoms?

A. He was extremely ill. His pulse was weak, but rapid. His heartbeat was faint, and his stomach and lower abdomen were sore to even a slight touch. His legs and arms were numb. His mouth and nose were red. There was vomiting and purging.

QS. Did you see the patient again?

A. No, he died early the next morning.

QS. Do you know the cause of death? Or what was given as the cause at the time?

A. I was told he died of acute nephritis, kidney failure.

QS. Did you agree with that?

A. I had no reason not to at the time. I had only seen the patient once during his last illness.

QS. Did you later question the cause of death being brought about by acute nephritis?

A. Well I had an uneasy feeling. You know, something that nags at you, telling you something is amiss.

QS. What did you do?

A. I thought and thought. I mean this was a healthy young man who became ill quickly and died. I got out my books and began studying those symptoms. Everything pointed to poison by arsenic.

QS. Are you now convinced that arsenic caused Albert's death and not nephritis?

A. Yes I am.

QS. One more question Doctor. Did Albert and Scyrel share the same symptoms?

A. Yes they did.

As Walsh stood for cross-examination, Judge Beach asked how long he would be. Walsh answered, "As long as it takes to satisfy my questions."

"Then I suggest we continue this in the morning," declared the judge. And, with a pound of his gavel, court was adjourned. Walsh felt he was losing ground. By not allowing him to question Dr. Conboy now, the jury would have all evening to consider what they had just heard.

* * *

The next morning Dr Conboy again sat in the witness chair, and Joseph Walsh began his cross-examination.

QWalsh. Dr. Conboy, you saw Albert before he died?

A. Yes sir.

QW. What did you think was wrong with him?

A. As I said, poison by arsenic.

QW. No, no. Not after he died. What did you think was wrong with him when you examined him on May second?

A. I really didn't know. Dr. MacGregor had told me the boy had suffered a fall and could have internal injuries. He also suggested the possibility of syphilis.

QW. And did Albert's symptoms indicate either of those maladies?

A. Not completely, but this was the first I had examined the boy and I didn't probe any more than necessary. He was obviously in great discomfort.

QW. I see. Now, you said after Albert died, you began to think of arsenic? Why?

A. It was just a hunch. A young healthy man just should not take sick to death so quickly.

QW. And you studied arsenic poisoning and decided that was what killed him?

A. Yes, I was almost one hundred percent positive.

QW. And whom did you tell, since you were so positive?

Dr. Conboy looked down and paused. Very quietly he answered "No one." Several people in the courtroom looked at each other and one juror was seen making a note. Dr. MacGregor leaned back in his chair with a small hint of satisfaction on his face.

QW. Do I understand correctly, Dr. Conboy, that you reached a conclusion of arsenic poisoning and told no one?

A. I was not one hundred percent sure.

QW. But you told Mr. Snow that you were certain Albert had been poisoned.

A. As I said, I was not one hundred percent positive.

QW. Then what percent were you positive? More than fifty percent? More than eighty percent?

A. I don't know.

QW. Were you more than ninety-five percent positive?

A. I should think so.

QW. Doctor, help me understand. You hold the answer to a great mystery in your hand and elect not to share it?

A. Who would I tell?

QW. Let me ask the questions please. But since you brought it up, did you tell Dr. MacGregor, or Sheriff McAulay, or Prosecutor Boomhower?

A. No.

QW. So you just sat on this piece of information. Is that correct?

A. You don't understand —

QW. You can say that again. Let's move on a few months. Is it safe to say Ubly is a small village?

A. Yes.

QW. Does the rumor mill operate efficiently in Ubly?

A. I live in Bad Axe and couldn't say.

QW. Are you telling this court that you and you alone never heard the rumors flying around all of Huron and Sanilac Counties after Albert died?

A. I may have heard a few, but I don't live my life by rumors I may hear.

QW. That is most commendable. So when Scyrel became ill I assume you took your secret knowledge to someone.

A. No.

QW. You continued to sit on the information you had gathered?

A. I didn't tell anyone.

QW. Can a person who has arsenic in his system through accidental means, or patent medicines, or even evil intent, survive arsenic poisoning?

A. It depends on a great many things.

QW. I'm sure it does. Such as identifying the cause of illness and treating it, providing someone knows the cause of illness and does not keep it a secret. I have no more questions.

Dr. Conboy was exhausted, but tried not to show it. Walsh had asked him the very questions he had asked himself over and over again. His answers were always the same. He was a friend to Dr. MacGregor. A colleague just did not, out of the blue, accuse a fellow physician of malpractice, or worse. He had also been a friend to the Sparlings for years. If he could not believe a mother capable of poisoning her family, whom could he convince? He left the stand with his head down.

Perry Cole took the stand next. He was a tall muscular young man with dark complexion and hair. Many a local girl had hopes of landing him. He appeared quiet, but was observant and very little escaped his attention. Besides being a good friend of Albert's, he had worked off and on at the Sparling farm. He told of watching Dr. MacGregor drop Mrs. Sparling's eyes.

QSnow. How long did it take?

A. Maybe two minutes.

QS. How long did he remain at the farm?

A. Hard to tell. Sometimes half an hour, sometimes longer.

QS. Was anyone else at the farm sick on those occasions?

A. Nope.

Perry also testified to seeing Dr. MacGregor throwing medicine bottles into the kitchen stove right after Albert died. Under cross-examination, he admitted he only saw bottles and did not know what they contained.

QWalsh. You really have no idea what Dr. MacGregor threw into the fire, do you?

A. I know what I saw. The doctor came from the sick room of my friend, looked around, reached into his pocket, and quickly threw bottles into the stove.

QW. Yes or no. Do you know what was in those bottles?
A. No.

Nicholas Prezinski, a neighbor to the Sparlings, followed Perry Cole on the stand. His testimony was also about the many visits Dr. MacGregor had made to the Sparling home.

QSnow. You are acquainted with the defendant?
A. Sure, Dr. MacGregor has been our doctor for three or four years now. A good one, too.
QS. And you saw him at the Tyre farm on a regular basis?
A. Yes.
QS. Did you ever have occasion to ask him about his visits there?
A. Kinda. He came out to our place one time right after being at the Sparlings, and I asked what was the matter with the family now. Two were already gone you see.
QS. What was his answer?
A. He said he was treating Mrs. Sparling's eyes.
QS. What did you say to that?
A. I said that poor family certainly had lots of troubles.
QS. Did he answer that?
A. Not exactly. He told me she was a wonderful and good woman.

Attorney Snow paused. With these words, knowing looks and smirks were exchanged in the courtroom and he wanted their unspoken voice to sink in. He looked at the jury. It was the effect he wanted. "Thank you Mr. Prezinski."
Attorney Walsh rose for cross-examination.

QW. Mr. Prezinski, did you know Mrs. Sparling well?
A. Sure, I already told that.
QW. Do you think she was a wonderful and good woman?"
A. Sure, everyone around there thought so.
QW. Thank you, I have no further questions.

Dr. Holdship was called next and testified regarding the post mortem he had conducted on Albert. He also related a conversation he had with MacGregor following the autopsy. "MacGregor asked me if I thought arsenic would be found and before I could answer, he said that he expected it would be found in all of them."

* * *

It was now Thursday, May sixteenth. Several jurors and spectators privately wondered when the prosecution would end. There had been continuous testimony from several witnesses regarding the house where the doctor resided, Scyrel's health before death, the frequent visits of MacGregor to the Sparling home, and symptoms of arsenic poisoning. It had nearly reached the point where the repeated testimony was ignored.

However, the prosecution was not finished and they called Tom Phillips, the Detroit newspaper reporter, to the stand. He recounted the conversation he had with MacGregor the previous August. "He told me all four died of syphilis and that they were taking arsenic in patent medicine as a cure." Attorney Walsh objected to the mention of all four deaths. His objection was sustained and the words were stricken from the record. It appeared at first glance to be testimony desired by the defense, because it showed that the victims used patent medicines that often contained arsenic. It caused some to wonder if the deaths were accidentally self-inflicted.

Those suppositions vanished, and the intent of the prosecution became clear when Dr. Vaughn took the stand.

QBoomhower. Dr. Vaughn, are you familiar with patent medicines?
A. I know of them.
QB. Do you know that arsenic is often an ingredient in them?
A. I am aware of that, yes.
QB. Would there be enough arsenic in a bottle of patent medicine to kill?
A. I hardly think so.

Boomhower thanked the witness and Walsh took over.

QWalsh. Dr. Vaughn, you are a well-known physician and have a great deal of knowledge. Can it be you are also an expert in patent medicine? I mean there must be hundreds of them available.
A. As I said, I am familiar with them.
QW. Then, can you inform the court how much arsenic is found in Dr. Simm's Arsenic Wafers? In Taylor's Electric Oil? In Trilene tablets? In Storey's Worm Cakes?
A. No.
QW. I could go on for some time, but I believe your answers would be the same. Would you at least concede there are many patent medicines available that contain unknown amounts of arsenic?
A. Yes.
QW. Thank you Dr. Vaughn.

Xenophon Boomhower did not want to let any suggestion of accidental death become embedded in the jurors' minds. He rose quickly to redirect.

QB. Dr. Vaughn, from what you know of patent medicines do you still maintain that there is not enough arsenic in them to be lethal?
A. Yes I do.

Boomhower returned to his seat, but then, as an afterthought, asked another question. It appeared unrelated, but he was actually laying ground-work for the next trial.

QB. Doctor, are you familiar with Paris Green?
A. Yes, my wife uses it to kill potato bugs. But she is very careful with it.
QB. Why is that?
A. It contains arsenic.

Walsh had no further questions and he wondered why Paris Green was even mentioned. Dr. MacGregor was not a gardener.

Court recessed for dinner. The crowd of spectators had thinned as the prosecution kept hammering at the same established facts. Dr. MacGregor's father was there, which was no surprise. What was a surprise was the appearance of Big Pete Sparling and his son George. Had the public known what was to occur later that afternoon, the Tribune Hall would have been full.

Boomhower called John Yauch to the stand regarding the defendant's purchase of an automobile.

QBoomhower. Did you discuss terms with MacGregor?
A. No.
QB. Why not?
A. I started to provide him with the information, but he stopped me, saying he intended to pay cash.
QB. Did that surprise you?
A. Sure, but I wasn't about to object.

Walsh now approached the car dealer.

QWalsh. Mr. Yauch, were you surprised that Dr. MacGregor planned to pay cash for his automobile?
A. Yes sir.

QW. Was he the first person ever to pay cash at your dealership for a new automobile?

A. Well no, but—

QW. Thank you Mr. Yauch. I have no more questions.

As John Yauch left the stand, the back door of the hall opened. The few in court gasped as Carrie and Ray Sparling entered the room. Judge Beach asked them to approach the bench. Ray was nervous. His experience in court had been painful. Carrie, however, seemed to be in a world of her own. She was nearly forty-eight years of age and still cut a fine figure, not lost on any who saw her. She had been in court before, but now the room had people, and a jury. And Robert. He sat at a table to her left. She had not seen him in months and as she drew closer, her steps slowed. Ray took her arm and quickened their pace to stand before Judge Beach. Paul Woodworth, her attorney, joined them. At that point, Big Pete and George were called to step forward.

Big Pete was appalled. This was all wrong. He had expected the courtroom to be emptied during this procedure so he could better explain his actions to Ray and Carrie. He wanted to try to make them understand why he withdrew the bond. But there wasn't time; the judge was moving quickly. Perhaps he could talk to them outside afterward.

"It has come to the attention of this court that Peter Sparling and George Sparling, bondsmen to Carrie Sparling, wish to surrender this bond," announced Judge Beach. "Is this correct, gentlemen?" Both men answered in the affirmative and the judge continued. "According to law, all parties must be present. Carrie Sparling, do you understand these proceedings?" She glanced at Big Pete with a sorrowful look and, turning back to the judge, answered softly, "I do." Judge Beach then addressed Mr. Woodworth. "Have you obtained new bondsmen for Mrs. Sparling and are they here today?"

At that point, three men stood. Attorney Woodworth answered, "Yes your Honor. Mr. Douglass, Mr. Gordon, Mr. Stambaugh in addition to Ray Sparling have agreed to a new bond." The judge asked the gentlemen to step forward and sign the document. It was over in less than five minutes. Carrie was excused and turned to leave. She saw Robert staring at her, but when their eyes met he lowered his head. "Oh," she thought to herself, "if I could just talk to you."

Ray, not wanting any more attention drawn to them, again took his mother's arm and quickened their pace to exit the hall. Carrie finally seemed to realize the awful truth of what was happening. Bert and Mae had made certain that no newspapers came into Carrie's hands. But they could not shelter her from this. As Carrie and Ray left the building, a reporter pushed his way into their path. "Mrs. Sparling, do you now believe that arsenic killed your family?"

Ray tried to ignore the man and kept moving, but Carrie stopped. She looked at him and replied, "No I do not." Mr. Woodworth, who had followed, made it clear that no more questions would be accepted. He then helped Ray and Carrie into his waiting buggy and drove them to the train station. Carrie said nothing on the ride to Port Huron. She kept seeing Robert's face, and a deep hurt filled her heart when she recalled how he had averted his gaze from her.

Big Pete had tried to catch up with Carrie, but by the time he got outside he saw Mr. Woodworth's buggy driving away. Maybe it was just as well. What could he have said anyway? He snapped at a reporter who was trying to talk to him and beckoned to George that it was time to go.

* * *

Back in the courtroom Judge Beach pounded his gavel. The presence of Carrie and the doctor in the same room had shocked everyone. The gavel shook them back to the matters at hand. John Dunlap, a juror from the post mortem on Scyrel, testified that MacGregor told him before the autopsy that he expected to be arrested. During cross-examination, he admitted that an expected arrest did not prove guilt.

Professor Warthin again took the stand, but he basically repeated what Dr. Vaughn had already said; the viscera of Albert showed the presence of arsenic. Taking a chance on overkill, Boomhower asked a long and detailed hypothetical question. He posed for the professor a scenario of a healthy young man; twenty years of age becoming ill; his progression and symptoms; the treatments given; his ultimate death; and the results of the post mortem. The professor was then asked for his opinion as to the cause of death. The professor answered, "My educated opinion would be arsenic poisoning."

QBoomhower. Professor, in your pathological tests did you find any signs of cancer or syphilis in either Albert or Scyrel?
A. No. I did not.

Joseph Walsh had only two questions.

QWalsh. Professor Warthin, in your examination did you find anything that could lead a physician to believe that the deceased could have died from kidney failure?
A. I suppose that might be a valid, though incorrect, conclusion.
QW. Could syphilis be present in a body and yet go undetected by any changes to the liver?
A. Yes, it's possible.

Sheriff McAulay was the last witness of the day. It had been a long session and Judge Beach was tempted to adjourn early. However, the entire trial seemed to be grinding on forever, and he allowed one more witness for the day.

QSnow. Sheriff, did you have any conversations with Dr. MacGregor before the trial began?
A. Yes.
QS. Would you tell us about it?
A. Which one?
QS. Let's start with the discussion after Scyrel's organs were sent to Ann Arbor.
A. Well, I saw him on the street and he asked if I had heard from Ann Arbor. I told him no.
QS. Did he have anything to say?
A. Yes. He wondered what people around town were saying. Before I could answer, he said that this deal would ruin him.
QS. Ruin him? How?
A. Doc said that Mrs. Sparling owed him money, about six hundred dollars, and she would be arrested and he would lose that money.

Robert MacGregor's brow furrowed. He had forgotten that conversation.

QS. What other conversation did you have?
A. When I went to get him for the second inquest, he said this thing was killing him.
QS. Killing him? What did you say?
A. I told him not to worry, that it would all work out all right.
QS. Did that relieve him?
A. No, he said I didn't understand. Said he would be boarding with me some day.
QS. Did the defendant ever mention poison?
A. Yes. I ran into him at Gibson's barbershop. We were still waiting on word from Ann Arbor and he said he was sure they would find poison. Said he told Conboy about arsenic and that they were both thinking of it at the same time. Then he looked at me and said, "Sheriff, I know a fellow who can tell you who gave it to them and make Mrs. Sparling confess." I told him to get busy and get that man. He said he would only have to look into a looking glass.
QS. Is there any mistaking what he said to you?
A. No sir.

Snow paused long enough for that statement to be digested before asking questions about Nurse Gibbs.

QS. Sheriff, you stated in your deposition last December that you and the defendant had a conversation regarding Nurse Gibbs. Do you remember that?
A. Yes.
QS. Please share it with the court.
A. Doc said the nurse was keeping an eye out for a breakdown in Mrs. Sparling.
QS. Breakdown?
A. You know, insanity.
QS. Continue.
A. He said the nurse searched the house for poison when everyone was asleep.
QS. Thank you.

It was time for cross-examination and Walsh hoped he could downplay some of the damaging testimony. He was prepared to question the sheriff regarding the looking glass, but had not been aware of any previous conversation involving money owed by Carrie to his client. He would have to address it and hopefully remove some of the sting.

QWalsh. Sheriff, you have been working closely with the prosecution, correct?
A. I been doing my job if that's what you mean.
QW. Was Dr. MacGregor the only one who asked you about hearing from Ann Arbor?
A. No, lots of folks asked.
QW. Now six hundred dollars is a lot of money. Would you be upset if that amount was coming to you and you found out you might not get it?
A. Sure.

Walsh felt confident that he had put those subjects to rest.

QW. Are you acquainted with doctor and patient confidentiality?
A. I suppose.

QW. Well, in case you aren't certain, it is the duty of a doctor to keep certain things regarding a patient to himself.

A. Sure, that makes sense.

QW. Now when Dr. MacGregor told you this thing was killing him; that he would be boarding with you one day. Could you look at those statements as coming from someone who is being framed? Could he have been in possession of facts that would clear him of any suspicions except for the fact that he holds his confidentiality dear and that it should not be destroyed?

A. I sure didn't take it that way.

QW. I didn't ask you how you took it. Being a fair minded individual, can you see those statements in a different light now?

A. I guess it's possible.

QW. Sheriff, when the doctor mentioned a looking glass, who was he saying should look into it? You or himself?

A. He meant himself.

QW. Could he have meant for you to look into the glass? For you to question Mrs. Sparling?

A. I didn't take it that way.

QW. Come now, there were just the two of you. Couldn't he have been referring to you as well as himself?

A. It wasn't just the two of us. We were in Ed Gibson's barbershop. He heard it too. No, I'm sure he meant himself.

QW. Sheriff, whose job is it to make a person confess? A doctor or a sheriff?

A. Usually a sheriff.

QW. Thank you.

Judge Beach banged the gavel and adjourned court until the twentieth.

Bert and Mae huddled with Ray in the kitchen. "She was doing better until last Thursday," Mae said with tears running down her face. "Now she just sits in that old chair, rocking and talking to herself." Ray patted her arm. "It didn't help any to have Big Pete desert her like he did. And all done with MacGregor sitting right there, and the jury too. It just isn't right the way they handled it."

Carrie heard voices, but the words were unintelligible. It really didn't matter. Her thoughts were of her mother. Did her mother realize she was losing her mind as it happened? Did she lose her mind because of the fires, or was something inside her that could have been passed on? Could she, Carrie, lose her mind and not even know it?

Chapter 59

On Monday, Snow and Boomhower submitted for evidence Scyrel's and Albert's insurance applications plus medical statements that accompanied them. Alma Coultard was then called to the stand. She had prepared for this and stood confidently. With a touch of her hat to be certain it was properly placed on her head, she strode to the stand. As she sat down, she scooted her chair to align perfectly with the small table in front of her. Satisfied that all was in order, she folded her gloved hands on her lap and looked at Boomhower.

QBoomhower. Mrs. Coultard, what is your involvement with the Gleaners?
A. That would be the "Ancient Order of the Gleaners" and I am the secretary and treasurer.
QB. Are you familiar with the application for insurance, and the medical examination forms used to obtain insurance?
A. Yes sir.
QB. Will you please take a few moments to read these papers I have just introduced as evidence?

Mrs. Coultard read the documents and handed them back to Boomhower.

QB. Have you seen these before?
A. Yes. They deal with granting insurance to Scyrel Sparling.
QB. What type of information do the Gleaners request when someone applies for insurance?
A. The same as any insurance company. Name, age, occupation, general health, and habits. We also want to know about the health of the applicant's family.
QB. Mrs. Coultard, I do not wish to take up valuable court time by having you read every question and answer, but there are some items that need to be put into the record. I will read certain portions and then ask you to give the answer as it was submitted. Do you understand?
A. I understand, but I want the court to know this is usually privileged and confidential information. I would not want people to think I pass on this information on a regular basis.

QB. I appreciate your concern, and I can assure you people will understand this situation. Shall we begin? Name of applicant.

A. Scyrel Sparling.

QB. Are you in good health at the present time?

A. Yes.

QB. Has your weight increased within the last year?

A. Yes.

QB. If so, how much?

A. Twenty pounds.

QB. Give cause.

A. Growth.

That brought a few chuckles and Judge Beach pounded his gavel for order.

QB. Mrs. Coultard, you may answer at the end of these questions unless a different answer is necessary. Have you ever had insanity, epilepsy, paralysis, convulsions, apoplexy, sunstroke, persistent headache, St. Vitus dance, neuralgia, delirium tremens, asthma, pleurisy, acute bronchitis, chronic catarrh, disease of the throat or air passage, shortness of breath, spitting of blood, chronic cough, consumption, palpitation of the heart, piles, dysentery, chronic diarrhea, jaundice, liver complaint of any kind, dropsy, gravel, difficulty in urinating, swelling of feet hands or eyelids, disease of the kidneys or bladder, persistent pain in the back, cancer, syphilis, varicose veins, ulcers on legs or elsewhere, rheumatism, gout, erysipelas, disease of any joint?

A. No.

QB. The answer to each was no?

A. That is how it reads.

QB. Let's continue. Have you ever taken patent or proprietary medicine during the past two years?

A. No.

QB. Have you ever undergone any surgical operation?

A. No.

QB. Mrs. Coultard, are you certain about that answer?

A. It says no.

QB. Are you ruptured?

A. No.

QB. Do you drink wine, spirits, or malt liquor?

A. No.

QB. Do you use tobacco?

A. No.

QB. Do you use opium in any form, or chloral?

A. No.

QB. My, but he was a healthy young man. How was this document signed?

A. By Scyrel Sparling.

QB. Now, if we can do the same with the medical examiner's report for insurance. I think we can skip his general health information such as pulse, heartbeat, and chest dimensions. Down to question number eighteen. Do you believe the organs of respiration to be perfectly healthy?

A. Yes.

QB. Did you discover any indication of gastric or intestinal diseases?

A. No.

QB. Now number twenty-one, please. According to your judgment, will the party survive the term of expectation?

A. Yes.

QB. Mrs. Coultard, can you tell the court what that means?

A. It is a person's life expectancy.

QB. Can you tell us what Scyrel's life expectancy would have been in December of 1909 when this policy was issued? I believe we asked you to bring this information.

A. Yes you did. According to the charts Scyrel, in December of 1909, was eighteen years of age and his life expectancy was to live to the age of sixty years.

QB. Number twenty-two. Is there anything discovered by you which might affect the risk not set forth in the examination?

A. No.

QB. Number twenty-seven. Do you believe the party examined, safely insurable?

A. Yes.

QB. Would you now please read the last paragraph for us?

A. Having this thirtieth day of December 1909 carefully examined Scyrel Sparling, in accordance with the above form, and having thoroughly considered the statements made by him in this application, I hereby certify that in my judgment as a physician he is of sound bodily health and so far as I can ascertain, there are no indications of disease, either from ancestry, present physical condition, or personal habits which should debar him from participating in the financial benefits of the order. I therefore recommend him as physically qualified for an endowment membership.

QB. Who signed this medical section?
A. R. A. MacGregor, M.D.
QB. Mrs. Coultard, I now ask you to read, to yourself, this document.

She read the paper and looked up at Attorney Boomhower.

QB. What did you just read?
A. It is an application for endowment membership in the Ancient Order of Gleaners.
QB. Is it identical to the one we have just discussed?
A. Almost. Except this one is for Albert.
QB. So except for name, age, and general body description, these documents are similar?
A. Except for those things, they appear to be identical.
QB. I have one more paper for you to study Mrs. Coultard.

She looked at the piece of paper handed her by Boomhower.

A. This is not a Gleaner paper. It is from Sun Life Assurance.
QB. I realize that, but in your position have you ever seen this type of document?
A. Yes, it is a Special Appropriation of Policy. It appropriates or transfers this policy to someone other than the original designation.
QB. Why would a person do this?
A. It is often done to avoid probate. Without this paper the insurance would be paid to the estate of the deceased.
QB. So it gets money to the beneficiary faster and without additional court time and cost?
A. Correct.
QB. Mrs. Coultard, were you acquainted with Scyrel Sparling?
A. Yes.
QB. Please look again at his signature on the application.
A. I see it.
QB. Now please look at the signature on the Special Appropriation.
A. There is a mistake.
QB. Mistake? What do you mean?
A. The signatures are different.
QB. How so?
A. Scyrel spelled his name S-C-Y-R-E-L and that is how the Gleaner application is signed. But the signature on this special appropriation is spelled with no S. Just C-Y-R-E-L.

QB. Thank you Mrs. Coultard.

Defense had no questions and Mrs. Coultard left the stand with a puzzled look on her face. Suzie MacDonald was sworn in next.

QSnow. Please tell the court your name and how you know the defendant.

A. I am Suzie MacDonald and I live in Ubly with my husband. I have known Dr. MacGregor ever since he arrived in town. Our only child died last August thirty-first. Dr. Corcoran was the attending physician and he called in Dr. MacGregor later. I think that was Monday, the thirtieth. My child died the next day.

QS. I'm sorry for your loss. I'll try to be brief. Did you have any conversations with the defendant relative to a nurse?

A. Yes. Dr. MacGregor told me we should hire a nurse as soon as possible.

QS. What did you say?

A. I asked him about the nurse out at the Sparlings. I knew she was still there.

QS. And what was his response?

A. He said that was impossible.

QS. Impossible?

A. Yes, I asked again. Couldn't we have her for just one night?

QS. What did he say?

A. It was odd. He said he was between the devil and the deep, and the nurse had to remain at the Sparlings.

QS. Did you have a nurse that night?

A. No.

QS. What did the defendant do after he made the remark about the devil and the deep?

A. He left.

QS. He just left?

A. Yes, I didn't even have a chance to say anything more. He just turned, went to his automobile, and left.

QS. Thank you Mrs. MacDonald.

Joseph Walsh ached for the mother, but he still had to ask her questions.

QW. Mrs. MacDonald, I too am very sorry for your loss, and I'm also sorry that you were even called here by the prosecution to have to relive it all. Had your son been sick a long time?

A. Yes. In fact he almost died when he was born. The doctors told us then he might not live long. But he tried so hard and fought for a very long time. I know he's better now, but oh how I miss him.

QW. Mrs. MacDonald, I have no further questions. I wish the best for you and your family.

Boomhower silently and begrudgingly congratulated Walsh. With one statement, Walsh had discredited the testimony and vilified the prosecution. Boomhower had planned to call Suzie MacDonald's sister, Eva, to corroborate the testimony, but thought better of it. Instead he called Chris Sparling.

QBoomhower. Mr. Sparling, what is your relationship to Scyrel Sparling?
A. I am, or was, first cousin to his father John Wesley.
QB. Did the family ever call on you for help?
A. Indirectly.
QB. Please explain.
A. I saw Albert during his last sickness and remember when he died. I was in Ubly the day after he passed and saw Dr. MacGregor. He had been asked to select a coffin and wanted me to go along.
QB. Did you go?
A. Of course.
QB. Were there any other requests for assistance?
A. The day after the funeral, the doctor came to me and wondered if my brother Peter would go the bond for the insurance.
QB. He was asking about the insurance money the day after the funeral?
A. Yes. He wasn't sure if they would need a bondsman. They had submitted appropriation policies, but he wasn't sure if they had taken effect.
QB. But do I understand correctly, the very day after Albert was buried the defendant was asking about insurance money?
A. Yes.
QB. Thank you Mr. Sparling.

Mr. Walsh rose for cross-examination.

QWalsh. Mr. Sparling, are you a wealthy man?
A. No sir.
QW. Did you grow up in a wealthy family?
A. No.
QW. What is the purpose of life insurance, as you understand it?
A. Why, to help with finances when a person dies.

QW. Exactly. Do you think, for example, a mother who has just buried a young son would be thinking about the insurance money the next day?
A. I wouldn't think so.
QW. And yet, would you agree that money would be very helpful, especially on a farm?
A. Of course.
QW. Mr. Sparling, do you have good and caring friends?
A. Yes, several.
QW. Good, caring friends step in to help even when not asked, right?
A. Yes.
QW. Is it possible that Dr. MacGregor, having known what Mrs. Sparling had to endure with probate after Peter died, stepped in as a good, caring friend to get her the money to which she was entitled?
A. I suppose so, yes.
QW. Thank you.

Boomhower had only one question on redirect.

QBoomhower. Mr. Sparling, do you know what the insurance money was used for?
A. I understand Dr. MacGregor purchased an automobile with most of it.
QB. Thank you, nothing further.

Ora May Hunter followed Chris Sparling on the stand.

QB. Miss Hunter, how do you know the accused?
A. Dr. MacGregor treated my father during his last illness.
QB. Could you tell the court when this happened?
A. It was about the time of the October inquest.
QB. And you are certain of the time?
A. Yes, he was at our house the day before the inquest began, on October eleventh. I remember because he had just told me my father would not recover and added there were worse things than death.
QB. Did he say anything else?
A. Yes, he said he would probably be arrested the next day and would gladly trade places with my father.
QB. Was arsenic mentioned?
A. Yes. When he came back two days later, he told my family they had found arsenic in Scyrel. He said it was in medicines.

Boomhower thanked the witness and Joseph Walsh approached for cross-examination.

QW. Miss Hunter, did your father die from his illness?
A. Yes.
QW. I hate to bring up sad memories, but did he suffer a lot before he died?
A. Yes, the pain was constant and terrible.
QW. Knowing what you know now, does the statement that there are worse things than death seem unusual?
A. No, I miss my father very much, but I would not wish him back if he had to endure the same suffering.

Walsh said he had no more questions, and Boomhower faced the judge. "Your Honor, at this time, the prosecution rests. I submit that we be allowed to call rebuttal witnesses if necessary."

The judge looked at Joseph Walsh. "Mr. Walsh, are you prepared to begin your defense?" After Walsh said he was ready, the judge spoke to the court. "I suggest we adjourn for the day and get a fresh start tomorrow." With a pound of his gavel, the makeshift courtroom on the second floor of Tribune Hall was adjourned.

The courtroom emptied and the drone of testimony was replaced with the sounds of departing automobiles and buggies. Ida touched her husband's shoulder and went outside to wait. He would follow when he was ready. He sat a few moments longer, listening to the sounds and staring at his hands.

In Port Huron, Carrie heard Bert's horse and buggy drive into the yard. She heard him enter the house and greet her daughter with a kiss. She heard the sounds of pots and pans as Mae cooked supper. She heard the familiar noises and wished she could help. But Mae's motions were too quick and Carrie's head was too slow and she couldn't concentrate. So she sat at the kitchen table hearing the noises and staring at her hands.

Chapter 60

On the twenty-first, the crowd of spectators, which had dwindled throughout the prosecution's presentation, now swelled. The courtroom was packed and hundreds more lined up to hopefully be admitted. Joseph Walsh cleared his throat and began a short presentation in contrast to the lengthy opening statement of the prosecution.

"Gentlemen of the jury, I thank you for the time and dedication you are showing with your presence. I am grieved that the honorable George Clark was too ill to lead this defense, but I'm sure you'll be relieved to know he is recuperating nicely. I tried to have this trial delayed until Mr. Clark could present the evidence he worked so hard to obtain. That request, as you know, was denied. At first I felt inadequate for the task. But I now believe the truth will come out. I do not intend to question the evidence of arsenic poisoning. In fact, my client will state that, after hearing testimony from the experts, he concurs with their findings. However, and I stress this, he had no connection whatsoever with the giving of said poison. It will also be shown that there is absolutely no foundation for ugly rumors of intimacy. And remember they are rumors, by definition unconfirmed gossip. It will also be shown that Dr. MacGregor acted as a friend of the entire family when he made inquiries as to insurance. He also acted out of kindness in performing the post mortem immediately rather than making the family wait through a long night with their dead son and brother in the next room. And finally it comes down to this. It is not the duty of Mr. Woodworth or myself to prove our client innocent. It is the duty of the prosecution to prove him guilty beyond any reasonable doubt."

Attorney Walsh took his seat and court adjourned until after the noon meal.

* * *

An hour before the trial was due to resume, a crowd of at least two hundred men and women of all ages waited for the courtroom door to open. They stood two to three abreast in a line that began at the top of the staircase and continued over thirty yards up the street. All appeared orderly until the door opened. Then a massive forward surge ensued, leaving the stairs so packed that many tried to gain access by scrambling up the railing. It was mayhem and many were disappointed to be on the wrong side of the door when it closed.

* * *

Alexander MacGregor was the first witness in his son's defense. He gave a glowing account of Dr. MacGregor's early life. "He was top in his class at Western University. Ever since he was very young he wanted to be a physician. He never gave his mother or me a reason not to be proud of him." He glanced warmly at his son. "And he never will."

QWalsh. Mr. MacGregor, how did the Sparling boys come to be insured with Sun Life Assurance Company?
A. I don't know the absolute beginning. I was visiting my son and—
QW. When was this?
A. In the summer of '09.
QW. Continue.
A. My wife and I were in Ubly and I believe two of the boys stopped by with cream from their milk route.
QW. Was insurance mentioned right off?
A. My no. We had an ordinary conversation and it came around to a recent tragedy. Three young men had been working on a barn when the scaffolding gave way. They were busted up pretty bad. One thing led to another, and one of the boys said it would be a long time, if ever, before the men would be able to work again. The possibility of death was mentioned and my son said if they carried life insurance, their families would at least have something. Before long I was asked about Sun Life and shortly after that all four boys applied for and received policies.
QW. Were they pressured into it?
A. Of course not. I know what you are thinking and yes, there are agents out there who use scare tactics. I have always held to the theory that my job is to give straightforward information. Then the person can make an educated decision for himself.
QW. Mr. MacGregor, do you think it is foolish for young healthy men to own life insurance?
A. On the contrary. I think it wise. Accidents can happen regardless of age or well-being.

Walsh turned to his seat as Snow approached the doctor's father. The seemingly arrogant attorney was now face to face with the professed proud father of a man he was prosecuting for murder.

QSnow. You stated that all four boys were in no way pressured to buy life insurance. Is that correct?
A. Yes it is.

QS. Yet all four received a policy with your company.

A. Yes. It is not unusual to insure more than one member of a family. In fact it is the norm.

QS. Now this discussion the defendant had with the sheriff—the one that suggested Mrs. Sparling still owed him money and if she was arrested, he would never receive payment owed him.

A. I heard the sheriff, but I do not remember that conversation.

QS. Do you deny the conversation took place?

Alexander MacGregor sighed audibly.

A. Mr. Snow. How can I deny something that I do not recall ever happening?

Snow handed the elder MacGregor the Special Appropriation of Policy, which Mrs. Coultard had already testified to.

QS. Is that your son's signature as a witness?

A. It is.

QS. What happens after these papers are filled out and witnessed?

A. I, or my stenographer, make a note of it and send it on to the head office in Montreal.

QS. Do you make a copy before you send it on?

A. There is no need. A duplicate is made when the original is completed.

QS. Why do they need a copy in Montreal if they have the original?

A. The copy, when stamped at the head office, is then mailed to the insured.

QS. Did you notice this signature mistake of C-Y-R-E-L when you received it?

A. No.

QS. Was it ever discovered?

A. Yes, someone in Montreal called my attention to it. I was told what to do to set the record straight and I did it.

QS. Do you have the corrected copy with you?

A. Of course not. As I said, Montreal has a copy, as does the insured.

QS. Can you give an account as to why a young man, who is not stupid, would sign his name incorrectly if in fact he was the one who signed it?

A. No.

Alexander MacGregor gave up his seat on the witness stand to Ed Gibson.

QWalsh. Mr. Gibson what is your occupation?

A. I'm a barber in Ubly, have my own shop.

QW. Are you a friend of Dr. MacGregor?

A. Sure am. Ubly was mighty lucky when he settled here.

QW. Do you recall a conversation in your shop between Dr. MacGregor and Sheriff McAulay about a looking glass?

A. Sure do. Doc told Donald that if he held up a looking glass he would see the man who could make Mrs. Sparling confess.

QW. Are you saying Dr. MacGregor meant for the sheriff to hold the glass to his own face?

A. Sure, that's how I remember it.

Boomhower approached the witness for cross-examination. Ed Gibson was a friend and, like it or not, he now had to question his reliability.

QBoomhower. Mr. Gibson, how can you be so sure Dr. MacGregor meant for the sheriff to look in the glass?

A. That's just how I remember it.

QB. Do you know who else was in your shop at that time?

A. I think it was just the three of us.

QB. Would you be surprised if I told you that two other customers were there and ready to testify that they heard the remark and interpreted it differently, that the doctor should look in the glass himself?

A. I don't remember. Two you say? Could have been the Worth brothers. They always come in together. But they don't like Doc. Hard telling what they might say.

QB. So now you think two other gentlemen may have been in your shop that day?

A. Well, I can't be sure.

QB. What if Sheriff McAulay again took the stand and said it was only you three in the shop?

A. But you just said others were there.

QB. No Mr. Gibson. I asked if you would be surprised to learn others were there. It seems your memory is not as good as you would have us believe.

A. So this was a trick?

QB. No sir. I'm just trying to obtain clear and accurate testimony. Let's move on. Did you ever receive money from Dr. MacGregor?

A. What do you mean?

QB. Isn't it true that Dr. MacGregor pays you to make collections for him?

A. I may have helped once or twice.

QB. Is your memory failing you again?

A. I have occasionally worked for Dr. MacGregor as a collector, yes.

QB. Do you have another job?

A. Nope.

QB. Have you had another job in the recent past?

A. What do you mean?

QB. Mr. Gibson, have you ever held the position of Justice of the Peace?

A. Oh that, yes.

QB. Please look at this insurance form and tell the court if you signed it as a witness and also as a Justice of the Peace?

A. Yes I did.

QB. Do you remember when this happened?

A. Looks like August eighteen.

QB. But do you remember it?

A. No, I had to sign lots of things and can't remember all of them.

QB. Do you remember all three boys being at your shop to have these special appropriations signed?

A. They must have been if I signed them.

QB. But you don't exactly remember it as fact.

A. If I signed these papers the boys must have been there.

QB. So your memory of them being there is only triggered by seeing your signature?

A. They must have been there.

QB. Look again at this paper. Did you know Scyrel Sparling well?

A. Well enough.

QB. Was he in the habit of signing his name incorrectly?

A. Don't know.

QB. You say you remember the looking glass conversation.

A. Yes, I already told you that.

QB. What were the exact words?

A. I don't remember the exact words.

QB. You don't remember three boys in your shop waiting for your signature. You don't know if Scyrel was even there. You don't remember the exact words of a short conversation.

A. Well, I can't account for my memory.

Boomhower said he was done with the witness and, as he went to his seat, made a mental note not to go back to Gibson for a shave in the near future. Judge Beach told Ed Gibson he could step down, and as he left the courtroom he mused how he would love to have Zen Boomhower in his shop for a shave.

Mrs. Gibson and her daughter Edna had expected to take the stand next. But the hour was late and Judge Beach adjourned for the day. Neither woman was happy when told they must return.

* * *

On Wednesday, May twenty-second, an officer of the court was stationed at the bottom of the hallway stairs to maintain order and ensure the safety of those wishing to attend the trial. The judge did not want a repeat of the previous day's mayhem.

The Gibson women were sworn in when the trial began. The purpose of questioning them was to try and confirm the date that all three Sparling boys, Albert, Ray, and Scyrel, had been at their home to sign the Special Appropriation of Policy. The misspelling of Scyrel's signature demanded an explanation. Their memories, however, were no clearer than Ed Gibson's had been. After lengthy questioning from both prosecution and defense, both sides resigned themselves to not knowing where Scyrel was on August eighteenth or why he had misspelled his name. If he had spelled it at all.

Ida MacGregor was called after noon recess. She was dressed plainly, yet handsomely, in a blue and white striped dress of poplin. She wore a matching hat, but did not bother herself with adjusting it. Ida appeared to be a very confident woman and seemed eager to take the stand in her husband's defense. She had suffered months of gossip and innuendos with strong outward fortitude. As Ida took the stand, she looked at her husband and smiled.

QWalsh. Mrs. MacGregor, how long have you been married to Dr. MacGregor?

A. I have proudly and happily been married to Robert for over fourteen years.

QW. Do you have children?

A. I have a daughter, Bonnie, from a previous marriage. Robert and I have a son, Douglas, who is ten years old.

QW. Mrs. MacGregor, are you a friend of the Sparling family?

A. Yes I am.

QW. Are you aware of stories being circulated regarding your husband and Mrs. Sparling?

A. I have been told that lies are being passed around, yes.

QW. Have you ever had cause to doubt your husband's faithfulness to you?

A. Never!

QW. Is it true that your husband goes to the Sparling farm every day?

A. I don't keep track of my husband's business. If he was there every day, there had to have been a medical reason.

QW. You and Dr. MacGregor took a trip in the summer of 1911, is that correct?

A. Yes.

QW. Can you tell us the reason for that trip?

A. It was a vacation. We had a new automobile and Robert's brother had planned an automobile tour.

QW. Oh yes, the automobile. Was this a planned purchase?

A. We had certainly talked and dreamed about it. An automobile would make Robert's job so much easier.

QW. So you took your new automobile on a vacation?

A. Yes, we took it to London to see Robert's brother.

QW. Did you have money to pay for all of this?

A. Of course we did. Otherwise we would not have gone.

QW. Mrs. MacGregor, did Carrie Sparling give or send money to your husband for this trip?

A. I didn't learn of it until later, but if she gave my husband money, it was because she owed him.

Ida MacGregor continued to put on a strong appearance, as she knew the worst was yet to come with cross-examination. Would Zen be questioning her? She thought of so many times when he and Jennie had been guests in their home. They used to have such good times together. Her eyes met Zen's, but it was Ernest Snow who stood.

QSnow. Mrs. MacGregor, I realize how hard this must be for you.

A. Mr. Snow, telling the truth has never been hard for me. What is hard is having my husband falsely accused.

Snow smiled, but privately told himself that the gloves were off.

QS. Does your husband visit all his patients every day?

A. I already stated that I do not keep track of my husband's patients. But I'll tell you this. He is the kind of doctor who would do whatever was necessary to help those in need. If that meant daily treatment, he would do it.

QS. Very commendable. Mrs. MacGregor, do you know how much a new automobile costs?

A. No.

QS. Would you be surprised to learn a new Ford would cost six hundred and eighty-four dollars?

A. I would not be surprised, as I know very little about such things.

QS. You stated that you and the defendant talked and dreamed of owning an automobile.

Ida MacGregor was tired of hearing her husband referred to as a defendant. She looked intently into Snow's face and spoke.

A. I stated that my husband, Dr. MacGregor, and I did so. Yes.

QS. Were you surprised to discover your husband paid cash for that automobile?

A. I did not know that at the time.

QS. Were you surprised to learn that the money for the automobile came from Albert's life insurance policy?

A. I only learned of that the day we picked up the automobile.

QS. So it would seem you and your husband share dreams together, but not reality.

A. Mr. Snow, shortly after Albert Sparling died my daughter was very ill and she remained ill for many weeks. I was worried about her and my husband did not put any extra burdens regarding his business upon me.

QS. So an automobile came into your life, and you did not question how it got there?

A. I do not question my husband, if that is your meaning. If he purchased an automobile, I supposed his practice to be good enough to afford it. My husband is not the only physician to own an automobile.

QS. But your husband is the only one on trial for murder.

A. And falsely, I will add.

QS. That, Mrs. MacGregor, will be for a jury to decide. Getting back to your vacation. Were you surprised to learn Mrs. Sparling gave the defendant money both before and during the trip?

A. When a patient pays his or her bills I am pleased, not surprised.

QS. You have stated that stories about your husband and Carrie Sparling are lies. How can you be so certain?

A. Mr. Snow, I have told this court that I was married before I met Robert. I now tell the court that the marriage ended in divorce. Believe me Mr. Snow. I know when someone is unfaithful!

Ernest Snow did not want this testimony to end in Ida's favor, but he was reluctant to push her any further in case the jury saw it as badgering a person of the weaker sex. He looked at her, sitting self-assured in the witness chair. Weaker sex? Hardly! He addressed the judge and said he had no more questions.

As Ida left the stand she looked at her husband. His face was full of admiration and pride. She smiled at him and took her seat, folding her hands in her lap to keep them from shaking.

Reverend Hurd was sworn in next and took his seat.

QWalsh. Reverend Hurd, do you know the accused?
A. Yes I do. He is a member of my church.
QW. What is your opinion of Dr. MacGregor?
A. He is a good physician and an honorable man.
QW. Are you alone in these beliefs?
A. I hardly think so. The Sunday after his arrest I alluded to that event in my sermon. I told the church that the doctor needed our support, and when I asked for a show of that support, the entire congregation stood.
QW. Thank you, Reverend Hurd.

Ernest Snow approached the witness for cross-examination.

QSnow. Reverend Hurd, have you had occasion to talk to the defendant during this trial?
A. Sure, Dr. MacGregor and I talk some.
QS. Do you talk about the case?
A. Only in generalities.
QS. Why is that?
A. I have felt all along I might be called to testify and just didn't think it proper to go into detail.
QS. So you have avoided it?
A. Avoid is too strong a word. Most of my discussions with the doctor have been about spiritual strength in hard times.
QS. You were present when Scyrel died?
A. Yes I was.
QS. And you remained during the post mortem?
A. Yes. I felt the family might need me.
QS. Did the doctor tell the family that Scyrel died of liver cancer?
A. I do not recall the exact words, but the general understanding that night was that cancer is what killed the lad.

QS. And you believed that?

A. I'm not a physician and in no position to question the diagnosis of a good doctor.

QS. Did the defendant ask you to testify for him?

A. No. I was subpoenaed to appear and am honored to do so.

QS. Reverend Hurd, doesn't one of the commandments tell us not to commit murder?

A. It certainly does.

QS. Thank you Reverend Hurd. I have no more questions.

Reverend Hurd stood and gave a parting shot. "Another commandment says we should not bear false witness against our neighbor." He stepped down and took a seat with the other observers. One was seen to pat him on the back.

This May 21, 1912, photograph shows people waiting to enter the courtroom (Tribune Hall) before the doors opened.

This photograph shows people entering the courtroom (Tribune Hall) after the doors opened on May 21, 1912.

Chapter 61

On Thursday morning, banker Darby Leach was questioned about the Sparling family finances. Ernest Snow objected to the questions as being immaterial and irrelevant. He was overruled. Leach proceeded to give a history of the Sparling accounts beginning in July of 1908. When asked for a brief summary of account activity since 1908, he read a long list of dates and amounts of notes paid. "They were in debt when Mr. Sparling died, but Mrs. Sparling did a better job than her husband, rest his soul, about paying off notes," he commented.

QWalsh. There were no names in what you just read. Why is that?

A. It's just a statement of numbers, not people.

QW. Do any records show names?

A. Yes, if they were paid to the order of an individual.

QW. I will not ask you to read the names as a courtesy to their privacy, but would you please check the list for Dr. MacGregor's name?

Mr. Leach silently checked the list and then looked back at Attorney Walsh.

A. I find only one note to Dr. MacGregor for thirty-five dollars and twenty cents.

QW. Are you certain Mr. Leach? We have been led to believe that Dr. MacGregor had full control of Mrs. Sparling, including her finances.

Darby looked through the file again.

A. I only find the one.

QW. Thank you Mr. Leach.

Boomhower conducted the cross-examination.

QBoomhower. Mr. Leach you say you only find one instance of a note paid by the bank from Mrs. Sparling to Dr. MacGregor?

A. Yes.

QB. Do you keep records of who brings in these notes?

A. We enter them in the name of the party whom they were against.

QB. Then if a note was signed by Mrs. Sparling to me and I brought it to you for cash, you would only record the amount against her account? There would be no record of who cashed it?

A. That is correct.

QB. Then can you accurately say that Dr. MacGregor never brought in notes from Mrs. Sparling for cash?

A. Mr. Boomhower, most of our customers are creatures of habit. Dr. MacGregor, when bringing in notes, always had them credited to his account.

QB. What if he needed cash?

A. He withdrew from his account what he needed.

QB. If he brought in a note and received cash, would there be a record of that transaction?

A. The amount would be deducted from the account of the person who signed the note.

QB. Can you assure this court that Dr. MacGregor never strayed from his habit of crediting notes to his account?

A. His habit has been—

QB. I'm sorry to interrupt you, Mr. Leach. But can you state, without a doubt, that Dr. MacGregor never brought a note from Mrs. Sparling to your bank and took the cash rather than crediting it to his account?

A. No sir.

QB. Mr. Leach, if a person brought a note to be paid to the bearer, would you have a record of who received the money?

A. Only if that amount were credited to that bearer's account.

QB. So if I brought a note, payable to bearer, into your bank and only wanted cash from it, there would be no record of who received the money. Is that correct?

A. Yes it is.

   Boomhower had no more questions for the banker and court recessed for dinner. Nurse Gibbs took the stand in the afternoon.

   Margaret Gibbs wore a black skirt with a white shirtwaist. Her light brown hair was in braids, which wound around her head. She was above average in height and her pretty blue eyes belied the steeliness she had shown to people during the time after Scyrel's death. Those eyes now looked at Joseph Walsh.

QWalsh. Please tell the court your name and occupation.

A. My name is Margaret Gibbs and I am a nurse.

QW. How long have you been a nurse?

A. At least twenty years.

QW. How did you come to be at the Sparling farm?

A. I received a telephone call from Mrs. MacGregor on the eighth of August. I agreed to nurse the patient, and arrived the next day.

QW. Were you told about the possibility of poison?

A. Yes. Dr. MacGregor reviewed Scyrel's case on the way from the train station to the farm.

QW. Were you told to look for poison?

A. No.

QW. What were your orders?

A. I was to make certain that the patient received no food, drink, or medicine from anyone except myself.

QW. Miss Gibbs, when did Scyrel die?

A. He passed on the fourteenth.

QW. And you stayed on?

A. Yes. I had already been paid for the first two weeks and that time did not expire until August twenty-third.

QW. Did Dr. MacGregor ask you to stay?

A. No. Mrs. Sparling was doing poorly and since I was already there and paid, I decided to remain and help her regain her strength.

QW. This was your decision alone?

A. Yes. And Mrs. Hurford, Scyrel's sister, asked if I could stay the two weeks. She lives in Port Huron and it was hard for her to go back and forth.

QW. Your two weeks was up on August twenty-third. Did you go home then?

A. I planned on it and even said my good-byes. But I missed my train and returned to the farm. I told them I would stay another week.

QW. Was this your own decision?

A. Of course.

QW. How long did you stay?

A. Until September seventh.

QW. Why did you leave on September seventh?

A. For two reasons. Mrs. Sparling's physical condition had improved and I was called to be with the McCreary family in Tyre.

QW. Were you paid for the extended time you remained at the Sparlings?

A. No.

QW. And yet you stayed?

A. I had become attached to them and felt great sympathy for their situation. Even though Mrs. Sparling had improved physically, there were times when I felt I was still needed.

QW. When did you leave the McCreary's?

A. On September twenty-first. And then I returned to the Sparling's.

QW. How long did you stay this time?

A. For three days.

QW. Did you then remain in Port Huron for good?

A. No. I came back for the inquest in October. I promised them I would be there for it.

QW. So you were back in Ubly. How long did you stay?

A. After the inquest, one thing led to another. Mrs. Sparling was preparing to move, and then there was another post mortem on Scyrel's brother. Time just got away from me. I felt needed and I stayed.

QW. But how long did you stay?

A. I was there for the auction in November and went home about the fifth of November.

QW. To stay?

A. No. I told Mrs. Hurford I would come back to help with final arrangements for the move.

QW. How long did you stay that time?

Nurse Gibbs hesitated and looked down at the floor. It was only a short pause and then she was again in control.

A. I was there until November twenty-second, the day I was arrested as an accessory in Scyrel's death.

QW. That must have been a very hard time for you.

A. That is an understatement Mr. Walsh. It was devastating to learn my good intentions were being changed into something sinister.

Walsh said he had no more questions and returned to his seat. As Boomhower approached, Nurse Gibbs looked over the crowded courtroom and thought about her own upcoming trial.

QB. Miss Gibbs, did you know Dr. MacGregor before nursing Scyrel?

A. Slightly.

QB. And how was that?

A. I used to work where his father practiced, St. Joseph's Hospital in London.

QB. Do you think other nurses, closer to Ubly, could have given the same care and attention to Scyrel Sparling?

A. I'm sure there are many who could have done so.

QB. And yet he called on you to come from Port Huron. That is several miles away. Don't you find that curious?

A. When I am called to attend a patient I don't ask questions other than regards that patient.

QB. You stated that you missed the train on August twenty-third.

A. Yes, I misjudged the time.

QB. Are you certain you did not miss the train because you had gone to Dr. MacGregor's office to report on Mrs. Sparling?

A. I am sure. I did go to Dr. MacGregor's after I missed the train, but only because I needed a ride back to the farm.

QB. I don't know if you have been following these proceedings, but Sheriff McAulay testified that Dr. MacGregor told you to look for poison when the family had gone to sleep. Is this true?

A. No sir.

QB. Then how did you happen to find a bottle of strychnine?

A. I found it sometime between the two inquests. As I said, I stayed at the farm to help Mrs. Sparling. That included cleaning and helping her prepare for the move. I had cleaned the top of cupboards under those conditions and for no other reason.

QB. And that is how you found the strychnine?

A. No.

QB. But you testified that you did.

A. I did not find it when I cleaned the top of the cupboards the first time. But one week later, Mrs. Sparling asked me to clean them again and that is when I found it.

QB. Are you certain you didn't just overlook it the first time?

A. I am positive.

QB. Why did Mrs. Sparling ask you to clean the area again? Rather odd isn't it?

A. Mrs. Sparling had suffered a great tragedy and she was not always clear of mind. Rather than tell her the cupboard top was already cleaned I thought it easier to just do it again.

QB. If the doctor did not tell you to check for poison is the sheriff lying?

A. I'm sure I don't know. I can only speak from my own memory. And Dr. MacGregor never told me to search the house for poison.

QB. Miss Gibbs, you stayed for almost three months at the Sparling farm without pay. Why is that?

A. Mr. Boomhower, there are times when a person does, or should do, acts of kindness just because they need to be done.

QB. It has been suggested that you were kept at the farm, at Dr. MacGregor's urging, to keep Mrs. Sparling from talking.

A. I was told, and rightly so, to keep reporters and curious onlookers away from Mrs. Sparling. After Scyrel died, there were many buggies and automobiles passing by the house. More than usual.

QB. But didn't you also keep family away from her? Didn't you keep her husband's cousin Peter from having a conversation with her?

A. At that time I did not know Peter Sparling. I had already chased one reporter away. Mrs. Sparling was too frail to talk to a reporter or anyone else about the case.

QB. So you took on the job of deciding whom she could talk to. You kept her isolated.

A. I never took on another job, as you phrased it. I was trying, as a nurse and a friend, to prevent further stress upon a person who was physically and emotionally exhausted.

QB. While you were there tending Scyrel, did the doctor come to the farm?

A. Of course. Every day.

QB. He was checking on Scyrel?

A. That, and treating Mrs. Sparling's eyes.

QB. Oh yes the eyes. Miss Gibbs, is it difficult to treat Mrs. Sparling's eyes?

A. No, it is rather easy.

Boomhower had no further questions and privately wondered if there was any case against the nurse at all. She had treated Scyrel, but had not been involved in the care of John Wesley, Peter, or Albert. The expense and labor for her trial could now possibly be avoided. After all, there was still Carrie Sparling.

Nurse Gibbs left the stand and, looking straight ahead, walked out of the courtroom, down the steps, and toward the train station. At least one trial was behind her.

Chapter 62

On Friday morning the courtroom was full, but not over crowded. Had it been announced that Dr. MacGregor was to take the stand there probably would have been standing room only. Dr. MacGregor walked determinedly to the witness chair. He had sat quietly through troubling testimony that tarnished his name and his practice. His wife had been subjected to whispers and stares. He knew his children would be teased when school started in the fall. Now he had the opportunity to tell his story, and he prayed the jury would believe what he had to say.

QWalsh. Dr. MacGregor, how long have you been associated with the Sparling family?
A. Since 1906, or maybe 1907.
QW. Whom did you treat first?
A. Peter, the oldest boy.
QW. What was the nature of his illness?
A. He just was not right, had some mental problems and hallucinations.
QW. How did you treat that?
A. I tried talking to him and encouraged him to stop taking patent medicines. Told him he needed to take better care of himself.
QW. Whom did you treat next?
A. I treated Mrs. Sparling about the same time as Peter.
QW. What was her condition?
A. I first treated her for pneumonia, and later she developed an illness of a private nature, female problems. She had to have an operation in 1907.
QW. Did that fix the problem?
A. Not completely. She continued to have trouble until—she still had some problems the last I saw her.
QW. Did she have any other problems?
A. Yes, she suffered a conical cornea and choroiditis, which are eye ailments.
QW. Is there medicine for these afflictions?
A. Yes. Atropine.
QW. What is atropine?
A. It is a poison derived from the belladonna plant.
QW. Poison?
A. Yes, but in controlled circumstances it can help a person with those optic diseases.

QW. Did you treat Mr. Sparling?

A. Yes, he came to my office in late spring of '08.

QW. What was his concern?

A. He could not get free from the grippe, and he had a dragging gait.

QW. Did he recover from the grippe?

A. No. Complications arose from it and his immune system was weakened.

QW. What was the cause of his death?

A. Diffusing Myolitis, an inflamed and diseased spinal cord. He was mostly paralyzed when he died.

QW. When did the oldest boy die?

A. I believe it was July of 1910.

QW. What was the cause of death?

A. Septicemia Pneumococcus, bacteria in the lungs.

QW. Dr. MacGregor, you have heard accusations from Henry Bacon and Anna Pieruski regarding your being in the bedroom alone with Mrs. Sparling.

A. Yes.

QW. How would you explain these circumstances?

A. First of all, if Anna Pieruski observed that, she would have noticed Mrs. Sparling's sons in the house. I was treating her for female problems that demanded privacy. I don't know of any woman who would wish to be examined in front of others.

Dr. MacGregor shook his head, trying to recall the only incident he could remember that involved Henry Bacon.

A. As far as Reverend Bacon, it had to be when J.W. was still alive. He wanted no part of a hospital, but I felt such action necessary. I needed to speak with Mrs. Sparling out of his earshot regarding the arrangements.

QW. And her eye treatments? We heard Nurse Gibbs say the eye drops were fairly easy to administer.

A. Yes, for a trained nurse or physician. I would rather err on the side of caution when atropine is involved.

QW. You dropped her eyes every day?

A. At first it was every other day, but her eyes responded better when done daily, so that is what I did.

QW. Dr. MacGregor, have you ever had improper relations with Mrs. Sparling?

The silence in the room was deafening. The jury sat up attentively and the spectators leaned forward in their seats to hear the accused's response.

Reverend Hurd sat beside Ida MacGregor for support. Dr. MacGregor, who had been calm throughout the trial, almost shouted his denial.

A. Never. Absolutely not!

Judge Beach decided it was prudent to take a short break at this time and he adjourned the court until after dinner. As the bailiff led MacGregor away, Ida reached out to her husband. Robert stopped as if to go to her, and his slight hesitation gave the guard opportunity to grab the defendant's elbow and whisk him out of the courtroom. Ida lowered her empty hand and watched him leave. In the afternoon session much of the testimony referred to Albert Sparling.

QWalsh. Doctor, you stated that Albert was often sick.
A. Yes. He had stomach and kidney problems. And, like his brothers, he was always worried about pimples.
QW. Let's go to his last illness. When were you called to the house?
A. On a Saturday. I think it was April twenty-ninth. He had been vomiting severely. I gave him bismuth and it seemed to help.
QW. Seemed to help?
A. Yes, he and his mother were in church the next morning and my wife invited them to dinner at our home.
QW. So Albert was better the next day?
A. I had hoped so, but he again became ill and Mrs. Sparling took him home.
QW. Did anyone else examine him?
A. Yes, Doctors Conboy and Corcoran.
QW. Did either of them give a diagnosis?
A. Some things were discussed as possibilities. Nephritis, uremia, and pancreatitis were all suggested.
QW. Doctor, Perry Cole has testified that he saw you throw something into the wood stove after Albert died. Did you do that?
A. Yes. Dr. Conboy had left strychnine powders for Albert and when the boy died, I threw what remained into the fire.
QW. Why did you do that?
A. Strychnine is a poison, and I didn't want it lying about the house.
QW. Dr. MacGregor, did you ask for a post mortem after Albert died?
A. Yes I did, but the family would not allow it. His brother Scyrel and sister Mae were the most vocal against it.

QW. What was given as the cause of Albert's death?
A. Dr. Conboy was inclined to think—

Snow interrupted with an objection as to conclusion, but was overruled.

QW. What exactly did Dr. Conboy say?
A. I don't recall his exact wording, but he seemed to believe nephritis might be the cause.
QW. Did Dr. Corcoran give a reason for death?
A. He agreed that nephritis might have killed the boy.
QW. When Albert died, had you thought of arsenic?
A. Indeed not.
QW. Had Dr. Conboy thought of arsenic?
A. I doubt it. He never mentioned it and, besides, he had agreed on nephritis.
QW. Dr. MacGregor, have you made money off the Sparling family?
A. Hardly.
QW. But you used Albert's insurance money to buy an automobile.
A. Yes, but that money was owed me.
QW. Doctor, you must admit that was certainly a hefty bill.
A. Mr. Walsh, I saw the family sometimes three or four times in one day. I did not become a physician to gain wealth, but there are bills to be paid.
QW. Yet it was testified that you told Mr. Yauch before Albert died that you planned to pay cash for the vehicle. How did you intend to do so?
A. I was owed money from several patients. Mr. Gibson was helping to collect on those debts. I really thought that between the two of us we would come up with enough for the automobile.
QW. And did you?
A. It wasn't necessary. Mrs. Sparling received one of the insurance payments and signed it over to me.
QW. I understand you live in a house owned by Mrs. Sparling. Do you pay rent to her?
A. The amount agreed to was twenty-five dollars per month.
QW. How did Mrs. Sparling usually pay you?
A. By note.
QW. Were these made out to bearer or to the order of Dr. MacGregor?
A. Usually to bearer.
QW. What did you do with these notes?
A. I paid my bills and supported my family.

QW. Dr. MacGregor, this may seem to be a foolish question but the prosecution has made a to-do about your helping Mrs. Sparling get Albert's insurance. Please explain why you did this.

A. When Peter died, his estate went through probate. It took a long time for Mrs. Sparling to get his insurance, money that was owed her and needed on the farm. When Albert died, I tried to be a friend and help her through the difficult times. One thing I knew I could do, and did, was to look into the insurance situation. I would do that for any patient or friend.

QW. Doctor, with capable nurses in this area, why did you call Miss Gibbs from Port Huron when Scyrel became ill?

A. Her name came to my mind first. This was a desperate time and I wanted a nurse that was proven.

QW. Did you tell her about the poison?

A. I did.

QW. And did you suggest she look for it?

A. I'm sure I did.

QW. But she has just testified that you did not ask her to do so.

A. Then she misunderstood.

QW. How so?

A. I told her in no uncertain terms that nothing—no food, no drink, no medicine— be given to Scyrel by anyone other than herself. I knew we had to stop the poisoning. I'm sure I asked her to search for it but, again, this was a desperate time and maybe she just didn't hear me correctly.

QW. Dr. MacGregor, did you call upon Doctors Conboy and Corcoran when Albert was ill.

A. Yes.

QW. When Scyrel became ill, you also called Dr. Herrington for assistance?

A. I called him, yes. After Albert died there was much second-guessing, and folks wondered why I hadn't called Herrington in to examine him.

QW. So your reason was to quiet the complaints?

A. Not completely. I hoped he might have a diagnosis or suggest a treatment the rest of us had not thought of.

QW. And did he?

A. No. In fact, he seemed upset that I had called him.

QW. You have heard the testimony about the Special Appropriation and the misspelling of Scyrel's signature. Can you enlighten us?

A. When my father sent the form, I signed it as a witness to the form. Scyrel was not there. I did not sign as a witness to the signature because I was not there when he signed it. I know nothing about a misspelling.

QW. Dr. MacGregor, did you telephone Doctors Morden and Herrington when Scyrel died?

A. Yes. They were to come out and perform a post mortem.

QW. And did they?

A. No, they were delayed by an emergency.

QW. So you and Dr. Holdship conducted the procedure.

A. Yes.

QW. Why didn't you just wait until they arrived? Couldn't it have waited a few more hours?

A. I suppose so. But that would mean Scyrel's body would have to wait, and that would mean Mr. McKay would have to wait. I felt there was no reason Dr. Holdship and I could not go ahead with the autopsy. I also was thinking of the family when I made the decision.

QW. Now much has been made of this post mortem. I will just ask you a simple question and you can give me a simple answer. Did you tell Dr. Morden that Scyrel's stomach had been opened?

A. No. I do not remember doing so and my deposition of last October will substantiate that. When I saw the condition of the liver, I was certain we had an answer and there was no need to cut further.

It had been a long day and a long week. Since court would be held the next day, a rare Saturday session, the judge adjourned earlier than usual.

On Saturday, the questioning of MacGregor resumed.

QW. Dr. MacGregor, the Sparling boys all carried insurance. In fact, three of them were covered by policies from two different companies. Can you tell the court of your involvement?

A. I knew nothing about the Gleaner policies when I suggested Sun Life Assurance to them. I believe they added those policies later.

QW. So you initiated the action?

A. No, Peter and Albert came to me and asked about insurance. My father was a representative for Sun Life and I knew the rate to be very competitive. When they learned that, they said it sounded good. My father was coming for a visit, the boys met him, and one thing led to another. The boys were examined, filled out the applications, and each received a policy.

QW. You did not pressure them into this?

A. No sir.

QW. When Albert died, what was given as cause of death?

A. Acute nephritis, kidney failure.

QW. You were satisfied with that conclusion?

A. Given his history of stomach and kidney problems, yes. And Dr. Corcoran said he believed Albert to be uremic as well. He and I agreed on the cause of death.

QW. Doctor, you heard Mrs. MacDonald testify that while you suggested she have a nurse for her child, you would not allow Nurse Gibbs even one night with the sick baby. Why is that?

A. My primary patients were the Sparling family. I was only called to the MacDonald home as a favor to Dr. Corcoran. I had to decide on nursing care for a baby who was near death, and a mother who was extremely weakened by the death of a third son.

QW. You also heard the testimony of Miss Hunter?

A. Yes.

QW. She said you told her there were worse things than death, that you expected to be arrested, and would trade places with her father. Did that conversation take place?

A. Yes it did.

QW. Did you also say that arsenic was used as a medicine?

A. Yes. But I also told her I never gave any.

QW. Dr. MacGregor were you, besides being a physician, also a friend to the Sparling family?

A. I was.

QW. Through this friendship did you come to control Mrs. Sparling and everything she did?

A. Absolutely not! I did things for the family out of friendship and for no personal gain.

QW. What kind of things?

A. I helped select a coffin for Albert and assisted with the funeral arrangements. I have helped the boys butcher hogs and I did general jobs to help them on the farm whenever possible. I even carried a set of work clothes on my rounds.

QW. You carried work clothes when you went to the Sparling farm?

A. I carried work clothes in case any patient needed help.

QW. Coming now to Scyrel's last illness. How long before you realized he would not live?

A. I don't know an exact time. A physician always works to heal his patients. My theory is to keep their hopes alive so they will use their will to live and fight off the sickness. There is much power in the human will.

QW. When Dr. Conboy came to the farm on August ninth, were you surprised?

A. Well, I had not known he was coming.

QW. Did he say why he was there?

A. Yes. He planned to scare Mrs. Sparling enough that if she was administering poison she would stop.

QW. Did you say you had already scared the devil out of her?

A. No. I do not remember saying those words.

QW. Doctor, you heard the chemist and doctors from Ann Arbor testify that arsenic was found in both Albert and Scyrel?

A. Yes I did.

QW. Do you believe that?

A. I cannot go against expert testimony, but I still find it hard to believe these boys were intentionally poisoned.

QW. You heard Sheriff McAulay's testimony. Did you tell him the boys had syphilis and that Ray would also die from it?

A. I conveyed those thoughts, but not in those words.

QW. Did you tell him that this deal was killing you?

A. I'm sure I said something to that effect.

QW. The sheriff also stated that you said this deal would ruin you because Mrs. Sparling would be arrested and you would never get the six hundred dollars she still owed you. Did he hear you correctly?

A. No. I did say that Mrs. Sparling owed me money, but I never said I would lose it if she were arrested.

QW. Dr. MacGregor, when you mentioned a looking glass to the sheriff who did you intend to look into that glass?

A. Why, the sheriff of course. It's his duty to go to an alleged guilty party and get a confession.

QW. Did you in any way administer arsenic to Albert and/or Scyrel Sparling?

A. No I did not. If they got arsenic, it wasn't from me.

Court was adjourned until Monday morning.

On Sunday, Ed and Cecelia Hurford went to Port Huron to visit their son and daughter-in-law. They spoke to Carrie, but she seemed distant and had little to say. At dinnertime, Carrie said she was not hungry so the Hurfords and Ray sat down to dinner without her. In low voices, Ed and Cecelia gave an update on the trial. "This whole case is unbelievable. They claim proof of intentional poisoning, yet there's absolutely no clear evidence that anyone actually gave the boys arsenic. MacGregor will be cross-examined on Monday. He claims he's innocent. In fact he seems to be casting blame toward your mother, Mae. She seems so weak. How can she ever survive a trial?" Silence came over the table and Mae fought back tears. "She was doing somewhat better until Big Pete surrendered the bond. Now she just sits in that old rocking chair. I don't believe she can get through a trial without a complete breakdown. But we don't need to be concerned until that happens. Let's talk about something else. We're trying to isolate her from news of the trial and it would be terrible if she heard it in this house."

It was too late. Carrie had decided to join the group for dinner, but paused outside the door when news of the trial reached her ears. Slowly and silently, she returned to her chair. In murmurs too soft to be heard, she kept repeating, "How could you?"

Chapter 63

Ernest Snow began the cross-examination on Monday. He had been looking forward to this since the trial began. Dr. MacGregor had worked with his attorneys to prepare for Snow's cross-examination. He had learned that Snow could be harsh in his questioning and the doctor hoped he was strong enough to deal with him. As he took the stand he looked at his old friend, but Boomhower appeared to be busy with paperwork on the desk in front of him.

QSnow. Dr. MacGregor, you gave your reasons for treating Mrs. Sparling behind closed doors when others were in the house. Did you also treat her behind closed doors when the house was empty?

A. Of course. A farmhouse doesn't remain empty for long. If I was treating her for her female ills, then yes, I always did so behind a closed door.

QS. Dr. MacGregor, when did you begin treating Albert?

A. As I said, I assumed care of the Sparling family in 1906 or 1907.

QS. His previous ailments, were they serious?

A. If you are the one hurting or uncomfortable, yes.

QS. But were they life threatening?

A. No.

QS. You stated he became ill the last time on April twenty-ninth. When did he die?

A. On May third.

QS. So, for someone not seriously ill, he worsened quickly.

A. Yes.

QS. You called both Dr. Conboy and Dr. Corcoran in for consultation and they concurred with your diagnosis of kidney failure?

A. Yes, acute nephritis.

QS. Did they do a thorough examination of Albert?

A. No, not thorough.

QS. So they agreed with you because of what you led them to believe.

A. I did not lead either doctor. I told them that Albert had been troubled with stomach and kidney problems for years.

QS. But you said those illnesses were not life threatening.

A. Correct. But over time his internal organs could have been affected for the worse.

QS. Then why did you ask for a post mortem?

A. Because I was not positive in my own mind that nephritis had killed him.

QS. But the post mortem was never done?

A. No, his family was firmly against it.

QS. When you and Dr. Conboy drove out to the farm in May, did you tell him Albert's condition?

A. Yes.

QS. Did you mention a fall?

A. Yes. Albert had fallen from a tree some few days before he took ill. It could have caused internal injuries.

QS. And did you mention syphilis?

A. Yes. I believed it was a possibility.

QS. Why did you think he might have it?

A. From family history and his carrying on at night.

QS. Did Dr. Conboy find any sign of syphilis?

A. No, but he only did a cursory examination.

QS. You heard the experts from Ann Arbor?

A. Yes.

QS. Then you also heard them say they found no sign of syphilis in Albert or Scyrel.

A. I heard it.

QS. But you thought it could be the problem?

A. Only that it was a possibility.

QS. What time did Dr. Corcoran arrive to examine Albert?

A. It was late on the second of May.

QS. Did you really think he could help Albert who by now was near death?

A. A doctor never gives up Mr. Snow.

QS. Before Dr. Conboy left, you asked him to tell Mrs. Sparling that her son was dying.

A. Yes. He had known the family longer than I, and I thought it might be easier.

QS. Easier for you, or Mrs. Sparling?

A. Mrs. Sparling of course.

QS. Now we have all heard the symptoms Albert experienced, tenderness of the abdomen, weak and rapid pulse, swollen and inflamed lips and nose. Aren't those indicative of arsenic poisoning?

A. I think so.

QS. You think so? Don't you know?

A. I do now.

QS. Didn't you know the symptoms of arsenic poisoning at that time?

A. Not as well as I do now. When Scyrel became sick with many of the same symptoms, I proceeded to study up on the subject. When Dr. Conboy came out to examine Scyrel, I was the first one to suggest arsenic.

QS. Are you saying you did not try to cover your tracks, or cast blame elsewhere by suddenly introducing arsenic into the conversation?

A. I felt no need to cover tracks, as you put it. Dr. Conboy and I had apparently arrived at the same conclusion that day.

QS. So you asked if he was thinking about arsenic?

A. Yes. And he said he was.

QS. And then you added how strange that you were both thinking about it at the very same time.

A. I do not recollect that.

QS. You did not say it?

A. I won't swear I did or didn't.

QS. Now when Scyrel was ill, you called Dr. Herrington.

A. Yes, I have already gone over that.

QS. You had been criticized for not having him out to examine Albert, hadn't you?

A. There were rumors to that effect.

QS. You were convinced from the beginning that Scyrel was going to die.

A. I thought he might.

QS. Didn't you tell Dr. Herrington that the boy was going to die?

A. I doubt I used those words. I was afraid he might die.

QS. Doctor, did you think Scyrel Sparling was going to die on August fifth when Dr. Herrington was called?

A. To a certain extent.

QS. To a certain extent you thought he would die, or you were afraid he might die. Can't you just answer yes or no?

A. I thought he might die.

QS. When you arrived at the farm on August fourth, Scyrel was walking around outside.

A. I don't recall if that was the fourth or fifth.

QS. Regardless doctor, did you on the fifth of August believe a man who was up and about on the fourth was going to die?

A. After checking his pulse, I thought his condition to be unfavorable.

QS. I did not ask about his condition. Just tell the court whether or not you thought this lad was going to die.

A. I said I thought his condition was unfavorable.

QS. Dr. MacGregor, this is getting ridiculous. Tell us, please, if you thought Scyrel Sparling was going to die.

A. I said I thought to a certain extent his condition was unfavorable and I thought he might die.

QS. Is that the way you want to answer the question?

A. That is as near as I can answer, Mr. Snow.

Judge Beach was exhausted after this tiring interchange. He looked at the jury. A few were fidgeting and some sat with a glazed expression on their faces. He pounded his gavel for noon recess. Cross-examination continued afterward.

QS. Dr. MacGregor, you stated that Dr. Herrington was upset because you had called him to come out.

A. Yes. He said Scyrel's trouble was merely a bilious attack.

QS. Did you agree with him?

A. I can't say that I thought exactly as he did.

QS. Is Dr. Herrington a reputable physician?

A. I believe so.

QS. And yet you did not agree with a reputable physician that the lad would be all right. In fact Dr. MacGregor, you knew he would not be all right.

A. No I did not!

QS. I refuse to enter again into the dialogue we had before dinner, but the record does show you thought the boy might die. Did Dr. Conboy also examine Scyrel?

A. Yes.

QS. What was his diagnosis?

A. He gave none, but suggested all medicines be stopped. He left strychnine as he did with Albert.

QS. Why didn't you call Dr. Herrington again when the lad's condition worsened?

A. I had more confidence in Dr. Conboy.

QS. Looking at the nurse's record, you prescribed several enemas for Scyrel.

A. Yes.

QS. What was the purpose in that?

A. To clean the boy's system.

QS. Wasn't it to eliminate any traces of arsenic that might be found in an investigation?
A. No sir.
QS. Would an enema eliminate arsenic from a person who was poisoned?
A. To some degree, yes.
QS. And you prescribed several enemas. If I count correctly, he had seven from August ninth to the thirteenth. That is seven enemas in a period of five days.
A. I already stated my intent.
QS. Doctor, you also stated that an enema would eliminate arsenic.
A. Yes, if there were any poison in the lower part of the bowels, an enema would have a tendency to get it out.
QS. Would vomiting have the same effect?
A. To some degree, but an enema would work better.
QS. So you ordered one enema and then more.
A. I knew if Scyrel lived long enough, any poison would be eliminated. I didn't know then that even if poison were removed, the damage would be done and that person could still die from its effects.
QS. After you and Dr. Conboy had your discussion on arsenic—
A. It was not a discussion.
QS. Well when you both were suspicious of arsenic, did you tell Mrs. Sparling of your concerns?
A. Dr. Conboy did. He didn't mention arsenic, just poison.
QS. And her response?
A. She thought he could have been poisoned by dust from threshing.
QS. Why did you have Dr. Conboy tell her?
A. I felt it better if she heard it from him.
QS. But you were the family physician.
A. Yes.
QS. Seems to me you would have taken the lead.
A. I answered the question Mr. Snow.

Ernest Snow was determined not to let his frustration show. Dr. MacGregor was giving him a much harder time than he had anticipated. He walked back to his table, took a drink of water, and returned to face MacGregor.

QS. Moving to August ninth. Dr. Conboy came to the farm at Attorney Boomhower's request to scare Mrs. Sparling.
A. Something like that.

377

QS. And you told him not to bother because you had already scared the devil out of her.

A. I have already testified that I did not utter those words.

QS. Doctor, did you say it in substance?

A. In substance I may have.

QS. On August thirteenth, Dr. Herrington, Dr. Conboy, and Dr. Holdship joined you at the Sparling farm.

A. Yes.

QS. And that is when you had a whispered conversation with Dr. Conboy about arsenic and about who else knew of your suspicions.

A. It was not whispered like you are trying to convey.

QS. Was it loud enough for the other two doctors to hear?

A. I don't think so, but that was not the intent. Mr. Snow, we were almost to the door. Do you think I would say the word arsenic loud enough for the family to hear?

QS. So you maintain this was not meant to be a secret conversation?

A. I do.

QS. Had you told the other doctors of your suspicions?

A. No.

QS. Then it was known only to you and Dr. Conboy, and kept secret from the others.

A. You are twisting words.

QS. I am only trying to give the jury a clear picture of events. When Scyrel died, you and Dr. Holdship did the post mortem rather than wait for Doctors Herrington and Morden.

A. I have already explained that.

QS. Is it true that you were once Huron County Coroner? And in that position, did you ever conduct post mortems?

A. Yes, to both questions.

QS. Then you must know the only way to determine inflammation of the stomach is to cut it open and look at the lining.

A. Yes, but we got to the liver first.

QS. I didn't ask you for sequence. Did you know that only by opening a stomach you could determine inflammation?

A. Yes.

QS. And by this time you suspected arsenic poisoning?

A. It was a possibility.

QS. Then why didn't you open the stomach?

A. Dr. Holdship was doing the cutting.

Snow let out a huge breath. Could MacGregor actually be this obtuse or was he just baiting him in hopes the prosecution would lose its temper in front of the jury? He leaned forward and put his hands on the table in front of the defendant.

QS. Then why didn't you tell him to open the stomach?
A. Because once we saw the liver, we believed we had found the cause of death.
QS. That being?
A. It appeared cancerous.
QS. You stated you did not wait for Doctors Herrington and Morden out of concern for the family.
A. Correct.
QS. Then why wasn't that family entitled to a more thorough investigation?
A. The boy was dead. It appeared to be a cancerous liver. I saw no need to cut any further.
QS. So you felt you were off the hook?
A. I resent that Mr. Snow!
QS. But you made a comment after determining there was cancer that now people would shut up.

Dr. MacGregor was becoming angry and his voice grew louder.

A. You are twisting words again. I saw what looked to be a cancerous liver. I also had heard whispers and accusations. I think I was actually relieved if it were cancer, because then people would know the truth and stop peddling lies.

Snow paused to let MacGregor's anger settle on the courtroom. He walked back to his table slowly for another drink before addressing the defendant again.

QS. Can we get back to the subject of cutting? Why would Dr. Morden testify under oath that you told him the stomach was cut open?
A. For the same reason I testified under oath, now and at my deposition, that I did not say that!
QS. So Dr. Morden is incorrect?
A. You would have to ask him.
QS. But I did, and he said you told him the stomach had been cut.
A. But I never told him that.

QS. Perhaps we need to call Dr. Morden to the stand again, but for now we need to move on. What did you do with the pieces of viscera you took from the body?

A. They were placed in a crock and a two-quart sealing jar. Mr. McKay covered them with embalming fluid.

QS. Did you request any of the viscera for yourself?

A. Yes, a small piece of the liver.

QS. Why?

A. I wanted my brother, who is also a doctor, to examine it.

QS. And did he?

A. Yes.

QS. What was his determination?

A. He said the liver had undergone a chemical degeneration, a toxic change.

QS. Toxic as in poison?

A. Yes.

QS. When did you receive this report from your brother?

MacGregor paused before answering.

A. It was about the end of August or early September.

QS. Dr. MacGregor, I have here the death certificate for Scyrel Sparling. Is this your signature?

A. Yes.

QS. What is given as cause of death?

A. Hypertrophic cirrhosis of the liver.

QS. And that means an enlarged, diseased liver?

A. Yes.

QS. What is the date of this document?

There was another hesitation from MacGregor.

A. September twenty-second of last year.

Mumblings quietly spread through the room and Judge Beach banged his gavel to silence them before they could disrupt the proceedings.

QS. So you knew from your brother by early September that the liver showed signs of poison, but did not include it as a cause of death?

A. The liver was enlarged and diseased. I did not lie.

QS. I didn't say you did.

Snow looked at the jury.

QS. Now who is twisting words?

He turned back to face MacGregor.

QS. Doctor, when you received the report from your brother did you go to Attorney Boomhower or the authorities with this important information?
A. No.
QS. But weren't you all working to the same end?
A. Yes, but by this time the prosecution was not sharing anything with me. I thought they were in a position to find out for themselves. After all, they had sent samples to Ann Arbor.
QS. Weren't you interested in finding out whether or not Scyrel had been poisoned?
A. I was.
QS. But you thought they could find it out on their own.
A. I would hardly say that.
QS. But you just did.
A. To a certain extent perhaps.
QS. Dr. MacGregor, you told Miss Hunter that arsenic is used as a medicine.
A. Yes. Two years ago a scientist claimed it could cure syphilis.
QS. But you also told Miss Hunter that you never gave arsenic as a medicine.
A. That is correct.
QS. Do you carry something called Fowler's Solution in your medical bag?
A. Yes.
QS. Does it contain arsenic?
A. It has some arsenic in it. I believe four grains to a fluid ounce. I never gave straight arsenic to a patient.
QS. But you gave Fowler's, which is an arsenic solution.
A. Yes. Every doctor carries it in his bag.
QS. But I'm not talking about other doctors.

Judge Beach interrupted. "Mr. Snow, it's getting late. Do you have more questions?" Ernest Snow declared he was only beginning. "Then I suggest we adjourn," proposed the judge.

Dr. MacGregor was not sure his legs would hold him when he left the stand. He didn't know how much more Snow planned to throw at him but he had to keep up a strong appearance. Somehow, he managed to return to his chair.

Ernest Snow appreciated the adjournment. His patience had worn thin and he needed to collect his thoughts for the next day. MacGregor had proved to be more formidable than he had expected.

Chapter 64

Questioning on Tuesday concerned MacGregor's financial status. Neither Snow nor MacGregor had enjoyed a good night's sleep after Monday's grueling battle and both hoped they were up for another day of confrontation.

QSnow. Dr. MacGregor, were you in debt when you arrived in Ubly?

A. I had a few debts from Burnside, but we paid them off quickly.

QS. You bought Dr. Griffin's practice when you moved here, correct?

A. Yes.

QS. But he would not sell you his house?

A. Correct.

QS. Why is that?

A. You would have to ask him.

QS. That might be difficult seeing as how he is deceased. But do I understand that he did sell to Mrs. Sparling?

A. Yes he did.

QS. And she fixed it up for you to live in?

A. Yes, it was most generous.

QS. Did you pay the rent directly to her or did you credit her account?

A. I believe it was credited.

QS. Where would we find a record of that?

A. It would be in my ledger.

QS. Is this the ledger?

A. Yes.

QS. But Doctor, there are several erasures in it.

A. That was a misunderstanding.

QS. How so?

A. Mr. Clark told me to be sure it was properly posted before the trial.

QS. This would be Attorney George Clark?

A. Yes.

QS. And he told you to make erasures?

A. No sir. He told me to post it properly and I misunderstood. I am a physician, not an accountant. He was not happy when he heard what I had done.

QS. So it wasn't posted properly?

A. No. Some months were missing.

QS. Missing?

A. I had not transferred them from my daybook.

QS. Continue.

A. Some entries only had a lump sum with no details.

QS. So you fixed it up?

A. I did not fix anything up. I only tried to properly post my ledger for this trial.

QS. Getting back to the rent. I have searched this ledger to find a credit, but have been unsuccessful. Can you find monthly credits for this court?

A. I don't believe they are posted.

QS. So you have lived rent-free?

A. No. I am sure rent was paid or credited.

QS. How can we know this if there are no records to prove it?

A. I'm sure I did not live rent-free. I may have paid her in cash.

QS. Do you have a cashbook that might help answer the question?

A. I did, but I can't find it. I had it with me at the last inquest, but it is now missing.

QS. Well that's convenient isn't it?

Joseph Walsh exploded from his seat to object. Judge Beach sustained the objection with a stern, "You know better, Mr. Snow."

QS. Now Doctor, you took both Albert and Scyrel to Detroit for hernia operations?

A. Yes, I went as a favor to the family.

QS. Did you charge for these favors?

A. Well, I had expenses. Mrs. Sparling gave me fifty dollars for each trip.

QS. Can you break down those expenses for the court?

A. Yes. For Albert, my ledger shows five dollars on Tuesday, ten dollars on Wednesday, and twenty-five dollars on Thursday. For Scyrel, I charged five dollars for Thursday, ten dollars for Friday, ten dollars for Saturday and fifteen dollars for Sunday.

QS. But each of those adds up to forty dollars and you said she gave you fifty dollars.

A. Yes. I didn't know ahead what the expenses would actually be so she gave me fifty dollars when we left for Detroit.

QS. So you actually wrote down the expenses when you returned home. What did you do with the ten-dollar overpayment in each case?

A. I must have credited her account.

QS. Did you?

A. It isn't in the ledger. I may have paid her in cash.

QS. And that transaction would be in the missing cashbook?

A. Yes.

QS. It has been established that Mrs. Sparling usually paid you with notes payable to bearer.

A. That is correct.

QS. Whose idea was that?

A. I have no idea. Many patients prefer to pay that way.

QS. When Peter died, his estate had to be settled through probate Is that correct?

A. Yes.

QS. And you assisted Mrs. Sparling in that matter?

A. Yes, as a friend of the family.

QS. Did you charge her anything for this?

A. Well, there were expenses. I don't know if I asked for money or she suggested it.

QS. How much did she give you?

A. I believe it was fifteen dollars.

QS. Was it for legal services or medical services?

A. Neither.

QS. Then I have to assume it was for friend services.

The obvious sarcasm raised the eyebrows of several in the courtroom.

QS. Did you credit her account?

A. I don't think so, but again it may have been her idea to pay me for helping. She was that kind of person.

QS. There is nothing in your ledger so I guess we'll just never know.

Snow looked at the jury and shrugged his shoulders. MacGregor seethed, but tried not to let the jury see his anger.

QS. Doctor, did you truly believe you could collect enough money from your patients to pay six hundred and eighty-four dollars in cash for a new automobile?

A. Many people owed me, Mr. Snow. Mr. Gibson and I planned to be very aggressive in collecting. Not in a mean way though. I planned to deduct a percentage of the bill if they would pay off what they owed.

QS. But you never had to do that, did you?

A. No. Mrs. Sparling received the Sun Life check and gave it to me to settle her account.

QS. My but she had a large account if it took one thousand dollars to pay it off.

A. I was treating the family almost daily. It adds up.

QS. Did you offer her a percentage deduction?

A. I don't remember.

QS. What amount did you claim she owed you before Albert died?

A. It came to nine hundred and sixty-three dollars.

The gavel hushed a collective gasp from the courtroom. Attorney Snow looked shocked at the amount, as if he had heard it for the first time. He shook his head as if trying to understand.

QS. Dr. MacGregor, what on earth did you charge for a house call?

A. I charged two and a half dollars.

QS. And what period did this nine hundred and sixty-three-dollar bill cover?

A. It was for the month of April—

Snow interrupted.

QS. Excuse me a moment.

Snow then pretended to cipher at his table, but the amount had already been calculated and he turned back to the doctor.

QS. That would be over three hundred and eighty house calls in one month.

A. I tried to tell you. It had an April date, but included previous unpaid bills, plus medicines.

QS. But I heard that Mrs. Sparling was very good at paying her bills on time.

A. Yes, but sometimes there can be a hardship and bills have to be held over.

QS. I can understand that, I suppose. Now, let's review. You gave her a bill for nine hundred and sixty-three dollars and she gave you a check for one thousand dollars. Is that correct?

A. Yes.

QS. Did you pay her back the extra thirty-seven dollars?

A. I don't remember.

QS. All right, let's leave that and move on to the six hundred dollars you said she still owed you. If she paid your bill of nine hundred and sixty-three dollars, in May, how did she come to again owe you another six hundred dollars by last fall?

A. Mr. Snow, I was at the farm sometimes three or four times a day to treat Scyrel.

QS. And you have an itemized record to equal six hundred dollars?

A. No I don't. That figure was conjecture on my part.

QS. Were you hoping to erase this new debt of hers with an insurance check from Scyrel's estate?

MacGregor's eyes flashed. He braced his hands against the table, looked past Snow to the jury, and shouted.

A. I was not!

Snow looked at MacGregor for what seemed like a very long time before continuing.

QS. All right, let's forget the additional six hundred dollars. After you bought the automobile, you took a trip to Canada.

A. Yes.

QS. And Mrs. Sparling gave you twenty dollars before you left?

A. Yes.

QS. Why was that?

A. You would have to ask her.

QS. I intend to. I will also ask her why she sent an additional one hundred dollars to you during that trip unless you can explain it.

A. I can't explain a person's generosity.

QS. Did you credit her account for this one hundred dollars?

A. No. I accepted it as a gift.

QS. Let me understand. You have no records that show credits to Mrs. Sparling for the two hernia overcharges, nor for the rent you owed her. You have no record to show credit for your services in Sandusky to clear Peter's estate. Nor do you have a record to credit her account for the thirty-seven dollars owed from the one thousand dollar insurance check. Your cashbook is missing and your ledger is full of erasures.

A. You make this sound worse than it really is Mr. Snow.

QS. I find it difficult to make it sound good, Doctor.

There were more questions regarding other accounts and debts, but the gist of the inquiry remained the same. Either Dr. MacGregor did not have book-keeping skills, or he was indeed making money off the Sparlings. In the early afternoon, all were relieved to hear Ernest Snow tell the judge he was nearly done with the defendant except for a few loose ends.

QS. Dr. MacGregor, I have a few questions regarding the boys and their insurance policies. First, the Special Appropriation of Policy. This was an amendment to change a beneficiary from a person's estate to a specific person, correct?

A. Yes.

QS. Who suggested this approach?

A. I believe it was Albert. He saw how long it took to get through all the paperwork when Peter died.

QS. These papers were filed before Albert died?

A. Yes.

QS. But after his death, you immediately went to Chris Sparling to inquire about the possibility of securing a bond.

A. Yes, I didn't know if problems might arise. Because the forms came from Canada, I wasn't sure of the timetable of their application.

QS. Was there a problem?

A. As it turned out, no.

QS. Now Scyrel also filled out one of these forms, but the puzzling thing is that he spelled his own name wrong. You stated that you witnessed the documents, but not the signature. What does that mean?

A. When I received the Special Appropriation, I signed where I was told to sign. The boys then came in, picked up the forms, and took them to Ed Gibson. He, as Justice of the Peace, was to witness the signing.

QS. That still doesn't explain how a young man incorrectly signs his name.

A. No, it does not. But as I said, I was not there when he signed.

QS. Perhaps Scyrel was ill and someone else signed for him.

A. I wasn't there Mr. Snow. The error was found and my father took corrective measures.

QS. When did the boys take out policies with Sun Life?

A. In the summer of '09.

QS. When did they have hernia surgery?

A. That was some time ago, but as I recall Albert's was done in spring and Scyrel's in October of 1909.

QS. Then can you tell me why hernia was not marked on the insurance application?

A. They were probably embarrassed.

That statement was easily believed as a few spectators shifted uncomfortably in their chairs.

QS. So to prevent their emotional discomfort you falsified the applications?

A. No. I did not. I knew they would have the operation. In fact, Albert already did.

QS. Let's assume those reasons are valid. You told Sheriff McAulay the boys all had syphilis.

A. I don't remember, perhaps.

QS. You told Dr. Conboy that Albert had syphilis.

A. Only that it was a possibility.

QS. Is it true you told Nurse Gibbs to be on the alert for reporters?

A. Did we change the subject?

QS. Please answer the question.

A. Yes, I told her that.

QS. Why?

A. You know, they want to snoop and pry just to sell a newspaper.

QS. Then please explain to this court why you told Thomas Phillips, a reporter for a Detroit newspaper, that they all had syphilis?

A. I didn't know he was a reporter at that time.

QS. So it was within bounds to tell a total stranger about the syphilis?

A. It wasn't like that. It would be hard to explain unless you were there.

QS. Apparently it's hard to explain even if you were there. Did you address syphilis on the medical application forms for insurance?

A. I don't believe there is a place so designated.

QS. Oh but I think there is. In fact, more than one. Here are some questions from Scyrel's application that might apply. Number one. According to your judgment will the party survive the term of expectation? You answered yes. Number two. Is there anything discovered by you which might affect the risk not set forth in the examination? Your answer was no. Number three. Do you believe the party examined safely insurable? Again you answered yes. Wouldn't syphilis be just cause to deny an insurance policy?

A. It would be.

QS. So you withheld that information?

A. I was never positive about the syphilis.

MacGregor wondered why his attorney was not objecting to the sarcasm Snow was heaving at him. But Walsh remained seated.

QS. Dr. MacGregor, you told this court the following. Cause of death for Peter Sparling, Septicemia Pneumococcus. Cause of death for Albert Sparling, Acute Nephritis. Cause of death for Scyrel Sparling, Hypertrophic cirrhosis of the liver. Were you positive about these?

Huron County Tribune articles

A. To some extent. I am not a pathologist.

QS. You heard the doctors and chemists testify that they found no sign of syphilis?

A. I heard that.

QS. When Mrs. MacDonald begged for Nurse Gibbs to sit with her child for just one night, you refused.

A. I have already tried to explain that.

QS. Why did you tell her you were between the devil and the deep?

A. If you had people talking about you the way they were talking about me, you would understand.

QS. But that does not explain why the nurse could not go to MacDonald's for one night.

A. I already explained. My first duty was to Mrs. Sparling and she was not well. And again, I do not remember the words you used, the devil and all that.

QS. So Mrs. MacDonald is wrong?

A. Perhaps she just remembered it differently. I don't think I used those words.

"I suppose wording is unimportant," Snow said. "But the fact is, you did not allow the nurse to tend a sick baby." Ernest Snow acted as if he would continue, but paused and then scratched his head. He looked through papers at his desk and cleared his throat. The judge asked if there was a problem and Snow shook his head. But then he paused again before turning back to MacGregor.

"Dr. MacGregor, I am at a loss. You have flatly denied statements made by witnesses under oath, and then stated perhaps you said something similar or in substance. You did not give credit where it was due and a cashbook, which might offer explanations, is missing. You have told people the boys had syphilis and then said it was only a possibility. You said you never gave arsenic, but you did administer Fowler's, which contains arsenic. You—"

Joseph Walsh stood. "Objection, your Honor. Is Mr. Snow giving his closing argument or does he have questions?" Judge Beach agreed. "Mr. Snow, do you have any further questions?" To which Snow replied, "Your Honor, I have many, but I am dizzy from all this evasion. I'm sure the jury has heard enough. I know I have. No further questions."

Judge Beach addressed the attorneys. "Gentlemen, unless there are rebuttal witnesses to be heard, prepare your closings. This court is adjourned until noon on Friday."

There were many sighs following that announcement. The jury, because they sensed the end was near and many of them had crops to tend. Snow, because he was certain he had done his best to put a murderer away. Boomhower, because soon he would not have to avoid his old friend's eyes every day in court. Walsh, because he wondered how much better things might have gone had George Clark not taken ill.

MacGregor's sigh came from deep within as he pondered the outcome. He had been made to look very bad indeed.

Chapter 65

Beautiful weather on Thursday ushered in Decoration Day. In Bad Axe, the usual customs were observed with one new exception. Veterans who had fought on foot or horseback were transported to the cemetery in automobiles. They left the Presbyterian church after services, followed by school children waving flags.

Jennie Boomhower had asked her husband to see if the judge would also grant Friday as a holiday. But Zen said it was better to proceed and be done with it. Jennie knew how hard it had been for him to prosecute a friend and she said no more.

Events in Ubly were celebrated as usual but before the concert band took its place, Mr. Slack read a letter to the boys.

> Mr. Slack,
> I thank you for inviting me to play again in the parade. But it would be difficult for me to come to Ubly this year. I will be thinking of you and know you will do a good job.
>
> > Your friend,
> > Ray Sparling

Robert and Ida MacGregor heard the happy commotion of a march from their home, but elected to remain indoors.

Port Huron also had customary practices to honor veterans, but Bert, Mae, Ray, and Carrie did not participate. The garden Carrie had prepared lay barren. If she gave any thought to the holiday, she would certainly think of the Tyre Cemetery. Then she might wonder about the condition of the Sparling family plot. If she could have seen it, she would know it had been properly tended. And then she would have to thank Violet Styles. But it was hard to know Carrie's thoughts. She spoke very little now.

Judge Beach had toyed with the idea of adding Friday to Thursday's celebration but decided against it. Better for all, whatever the outcome, to proceed as scheduled.

* * *

Robert MacGregor watched Boomhower stand and walk toward the jury. Zen had not questioned him during cross-examination, but was now going to give a speech that would paint a very dark picture. Boomhower began by

393

thanking the jury and telling them how sorry he was to have to prosecute a one-time upstanding citizen of the community. His voice droned on.

"They were cut down before their time."

MacGregor observed a fly at the end of the table. He watched as it struggled to take to the air. But something was wrong. It couldn't fly.

"If injustice or revenge is not the motive, we must look elsewhere. And when we look, we find passion — passion for money."

MacGregor looked down again but the fly was gone. He glanced at Ida, sitting behind him. She deserved so much more. He had not done enough for her. He had tried but, like the fly, had only struggled.

"He claimed to have helped Mrs. Sparling obtain insurance money as a friend. But this friend then used half of it to purchase a new automobile for himself."

MacGregor noticed the courtroom silently listening to Zen, but he heard outside noises coming through an open window—horses whinnying and an occasional automobile. He also heard the happy chatter of children out of school for the summer. No matter what the outcome of the trial might be, he would not let Bonnie and Douglas return to their old school in the fall. He looked at the open window. Maybe the fly had found new strength and escaped out of the courtroom and into the bright sunny day.

"Patent medicine? Hardly! Even though some might contain arsenic, the amount is not lethal. If it were, we would have people dropping dead all around us with a bottle of snake oil in their hands."

MacGregor felt sweat running down his back. He looked at the jury. Not all the men were looking at Zen and he wondered if their minds were already made up. His leg itched. As he leaned down to scratch, he saw the fly dead on the floor.

"Gentlemen of the jury, it is clear that Dr. MacGregor was responsible for the deaths of Albert and Scyrel Sparling. This trial, however, is only for the death of Scyrel and I ask that you do the right and proper thing to avenge the death of this young man. I ask that you find Dr. Robert MacGregor guilty."

Judge Beach anticipated a long speech from Joseph Walsh and adjourned to Monday. Walsh was of two minds. It gave him extra time to prepare his closing, but it also gave the jury the weekend to absorb Boomhower's remarks.

* * *

On June third, Joseph Walsh addressed the panel.

"Gentlemen, I am not here to argue what caused the untimely death of Scyrel Sparling. We are all saddened by it. However, casting blame on the wrong person will not bring the lad back. Nor will it truly satisfy a need to punish. Dr. MacGregor has been falsely accused of murder. He took an oath to save lives, not take them. He is an honorable man who is still highly thought of in his community. Many there will tell you they strongly believe in his innocence and will not be swayed by circumstantial evidence to the contrary. And gentlemen, please do not forget. The prosecution's case is totally and completely circumstantial.

"Was Doctor MacGregor guilty of poor bookkeeping? It would appear so. Does that make him a murderer? Absolutely not! The erasures in his ledger were a mistake and nothing else. We heard Mr. Leach testify that Mrs. Sparling paid her debts in timely fashion. That type of individual always expects the same from others. I have no doubt she would have approached the doctor for the house rent had it been withheld. If it was not credited, it must have been a cash payment. Oh yes, the cashbook. Much has been made about the doctor losing that cashbook. Gentlemen, this book was last seen seven months ago at a very public place, an inquest attended by many people. The fact that Dr. MacGregor cannot now locate the book does not single him out as the only person who could have lost it. Or made it disappear.

"Let's not forget the automobile and the insinuations we have been subjected to over that machine. Doctor MacGregor was owed the money he received from Mrs. Sparling. Hardly a crime. In retrospect, I should have asked Doctor Herrington while he was under oath if malicious gossip followed him when he bought his automobile.

"We heard about the money Dr. MacGregor received related to the Canada trip. Where is the crime if a grateful patient gives a gift of money to her doctor and his wife? This present was given openly to both Doctor and Mrs. MacGregor. It is a sad thing to question the motive of appreciation.

"Doctor MacGregor has also been accused of bringing in other doctors as a way to cover his tracks. Nonsense! He called in other physicians to help him save Scyrel's life.

"The doctor has been maligned for giving a different cause of death while he was suspicious of arsenic. May I remind this court that a legal document, such as a death certificate, is never signed as to a physician's suspicions. Other doctors agreed with him as to the cause of death. They agreed. They did not suspect.

"The prosecution claims a passion for money as the motive for Doctor MacGregor to commit murder. Gentlemen, anyone who renders a service expects to be paid for that service. The butcher is paid for his services, as is the dressmaker. There is no motive here. It's the way we live.

"Did Doctor MacGregor have opportunity? Yes. He was there, and often. As were friends, hired help, and neighbors. And let me share some information I have regarding the procurement of arsenic. My intent is not to cast blame. It is to inform. I am reading from the book *Medical Chemistry and Toxicology* written by Doctor Robert Holland and first copyrighted in 1905.

> White arsenic, ratsbane, is a favorite poison because
> it is cheap, can be bought as vermin-killer at any drug
> store in the United States and, owing to its very feeble
> taste, can be mixed with food without the victim recognizing the
> foreign ingredient.

Walsh put the book down. "Did you know common fly paper is coated with arsenic? Buffalo Carpet Moth Annihilator contains arsenic. Paris Green, touted as a remedy for potato bugs, contains arsenic and was previously used as a pigment in wallpaper. I am holding an advertisement for arsenic wafers which claims its use will give beauty of face, skin, and form.

"Gentlemen of the jury, arsenic is everywhere and available to everyone. I will close as I began. The prosecution has presented a case based upon circumstantial evidence. It was their duty to prove Doctor MacGregor guilty beyond a reasonable doubt, and no proof has been given to support those claims. It is not the job of the defense to show who committed this crime. Nor is it our duty to prove our client innocent, although I believe we have done just that. I thank you for your time and attention and pray you do the right and moral thing and find Doctor Robert MacGregor not guilty."

* * *

Court adjourned shortly after Walsh ended his speech. As the room emptied, he called to MacGregor's wife and father. "We are very near the end and I expect the jury will have this case by Wednesday. I have taken the liberty of reserving two hotel rooms for you here in Bad Axe. I think it's wise you be nearby while the jury convenes." The finality weighed heavily on the MacGregors.

* * *

On Tuesday June fourth, Attorneys Paul Woodworth and Ernest Snow gave their closing arguments. Boomhower and Walsh had already given fine orations and covered every phase of the case. But Judge Beach did not want to take any action that could be construed as reason for mistrial and he allowed both to speak. They each had their say, in their own style, but nothing new was offered and many observers left before day's end.

On Wednesday June fifth, Judge Watson Beach charged the jury and his words summed up the case and the job of each juror impaneled.

"There is no room for any intermediate grade of crime in this case, and a verdict, if you arrive at a verdict, must be either murder of the first degree or not guilty. You have undoubtedly learned, as the testimony progressed, that no eyewitness has testified to seeing arsenic administered to Scyrel Sparling by any person. The prosecution introduced testimony of a postmortem examination of the body and organs of Scyrel and testimony of subsequent tests for the presence of arsenic in the organs.

"The weight to be given to Albert's death depends upon the finding by you on similarity of deaths and circumstances in each case. If you are not satisfied beyond reasonable doubt that the cause of death to Albert was arsenic poison, administered by Dr. MacGregor, or by someone aided and abetted by Dr. MacGregor, with intent to kill Albert, you will not consider the testimony as to Albert's death in this case at all.

"Circumstantial evidence is entitled to the same consideration as the testimony of eyewitnesses.

"It was not incumbent upon the prosecution to show a fatal quantity of arsenic in the body of Scyrel or Albert after death; but the presence of arsenic and the preceding symptoms, the claimed pathological conditions after death, and the opinions of the experts are relied upon to establish death from arsenic in both cases.

"If, upon considering all the testimony as to the cause of death, you are not satisfied, beyond reasonable doubt that arsenic poisoning caused Scyrel's death, your verdict should be not guilty.

"If you find beyond reasonable doubt that Scyrel died from arsenical poisoning, but do not find beyond reasonable doubt that it was administered with intent to kill, your verdict will be not guilty.

"If you find beyond reasonable doubt that Scyrel's death was the result of arsenical poisoning administered with intent to kill, you will proceed to the consideration of the question of whether or not Dr. MacGregor had any connection with such crime.

"If other evidence in this case does not convince you beyond reasonable doubt of Dr. MacGregor's connection with the death of Scyrel, he must be acquitted notwithstanding you may believe him connected with Albert's death. He is on trial charged with the death of Scyrel only.

"Aiding or abetting in the law, as to be applied in this case, means that Dr. MacGregor must have counseled, helped, assisted, commanded, persuaded, procured, or induced another to administer arsenic to Scyrel with the specific intent in his own mind to kill Scyrel. Active participation, personally or by causing someone else to poison Scyrel, must be found beyond reasonable doubt to warrant a conviction.

"These matters of fact in cases of poisoning are difficult to prove, because the act of poisoning is usually a secret and can seldom be made out by direct testimony. In the absence of direct testimony, the prosecution may seek to identify the guilty person by showing that the accused had the opportunity and had a motive. Opportunity, standing alone, has no great force as evidence of guilt. It is the claim of the prosecution that he had a motive in the desire to profit by Mrs. Sparling's access of property and insurance money that would be caused by the deaths of Albert and Scyrel.

"Motive is the impelling reason for any act. When circumstantial evidence is relied upon, motive may be an important circumstance. Absence of any motive to cause either Albert's or Scyrel's death would be a circumstance favoring the theory of innocence of the crime charged. It is for you to say whether the motive alleged existed in Dr. MacGregor's mind.

"It is claimed by the prosecution in this connection that criminal sexual relations existed between Dr. MacGregor and Mrs. Sparling. This is charging the accused with an independent crime for which he is not on trial in this case, namely adultery.

"Your verdict should be arrived at by a careful consideration of all the testimony both on the part of the prosecution and the defense. It should be based upon the evidence produced in open court alone and not influenced by sympathy for the defendant and his family, nor by prejudice aroused by the enormity of the claimed crime nor by the wishes or feelings of anyone, witnesses or other persons. Claims or statements of counsel on either side are not evidence.

"You will take the case as I have before instructed you, and if you have no reasonable doubt that Scyrel Sparling died of arsenical poisoning and no reasonable doubt that the defendant either personally administered the same with intent to kill Scyrel Sparling or actively aided and abetted some other person in administering the arsenic to him, with intent in his own mind to kill Scyrel Sparling, your verdict will be guilty.

"If you are not so satisfied beyond reasonable doubt as to Scyrel's death from arsenical poison intentionally to kill him or not satisfied beyond reasonable doubt as to defendant's guilty connection with his death, you will say not guilty."

When the judge finished, the jury was escorted to a room for deliberation. Alexander MacGregor had dinner at the hotel before retiring. His son and daughter-in-law were not hungry and immediately retired to their room. A light rain had begun to fall.

Bad Axe was nearly closed for the night when word came from the jury room; they had reached a verdict. Officers of the court were sent to notify the judge, sheriff, attorneys, and defendant. Word spread quickly and as the major parties reached the makeshift courtroom, they were joined by reporters and several people who had not yet gone to bed. Dr. MacGregor, with his father beside him, listened to the rain and waited. Reverend Hurd sat behind them with Mrs. MacGregor.

At 12:15 a.m., on Thursday June sixth, Judge Beach gaveled the assembly to order. "Have you reached a verdict?" he asked.

The jury foreman stood. "We have your Honor. We find the defendant, Robert A. MacGregor, guilty of the murder of Scyrel Sparling." Each juror was polled and repeated the verdict. Dr. MacGregor was allowed to embrace his wife before being led by Sheriff McAulay to the jail.

Chapter 66

Dr. MacGregor was sentenced on June 10, 1912, to life imprisonment at Jackson State Prison. After sentencing, he met his wife and children in the jail office and then, for the first time, broke down and wept bitterly.

He arrived at Jackson on June twelfth, and within one month became a lay nurse to the prison physician, Dr. Pray. There he awaited word from his attorneys, including a completely recovered George Clark.

On December 23, 1912, these attorneys petitioned for a new trial, but the request was denied. They then appealed the case to the Michigan State Supreme Court on November 13, 1913. That decision of denial came on January 5, 1914.

On November 28, 1916, Governor Woodbridge Ferris, before leaving office, granted Dr. MacGregor a full pardon. No explanation or record of circumstances leading to the pardon by Governor Ferris has been found. Shortly after MacGregor reunited with his family, Jackson Prison offered him a position as prison physician. He accepted and served in that capacity nearly twelve years. In March of 1928, he died, at the prison, after a lengthy illness.

* * *

Charges against Nurse Gibbs were dropped shortly after Dr. MacGregor's sentencing. The expense of another trial for a person only present during the last death was determined to be inadvisable, and a conviction was doubtful.

* * *

On January 26, 1914, a motion by Paul Woodworth, with consent of Xenophon A. Boomhower, was accepted at the Circuit Court of Huron County and the case against Carrie B. Sparling was dropped. Boomhower felt he lacked evidence for a conviction and believed it would be difficult to convince a jury that any mother could intentionally murder her family.

No. 9612 Name Robert A. MacGregor Alias Robert A. Wagner County Jefferson

Sentenced June 10th 1912 Received June 12/12 Term Yrs. Mos.

Min. Term Yrs. Mos. Max. Term Yrs. Mos.

Crime Murder of the first degree

Measurements 182.6 5.117 1.83 94.3 6.5 17.8 14.1 13.9 16.3 ⊢ 22.6.11.7 9.3 47.7 16.2

General Description	Age 36	Born Perth Co. Ontario	Nationality Scotch
Complexion	Hair Mxd 2/6 Grey	Forehead Recd. Hi. Brd.	
Eyes Grey blue & Gr. flt.	Nose Exp. Str. bar. Sli. El.	Brd. Broad Grey Mxd.	
Mouth Med.	Lips Med.	Chin Med. Mas.	Build Stout
Ear Border Full	Ear Lobe Gulped Med.	Cheek Dep.	
Conjugal Married	Home Residence Mtg. Med.	Occupation Physician & Surgeon	

Former Imprisonments

Remarks Pardoned by Gov. Ferris Nov. 28 – 1916

Smokes and ~~Chews~~

Paroled

Discharged

Died 3-21-1928

Prison record and photo of Dr. Robert A. MacGregor

Huron County Tribune articles

Executive Pardon of Dr. Robert A. MacGregor
by Michigan Governor Woodbridge N. Ferris

Case dismissal for Carrie B. Sparling
Huron County Court Records of January, 1914

Epilogue

January 18, 1933

Violet heard the operator put her telephone call through. Cora answered and gave Violet the information she had called about. "The funeral will be tomorrow at the Tyre cemetery, where she will be buried," Cora informed her. "Reverend Hurd has agreed to do the service. Violet, you mentioned before that you were surprised Carrie remembered you. As you may know, my sister had many problems these last years, but she did remember you, and fondly. In fact, she talked about you a great deal the week before she passed."

Violet thanked Cora and said, "I hope Carrie is finally at peace. Her troubles have come to an end." To which Cora replied, "If she isn't at peace, there's nothing we can do about it. Lord knows we've tried through the years. At least I can get rid of that old rocking chair. Did I tell you she was sitting in it when she died?"

* *

Only a handful of people gathered at the cemetery. So many years had passed since the trial that not even the curious were in attendance. Reverend Hurd kept his message short on that cold January day. And then it was done. Mae, Bert, and their son lingered, as did Ray, his wife, and daughters. Big Pete and his Mary were there as well as William and Ellen. Little Pete had died two years prior. The family plot looked stark and cold. Carrie never had ordered those headstones for her sons.

A few yards away stood a tiny woman, holding a package. It took a while, but Mae finally recognized her. "How wonderful to see you. I'm so glad you came." They shared a few words of condolence, but the bitter wind soon forced everyone to head to their automobiles. "May I walk you to your car, Mrs. Styles?" asked Mae. Violet smiled, "No thank you dear. I would like to stay a bit longer." Violet was still standing at Carrie's grave when the last car pulled away. "Be at peace my dear friend," she said before leaving.

* *

The few flowers from the funeral were quickly freezing on the mound. Next to them, unseen by any save two birds and a squirrel, was a loaf of bread.

Possible Scenarios

If you find the ending to this story to be abrupt and begging questions, you are not alone. For years I have been baffled by what really happened to my ancestors. What follows are possible scenarios; feasible plots formed from my imagination, but based on many facts. I never found a smoking gun (or arsenic bottle) and if any telling diaries exist, I have not discovered them.

WHY MACGREGOR MIGHT HAVE BEEN INNOCENT

Even though testing after the fact found no sign of syphilis, Dr. MacGregor could have believed these men carried the disease. He may have used arsenic in Fowler's Solution, for instance, as a treatment. Arsenic had been touted as a cure for the disease. If the Sparling men were taking additional arsenic from Carrie and/or patent medicines, the dosage could have been lethal.

Perhaps he suspected Carrie and that is why he was at the farm so often — to keep an eye on her. He might have involved the other physicians not to cover his tracks, but in hopes they would suspect Carrie and take action he felt he could not take alone.

The repeated enemas ordered for Scyrel could have been a way to eliminate arsenic that he speculated had been given by Carrie, not initially knowing the internal damage had already been done. MacGregor wanted a post mortem done after Albert died. If he was guilty, it seems odd that he would push for the autopsy.

WHY MACGREGOR COULD HAVE BEEN GUILTY

Dr. MacGregor's frequent trips to the farm gave him ample opportunity to administer arsenic in what he referred to as medicine. Those repeated visits also could have caused Carrie to rely on him more and more. He might have manipulated a lonely, vulnerable woman by paying great attention to her, especially after observing a distinct coldness between her and her husband. He could have poisoned J.W. to get even closer to her. Peter, being the oldest, had to die before he could assume control of the farm and Carrie's finances. When Albert became the oldest son, MacGregor would have to eliminate him as well. His death would have an added bonus. Scyrel had moved to Tyre to work in the general store. If MacGregor planned to do away with all the boys, he would not have the same opportunity to administer arsenic if Scyrel remained in Tyre. Kill Albert, and Scyrel will return to the farm to help Ray.

Dr. MacGregor wanted money for a number of reasons—to pay old bills, feel more prestigious in the community, and/or to buy nice things for Ida. Not only did MacGregor want more money, he also desired the Sparling farm as an additional asset. After eliminating the sons, would he have killed Carrie as well?

As a former coroner, he would have known during Scyrel's post mortem to open the stomach and intestines.

He ordered repeated enemas on Scyrel to eliminate arsenic to cover his tracks not knowing the evidence could remain. Another way to cover his tracks was to involve other doctors and get them to agree on illnesses and causes of death.

If he thought Carrie was mentally unbalanced and poisoning her family, why would he take a chance and let his son work and eat with the Sparlings?

My biggest problem in believing MacGregor innocent is the car. He ordered the automobile shortly before Albert died and told the dealer he would pay in cash.

WHY CARRIE MIGHT HAVE BEEN INNOCENT

She could have consulted medical journals after syphilis was diagnosed and tried to cure her family privately, not wanting word of "bad blood" leaking into the community. It is also possible that her poor eyesight caused wrong dosages of arsenic that she innocently used as a cure for the syphilis.

Carrie could have fallen totally under MacGregor's control and innocently given arsenic, prescribed by the doctor, as a medicine to cure the syphilis diagnosed by MacGregor.

WHY CARRIE COULD HAVE BEEN GUILTY

The events in 1907 in which many of Carrie's Sparling family moved or left are factual. This could have affected her mind greatly, causing her to vow that no one else would ever leave except under her conditions. Being obsessed with the thought her sons might also leave her, she had the advantage of their living at home making it easier to administer poison. When Scyrel moved to Tyre and opportunity to eliminate him became more difficult, she solved the problem by killing Albert, knowing Scyrel would return to help Ray.

Continuing with a possible mental condition, Carrie could have had Munchausen Syndrome by Proxy long before it was even given its name. To get and keep the doctor's attention she needed sick children. Keep her children ill by poisoning them separately, and the doctor's visits would be prolonged. Her intent may not have been to kill, but she wouldn't know that arsenic continued to do damage to organs long after the poison had been given.

Carrie might have fallen in love with her doctor and didn't believe divorce from J.W. was an option. After murdering J.W., it would have been easier to do away with her sons. After all, MacGregor might not want to take on such a large family.

Carrie had Paris Green at her disposal. And if she didn't use that, arsenic was readily available, no questions asked, as rat killer. Poisoning is usually the choice of women who commit murder.

COULD THERE HAVE BEEN A CONSPIRACY?

There might have been an affair between Carrie and MacGregor. (This belief is still widely accepted by many in the Thumb.) The plan would be for the doctor to leave his family, and for Carrie to eliminate hers. They would then use money from insurance policies to leave the area and continue their relationship far removed from the Thumb.

Perhaps they had an affair and the boys found out. They would have to be eliminated to be silenced.

MORE QUESTIONS

Why did Mae survive? She had married and moved away shortly before her father died. Perhaps that alone would keep her from inheriting the farm, even though she was the oldest child. I have no other explanation as to why she didn't die. Most puzzling to me is why Ray didn't die. Early in my research I had read that Ray stated he would never leave Carrie. So I began to write the story under the assumption that Ray was Carrie's favorite and would be allowed to live. The Sparling men were killed, with the exception of Ray, in order of age. But further research showed that Ray was not healthy and MacGregor made the statement during Scyrel's illness that Ray would be the next to die. Was it a fluke that Ray survived?

PURELY ACCIDENTAL?

It is remotely possible that Dr. MacGregor gave arsenic, in small medicinal doses, to cure the boys of syphilis. MacGregor said they all had syphilis, although that disease was never found in exhumations or autopsies. Syphilis, in those days, was often misdiagnosed as the cause for an unknown illness.

It is also possible that while the doctor was administering arsenic, Carrie was doing the same but neither knew what the other was doing. By stretching the imagination, it is also possible that while Carrie and MacGregor were giving arsenic separately, the boys were adding to the dosages in the form of patent medicines.

And finally, imagine my surprise and wonder in August of 2005 as my manuscript was nearing completion. The following headline appeared in the August 5, 2005, issue of *The Huron Daily Tribune*:

"UBLY TO BEGIN ARSENIC
REMOVAL TECHNIQUE TESTING"

It seems at the time of the article, the arsenic level in Ubly was not quite at the level allowed by federal drinking water safety requirements. Hmmm. . . .

I WONDER WHAT EVER HAPPENED TO . . . .

Carrie Sparling

Oral history puts Carrie in a mental facility after Dr. MacGregor's trial. I know she lived for a while with son Ray, and that she died at the home of her sister. However, I could not find any evidence to validate the rumor that she was institutionalized.

Big Pete Sparling

Big Pete was my great-grandfather. He and his Mary had twelve children, eight of whom reached adulthood. He died before I was born, but I remember great-grandmother Mary who lived until 1961. I am so sorry my interest in this story had not piqued while she was still living, as I'm sure she could have given valuable first-hand information.

Violet Styles

Violet Styles, at the time this story took place, was in no way related to any Sparling. The closest she would come was in 1915 when her niece, Nellie Styles, married Big Pete's son, Roy. Nellie and Roy are my paternal grand-parents. Violet is a main character in this book, as I can recall my father saying,

Aunt Violet (on right) as I remember her. Lady at left is my grandmother, Nellie Styles Sparling.

"Aunt Violet took the secret of the case to her grave." However, I have no proof that she and Carrie even knew each other. Aunt Violet could also have given valuable information (if she knew the secret and was willing to share it), but I was too young to have the deep interest I later formed. I remember her as a quiet, tiny, gray-haired lady, and I now know she had much sadness in her life. Her husband Ed died in 1940. Her son, as told in the story, died after birth in 1901. Daughter Marie, born in 1903, died in 1919 and Aletha, born in 1895, died in 1920. Violet died in 1958.

George Sparling

Eldest son of Big Pete. His youngest daughter, Eunice Sparling Armstrong, has given me wonderful oral history of those involved in the story. An interest-ing, to me, side note about George concerns a dream I had when I began to think about writing a book. In the dream George said, quite sternly, "Do not go that way," referencing my approach to the book. The trouble is, at the time of the dream I had not formed any ideas of where to go at all.

Xenophon A. Boomhower

He went on to become a judge for the Huron County Circuit Court.

Ernest Snow

He became a Michigan State Supreme Court Judge in 1926, but his term was cut short by an untimely death in 1927.

George Clark

He also became a Michigan State Supreme Court Judge and served from 1919 to 1933.

Judge Watson Beach

The judge actually did serve with Rudolph Pabst during the War Between the States. Judge Beach served as Judge of the Circuit Court for forty years and died in 1927.

William Sparling

J.W.'s brother died in 1949.

Juror Henry Binder

Juror Henry Binder's grandson, Carl, married Big Pete's granddaughter, Wanda. They are my aunt and uncle. There is a joke that if Henry had lived to see the courtship of his grandson to a Sparling, he might have discouraged him from those pursuits. At this writing, they have been married over fifty years. Uncle Carl provided me with much valuable information on corn shredders and wood buzzers. Henry is standing fifth from the right in the jury photo in Chapter 52.

Mae and Ray Sparling

I learned a few things about the surviving children but my focus was on those who died. Mae and Ray suffered enough throughout the illnesses, deaths, rumors, and trial. Even though both are now deceased I see no reason to probe any further.

Nurse Gibbs

Nurse Gibbs' journal during Scyrel's illness appears in Chapter 43. She disappeared in my research and I was disappointed to not even locate a photograph of her. The only account I have of charges being dropped came from an old newspaper article written by Boyd Simmons. It states, "Charges against Mrs. John Sparling, whose husband and three sons were the victims and a nurse, Miss Marguerite Gibbs, were later dropped."

The Bodies

Oral history stated that after Peter's exhumation, his brain was kept for study at the Pontiac State Hospital. I could not prove or disprove the story. If it happened, what did they learn and how did they later dispose of it?

I was unable to determine whether or not the bodies were returned to the Tyre Cemetery. At the time of exhumation, Carrie, Ray, and Mae were all very involved and burdened with a possible trial. The upheaval of their lives could have prevented them from making certain the bodies were returned to the ground.

I know Carrie was buried at the Tyre Cemetery but that cemetery is now defunct and I cannot find a record of her plot. Cemetery plots come in fives – thus the Sparling plot is filled (IF the exhumed were returned). (1) baby – (2) J.W. – (3) Young Pete – (4) Albert – (5) Scyrel. So, where is Carrie?

-- Jacki Howard
May 31, 2008

Author's Notes

This book is historical fiction, meaning it is an account of a true family tragedy/scandal that occurred in the early 1900s. I remember hearing parts of this story as I grew up. While the main story is based on facts, I have included the thoughts and many of the words of people I never knew. I used facts as I knew them, but often had to fill in the gaps with my own ideas of what may have happened. I also rearranged some facts to suit my story. For example, Carrie was not the oldest daughter. A few minor characters came from my imagination. Having said this, some things that might seem fictional in the book actually took place. They include the conversation about being "between the devil and the deep," MacGregor's comment about the looking glass, the misspelling of Scyrel's name on the insurance form, the account of Perry Cole observing Dr. MacGregor throwing a bottle into the stove fire, and Reverend Hurd's sermon asking for a show of support for the doctor.

The forest fires mentioned in this book were both devastating. The fire in October of 1871 did not take many lives in the sparsely populated Thumb. It did clear land for new settlers and when the firestorm of 1881 occurred, the loss of life and property was much greater. It became known as "The Great Fire of 1881." As mentioned in Chapter 3, the American Red Cross sent supplies to Bad Axe after the 1881 fire. The first local chapter, headed by Clara Barton in Dansville, New York, was formed August 22, 1881. Thirteen days later, they undertook their first disaster relief effort to aid victims of that fire.

To those knowledgeable in agriculture, you may question, as I did, certain practices conducted during unusual times. For example, hay pressing in February or bean threshing in spring. Think back to the time of this story. Not every farmer had a hay press or threshing machine. Those procedures could only be done when the man who owned the equipment was available.

There are law practices used in the trial which would probably not be allowed today. For example, future witnesses were allowed in court before their testimony was given. I also found it unusual that a lawyer defending Carrie, whose trial was pending, was chosen to help represent Dr. MacGregor during his trial. However, I found no questions were raised during the trial regarding either situation.

To get a feel for day-to-day living in the Thumb, I used my Grandmother Sparling's 1915 diary. Though written three years after the trial, much of the routine of daily life remained the same.

I had some concern regarding the surrender of Big Pete's bond and apparently the defense did as well. They brought it to the Michigan Supreme Court as an assignment of error. The Michigan Supreme Court stated that: "The thirty-eighth and thirty-ninth assignments of error complain of the action of the trial court in the matter of the surrender of Mrs. Sparling by her bondsmen and the taking of new bail in her case, in the presence of the jury. While this was a practice not to be commended, yet, owing to the part taken by one of the respondent's counsel, in the matter, and it not appearing that the prosecution had anything to do in bringing on the transaction, we do not think that the case should be reversed for that reason. It is mere conjecture to say that respondent was prejudiced by the occurrence."

A great percentage of the story has been taken from newspapers, depositions, and the ruling by the Michigan State Supreme Court. I was unable to find the transcript of the actual trial, but did obtain, through the Clerk of Court in Huron County, a copy of "The People's Amendments to the Proposed Bill of Exceptions of the Defendant." By using this document, along with newspaper accounts and the Supreme Court ruling, I was able to reconstruct the major aspects of the trial. However, not having the actual transcript, I at times had to use my imagination to make the story complete.

The judge's instructions to the jury are his actual charge but in an abbreviated form.

My mother and several others always heard that the arsenic was given in orange juice. Some said it was given via the cereal. I introduced lemonade into the story as a means to show how arsenic could be administered IF Carrie was the culprit. Since orange juice would not be part of a daily diet I used lemonade, as I had found ads for lemons in old newspapers. I've been asked what Carrie's secret ingredient was. For story purposes, she added apple juice. It would give a unique taste to the lemonade and make hers stand out. She did not add arsenic to it—or did she?

Patent medicines were not regulated by the government until the early 1900s when manufacturers of these cures were required to list ingredients. It was then learned they contained, among other toxins, arsenic, mercury, and strychnine. I personally believe all four men died of arsenic poisoning. Though it didn't appear in the exhumed bodies of John Wesley and Young Pete, it is a fact that arsenic can be totally eliminated from a body. Strychnine is a cumulative poison, meaning it remains in the body for a long time, even after death. I believe strychnine was used as a stimulant in both men and, even though it was found in them after exhumation, I don't believe it caused their deaths.

I have also been asked what Carrie told Violet in the jail. Going on my father's words that Aunt Violet took the secret to her grave, I used her as a means for Carrie to confide in, and that is why something was said in the jail that shocked Violet. What could she have said? Perhaps Carrie admitted to an affair. She may have told Violet that she did in fact kill her husband and sons. She may have innocently admitted to being in love with the doctor. If Violet took any secrets to her grave, something had to be said at some time. Why not in jail?

Acknowledgments

Many people helped with this book and their importance should not be judged by where they appear in this list.

My husband Bob. Not only was he a great supporter and encourager, but my editor, banker, and advisor. He also helped greatly in abridging the judge's charge.

Daughters Aimee and Jenny and son-in-law Chris. They had faith in my ability, and constantly encouraged me in this project. I would not have been able to finish without their technical support regarding their computer and editing expertise. And their marketing knowledge has been greatly appreciated.

My late father, Verl Sparling, for the initial and ongoing inspiration. Dad, how I wish you could have helped me research this story.

My mother, Aimee Herford Sparling for patience and company as we traversed the Thumb getting information. Mom went above and beyond on our first trip to the now defunct Old Tyre Cemetery. As we drove up, we observed the feet of someone hiding behind a large evergreen tree. If I moved the car forward, the feet moved backward. If I put the car in reverse, the feet traveled forward. Needless to say, Mom and I didn't get out of the car. In fact we made a rather hasty exit from the area to return later, fortified by several other family members.

Bud Sparling, my uncle. He shared documents pertaining to the story and also gave oral history regarding some of the characters.

Aunt Wanda Sparling Binder and Aunt Doris Sparling Cummings for family information regarding the Sparlings.

Uncle Carl Binder for his agricultural expertise in corn shredding and wood buzzing.

Attorney Donald Clark, great-nephew to Attorney George Clark. Don Clark provided me with magazine articles that featured the case and also sent me a copy of the Michigan State Supreme Court ruling.

Jeanette Jacobs for her book about the history of the Sparlings and Martha Maitland, descendant of Little Pete, for sharing her copy with me.

Diana Hebner who copied and mailed plat maps of Bingham Township.

Eunice Sparling Armstrong for her oral history, part of which was "Oh Grandpa (Big Pete) said none of them had syphilis."

Dr. David Chernoff for information on arsenic.

Katie Still and Larry Sparling for genealogical information.

Nancy Sorrells for agricultural information on hay pressing.

Bear Funeral Home for information regarding cooling boards.

The Huron County Tribune and Trisha Tyler who recopied and mailed hard-to-read copies.

The Bad Axe Public Library for assistance in obtaining newspaper articles.

Bad Axe Librarian Mimi Herrington (yes, she is related to Dr. Herrington) and her helper, Erika Goebel, for transcribing and typing a very faint article I needed for the book.

Cliff Willett of the Bad Axe Historical Society who led me to Mark Green.

Mark Green of Green's Photography and Framing who provided me with the pictures of the jury and the photographs of the people waiting to get into the courtroom.

Tammie Woodson, an employee with the Virginia Department of Health, for answering my questions about syphilis.

George Behonick, Ph.D. Forensic Toxicologist for the Commonwealth of Virginia for information on poisons.

Bad Axe Courthouse and Clerk of Court, Peggy A. Koehler

Former Churchville, Virginia Librarian Debbie Sweeney for locating inter-library loan books on poison and about women who poison.

A Bank of America employee who explained 'notes payable to bearer' to me. He wished to remain anonymous.

Ellen Bell who read an early manuscript with fresh eyes looking for flow of story.

Other sources:
My Grandmother Sparling's 1915 diary.
Michigan Secretary of State for copies of Dr. MacGregor's prison
 photograph and pardon.
Articles from the *Huron County Tribune* (now the *Huron Daily Tribune*).

Books and Pamphlets:
Village of Ubly Centennial Book
Big Burning School Centennial Book
Port Crescent Centennial Book
Medical Chemistry and Toxicology by Dr. Robert Holland
Bad Axe Historical Society booklets:
 Homes of Bad Axe
 Good Old Days
 Log Cabin Days
 Mud Trail Days
Articles from the *Sand Pointer*

Photographs:
The photographs are from my personal collection, the *Huron County Tribune* Newspaper, and Jeanette Jacobs' book on the Sparling history.